I0797122

ROWAN JUN

Pathos, Book 1

2nd Edition

Tamara Henson

Tamara Henson Studios, LLC

Barbourville, KY, USA

Thank you for supporting the creative work of Tamara Henson!

Copyright © 2012 Tamara Victoria Marie Henson
as *The Pathos of Rowan Jun*

2nd Edition:
Copyright © 2025 Tamara Victoria Marie Henson

All rights reserved.

Published by Tamara Henson Studios, LLC
Barbourville, KY, USA
www.tamarahenson.com

ISBN-13: 978-1-968677-02-2

DEDICATION

To my mother Mary, who shoved my nose in a full length novel when other kids were reading short verse, who encouraged me to dream big as the world fell around us, and who gave up more to raise me than I'll ever know.

I love you, Mom!

*   *   *

CONTENT NOTICE:

This work mentions and depicts violence and battle that pertain to but are not limited to slavery, violent parental death, infanticide, desecration of corpses, funeral pyres, war, fighting, and death. Plus huge dragon-like horse creatures that chomp bad guys and spew their remains on other bad guys for intimidation, so that other stuff is more forgivable, right?

CONTENTS

1: QUELLTRUTH

Little Ayli was born a slave, like every other human aboard the Slaveship QuellTruth. Rowan Jun gazed into Ayli's big hazel eyes, saw them crinkle with her innocent smile. He pressed his lips into a tight line. She should never know the snap of a whip on her shoulders nor the humiliation of being inspected like livestock. Rowan ground his teeth, knowing that her treatment would be so much worse as a female. Rowan wanted Ayli to grow up free. She had a chance to do that, but only if he acted soon.

Rowan listened to the infant's coo, watched her perfect face scrunch up right before she yawned. He held her in his arms so awkwardly, unfamiliar with much in the way of human touch. He stared at her tiny hand as it wound around his finger. *How could this perfect thing ever be considered property?*

"Out, now, slave," ordered the Slaver. He gave a point-toothed smirk behind his sallow skin. "You've been outside your cell for too long. Imelda will be concerned that you may strain those dark eyes or bruise your perfect skin." The towering figure laughed heartily, his yellow eyes closed tight, and his green face tilted back. His long black braids shook with his movement.

Rowan bit his lips together by habit. Without a word, he stood and carefully placed the child in her mother's waiting arms. The woman nodded an unspoken acknowledgment to him. The ghost of a smile alighted on her lips. The purple splotches beneath her elegantly upturned, dark eyes betrayed her exhaustion. Ayli was his mother's seventh child in as many cycles, and only the second with his father as sire, making Ayli Rowan's full sister. At that birth rate, though, Rowan knew her body would give out before her willpower ran its course.

He left the room, feeling his mother's eyes on him, as little Ayli cried. Don't give the Slaver reason to suspect you. One foot in front of the other. Step lively. Get where you're going. Don't dawdle. Don't speak unless questioned. And never tell the full truth. He repeated his self-made instructions like a mantra in his mind. It helped him focus on what was to come, instead of the captivity before him.

"Move, now, Breeder!"

An olive-colored, black-clawed hand on his shoulder, an unexpected shove. Rowan realized he had stopped outside the huge plate window into his mother's cell, catching a glimpse of Ayli, committing her beautiful face to memory. He stepped forward obediently, suppressing how the Slaver's words rankled him. A breeder he would indeed be if he stayed here, creating child after child fated to slavery aboard the human slaveship QuellTruth, then sacrificed to the mysterious and terrifying fate of those who are purchased from the Slavers for purposes beyond Rowan's full understanding.

He moved on, again maintaining his silence

and, as the Slaver perceived, his ignorance. The Gangre-tan employed by the Slavemaster as his Slavers possessed all the tact of a metal floor panel, and half the use. These had about the same intelligence, as well. Rowan heard rumors of elite Gangre-tan fighters taking over and occupying entire cities with far fewer numbers than occupied the QuellTruth. But Slavemaster Imelda's employees were just big, strong, and dumb. Occasionally, they reveled in a power trip and he set them to rights for damaging company property. But overall, he only permitted them to be violent when unleashed by the Slavemaster for his own reasons. Rowan simply knew his limits when dealing with them.

The cold metal shocked his bare feet with each step, sobering his thoughts. The Insurgency he led swelled in numbers among the surly youth who had never seen the green of a mountain nor the blue of the sky with their own eyes. Just like Rowan. They often spoke of how the metal above and below felt like a cage that shrank with each passing day. Their hopes and dreams rested on his shoulders as much as their strength in numbers made his lofty plans possible. They placed complete trust in his ideals, it seemed. Smothering though their expectations felt, he remembered the shining eyes of his biological sister and knew her freedom would be worth any price.

Deep in conversation with his cellmates a short time later, he discussed his next step in moving forward with the Insurgency. When the opportunity arose, he would use his stolen access codes for the navigation module and adjust course.

“We will make for whatever free planet we're near,” he whispered, with a glint in his eyes born of determination, "and by their planetside rules, we should be liberated."

The stern young faces around him flashed with excitement. One young man leaned forward with a harsh whisper. "I should be able to access the manifest tomorrow, when I'm scheduled to serve on the bridge. I'll know then where we are headed."

"Good, Cadin," Rowan answered. "We have but one chance, with the right free planet, so we must gain every bit of information we can to act at the right time."

Rowan cut his voice when a Slaver banged on the door with a thick fist. "Slavemaster wants to see Rowan Jun. Now."

"Yeah," Rowan said with a bright tone, eyeing his co-conspirators warily as he stood to comply. "She's absolutely beautiful. Hazel eyes and my mother's smile. Surely, she'll be an asset aboard the QuellTruth!" He doubted the dumb Gangre-tan would catch the acid Rowan infused in that last line, nor the instant change of subject he employed.

"Now, Breeder." The Slaver slid open the door with a frustrated sigh. "Keep your thoughts from the Slavemaster's property, lest he takes notice." His yellow eyes gleamed even in the brightness of the white room.

Rowan followed obediently, dropping his chin to his chest in a fake show of submission. He stared at his bare feet, counting each step until he stood before the Slavemaster's quarters. He raised his eyes on the closed door, waiting for the monster to answer the Slaver's rapping.

At long last, after several moments and muffled sounds behind the door, Dargin Imelda stood before them in all his casual finery—an open red velvet robe, darkened loose-fitting pants of soft material, and sandals that tied at the ankle. He took a long draught of the purple liquid from the glass stemware in his hand. He tossed back his long brown hair and, with a grand gesture, indicated that Rowan should enter.

"It's been a long time, my lovely," Imelda said, his velvet voice crawling under Rowan's skin.

"Less than five days, Slavemaster," Rowan whispered, his voice held even and smooth.

"Ah, I must've forgotten." Imelda pursed his lips and stared deep into the wine in his glass. "Work has kept me busy beyond measure of late!"

"Work?" Rowan snarled. "Do you mean the business of trading your fellow humans for financial gain?"

"Ah, that spirit rises in you again! I terribly miss our discussions, Rowan Jun." Imelda eyed him with genuine mirth. "The concept of a human selling humans still seems bizarre to you, though you were born to it?"

Rowan shrugged, accustomed to such candid discourse. Imelda's ego allowed him the luxury of humor to distract him from Rowan's real motives. The man seemed to enjoy Rowan's jabs at his profession, having Rowan disciplined only twice regarding his sharp tongue.

Two men—Imelda's constantly attending slaves—cleared Imelda's enormous bed and placed clean sheets on the surface. They wore underwear and sheared their heads for his preference. Their hollow expressions displayed neither pain nor discontent. He saw nothing of the several, much younger slaves Imelda kept for his humor. Rowan suppressed a shiver of fear.

"I have pressing chores this afternoon," Rowan said, allowing his annoyance to surface. He stood at attention in the center of the large room. "What brings me before the Slavemaster today?"

"Concise, as always." Imelda laughed, throwing his head back in a carefree way. "Very well. I understand that your sire and dam produced their first mutual offspring, since you, today?"

Rowan's stomach churned. "Yes, that is my understanding as well."

"A lovely product, I do believe." Imelda studied Rowan. "She will make a fine breeder one day."

"No doubt." Rowan forced his tone to be level. "She is from the finest stock aboard the QuellTruth, in my understanding."

Imelda laughed. "I suppose you are encouraged to believe just that. Which brings me to my point. I believe that both this new property and you are the future of my breeding program here on the QuellTruth! I have reports of perfect health and incredible genetic results in both of you."

"I don't follow, Slavemaster."

"Well, the combination of physical beauty and spirit in a slave is of great interest to my investors and clients. You're my future, Rowan Jun! You'll lead the QuellTruth Program into a glorious new direction. We've tried to duplicate what we've achieved in you, and now finally we have a female."

"I see," Rowan answered. His stomach roiled in protest to what Imelda implied.

"Oh, I doubt you see just yet," Imelda said, gloating over the secrets of his great human trafficking operation. "But soon."

"Ah," Rowan managed past the fear in his throat. "Then soon, Slavemaster."

"Yes, Rowan Jun." Imelda leaned into his

face, his chest rising and falling. Rowan closed his eyes. "I've received some hefty offers for you, just as you are. But I wanted to tell you personally, that I've turned them all down. And do you know why?"

Rowan shook his head, feigning ignorance.

"Because you are mine, and shall be mine until the day I die." Imelda's voice came sweetly and calmly, a mere statement of fact.

Rowan shivered inside, his nervous stomach tensing. *Then die*, he thought fervently. The only thing worse than being sold as a slave was being kept aboard this horrid ship as the personal property of Dargin Imelda.

"Now don't think you get that gift for free, Rowan Jun." Imelda studied his face. "You will still be considered a breeder, but in a much more expansive system. A true position of honor. How does it feel knowing that generations of perfect property will be created from your seed?"

"I...I have no words to express how that makes me feel, Slavemaster." Never tell the whole truth, Rowan repeated in his mind. "No words at all."

"Speechless, for once? I'm impressed!" Imelda drained his glass and dismissed him. "When you reach the age of maturity in the next cycle, we'll convene for a more formal meeting."

"Yes, Slavemaster."

And then, to Rowan's immense relief, Imelda dismissed him to leave by the escort of the Slaver waiting outside the door. Again, he stared at his feet, counting the steps and turns until he stood outside his cell again.

The Slaver didn't talk to him this time, which was just as good, since Rowan sank deep into thought. Rowan's mind felt tangled with threats of fathering masses of slaves. His sister's future threatened by a worse fate than simple slavery—by the same fate of his Breeder mother—Rowan let the sense of urgency refine his plan to lead all ten thousand souls aboard the QuellTruth to freedom.

He patiently waited for the next day, which would bring word from Cadin on their current trajectory in space. He waited, and he planned.

2: INQUISITION

Cadin did not report. He didn't show up for his meal. He didn't show up to sleep. The other boys murmured, afraid and worried. Their brave leader maintained a convincing front. However, Rowan felt a deep pang of worry and doubt well into the night and all throughout his chores the next day. Somewhere in the pit of his stomach, Rowan felt the stirrings of something worse than worry. Dread froze his mind. He couldn't focus on the task before him, least of all his great plan.

A Slaver pulled him from the last of his chores to attend the Slavemaster. "He's got big, important company. So keep your mouth shut."

Rowan obeyed, keeping his shoulders back and his eyes cast down, staring at his feet as they made their way along the familiar path to the Slavemaster's quarters. Then the Slaver veered off to the right. Rowan faltered and corrected his course. His stomach rumbled again.

Wide windows lined the corridor, giving the Slavers a panoramic view of goings-on regarding slaves. On the right, Rowan saw the entrance to the mess hall, all the walls glowing white. Workers climbed a ladder at the far glass wall that enclosed a Slaver booth. The Slaver paused to call out through the open doorway to the other Slaver supervising the workers.

In the moments they chatted, Rowan paid attention to the slave workers as they labored. They bent over with ropes and began tying knots, obscuring their task from his sight. The Slavers laughed together from the distance.

"Haul it up, men," the supervising Slaver called out. "Careful, no! Make it even on each side. Now heave!"

The workers pulled at the ropes to reveal a gruesome cargo. A human body—carved, bruised and beaten—dangled from those ropes. Rowan's blood ran cold. He recognized Cadin by curling red hair and slight build. Rowan's stomach lurched and he vomited at the door.

"Golden boy here has a weak stomach," his escort said with a vicious chuckle. "Get your boys to clean this mess up! We're due at the Slavemaster now." He waved off his Slaver friend's curses and rude gestures and whisked Rowan back down the hall. Then he shoved Rowan into the nearest restroom and growled, "Clean your face and get the bile out of your hair. I can't take you before Imelda as you are."

Rowan stared into his reflection in the two-direction glass. Even the restrooms had those wide windows for Slavers to keep an eye on slaves. His pale face held the air of death with dark circles under his eyes.

He forced down his next wave of nausea. They got to his friend and fellow insurgent. But how? And what all did they learn from him. Clearly, he either gave them nothing at the cost of his life, or gave them everything, still at the cost of his life.

The Slaver led him all the way past the slave quarters to the front of the ship, where

Imelda waited for them.

"Ah! Rowan Jun, at last." He threw open his arms as though welcoming an old friend. "Come. Stand here."

Rowan stepped up onto the block for inspection, as he had a hundred times over the course of his life. He squared his shoulders and looked straight ahead, as Imelda required of him. He glimpsed the man and woman in his periphery. They weren't quite human, though human-shaped, with purple and gray skin, hair coiffed in unnatural shapes, and clothing far tackier than any Rowan had seen in the archives.

Imelda brandished two pairs of soft white gloves and placed them in the visitor's hands. He gestured to Rowan. "If you please, good friends."

Their prodding hands raked down his muscles, squeezing to feel the strength of muscle over bone. They pushed his full lips up over his perfect white teeth to inspect them. They pried his mouth open to stare down his throat. The woman inspected other parts of his anatomy with an intrigued smile, much to Rowan's intense embarrassment.

"This Breeder would do wonderfully among our livestock." The man spoke in a constant falsetto that grated on Rowan's nerves. "Diversifying my program is of top priority."

Imelda laughed, his own voice tightening into a higher pitch. "I acknowledge your interest, my dear friend Katir, my lady Janta. You must understand that Rowan Jun is a unique specimen, the result of selective breeding for many generations. As such, he is not available for sale currently. However, he is the first of many in a glorious new product that we wish to provide. And you'll be among the first invited to place an order, with the minor consideration of perhaps a sizable deposit?" Imelda chuckled again, nervously this time. "Let us discuss further business in my office, and we'll make this fine specimen available at our leisure afterward."

Standing at attention for untold ages, on display for the Slavemaster's clients, who glanced at him often through the glass wall of Imelda's office as they negotiated sums, Rowan had too much time to dive deep into his thoughts and worries. Outwardly, he showed a deliberately blank expression. Internally, his fidgeting mind drew him in a dozen directions, all more confusing and worrisome than the last.

"Well, we'll be back through your system within the next cycle, by which time the product on which you've paid a generous deposit will be fulfilled," Imelda said, raising his voice as high as his vocal chords would allow, in an attempt to match the man's high-pitched tone.

What an odd courtesy, Rowan mused, laughing internally at how silly the powerful Slavemaster sounded. He felt sure now that he wouldn't be able to do anything about the ship's navigation in this system. Too many planets supported slavery in this area. The so-called clients and any of their kin would simply claim the slaves for their own, or return them to the company for a reward.

Rowan raged against the terms *client*, *deposit*, and *product* in his mind, when another interesting bit of conversation made its way to his ears.

"Oh, yes, my lady Janta. We'll be passing closer to Unata than Azela within a few months," Imelda said with his strained voice. "Unata lies on the outer rim of the Pazelian system at this point in their orbit. Azela lies much farther to the interior."

"Is Unata as brutal as we have heard?" The female sounded more intrigued than scared. "We hear they kill all who venture into their atmosphere."

"Oh, I'm sure the rumors inflate as they expand from the source." Imelda waved off her concern. "You know, my dears, that every self-knowing creature has their own specific motivating interests, usually monetary. However, the place is known as Fear Planet for a reason. Their citizens do have skill in combat. And their jungles are said to harbor some of the deadliest creatures in the whole wide universe!"

The man, Katir, voiced his agreement to all parts of the conversation. Janta exclaimed about deadly creatures, an elation sounding in her voice. They continued that part of the discussion for some time in conjecture, for none of these creatures had ever been confirmed.

Rowan dismissed the vile musings of those humanoid creatures in consideration of Unata. He knew the same rumors. He also had no reason to disbelieve them. Why would every unrelated survivor tell the same story? Rowan just assumed that Unatans released survivors to ensure that the universe would take the hint to stay away. He didn't know if that world supported slavery. And suddenly, knowing that the monster Imelda would be either selling or otherwise using them both within a cycle, he didn't care. For Ayli to live free, Rowan would have to take his chances with Unata.

Finally, Imelda walked his guests to their ship, following their final cursory inspection of Rowan, the ever-attentive slave. Rowan retched with the nervous twisting of his stomach again. This, along with everything else, he suppressed. He felt hungry and exhausted, swaying on his feet only slightly. Feeling for a moment that maybe Cadin died with his secrets, Rowan breathed deeply of the cold air.

Then Imelda returned. His false smile disappeared with his falsetto voice. “You’re a valuable asset, Rowan Jun.”

Rowan acknowledged him by bowing his head.

“So valuable that, for now, until you’ve fulfilled your purpose, you are absolved of your many transgressions.” Imelda stared up at Rowan, his eyes welling up with feelings of betrayal and anger in merely a second. “However, to think you would escape without a proper punishment is absurd.”

“Slavemaster?” Rowan choked on the word.

“Your fellow slave Cadin provided some interesting information about you,” Imelda began, his voice all velvet and calm. “My Slavers spent some time convincing him to speak, at length, before he said anything. But it’s amazing what fiery knives, blunt force trauma, and the removal of toenails and fingers will do for loosening the tongue.”

Two Slavers entered the display room behind him, laughing at Imelda’s words. Rowan’s blood boiled in righteous anger, then froze in fear. He couldn’t retaliate or run with the Slavers behind him. But where would he run? He understood for once what the other boys had meant. The walls felt closer on all sides. The floor and ceiling seemed to converge. He choked down his dizziness and managed to glare at Imelda.

“You have nothing to say?” Imelda crooned. “No denial? No additional names to provide that may save your skin the worst punishment?”

“There are no others left.” Rowan shivered despite his resolve. “With Cadin dead, there is only me."

"My gut says that is untrue, my pet," Imelda said. "Cadin wouldn't provide other names, either. But when we caught him digging through the manifest, he clearly had others in mind. He just wouldn't name them."

"There are no others!" Rowan's wavering voice came out as a shout. "Only I remain."

Rowan stared into Imelda's burning gaze and willed him to believe him. The lives of dozens of slaves rested solely on his ability to keep his mouth shut. He owed them that much.

"Well," Imelda said with a languid drawl, "I can't say that I believe you are the only one remaining. However, I am sure that removing Cadin and you from the equation will end this little insurgency you've organized. Come. Now."

Removing me? Rowan's mind fluttered through possibilities. Slavers dragged him off the block and down the hallway, behind Imelda. The Slavemaster took purposeful strides and made all-too-familiar lefts and rights until he stood before a wide window outside the nursery.

Gazing inside, unknown terrors arose in Rowan. Wordless fears he couldn't control. Little Ayli lay there, cradled in her mother's loving embrace. His precious little sister nursed and waved her chunky little hands overhead at a shiny golden object that her mother dangled from a chain.

Rowan recognized the object as the familial identity locket assigned to each mother upon the birth of a child. Aboard the QuellTruth, a woman would likely be bred again before her milk dried up. At that point, they took any surviving infant to be raised in a communal setting by unrelated slaves. The Slavers kept excellent records on all breeding programs. Therefore, the lockets served merely as a distracting comfort to bereft mothers, allowing Slavers to identify how many children a breeder had birthed at a glance. Rowan's mother carried a dozen lockets, one of which heralded his birth almost eighteen cycles prior and a shiny new one for Ayli.

His mother noticed his face through the clear glass. She appeared both elated and confused, then worried. The Slavers pulled him to the door, then followed Imelda into the room.

"Evening, Slavemaster," Rowan's mother said, eyeing the Slavers around her. "Pleasant having the man himself come see his newest."

Imelda ignored her. "Rowan Jun, come hold this child."

He stepped forward and did as he was told. His mother stared into his eyes. He saw the fear and confusion therein. Rowan mouthed, *I don't know*, and *I'm sorry*. One of the Slavers pulled a chair into the room beside the bed.

"Sit," Imelda instructed.

Rowan sat, cradling Ayli in his arms. She whimpered. He bounced her in his arms until she calmed down. Feeling Imelda's eyes on him, Rowan glanced up.

"Your son has gained a following and attempted to begin an insurgency aboard the QuellTruth." Imelda stared at the woman, satisfied she seemed genuinely surprised. "Now, he's been caught. But he's too precious a specimen to simply discard. His mind is the faulty part. Not his body. So, discipline is in order."

Rowan pressed his lips into a tight line, staring from his mother to little Ayli and back. "Imelda, please don't..."

"No," Imelda interrupted. "You are property which has disobeyed. You have no rights. You have no permission. You will do what you are told when you are told and the way you are told. You are bred for this purpose, and for this purpose alone."

"I'm sorry, Imelda," Rowan pleaded. "I'll do whatever I can to earn my forgiveness. I'll take any beating you want to purge me of my sin. But please..."

"This is your punishment. Your father has been purged as of earlier this morning, by the very Slavers who attend now. And next, your mother." Imelda leveled his handgun at Rowan's mother's chest and pulled the trigger.

Imelda's words did not have time to sink in before his mother slumped forward. The gunshot still rang in Rowan's ears, robbing him of clear hearing. Ayli squealed, her ears ringing with pain and her heart pounding in terror, her tiny face contorting as she gasped between screams. Rowan held the baby close, rocking her in the chair, too fast and too frantically. Tears rolled down his cheeks. Tears rolled down the baby's cheeks. Rowan wailed in wordless agony.

"Well, hurry and harvest her ovaries," Imelda ordered. "Set up in vitro with the new amniotic pods immediately, using the fresh samples from what we harvest today. Then we'll be on a time crunch to develop the rest of the follicles for our frozen bank. We have orders to fill, after all."

Human medics—slaves with extensive training—rushed forward, hacking on the woman's body to follow Imelda's instructions. Rowan rose to his feet and stumbled toward her body. Both Slavers shoved him down by the shoulders. The medics left to fulfill their remaining orders.

Ayli's wailing had reduced to gasping, wet moans and hiccups. Rowan still rocked her frantically, to keep from lunging at the man. He wanted nothing more than a miracle, for little Ayli to somehow live free on a planet far away from monsters like Dargin Imelda.

"You really are a monster," Rowan growled past his trembling lips.

"Oh?" Imelda smiled. "Are those true feelings at last from my favorite pet?" He bit off that last word with a snarl.

"Imelda, you lie to yourself," Rowan grumbled. His throat tightened. "You pretend to own people, to own humans. But you can't. Don't you see it in her eyes? She deserves to be free. Please, see what I see. I don't care what you do to me. But please set her free."

Imelda pursed his lips and narrowed his eyes at Rowan for too long. He stared at the trembling baby in Rowan's arms. "If I set her free, you will submit to whatever future I set for you? Freely and without argument?"

Rowan felt his future slip away with the glimmer of hope that Ayli would live free, somewhere far beyond the reach of Dargin Imelda. He nodded blindly, his tears flowing again.

"For all your machinations in your ill-timed insurgency, you are an idiot, Rowan Jun." Imelda grinned ear to ear. "I'll have your compliance. And I'll free your sister. You should have this to remember her by."

The Slavemaster tossed the dead mother's golden locket at Rowan's face. He turned his head aside. The locket bounced off his head and landed open on the floor. On one side of the oval, Ayli's smiling face shone out, her bright hazel eyes glowing happily. On the other, a laser had engraved her identifying numbers.

Dread and tears slowly blurred her face in

that picture. The tears dripped from his chin onto Ayli's head. She had cried so hard that she nuzzled against his chest, fully asleep but whimpering on occasion. He watched her little chest rise and fall. But his tears wouldn't stop.

"Do you know why you are an idiot, Rowan Jun?" Imelda had remained silent too long, pensively staring at them, dark clouds drifting through his possessive eyes.

Rowan cast his eyes upward to the monster before him. Full of hate, contempt, anger, and pain, the young man entertained a glimmer of hope mixed with dark, nauseating foreboding.

"There is only one way this bit of property," Imelda said with a broad gesture, "will ever be free."

He withdrew the pistol from his long robe and leveled it at Ayli. The next seconds passed in a blur. Rowan bellowed in shock and sprang to his feet. He pulled Ayli's head up to his shoulder. He turned to his left to flee. A bullet cracked through the air. Searing pain shot through his left hand. A Slaver grabbed him and shoved him into the chair. Then he felt the blood trickle from his hand down his arm.

His adrenaline set him to run. The Slaver pressed hard on his shoulders. Ayli hadn't awoken with that shot, screaming again like he expected. Then he looked down to see why she didn't cry out. The blood trickling from his hand mingled with the blood draining from the bullet wound in her head.

Eyes wide and a bloodcurdling scream escaping his lips, Rowan clung to the child in his arms until finally he collapsed on the floor, blissfully unconscious.

3: VALKYRIE DESCENDS

Rowan's hand wandered to the locket hanging from his neck. His heart felt so hollow. Weeks passed with his mind broken, hysterical, and inconsolable even on the threat of physical beatings. *There's nothing that can hurt me anymore,* he thought in a detached way. Or rather, he knew. Nothing in the cosmos could damage him the same way as Dargin Imelda.

The young man moved through his chores without a word, acknowledging only the Slavers if they spoke to him. His hollow eyes turned neither left nor right in nearly an eighth cycle. He ate when told, slept when told, submitted to exams when told, and maintained his fitness goals when told.

He pulled a mop across the floor and flinched. The twinge of pain in his left hand shot up his forearm. The bones shattered by the bullet that killed little Ayli had taken a long time to mend. On the surface, he was barely scarred, thanks to the expert stitching of the medics. Deep inside, the bones healed well enough, but held an ache that need not affect his real purpose aboard the ship—breeding.

"Breeder," a surly Slaver called him by title.

"Slavemaster Imelda orders you to mess hall duty today. Now."

Screaming inside, in a hollow way, Rowan blanked his face and nodded to the Slaver. He headed toward the mess hall, watching his bare feet and counting his steps. With his final step, he gazed up and out across the room. His breath came in ragged gasps for several minutes before he could continue into the room.

There, on the glass partition to the Slaver's cubicle, hung the desecrated bodies of Rowan's father and mother, stripped naked and sprayed with some type of preservative. The infant Ayli hung between them, her tiny arms bound in the same thick ropes as her parents.

Reliving the nightmare of Ayli's death, Rowan froze in the hallway. The room spun and he grasped at the door facing to keep his body upright. Imelda sent him here frequently as an ongoing lesson. The locket he awoke with the next day served more as a warning than a memorial. Imelda had been right. Rowan would be subjugated with Ayli *freed*.

The thought of that monster, of his many unspeakable actions, left Rowan breathless. He gathered his cleaning supplies, ever the mindless yet dutiful slave. He cleaned all around the room. He wiped the tables and polished the glass and metal fittings. No one else showed up for duty in the mess hall this evening, as was the case when they delegated the task to Rowan.

Lately, he felt more clarity as he worked. He carefully guarded his facial expressions, but let his mind wander to anything but the memory of little Ayli. The Slavemaster made sure he spoke to only the Slavers by removing other slaves from any path he ordered. But Rowan refused to condemn another innocent slave with his words or actions.

Rowan had wandered the halls for many days on assignment, feeling as if he were smothered under a dense fog, thick in tongue and body. That atmosphere had followed him from the event through every day. He knew it must be the deep depression he sank into, at least at first. But the fog never lifted from his mind so that he could face the full pain of his actions. This felt wrong, artificial. When he found a suspicious powder on his plate earlier that week, he began trimming his generous rations. In mere days, his lucidity improved so that he could reason more clearly.

As he mopped closer to the defiled bodies of his family, Rowan felt his skin crawl, like his limbs awakened after dangling his feet from a ledge. The feeling started at the top of his head and continued down his limbs. His left hand throbbed with each heartbeat. His heart pounded as the veil of his intoxication peeled back from his eyes at last.

The hefty rations he consumed until that week had no doubt been laced with some drug that kept him locked in his mind. When the righteous anger had arisen, he felt it choke down of its own accord. Depression crippled him for a time, but these drugs made him numb and functional for the Slavemaster's uses. The pain still threatened to smother him. He let it flow through him and reignite the flame within his heart.

He stood before his family, leaning on a mop until his legs stopped their pinpricked tingling. He stared up with clear, determined eyes once more. *I'll take up the banner again.* His heart pounded, the last of the drug filtering from his body. *For you, mother and father.*

He pulled his lips tight across his teeth, in

pain and in determination, ready again to bear the mantle of martyr. “But mostly, for you, Ayli.”

* * *

Starving took its toll after a week. Rowan, however, needed his wits about him. That was only possible when he avoided the drugged food they heaped before him. After another week, he noticed the traces of powder around his starches and couldn’t find any on the meat they fed him. Protein alone sustained him after that, as he flushed most of his meal in disgust.

His mind wandered constantly to the future he couldn’t provide to little Ayli. Luckily, he hid most of his drug withdrawal in the privacy of his solitary cell. If any Slavers noticed his sweating and pain and mumbling in reaction to hallucinations, they dismissed it as a manifestation of his guilt. During the day, during his chores and inspections, Rowan suppressed the worst of it. He seemed merely sullen and completely subdued, like a good slave.

When at last he heard that the QuellTruth would pass near Unata, he acted, knowing he could not miss his chance to help the other slaves find their freedom. With Ayli’s cause at the forefront, Rowan’s heart pounded as he made his way to the navigation wing of the slaveship. The Slavers considered him defeated in spirit. He found it easy enough to slip past them with some excuse to clean, his mop bucket in tow.

The warm rush of air flowed across Rowan’s face as the navigation wing opened before him. With the warmth came a distinctive electrical scent. Rowan stepped into the room to gain his bearings. Lights glowed to life around him and revealed a large, empty room. He breathed a sigh of relief. The navigation module spanned a garishly lit rectangle holding banks of glowing lights, buttons of various function, and flickering screens that constantly flashed information of little interest to the current intruder.

Rushing toward the control panels in his mental diagram, he punched in codes he read on a piece of paper and remembered, from a conversation held in confidence while he stood on the slave block for inspection. Rowan hoped the codes had not been updated since that conversation. He knew the navigation crew to be a lazy lot, and hoped they continued their confidence in his ignorance for just a little longer.

To Rowan's relief, the codes gained him access to the autopilot controls. Thankful for the continued sloth of the QuellTruth's crew and their dependence on the antiquated autopilot technology, Rowan pulled up the coordinates for Unata. He selected a random place on the map that looked like heavy forest or jungle. He engaged autopilot and locked in the coordinates, selecting commands for emergency landing protocols, stating in the emergency beacon that the ship was in distress and needed repairs. Rowan found that he could not edit the protocol with anything slavery-specific. Not surprisingly, there were no beacon options that stated anything about violating the rights of sentient beings, as those would arouse suspicion from authorities of worlds against slavery.

With the instructions locked in, Rowan dismantled the input devices that served the navigation module. He pulled enough wires and broke enough keyboards and dials and buttons to ensure that no one could alter the course of the QuellTruth.

The Slavers took no notice of Rowan's

activities until he started destroying the input devices. Crashes and sparks and dying flickers of light drew their attention. Two big, lumbering green monsters with black rope-like hair rushed into the room. Just as he turned to run from them, red disaster lights began flashing along the wall. Overhead, loudspeakers sounded the emergency landing tone. He grinned at them, a delighted, maniacal sheen of accomplishment in his crazed eyes. The QuellTruth's mechanical announcement began: "Prepare for emergency landing! Sensors detect course alteration is not possible! Distress beacon activated! Entering unapproved airspace imminently!" Rowan had no idea the ship had been so close to Unata's atmosphere!

The Slavers lunged at him, cursing every breath. The announcement droned on overhead, repeating. One Slaver caught him by the shoulders and lifted him into the air. The Slaver's foul breath flowed over Rowan's face. He sternly cursed and slurred a scolding to Rowan, punctuating each growl with a shake of Rowan's body in the air. Then the QuellTruth dipped into the atmosphere of Unata.

The Slaver, thrown off balance, simply flung Rowan as the ship's floor tilted with the sudden reentry. The air rushed past Rowan until he smashed against a glass partition with a sickening thud. The pain engulfed him. He fell to the floor, hitting his head on the edge of a console on the way down. One counter tipped over onto his foot. Rowan knew for sure it must be broken. He cried out in agony. Each jolt of reentry jarred his pinned foot. Breathing proved difficult with what must be broken ribs. He struggled to maintain consciousness, feeling the blood trickle down the side of his face.

The Slavers received some vocal transmission and cursed again, scrambling out of the room. Rowan would have been relieved if not for his fear of dying on this cold floor. He shoved at the counter edge with no effect. Between his pain and blood loss, he had no strength to move the counter. Then the reality of his situation dawned. Even as he suffered greatly, the freedom of ten thousand slaves lay ahead! The small comfort lulled him for a moment.

A new announcement sounded overhead: "Slavemaster override code approved. Cargo preservation protocol initiated. Lockdown in progress. Gravity and temperature controls adjusted. Power rerouted."

Rowan's gut twisted. He did not know about any override codes. Imelda wasn't one to preserve cargo in favor of his own skin. However, Imelda had managed such a code from wherever he stood aboard the plummeting QuellTruth. He cursed that horrible man for whatever plans he set in motion against the possible freedom of his slaves. But this big, old ship was sturdy, though it rarely landed planetside. Then, as if retaliation to Rowan's faith in the QuellTruth, came another, more chilling announcement:

"Danger! Emergency thrusters offline. Landing gear non-functional. Execute emergency landing protocol. Brace for impact."

Rowan's blood ran cold. His mind blanked. His smug martyrdom fell away. His panic arose. The icy hand of terror gripped his heart. He felt every moment of the ship's descent as a jolt to his ego, battered body, and his lofty plan.

The QuellTruth plunged nose-first toward the jungle. She rocked backward in the air and wobbled just before she hit the canopy and began her long slide to a crushing stop.

With the QuellTruth's first grazing into the ground, the console pinning Rowan's foot flipped over and skidded across the room. The sudden release of pressure caused him to shudder, groaning in fresh, nauseating pain. He blinked hard and willed the room to stop spinning. Deafened by the grinding roar of the ship's impact, Rowan struggled to focus. Red disaster lights flashed along the wall in unison with the constantly wailing siren. Then the siren sputtered and crackled into a hiss of white noise. The room lights flickered once more, then died. In the intermittent flashing of the red emergency lights, Rowan saw the upended room as completely unfamiliar.

Rowan groped blindly across the shaky, uneven floor. When shards of glass cut his hands, he snatched them back and clenched his fists, ignoring the pain in the face of his rising panic. The floor still rumbled, bucked and churned beneath him as the bulky vessel skidded to a lurching stop. He collapsed in numb silence, shivering and struggling against his body going into shock, until the sound of grating metal faded in the distance.

He reached out again and grasped the edge of an upturned computer console. With a grunt of exhausted agony, he hauled his body upright. Rowan's injured foot buckled under his weight. He bit his lips together, gasping in air. He sprawled across the hard counter and lowered his uninjured foot to the floor. Leaning heavily on the console, he stood.

Rowan wiped the sweat from his brow, tracing fresh blood from his temple to his chin and back into his matted hair. His chest and side burned with a dozen long cuts from broken glass. He felt the stickiness of drying blood all the way down to his hip. The reality of his condition set in. *At least the Slavers are gone for now!*

Intermittent red illumination sputtered across upturned furniture and twisted metal that had once been the control room. Jaw set in some newfound determination, Rowan sifted through the debris. His hand closed on part of a broken metal cart. He snapped off a hollow tube of metal with a smooth curve at the top that would serve adequately as a crutch. He hobbled across the uneven floor to a twisted cabinet. Using his crutch for leverage, he pried the door open and pulled down a large metal medkit full of bandages. He leaned back against a broken countertop and wrapped the gauze around his ribs, trying to stem the flow of blood from cuts that continually reopened with his effort.

After that, he turned his attention to his foot, which dangled, aching monstrously. Flashes of electrical sparks and damaged red lighting revealed a bloody, purple mess at the end of his rapidly swelling leg. He groaned through clamped lips and focused on the floor, trying not to succumb to the dizziness he felt. He wrapped his broken foot tightly in a thick compression bandage, though it robbed him of breath and left him woozy with pain. He stood for a long time, gasping in the thick air, unsure of his next step and gaping around him at the evidence of his great sin.

Rowan barked his shins on scattered consoles, stubbed his toes on the irregular floor, and stumbled more than once as he headed toward the door. He muttered curses under his breath until he finally made it to the corridor. He breathed deeply of his newfound hope and then froze where he stood.

Mingled with the frayed, burnt electrical

wires and the normal human waste stench of the vessel, the metallic smell of fresh blood arose to taunt him. Rowan swallowed the bile that filled his mouth and crammed his lips into his shoulder. He leaned against the smooth wall outside the control room, readying himself to move. *Or I could stay,* he thought. The brief consideration echoed as a deep reckoning in his conscience. *How many survived?* He listened closely for several minutes.

Utter silence answered him. Is everyone dead? Was it possible that all the cargo, all the fragile human slaves died in the crash? All but Rowan. Remorse paralyzed him. His heart pounded in an uneven rhythm. He gripped his agonized chest, felt the metal crutch dig into his flesh, reminding him of the numbness of shock that threatened to overwhelm him. The coldness of sorrow crept into his bones, shutting him down moment by moment. He remembered the Slavemaster's last minute protocol override. He hoped Imelda's "cargo preservation protocol" proved as promising as it sounded.

Then a more terrifying sound rose above his ragged breathing—the rhythmic sound of sharp clicks on metal. Feeling detached from the danger, he listened. One, two, three, four, he counted. Footsteps, he realized with a start. Rowan's hands trembled. Someone survived! The sound ceased, followed by the groaning of metal and a shuffling of cloth, then more footsteps. Five, six, seven, eight, nine.

He strained his ears to determine who had survived. Then terror replaced his sudden joy. The abrupt noise that accompanied each step was the clicking of boot heels. Only the Slavers wore shoes. This shuffling gait sounded oddly familiar to Rowan. Other footsteps joined the first, Rowan judged over the sound of the blood roaring in his ears. Slavers proved much sturdier than humans, and meaner, too. More likely to survive a spaceship plowing into a planet.

Yet someone with swinging, disdainful steps led the heavier ambling of the Slavers. Only the Slavemaster swaggered like that. The fact that the man still breathed rankled Rowan. Dargin Imelda may have been just a human. However, he had a knack for preserving himself as only a monster of his caliber could. A traitor to his own species—buying, selling and breeding his own kind—always finds a way. Rowan pressed his lips together, determined to control his mixture of fury and fear, to halt his body's violent shaking. He struggled to silence his rasping breath. Too late. The direction of footsteps angled down a hallway near the Slaver quarters and grew louder. They headed toward the control room, toward him.

Rowan pushed his body from the metal wall and leaned heavily on his good leg and the crutch. He plunged down the nearest hall that led to the outer hull of the ship. His pulse raced. Rowan forced his brain to focus on his ungainly footsteps. He counted the Slavemaster and two remaining Slavers, at least. None of the three moved as if severely injured. Rowan cursed under his breath.

Strange voices rose excitedly in the corridor beyond. "Rowan Jun?" Then Imelda grumbled, "I hardly believe he survived!"

"I told you, Master," snuffled one of the Slavers. "I just flung him."

Imelda called to Rowan again in a velvet voice. The veiled contempt in his tone chilled Rowan to his core. This was by far the worst thing Rowan had done, short of failing to save little Ayli.

No amount of lashing Rowan would satisfy the sadistic Slavemaster's anger now. And beyond the actual crash, Rowan wanted more than anything to confirm how many slaves had survived. But such thoughts clouded his mind. He blinked hard and refocused on moving forward.

Hand-lights glared into the flickering darkness, a revealing constant that proved Rowan could not escape. Rowan cursed again and launched his body toward a blackened hallway, and hopefully, to freedom. His foot smacked into an upturned floor plate, taking his breath for a long moment. Then he lurched forward once more, teeth clenched as pain seared through his vision.

Rowan flicked his chin to the side to move his sweaty black hair from his grimacing face. He glared ahead, near crazed with fear, his mind flashing a hundred incoherent scenarios for how he could survive. The white lights flickered on, mingling with the red. Using the brief revealing light, Rowan hastily plotted his next few steps over dangerous wreckage. He progressed more slowly in the pitch blackness.

In his mind, he struggled onward. *If they didn't survive, my only penance is death!* But death would be a waste! He spent his whole life—all seventeen cycles of it—as a wretched slave aboard the Slaveship QuellTruth. For the first time ever, freedom awaited him! *I deserve death more*, his anguish whispered. When the garish light subsided, another dark hallway swallowed his stumbling form. Cursed conscience or not, Rowan clung to his chance for liberty.

Rounding the corner into the exterior hallway, Rowan moved ever forward, albeit slowly, dragging his injured foot in a bloody trail behind him. The floor felt icy cold and appeared frosted at the edges. He paused to pry open a door with his crutch, heaving with all his might until the metal gave way and slid back with a scraping groan.

The air around him felt sweltering. The impact in the deck below must have damaged the temperature regulation mechanisms. The tanks would have exploded, spewing their volatile contents on anything in the way. Or anyone. *Think of all the slaves who may have died in agony*, his anguish whispered. *Not now!*

"Hahaha! Look. He's running *away*, Dargin!" a Slaver cried, rounding the corner.

"Does he think so?" answered Imelda softly.

Instead of freezing like his mind desired, Rowan broke into a hobbled run, crying out in pain at each jolt. The hand-light beams stabbed into his secure darkness, swinging to and fro, glaring across his blood-caked pale skin and blinding him. He wondered why he still ran, still struggled, after all he had done. *So much death!*

In the darkness and panic, his left arm collided with a large round metal object on that side of the hallway. Rowan heard a muffled pop as the bone snapped. He cried out first in searing pain, then in realization. An escape hatch!

Rowan gripped the round metal tube with his right hand and wrenched it in a half circle to unlock the door. He leaned in with his shoulder and pushed as hard as he could. The metal did not yield. He glared at the door and pulled inward. He roared in rage as much as pain when it didn't budge. Rowan threw all his slight weight against the metal repeatedly. Nothing.

Defeated, Rowan turned to face his enemy, to atone, finally. Fear sobered him. Defenseless, he searched for a weapon and found only the metal crutch he fashioned. Feeling death was imminent and possibly deserved, he knew this must be the only right, just way to end it all. He had sinned and sinned greatly.

Flanked by the grotesque, knobby-shouldered Slavers, the Slavemaster Dargin Imelda stepped forward into the flickering light. To Rowan's perverse satisfaction, the man's face appeared thoroughly roughed up, with bruises and cuts all over the left side. He wore a tattered version of the finely embroidered red robe he used for special occasions, open to the navel and burnt where once it flowed to the ground.

Imelda stared at Rowan with the calm detachment of nobility. The human who owned humans. Words failed to describe him fully. Slavemaster, Leader, Human. Monster. One word came to Rowan's mind.

"Bastard!" Rowan whispered, swallowing past the tightness in his throat.

Imelda laughed. The Slavers joined in until Rowan could no longer suppress the shudders of terror raising the hair on his neck. Imelda spoke up. "My little pet! One thoughtless action," he held up his long finger, "and you cost me a substantial sum, an entire section of my empire. You just proved that you are faulty merchandise, after all... a property liability. And *I'm* the bastard?"

Rowan gulped. "I'm no one's property!"

Another laugh rang out from the man. He straightened his robe and brushed his dark, dirty hair behind his ear. He leaned forward and lowered his voice. "My property caused a great deal of damage." He took in the ruined ship with an expansive gesture. "I, of course, take full responsibility for this. A business management mistake that will not be repeated."

Dizzy for lack of blood, Rowan fell against

the door, his last effort before he welcomed death. He feebly leaned back. He turned his face from Imelda's sneer, preferring to merge with the metal than have the terrifying creature come an inch closer. Yet the door would not budge. The Slavemaster's property. A human slave. *Me*, Rowan thought. *Mere property*.

Rowan stared at the Slavemaster's sarcastically extended hand. His fingers showed no callouses. His palms remained clean in the horrible aftermath of this crash. This man never worked. He only ordered work. He was the human who tried to own other humans. He was a monster who didn't think he was wrong. A dangerous man of power. *A man whose power I shattered*, thought Rowan with a crazed smile.

When Rowan smiled viciously, the man withdrew his hand with a frown, scrubbing his already clean palm on his pants. With perfect teeth revealed, the Slavemaster smiled and said, "Of course, I forgive you, my pet, as always. I have plans to rebuild in the most glorious manner, using the embryos I have saved on the inside."

Rowan frowned at the thought of another slave ship full of terrified, subjugated people.

"However, the others insist that punishment must be dealt to misbehaving property. As you know, given the circumstances, my hands are tied." Imelda demonstrated by spreading his hands at his sides and then clenching them behind his back.

As the monstrous Slavers circled to flank Rowan, he shivered. With yellow eyes glaring outward, they moved deliberately with their tall green bodies hunched over under the low clearance of the ceiling. Black ropes of twisted hair fell forward and obscured their scarred faces. The Slavers closed in on both sides of the boy;

Rowan looked left and right in the flickering light, shivers of terror and hopelessness reducing him to a quivering, crumpled form.

"He's rather damaged already, so don't kill him. He's unbelievably valuable to me. Strong, beautiful." The Slavemaster's voice trailed off on a gravelly note. "He'll still make a lovely Breeder when we acquire new stock."

The young man whipped his face toward Dargin Imelda, ignoring the Slavers. Rowan glowered at the arrogant fool. Every inch of his body burned with fever and hatred for the man. Then he lifted his metal crutch and swung it in a wide circle, keeping the Slavers at bay. He saw their blunt weapons and lashes and gritted his teeth. He fell back against the door once more, a gesture of defeat.

His eyes snapped open in alarm, for the door creaked and gave way. As the hatch swung outward, weapons snapped past Rowan's face and clanged off the metal wall. The sensation of relief replaced the rush of air and even the pain of hitting the ground. He managed a sloppy tumble and rolled to his back, trying to regain his breath. The new fractures and bruises, lacerations and reopened injuries couldn't encroach on the euphoria Rowan felt with his potentially brief getaway.

"Free, finally!" Rowan managed as his euphoria wore off. His laugh terminated in a series of sharp coughs. But the breath he drew was free!

He curled up on his side, clutching more ribs that had broken in his fall. He stared upward to judge the distance and froze in alarm. Large armored boots crowded him from all sides. Rowan scrambled to his knees, spreading the fingers of his right hand over the ache in his ribs. He looked up to face his new enemy. All five glowed, backlit by the setting sun. All five held metal weapons high above their heads. He closed his eyes as the weapons descended, upset at the turn of events. He didn't raise his hands in defense or cry out. He merely waited. He would at least *die* free.

Someone spoke in a stern, vaguely annoyed voice to Rowan's right. He didn't understand the language, but it sounded enough like a curse to his ears. Of their own accord, Rowan's eyes snapped open and followed the sound. The warriors lowered their weapons and obediently retreated. A figure stood beyond them, in full silver and black battle regalia. The woman appeared to be an angel, a Valkyrie, from his mother's ancient stories. He felt as if he died at her feet, weak and pathetic. Rowan looked for his metal crutch, but it was beyond his reach. He had no sword in his hand. She looked down at him and knew he was no warrior. *She will pass me by,* Rowan thought. *I don't even deserve eternity. Does eternity even exist?* He stared at the woman in awe, until he lost the strength to stay upright. He lay crumpled on the ground. He never knew dying could be so complicated.

"What are you, boy?" asked the Valkyrie as she stepped forward.

He stared at her shadow on the ground, taking a long moment to realize she spoke his language. An odd question, too. But he knew the response. The answer echoed in every fiber of his heart and every waking thought. He clenched an impotent left hand, digging his dirty fingernails into the jungle floor.

"A murderer," Rowan replied, his tone dead serious. "Nothing more."

For a while she stood in silence. He felt her gaze on the back of his head. "I will be the judge of your worth, now."

Rowan gazed up at the woman and felt his choices slip away, along with his consciousness. As her profile blurred in his eyes, he clung to the ringing resolve in her words. Perhaps the Valkyrie would not pass him by. His eyes closed. He finally felt ready for death.

* * *

A warrior knelt at Rowan's side. He placed two fingers on the boy's throat. "Hmph! He's alive, Garyn!"

The woman glared down at the boy, lost in thought. "After such a horrible crash?" she murmured. "And a human at that!"

The warrior cried out as he swung his axe at the young man's throat.

"Wait, Collern!" Garyn ordered, her hand raised. The blade stopped. "He's in my care now. And for God's sake, bandage his wounds! A solid field dressing will do until we get back. What do you say, Te-Dasuka?" She looked over her shoulder.

Te-Dasuka stepped forward, a dignified man with a leathern face lined with war and age. "You know my opinion on your habit of taking strays, Queen Garyn. Why, that Chard infant you fostered is only half Unatan and he'll have a hard time!"

"Chard was born to a Unatan mother in Parisia. This is his home." She waved his concern away with a gauntleted hand. She stared at the boy's strained, bloody face with forced detachment. "And this one's hardly a stray. More like a refugee, in fact," Garyn began, her hands on her hips.

Te-Dasuka laughed and shook his head. "I

suppose if I told you that humans are fragile creatures, that he can't withstand life in your kingdom, it wouldn't sway your decision?"

"He'll pull his own weight." Garyn's pale green eyes flickered behind her helm. "Mark my words, old man!"

"Marked and remembered, young Queen," he said with a sigh, "but I often wonder why you ask my opinion when you're already set."

"Because *you're* not afraid to oppose me if my decisions threaten this kingdom." Her smile went unseen behind the black and silver face plate. She knew Te-Dasuka understood. Since she took the Throne at eleven, he had been ever by her side. She shuddered at the memory of her first day, when Te-Dasuka alone had knelt in the blood around her and vowed to protect his new Queen.

A low sound reached her ears. Garyn turned to her left, toward the crashed spaceship. "Show yourself!"

The men grew silent around her. Collern paused in his task of wrapping the crumpled human boy in yards and yards of cloth dressings. He wiped his calloused hand clean of the pungent searingsalve that sanitized and cauterized the boy's wounds. He watched smoke drift from the chemicals under each bandage and felt comfort knowing that his patient remained blissfully unconscious. Collern stood, pulled his light metal gauntlet back over his hand, and followed the Queen's gaze. A tall human stood in the open door overhead. He leaned out and grasped a branch to steady himself. He began to speak and Collern did not understand the language.

"One guest is near-dead, and the other is quite rude," Garyn whispered to her warriors. "Identify!" Garyn demanded of the stranger.

"Forgive my ill manners. I am Dargin Imelda, Chief Executive Officer of the VuDega Merchant Company." He executed a curt bow from his precarious position. "It seems our business has suffered a minor setback. However, I can guarantee compensation for your damages once we reacquire our course."

"What is he saying, Majesty?" Te-Dasuka asked. "The words sound familiar."

"A dialect of Gangre-tan with a high-echelon inflection," she answered. "Not widely taught, but—" She shrugged. To the human, she called out in his language, "What business brought you to Unata, human?" Garyn spat out his species, intentionally disrespecting his name and title. His demeanor, his very aura, unsettled her.

"Ah, Unata, the Crossroads of the Universe! How fortunate!" The false relief he voiced made Garyn smile. She smelled fear. "We were en route to another merchant vessel when we suffered a fatal system malfunction. Gravity did the rest." He gave a short, disconcerted laugh. "My deepest apologies for the incon-venience our presence has caused Unata." This time he bowed deeply. His dirty hair bobbed forward and swayed in the empty space beneath him.

His palpable insincerity dripped through the air to Garyn's waiting ears. "An old sentiment," she replied. "Unata is not a welcoming home, as you may have heard. I trust that you notified your mothership to deploy a rescue vessel?"

"Madam, if I may join you to finish our discussion?" Imelda yelled down, teetering unsteadily out the hatch. "I feel rather unsafe at this height."

"Suit yourself!" Garyn called back. She

turned to her men, the smile evident in her voice. “He’d like to join us for a talk.”

Collern chuckled and murmured, “May be safer up there.”

“Show him some Unatan hospitality, men!” Te-Dasuka ordered. The others stood at attention, weapons at the ready. To Collern, he said, “Look after the boy. We can handle one human.”

Collern smiled and returned to the boy, who was soon more bandage than dirty skin. Garyn stared down at the kid, thinking he couldn’t be much older than her eldest warrior recruits. But for a human, he looked incredibly young. As she mentally plotted his training path, the heat assaulted her from the sun and the various fires that reduced her jungle to char.

Garyn gripped either side of the black and silver helm and hefted it from her head. She then pinned it against her hip with one arm. Her sweaty white hair dropped in front of her pale-lashed sea green eyes. She raked a hand through her hair as she watched Collern work. Then an electrical whirring drew her eyes away from the unconscious boy. Above them, Dargin Imelda hooked his metal belt harness to a mechanical device and waited for the zip line to lower him to the scorched jungle floor.

The businessman sauntered over to the warriors, pretending every moment that their appearance didn’t terrify him. His trying ordeal evident in the tattered and burnt robe he wore, his pale skin appeared unaccustomed to dirt. He greeted them formally with a quick bow. Then he jerked a thumb toward his back. “*That* is what’s left of *my* mothership. Our communication station inside was destroyed. And even if it worked, my VuDega partner’s mothership is out of range now."

Garyn considered the truth in his words and then met his eyes. "A sanctioned trade freighter arrives in three weeks. I'm sure as a favor to the *Queen*, they will take you to the nearest planet with com capabilities." She challenged him with her glare. His eyes went wide.

"Many thanks, your M-Majesty," he stammered, realizing his fault in not addressing her appropriately. He clenched his eyes shut during his long bow. He assumed that all the warriors were scouts. He had been mistaken. *What kind of civilization allows their royalty to go on scouting missions, anyway?*

When he raised his head finally, Dargin looked past the pale hair and dark skin of the Queen to the group behind her. Collern stood, removed his helmet and arched a pale eyebrow at him. Dargin stared at the warrior's chiseled jaw and severe eyes, the cleft in his square chin. Then Collern cocked his head to the side and shook his head, grinning all the time. *That one would fetch a high price*, Dargin realized, trying to hide his excitement. *So would the Queen!* An unlikely plan started to form in the businessman's mind.

"Garyn," Collern said with a smirk, "this guy's staring like I'm dinner. You sure humans aren't cannibals?"

Garyn sighed. "Just work. Let me worry about him."

Then Collern and another warrior knelt to work on something lying on the ground. Imagining Dargin a threat, the others advanced a few feet. Dargin craned his neck to see around them. The tall Unatan smeared salve and wrapped cloths around a boy's shoulder while the other twisted hard on his left arm. The bones popped back into place. Dargin recognized the blood-smeared face of Rowan Jun.

"Ah! My property lives!" Dargin cried in ecstasy.

"Property?" the Queen asked in a menacing low voice that drew Dargin's eyes back to her face.

He mustered his best smile. "Yes. This creature is my property," he answered, keeping his voice amiable. "The last living slave aboard the Slaveship QuellTruth. You'll be reimbursed your treatment of him, and I thank you."

The businessman rushed past the Queen to kneel by the young man. Dargin Imelda's head darted this way and that as he wrung his hands in manic worry. Garyn slowly turned and strode after him. She stared wide-eyed over his shoulder. She rested her hand on the grip of her katana. She clenched her teeth. *A slaveship? So that's why it wasn't registered!*

"A human who owns other humans?" Garyn asked. She managed a conversational tone but couldn't fully keep the anger out of her voice. "And here I thought slavery abandoned ages ago."

"That is why I'm willing to front a large sum to maintain that assumption, My Lady." Dargin's eyes snapped up from the unconscious boy.

The gray depths of his eyes held a note of lusty challenge. Garyn studied his bruised, blood-crusted face. His long light brown hair—dirty from the smoke of the crash—had been pulled back neatly. His square jaw worked in thought. His soft lips parted to entice her. He had to be charming in his social circle, a beautiful man. Seeing her small smile, the man stood and leaned in to speak privately to the armored woman. Garyn heard metal shift all around her as each warrior half-drew his weapon. Her hand tightened convulsively on the katana.

"At what price comes your silence about this little misadventure?"

His soft, manipulative voice lowered, just for her ears. He didn't know about Unatan hearing. She could hear the fearful beating of his heart. *A human who owns humans.* So this is what one feels like. Inward a coward, outward a lover. She grinned at the comical duality. Dargin Imelda mistook the grin for something else. He narrowed his eyes slightly and took her gauntleted hand to kiss.

Garyn's vicious smile held no desire. "At what price? Hmmm. Let us consider."

Garyn walked forward, passing the man and casually withdrawing her hand from his. She spared a furious glance at the injured young man. Then she gestured to the scar in her jungle that housed the wreckage of a spaceship.

"First, you have the massive cleanup of our jungle. And don't forget scrapping the ship." She paused a moment for effect, then turned back to him. He stood nodding, obviously crunching numbers in his ambitious mind. Garyn let her fury form another question. "In what numbers are your casualties?"

"In the tens of thousands, at least," he responded with a regretful sigh.

"In slaves alone?" Garyn ventured, seething.

"Yes. Our entire cargo." His throat grew dry. He coughed.

Too late, Dargin realized the trap of her stilted questions. Garyn heard his heartbeat double. She smiled at him, this time in sympathy.

"My men noticed that your ship is not registered. And given your trade, no one could look for you discreetly," Garyn whispered.

Dargin's eyes widened in fear, and then

narrowed in anger. "With what are you threatening me, *Your Majesty*?"

Garyn paused to consider. "I have never *threatened* a weakling in my life." He bristled in fury at her insult. She turned idly away, watching Collern and another warrior roll the boy's injured body onto a makeshift stretcher. "I may be the Queen of Unata, but my people follow me out of respect. I offer leadership and livelihood, and they answer with reasonable servitude. And in my kingdom, on *my* soil, freedom is a basic right."

"That has nothing to do with me!" Dargin Imelda cried. "Return my property and make good on your promise!" He lunged at the Queen.

Te-Dasuka appeared at Garyn's side and swatted the man down with the back of his hand. "Her Majesty has made no vow to you, whelp."

"Weaklings who become my enemies, who break the laws of my land," Garyn said with a sigh. "*They* get a promise." She turned to the man as he sputtered on the ground. "I promise you will cower. I promise you will die, and that your death will be swift. And in this case, I promise I will *not* kill you unless you refuse my quite simple request."

The businessman pressed a hand to his mouth and his fingers dripped with blood. Wide-eyed, Dargin struggled to his knees, looking wildly about for a weapon. He flung his body upward and rocked on his feet. But his heart pounded. He didn't want to die in this place. So he asked, "What do you want?"

"For starters, I have no intention of returning this boy to you, simply because a person cannot be owned," the Queen responded. "I *do* give you permission to live until which time an Enforcer ship collects you as a prisoner and you are arraigned before the Alliance's High

Courts regarding your slave trade."

His face blanched. With the Unatan Queen's testimony and glaring evidence, Dargin's name would be smeared across the galaxy by the harsh High Courts. His case would be a brutal warning to the other black-market Slavers. And only then would they execute him. In his terror, he began shaking his head. *Why would she not name a price?* Then he gawked at the Queen, pleading.

"Foolish woman, I can give you all the riches you desire!" Dargin cried desperately. "Just for looking the other way!" He closed the distance between them, reaching for Garyn's hands. Two of her warriors forced him to his knees before her. Cold metal found its way to his neck.

"Do you really think that money is power?" Garyn threw her head back and laughed. "You sit here with weapons at your throat and *spit* in the face of real power."

Garyn drew her katana, a fine weapon in black and silver with a long blade and a tasseled handle. The light from her sun glinted off the smooth surface, reflecting Dargin's scared and angry reflection back at him. "I tend not to give second chances, but seeing as how you come across as extremely dense, I will make an exception."

Garyn's eyes followed the length of steel until it merged with the intricate hilt. Then she leveled her eyes and her blade on the businessman. "Will you, Dargin Imelda, bend to the will of the Sovereign of Unata, Queen Garyn Kei, and face the crimes you have committed?"

His bottom lip quivered. Defeat etched lines across his handsome face. Then he scowled. "Why would I bend to the will of *old money*, Woman?" He spat on the ground at Garyn's feet.

She arched an eyebrow, smiled devilishly, and whispered, "So you choose to disappear."

The man's eyes narrowed and flashed indiscreetly over her shoulder. His foolish smile infuriated her. Garyn's senses flared as she acknowledged a new threat to her men.

"Behind you!" she cried, all too late.

One of her men withstood a crushing blow from a metal club. Another dodged a long, curved dagger. The cloaked figures, easily a head taller than the Unatans, were two in number but very agile. To Garyn's surprise, they had flanked the group in silence.

Collern swung his battle-axe at one of the attackers. Garyn saw his surprised expression when the creature deflected his attack with a much smaller dagger. The distraction cost Collern a hard blow to the stomach.

He rolled to avoid the dagger, scrambled to his feet and dove at the Slaver. Collern drove his axe deep in the enemy's sternum. The giant creature screamed. Collern yelled in surprise as the enemy wrapped a green hand around the axe handle and tore it from his chest. Then he shoved a hand into the mortal wound, continuing the fight as his dark blood spilled over the ground.

Garyn studied their movement and green-tinged skin. "They're Gangre-tan! Their skin is fused with organic armor! Their throats are not!"

Te-Dasuka stood at Garyn's back as she held down the squirming Slavemaster. One of her warriors fell to the ground. The uninjured Gangre-tan swung a metal club at the man's armored back. The old warrior clenched his fists in anger and turned to his Queen.

"Go," she told him. "I can handle this one." She pinned his shoulders, forcing Dargin to be still.

Te-Dasuka rushed to the aid of the young warrior, leveling the Gangre-tan Slaver with the flat side of his broad sword. The old man shoved the scout's helmet back into his hands and hauled him to his feet. Meanwhile the Slaver regained his footing. Te-Dasuka took an offensive stance and waited, his experience and training grounding him, calming him.

The Gangre-tan creature lunged again, dangling a freshly broken arm. In his anger, the Gangre-tan left his throat unguarded. Te-Dasuka swung the blade neatly between the Slaver's shoulder and head, slicing through his neck. The creature's head bounced across the burnt ground.

Watching Te-Dasuka work always impressed Collern. *Old man's just gotta be flashy!* But Te-Dasuka had come to the same conclusion as Collern. In revealing the enemy's weakness, Garyn just gave a kill order. *So, they have a weak throat*, Collern mused. He had worried that his weapon had dulled from disuse on real flesh in the last year of peace. Now, fighting against a superior enemy, he smiled.

"Looks like I'll pay you back for that gut shot, Gangre-tan!" Collern said as he slipped past the creature's dagger and sliced into his armored shoulder. He could finish what he started when the Gangre-tan's first blood fell. The battle dragged on. His fellow Unatans watched and waited at a respectful distance. Finally, in a risky dive, Collern lopped off the Slaver's head, which rolled to rest next to the other.

When his last Slaver fell, Dargin Imelda kicked the Queen in the stomach and scrambled away on his hands and knees. He grabbed a discarded dagger and hovered over the unconscious Rowan.

Queen Garyn rose slowly to her feet, every fiber of her being enraged. The foolish man started shaking the boy, desperate to awaken him. Garyn took slow, measured steps across the space between them. When she came close to the man's back, he lifted the dagger into the sunlight.

"Listen, Queen," he began without a backward glance. He clenched his fist around the dagger handle. "You should really stop to contemplate your next step."

Garyn set her foot back down. "As you wish. Are you ready to talk, to discuss the situation, Mister Imelda?" Her words came easily, sweetly.

She raised her hand to stop Collern and Te-Dasuka from advancing. Collern glowered at Imelda but didn't move. He had spent too long in the Queen's presence to trust that innocent, calm singsong voice she used with the Slavemaster. Collern glanced at Te-Dasuka for confirmation. The tension faded in the old man's face. Their Queen was probably at her most dangerous at that moment.

"Talk? With nasty *old money*?" Dargin scoffed, then laughed.

"Clearly, Mister Imelda, you hold the advantage now," she answered, her voice calm and even. "What demands do you now make?"

"For what? To what end? For the boy's life?" Dargin's voice grew shrill.

"If you truly believe you own him, yes," Garyn said.

She lowered her arms to her sides, feeling electricity rush throughout her Royal birthmark. She reached out with her senses, allowing her power to peak with the influence of her Royal blood. She heard the man's heart beating in an irregular pattern. Like a glove, her senses enveloped him. She felt the tension in his muscles. She could tell that his muscles were bulky instead of lean, and unaccustomed to the slight exertions of fighting. She felt the tremble of fatigue slip into his raised dagger arm. She narrowed her eyes and waited.

"Ha! I'll end his life now rather than let you keep him!" Dargin said, but his dagger remained aloft.

"That would benefit neither of us," Garyn said.

She saw the boy's eyes flick open. He gazed up at the Slavemaster with momentary surprise, then at the dagger. He blinked and swallowed. He felt the pain of his field dressings but refused to respond to it. Garyn heard the boy's heart beating fiercely strong, not in the flutter that indicated fear. She watched him close his eyes and tilt his face back in deserved resignation.

Dargin saw the boy give up and it infuriated him. "What are you doing? Are you really this worthless?" He slapped the boy with his free hand and again when the boy didn't react.

Garyn saw the dagger finally descend as Dargin lost his last shred of temper. She gripped the katana, ready to charge the man, to finally kill him. But something flickered within the crumpled human boy, some shred of power and will and dignity she couldn't deny. Her Royal blood, her very will, cried out to him—*Live!* In that instant, her birthmark erupted with power that glowed from beneath her armor. With all the feeling she could muster, she screamed, "*Live!*"

The young man's eyes snapped open on her, wide with confusion. Dargin's dagger plunged into the charred earth as Rowan rolled out of the way. His legs snapped underneath him into a crouch and then a stilted slump, for his broken foot had been splinted. He clenched his teeth in pain.

He stood and hopped out of Dargin's reach. The Slavemaster lunged. Rowan grabbed the back of his head, throwing him off balance, and sent him crashing to the ground. Before the boy could move, Dargin lashed out with the blade and raked Rowan's calf, sending him back to the ground. He scrambled above Rowan and plunged the knife down once more. Rowan deflected his dagger with his right hand.

Rowan recovered and rolled to his side, forcing his body into a hobbled crouch. He turned to his enemy. The Slavemaster leapt forward and sank his knife into Rowan's protective arm. The boy lowered his head and gritted his teeth but made no sound. His useless arm dangled. Dargin swung wildly again, aiming for Rowan's heart.

Garyn screamed, "Dammit!"

She opened and flung her war fan at the Slavemaster. The blades sank deep into his shoulder. Imelda sprawled on the ground, his blood sinking into the charred earth. She approached his prone body. Grasping the grip of her war fan, she ripped it from his back. He groaned. Garyn sighed and walked over to the boy. She knelt at his side and compressed his open artery with one hand.

"For someone untrained, you did well." When he didn't respond, she reached for her medpack. "This is going to hurt," Garyn said, staring into the young man's black eyes.

She wiped away the blood and smeared a yellow paste into the opening. She pressed the edges together. When they sealed, she pulled out the cauterizing searingsalve. Rowan bit his lips together all the while that smoke drifted from the injury. Garyn began wrapping his fresh wound in cloths, wondering at his resilient nature.

Rowan looked up wide-eyed, but hatred dripped from his voice. "Imelda!"

Garyn turned in time to see the Slavemaster bearing down on her, blood staining his pale skin and the dagger raised high over his head. She grabbed her war fan and knelt before her charge. She braced herself for the impact from her much larger aggressor.

"Garyn!" Te-Dasuka screamed and rushed forward.

Dargin froze in his stride and looked down in confusion. A large blade protruded from his chest, the wound spraying Garyn and Rowan with blood. Te-Dasuka grunted in his exertion. He flung the man face-forward onto the ground and tore his broadsword from his back. Dargin reached feebly for Rowan once more, his fingers tearing at the burnt ground. Garyn watched the light in his eyes dim. She heard the choking sound of his last labored breath. Then he died, still reaching for the boy. Garyn caught Te-Dasuka's eyes in gratitude. Collern and Te-Dasuka glanced behind her, suddenly alarmed.

Rowan held Garyn's katana, having drawn it in the confusion of his captor's attack. He forced his crippled arms outward. He held a bloody strip of cloth between his teeth, a bandage he had wound around his knuckles to bind his immobile fingers to the sword grip. He breathed heavily past his gritted teeth in great gasps. His haunted eyes stared in horror toward the dead man at her feet.

The boy's eyes tore from the dead man to settle on Garyn. She couldn't read their black depths to understand what feelings coursed through him. He had witnessed death, but his heart calmed down to beat in a steady, strong rhythm. She wondered what other, worse horrors he had witnessed that could negate a mere human's full emotional response to terror.

Rowan's teeth opened to release the end of his bandage. The cloth unraveled from his hands. The sword clanged to the ground. Garyn heard his heart falter for lack of blood. His eyes rolled back in his head. He collapsed into merciful unconsciousness.

Collern knelt before the boy again, sighing over his ruined handiwork. He began to seal up the boy's wounds and wrap them again. He gestured for the others to help move him to the stretcher. Garyn stood looking down at him, the wheels turning in her mind. Te-Dasuka joined her, wiping the length of his sword with a cleaning cloth.

"Slavery." She shook her head. "In this day and age!"

"So, you'll be the judge of his worth, now, huh?" Te-Dasuka said with an amiable chuckle. "With all the dramatic flair of your mother, no doubt." His voice sounded soft.

Garyn smiled. "How many recruits does Dresden take this season?"

"I'm sure he will take one more for training, at the request of the Queen. Although this one is a little old," Te-Dasuka answered. "We'll have to do some remedial work, and there's that fragile body!"

"If he lives, we train him," Garyn said, a note of assertion in her voice.

She glanced at Te-Dasuka, bent to the task of cleaning his weapon. He smiled broadly, his teeth white amid leather and scars. He didn't rise to her challenge. When he didn't rise, Garyn knew he was on her side or too tired to pick a fight.

"Begging your pardon, *Your Majesty*,"

Collern said. His tone was practically frantic. "But that's a big 'if', especially if we don't get him to Kadray for proper care."

Garyn smiled again, recognizing the urgent tone that Collern's mother often used on her. "My apologies, Collern." The young man blushed, clearly embarrassed at his impatience. "As his attending physician, you have my permission to proceed." She poked the Slavemaster's body with a toe. Collern saluted and hurried away with his team.

"He said that the slaves numbered ten thousand," Te-Dasuka said as he turned to the hulk of a metal ship.

"That ship is just a giant tomb, now," Garyn said softly. "When the boy's fever breaks and he wakes up, we'll bring him back here. He deserves to attend the funeral rites. We'll have the men set up the large pyres. Or we'll burn the whole ship. I want nothing salvaged from such a place."

Garyn knelt before the pools of blood that marked the boy's exit and retrieved her katana. Something gold glinted in the light. She reached for the object and lifted it from the dirt. From a crumpled and kinked chain hung a golden oval locket, charred and bloody and crushed beyond opening. She frowned at it for a minute and tucked it into her armor. She willed the child to survive and thrive. She wanted him to learn about freedom.

4: BROTHERS

Rowan awoke to searing pain. At first, he couldn't remember where he was or what had happened to bring him there. Every smell assaulted him. Every light cut into him. The air rushed against his skin like pinpricks. Both arms and legs refused to move when he willed them. He cried out, feeling frustrated and bound, but the sounds came out garbled. He felt alone and fought the fear born of helplessness.

A cold hand pressed to his forehead. A smooth voice told him to relax. A firm grip forced the strong, bitter drink down his throat. Then he sank into stillness again. If only the stillness stayed silent! He heard the Slavemaster calling to him, the Slavers threatening him, and his parents screaming for him. Somewhere, a baby cried shrilly. The sound cut into him, dragging him down into infinity. He forced his gritty eyes open. His dream shadows followed him, shifting and receding in the dim room with smooth stone walls.

The darkened room pressed in all around. Strain as he might, he could not find a window along the black walls. He felt a tightness in his chest that reminded him all too much of his claustrophobia on the slave ship. His rapid breath rasped past cracked lips and down his parched throat. Rowan sat up on the hard cot, determined to find a way out of his constriction.

He regretted his movement immediately. Mingled with the fuzzy, drugged feeling that muddled most sensation in his body, Rowan felt the pain of a broken arm and leg. His leg was heavy from some dense substance encasing it; someone had bound his arm across his chest with wide strips of cloth. He slowed his heavy breathing, closed his eyes and counted his heartbeats. When the number dropped to an acceptable level, he opened his eyes again.

"He's awake!" sang out a scratchy voice on his right. A child's voice.

"So he is," a young man responded.

"Can I turn on the light now? It's so boring in the dark!"

"Oh, go on!" the other responded. "You'll never be a good warrior if you can't show a bit of patience, Chard!"

The electronic lights glared off stone walls whitewashed in lime. Rowan threw his unbound hand up to shield his eyes from the sudden brightness. The thin mattress on which he sat threw off the same amount of glare. His heart began pounding again as he drowned in the light from his former life.

Squinting into the room, he saw a tall, muscular young man, a few years older than Rowan. His rich complexion and wild white hair seemed exotic. He wore a tan, sleeveless tunic and brown drawstring pants. A few white scars stood out on his left shoulder. His pale blue eyes bored into Rowan. He smiled genuinely.

"Her Majesty was right," he said. "That fever almost killed you!"

"What's a Valkyrie?" said the younger boy. "You kept saying something about one taking you somewhere."

Rowan stared at the boy, realizing he looked a bit older than his rasping voice suggested. *Twelve?* he thought. *No more than thirteen, surely.* He had the same dark skin as the other one, but his deeply set eyes tilted upward at the edges and had the unsettling color of amber. The shallow bridge of his nose had a wide, flat feline tip, an effect enhanced by the long, shaggy pale hair that framed his face. He stared expectantly, inspecting Rowan as much as Rowan inspected him. The dialect flowed like a language Rowan had learned aboard the QuellTruth. He deciphered it with much effort, and responded carefully, wrapping his lips around the unfamiliar words.

Rowan looked from the cat-boy to the older boy. "You're the one in armor."

"Hmph, we were *all* in armor," he responded with a smile, leaning forward in his chair. "And you've been out a full two weeks in fever. At least you remember *something.* The doctor was expecting some brain damage with temperatures that high."

Rowan shuddered. "Some events are still… unclear."

"It'll all come back," he said, his voice trailing off. "Besides, I'm to present you to the Queen, once you're presentable."

Rowan looked down at his battered body, more bandage than skin. Some of the fine cloths had leeched blood from fragile scabs. Then the blood had dried. His broken arm and leg had been encased in a smooth, stone-like casting—the only clean-looking parts of him! He inhaled deeply and grimaced at his unpleasant scent. For once, he wanted a long shower, or at least a chance to scrub off some grime. *I can't go before the Queen like this!*

"Problem is, you don't get a full-on soap and water bath until you're fully healed, so we don't reopen those deep cuts! Healer says no immersion," the older boy said, grinning in apology to Rowan's disdain. "Well," he said, rising to his feet. "I've been your 'keeper.' My name is Collern Maraba."

He extended his hand. Rowan stared for a long moment, then he gripped it firmly with his right hand. Collern jerked a thumb at the cat-faced kid.

"The kitty here is Chard. The Queen's little fosterling," Collern said fondly, ruffling the boy's hair.

"Don't call me kitty, Cawl-een!" the boy said indignantly. He walked over to Rowan with a serious man's face and shook his hand with all the strength he possessed.

"My name is Rowan Jun," he responded, making a short bow with the little mobility he possessed. "I apologize for the inconvenience you've had in treating me."

"Are you kidding?" Collern asked, a wide grin plastered on his face. "Aside from the mess in the jungle, you're the most interesting thing that's happened on Unata in a long time!"

Rowan's blood ran cold. The *mess* in the jungle? The totaled ship. All those dead slaves. What a horrible accident! What a horrible secret that he buried deep in his heart! He froze where he sat. He entangled his fingers in the white sheet draped across his waist. *No, there's no way I can tell them now!* he thought frantically. *I will tell the Queen, only.*

I'll be the judge of your worth now, said the

Valkyrie in his blurred memory.

"Well, that's my fault," Collern said into the awkward silence. "Mother always says I'm callous and unthinking and, well, an ass."

Rowan opened his eyes wide and looked at Collern's sympathetic face. Chard stared down at his feet, rocking back and forth silently.

"Look, I'm sorry," Collern began. "I know that you're still going to have rough times. Life here has taught me that. But we do what we must and move on, right?"

Rowan nodded bleakly. Collern extended his hand toward Rowan's shoulder. Rowan, accustomed to the physical contact of beatings, flinched.

Collern smiled and clapped Rowan on the shoulder. "Well, step one to understanding Unatans is that we are prone to hugging," he said. "And by Royal Decree, you're one of us. We're family now, Brother."

Rowan puzzled over the concept of family and acceptance. Chard had stopped staring at his feet and now had a look of pure mischief smeared on his sharp face. The boy threw himself at Rowan's few unbroken ribs and squeezed profusely. Collern read Rowan's face easily and dragged the boy off, laughing all the while.

"For some non-Unatans, the Unatan transition is natural," he said. "For others, it takes a while." He set Chard down beside the cot. "But this one was born here and already has the cuddly half of the Unatan psyche down pat."

"Forgive me, I may be mistaken, but I also mean no disrespect," Rowan stammered. "Doesn't the Unatan Planetary Profile indicate your race as that of bloodthirsty warriors?"

"Haha! I suppose that's how they would interpret our culture," Chard answered. "They do call us 'Fear Planet' for a reason, you know. We prefer it that way."

Rowan became a bit nervous at this admission. He nodded obediently.

"But every battle has been fought—quite *effectively*—to protect our home," Collern answered. "We all love it. It's in our blood, to love the land and our Queen. And, like cornered rats, we'll turn on the attacking... kitty... every time."

Chard pouted. Rowan thought he acted several years younger than his physical age hinted. Like his body outgrew his mind. Yet he had an air of empathy, of understanding, in his amber eyes, which left Rowan puzzled. Rowan remembered his question.

"The Valkyrie comes during battle to take deserving warriors to their final resting places," he explained. "It's a story my mother used to tell me."

"Well," Chard began, "I'm going to tell Queen Garyn that... that she has to tell you... that you're not allowed to go with the Valkyries! So there!"

He turned and stomped off, pushing aside a sliding white door and disappearing down a dim corridor. Collern and Rowan exchanged surprised glances. Collern began to smile.

"*So there*," he said in a perfect mockery of Chard's scratchy voice. He made a dramatic turn and stomped to the open door. He shut the door and turned back to Rowan with tears in his eyes.

"So there," acceded Rowan, with a wistful expression.

When they looked at each other this time, Collern couldn't keep it together. He burst out laughing. He laughed until he had to grasp his sides in pain.

"So, you don't know you're funny, huh?"

Collern asked. He wiped at his eyes. “Well, looks like it’s time to drag you off to the Queen. Chard’ll already tell her in person that you’re awake if we don’t hurry.”

“I see. Please, lead on,” Rowan said, his goal firmly in mind.

“No. Wait! Garyn’ll have to wait. We need to get you to the Healer first. He’ll want to get a hold of your dirty bandages,” Collern explained, eyeing the dried blood. “Now, you may be a glutton for punishment. I guarantee that removing dirty bandages from seeping wounds was rough when you were asleep. But, now…”

“I will try to manage,” Rowan said with a hint of challenge.

“Then here!” Collern handed Rowan a tall, sturdy crutch. “We’ll see you manage, then.”

Collern pulled Rowan to his good foot and helped him balance on the crutch. Then he helped him hobble off to the healer. Rowan spared a glance in the dim hallway lighting at his seeping wounds. The burning salve had only stopped his bleeding temporarily. And that had hurt horribly!

He knew this to be one inspection he couldn’t just idly stand through. For some masochistic reason, though, he determined not to make a noise of pain. To prove Collern wrong, that he wasn’t just a weak human. The defiance crept into the fibers of his being like a perpetual mantra. He would win this challenge!

5: PARISIA

Rowan ached from head to foot. All through the rough treatment by the torture expert Collern called Kadray, Rowan kept his mouth shut. Through sheer stubbornness, he didn't react to the pain. None of the bodily tortures aboard the slave ship prepared him for the physical ministrations of a Unatan healer. At least the Slavers had to keep him presentable. According to Collern, the Healer just had to keep him functional for battle.

The human boy hobbled dutifully and silently alongside Collern, who slowed his natural long stride when he noticed Rowan's struggle to keep up. Determined to ignore his body's fresh agony, Rowan focused on his surroundings. Rowan saw no one else roaming the outskirts of town. He breathed deeply. The salty breeze pulled at the small amount of short, green foliage growing among the rocks and yellow sand. The sandy plateau on which he stood terminated twenty feet in front of him. The cloudless lavender sky stretched over a dim streak of blackened ocean.

"Unata is beautiful, isn't it?" asked a

woman's voice from Rowan's left.

"Huh?" Rowan startled and blinked. He'd stopped walking to stare openmouthed at the sky. "Yes, it is." He tore his eyes from that beauty to look at the woman. Again, his jaw dropped.

"Has Collern treated you well, Stranger?" she said, her silver eyes dancing.

"Yes, ma'am," he answered. "My name is Rowan Jun." He looked at her open palm for a moment. Then he extended his crutch-hand, which she took with a winning smile.

"Rowan, please meet my mother, Maraba," Collern said.

Rowan stared at her silver hair and silver eyes. Her natural pigment did not appear to be the color of the aged, for she seemed young. By Rowan's limited human standards, Maraba looked tall for a woman, almost as tall as Collern, which explained a lot if she served as Collern's dam. But Collern had to be at least several years older than himself.

"Forgive me for staring," he began, "but I don't see the lines of childbearing on your face."

"The lines of..." Maraba said, her eyes wide. Then she laughed, tossing her head back in a sound that rippled through the stillness of the day. She laid her cheek gently on his shoulder and cast a vibrant smile at Rowan's face. "Garyn'll love this one for sure. Son, you could learn from young Rowan Jun." Then she turned to Rowan again. "Unatan warriors tend to age gracefully in order to keep fighting."

"I see," Rowan said with deep admiration.

Maraba laughed again. "But enough with the flattery. Garyn sent me to see why you two took so long. Chard showed up with a list of demands."

Collern groaned. "Other than the brief sky-watching incident," Collern began, "we did go to Kadray for the better part of the morning."

"Ah, that old geezer! I haven't been to see him in so long!" Maraba said gleefully.

"Your father may want to see you when you're *not* injured, Mother!" Collern scolded. "And *I* have to hear about it when you don't!"

Maraba sighed and slumped forward. "But he always checks my ears." She pulled on one pointed ear with her thumb and forefinger. Then she looked at Rowan. "One month of deafness after one battle, and Father never let me live it down!"

Rowan nodded earnestly. So that's what the Healer meant by his cryptic question to Collern about someone's ears. Rowan felt queasy. *I wonder if the daughter inherited some of the father's torturous tendencies,* he thought. He looked up at her pensively. Then he decided she couldn't be as bad, not with such kind and beautiful features.

Maraba studied his face. She smiled and turned his face this way and that with her thumb. She gave him a final calculating glance and released his chin. She tweaked his narrow nose and spoke in a gentle, slightly teasing voice. "If you end up as strong as a Unatan, we'll have trouble keeping the young ladies at bay."

Rowan blinked, clearly surprised at the exchange. He felt awkward, sure that her imagination got the best of her, and sure that such things drifted far from his mind at present. Rowan shifted his weight onto his crutch, trying to think of an appropriate and respectful response to Maraba's well-intentioned comment.

"Now you've got him all flustered, Mother!" Collern said, making matters worse. Then he leaned into Rowan's ear and whispered, "Pay her no mind. She's the Event Coordinator for the Queen. She's probably already got your clothes picked out for a wedding!"

Rowan felt his face flush profusely. Collern chuckled. Maraba laughed again. They both angled him toward a series of low stone and metal buildings, where Rowan saw his first townspeople of the day. Some of the men and women wore thin, frail-looking metal armor. Some wore flowing tunics and dark breeches with high leather boots. Others appeared to be couriers, running in shorts with bags draped across their backs. One young courier afforded a quick bow to them and a curious smile to Rowan. Rowan bowed back, feeling too unsettled to smile.

He turned in time to plant his face in the shoulder of a very tall warrior wearing a long coat with some sort of symbolic notching at the collar and edges. Rowan stammered an apology and bent for a bow.

"Hey, I'm the careless one," he said with great sincerity. "I'm sorry. I get clumsy when I pass the Weaponmaster's shop."

Rowan raised his head and stared at the man, clearly confused. The man's concerned blue eyes scanned Rowan's face, looking for injury. Finding none, his look turned mischievous. He nodded to the double doors of a large building. Young men ran to and fro beyond the open metal doors. But those were of no concern to either man. Two young women hauled metal, buckets, finished weapons, and pushed carts around the stone-paved patio before the shop. The two girls—one with short white hair, the other with a long cream ponytail—stole glances at their admirers, casting them alluring smiles. Rowan blushed, but the blue-eyed man paid them no mind.

"Trayba! You louse-ridden lay-about!" came

an authoritative voice from the back of the long Weaponmaster hall. "Quit ogling my assistants! Shouldn't you be scouting for the Queen?" Then as an aside to someone else, in a quieter, gentler voice, "Go ahead, Ikaria. He won't leave until he sees you."

The women scattered, completing tasks that looked every bit as difficult as that of the young men. A small, frail-looking girl appeared at the door, wearing a long leather apron over her clothes. She jammed her fists onto her narrow hips and glared at them. From a distance, Rowan saw her angry oval face and spiky white hair and little else.

"We're busy, Trayba!" Ikaria said in an unaccountably angry voice.

Unmoved by her rudeness, Trayba smiled. "Your father's right. I only wanted to see *you*."

"It's time to go, Rowan," Collern said, seething for some reason. He grabbed the human's arm and helped him hobble away.

Trayba absently waved goodbye and called out "Later!" But his eyes stayed on Ikaria.

"What's wrong?" Rowan asked, piling on more confusion.

"Later, Rowan," Collern replied through clenched teeth.

Rowan dropped the subject for now. Maraba chuckled at the spectacle, but helped Collern drag Rowan along the streets. The faces that blurred by all had a shade of rich, dark skin, light eyes and pale hair. Everyone carried some type of martial weapon. However, the atmosphere wasn't threatening or foreboding or even overly concerned about warfare.

Social status remained unclear to Rowan's prying eyes. Each person smiled pleasantly and bowed to both his escorts and him. They talked in flowing tones to individuals in greatly varied dress styles, sharing stories and discussing trades and laughing with all levels of enthusiasm. Rowan felt disoriented. On the ship, he always knew who ruled who. Now, he only knew the Queen's place in this strange society.

Rowan, a one-man spectacle, hobbled onward, taking in the town as much as the onlookers. He felt relieved again, knowing some of their familiar language. He picked out bits and pieces of their discussions. Some made brief comments identifying him as the rescued human boy. Others mentioned "the incident" in whispers. Rowan knew they said far more that he couldn't understand. He felt foolish and clumsy, scrutinized and insignificant.

He remembered some of the Valkyrie's words. She defended him—though the incident still proved to be a fuzzy memory. Could he really trust her intentions as more than just a passing whim? *She is Queen of an entire world, after all!* What if she just didn't have the time or patience to see him more than this one time? *I'll have to say everything I need to say now, then.*

The Throne Bunker loomed in front of him. Guards pushed the metal doors back on oiled casters. A heavy feeling dragged his resolve down out of his chest and settled into his gut. He froze in the doorway, gaping at the woman. His jaw dropped.

The Queen sat on a black and silver marble throne. She wore full battle regalia. Her right leg swung back and forth over the armrest, making a rhythmic metal-on-stone clinking noise. She folded her gauntleted arms across her chest and discarded her helmet on the floor. Her head tilted back into the concavity of the throne back. Her eyes stayed closed.

The electrical lights buzzed periodically, casting the Queen in garish light. Maraba cleared her throat dramatically, preparing to speak.

"It's about time, Maraba!" The Queen pitched forward in the seat, her elbows on her knees. She growled in a nasty tone. "Do you know what a beautiful day it is outside? Chard gets to run off and play. But what do *I* do? Sit here! Do you know how boring it is, just sitting here in armor, trying to look all regal, waiting for official business?"

Maraba sighed. "Yes, okay and yes, Garyn." She stepped forward, expecting the others to follow. "And I also know how... how *difficult* you get right after the Festival of Proving each and every year."

"Difficult, am I?" Queen Garyn harrumphed and slumped against the backrest.

"Which is why you finally delegated the planning part to me," Maraba continued, full of fire, "to reduce the stress of the festival and to make it perfect for you. And yet you still insist on being *difficult*—"

"Oh, okay! Point taken," Garyn interrupted. She smiled broadly. "My apologies to the best Coordinator and one of the best Warriors Unata has ever witnessed."

"Hmmm... Now, that's more like it!" Maraba preened with a sly smile. "And you can thank my father for taking forever with his treatment!"

"That old coot?" Garyn asked. "I could've died of old age before he was finished!"

"You're telling me!" Maraba's eyes welled in tears from hiding her laughter. She tugged on her ear for effect.

Garyn laughed, a disarming and engaging sound, making Rowan's heart race. The young man blinked for a long moment, realizing that they just kidded with one another. *And Maraba is one of the best warriors Unata has seen?* The thought of a powerful woman rivaling the Valkyrie intrigued him.

He glanced now at Collern, who had plastered an amused smirk under otherwise bored eyes. The older boy clearly had witnessed that type of exchange before, and not only seemed unimpressed, but comfortable. Clearly, his mother had grown close to the Queen. *Or does everyone treat their royalty this way?* Rowan wondered.

"Now," the Queen began, "I want an official introduction to my new citizen."

She trained her eyes on Rowan, who looked up, feeling unsure and awkward again. From the corner of his eye, he saw Maraba fold her body to sit on the second step leading up to the throne. Collern smiled encouragingly at him from the other side. He lowered himself to the bottom step. He nodded to Rowan. Rowan stood between them on the floor and laid his crutch on the stone squares beneath him. He knelt there on the stones, as much as his leg cast would allow, and lowered his upper body onto his unbound hand. His long hair brushed the ground as he stared at the point directly under his nose. He couldn't decide on exactly what to say, but his heart pounded before the commanding presence of the Queen of Unata.

"Your kindness and generosity are unmatched, Queen Garyn Kei of Unata," he said finally, into the dust. "I, Rowan Jun of the Slaveship QuellTruth, offer my body, mind, heart and soul to whatever use you see fit in service of Her Majesty and her kingdom." He paused, feeling her eyes bore into the back of his head. "And if my life is the cost, in penance for my sins, then I pray you permit me to die."

A long moment of silence followed in which Rowan's words echoed from the stone walls and then died down. He held his difficult bow, waiting on her judgment. Then she spoke, her voice low and calculating, but gentle.

"When I said I would be the judge of your worth, I did not mean that I owned your life, Rowan Jun." Rowan heard a rustling of bootheels on stone. He bowed lower and closed his eyes.

Rowan felt the heat radiating from her armor. She spoke in a low voice immediately above him. "But if you want judgment, my commandment of you is to live and die by your own choice, not by mine. Nor by that horrid man's choice. An ended life serves no one, not even oneself."

"I don't deserve to live," Rowan replied, gritting his teeth in memory of every death he didn't prevent.

"Life is never deserved," she answered. "It is a gift we can never repay. We can only waste it by ending it without achieving some purpose. If you genuinely believe yourself a murderer, then look around. Everyone in this room has killed. I kill to protect my people." She nodded to Maraba. "To save her father's life and mine." She nodded to Collern. "On the battlefield. And again, to save my foster-child Chard. And you," she placed her hand on his head, "for reasons you may share when you wish."

Rowan looked up at all three. Each held the grim light of death in their eyes. He had been foolish to think that this warrior world was sinless, that they couldn't possibly have suffered as much as he. Lastly, he looked into the Queen's pale green eyes. Stern and soft all at once, she glimpsed deeper than his soul. His heart pounded faster. She was a rock! Solid and strong. He wanted to learn how to be strong like her. He wanted to live if it meant being near her wisdom. And if he could learn to protect anything, anyone when he had failed so often before, he knew she could educate him.

He bowed again. “Please teach me.”

“What do you want to learn?” She removed her hand from his head and crossed her arms.

“I want to earn my redemption,” Rowan said. “I...I want to fight against those who would harm what I hold precious. I want to learn to protect... someone. I will become strong enough to be your Champion, My Queen!”

“Life on Unata is hard,” she said, but Rowan could hear the smile in her voice. “With a spirit like that and determination to boot, you may survive the training.” She laughed. “But my Champion, huh? Wonder what Te-Dasuka would say about that?”

To his side, Maraba gasped. Collern mumbled, “He may not take kindly to having a kid take his place, especially a human!”

Rowan pushed his body to his feet suddenly, his face a mask of resolve. He glanced at Collern. Then he leveled his gaze at the Queen. “I vow that I will become the most powerful man on this planet, despite this human blood!”

Maraba scrambled backward in surprise, colliding with the wall. She let out an echoing cackle before she stifled it with the back of her arm. Collern simply gaped at him, then shook his head with a smile.

But Queen Garyn Kei of Unata didn’t budge. In fact, she smiled viciously at the boy. “The most powerful, huh?” She moved her hands to her hips. “Then as my new trainee and as a citizen of Unata, you have one order that you must obey above all others."

"Your Highness may command me as she wishes," Rowan replied, pulling his shoulders back and dropping his head in a curt bow.

She threw her head back and laughed again, a sound of pure challenge. When she looked at him again, the green in her eyes looked more like ice. She smiled.

"Live," she ordered.

6: MURDERER

The old Healer drew his razor-thin sword, making two swift swipes at Rowan's leg cast. As the young man flinched, Kadray sheathed his sword. The cast fell cleanly apart lengthwise, without a nick on Rowan's skinny, pasty leg. His arm cast came off in the same fashion, and Rowan still flinched. He sighed deeply.

"Thanks, Kadray," said Rowan, swinging his legs off the narrow table. His broken leg still hurt when he put pressure on it.

"Don't thank me yet, kid. And sit back down!" The old healer grabbed the broken leg and prodded its length. Rowan clenched his teeth in pain. "Fused, but not completely healed yet. Atrophied muscle aside, well on the way to healed. If I had my way, you'd be in that cast for another three weeks, at least. Here," he said. "You'll need it today."

Kadray shoved a cup of hot sourroot tea into his hand and dumped in a measurement of powder and herbs. "Drink it all. It'll last several hours. But then the pain will catch up to you all at once."

The old man pulled on and tightened Rowan's leg brace. Kadray strapped on the arm brace as well. Then he stood with his hands on his hips, pursing his lips and staring at his patient. Rowan hadn't even sipped the smelly concoction in his hands. He obediently chugged the vile contents of the cup and set it down beside him on the table. Kadray harrumphed. Rowan flexed his leg. The near-weightless metal brace moved like it was made for him.

"As long as you don't do anything stupid," Kadray looked from Rowan to Collern, wagging a finger in Rowan's face, "you'll not further damage your arm and leg. And if you're *smart*, you'll be back before the drugs wear off."

"Where's mine?" Collern said playfully, reaching for the old man's drug case.

Kadray snatched the case out of his reach and eyed Collern. "These drugs are for honor and duty, not a good-for-nothing lay-about like you!" he said in his own gruff version of humor. "Now get going! You don't want the Jungle to swallow him up before he gets home, do you?"

Rowan swung his feet to the floor and stood. He managed several pain-free steps. Just when he wondered what Kadray meant by the jungle swallowing him up, heat welled up in his stomach, spreading down his limbs. Then his leg began tingling at the break point. His arm started prickling as well. When the feeling escalated to burning, he turned to Kadray.

"The meds have to bond to your injury sites," Kadray said. "So it tingles a little for a while. Once that stops, *then* you'll have several hours of no pain. And you'll love the side effects of this one!"

Rowan hobbled off, fire shooting up his leg with each step. He mumbled, "Of course, even his *medicine* hurts!"

Kadray still laughed heartily as Rowan and

Collern disappeared around a corner in Parisia. Rowan's leg muscles had atrophied from disuse. However, even in pain, he enjoyed walking without the bulk of his heavy cast and a crutch.

When Collern retrieved their rites-supplies from his home, he handed a pack to Rowan.

"You sure you can carry this?" Collern asked.

Rowan winced under the weight of it. "I'll be fine," he said, "if the pain really *does* go away like the old man said!"

Collern chuckled—a habit that reminded Rowan of Maraba—and shrugged. "All right. Let's go!"

* * *

From Parisia, Unata's main city housing the Queen's Throne bunker, Collern could still see a smudge of smoke on the horizon. Most of the fires had died in the recent rainfall. As they trekked through the understory of the Upper Jungle, Collern lengthened his stride to keep up with Rowan. The young man seemed drawn to the smoke, like he knew where he was going even though the jungle canopy blotted out the sky. He'd been staring in that direction from his bed in Parisia for a week. *Odd kid.*

"You do realize that outsiders call this whole place Fear Planet, don't you?" Collern asked to break the silence. Rowan's vow first concerned and then decidedly inspired him.

"Yes," Rowan replied. "A planet full of warriors, highly effective killers. Even if the outsiders have guns and lasers and the bulk of spaceships, it would be intimidating."

"In peacetime, Unata is warm and inviting to some, and very productive," Collern said. "But in war, that's when she gets her reputation. And there's a lot of war here. I've seen several in just my life. You know I don't want to discourage you," Collern began.

"Then don't," Rowan replied. He stopped and turned to Collern. He smiled a kind of resigned, longsuffering smile that didn't quite reach his eyes. "You were born to this life. To a degree, it defines you."

Collern nodded, considering all his experiences.

"But for the first time in *my* life," Rowan said, looking up at the bright green of the canopy, "I saw the sky and felt the grass beneath me. For the first time, I got to choose the next step without sacrificing someone else."

Collern furrowed his brow. Rowan's reasoning hinted at that part of his past he didn't want to discuss. And since his meeting with Garyn, he couldn't possibly ask Rowan for details. He nodded again. "Then it looks like we'll be training together for the rest of our lives."

"Sounds good to me. But you won't be ahead of me long. Give me a year, and I'll catch up to you," Rowan said. His eyes held a friendly challenge.

"Yeah, right! A year, my foot!" Collern said. "I'll eat my own boot if you can beat me in a fair fight in just a year!"

"This time next Festival, then," Rowan said. "We'll have a little exhibition. That's the challenge custom, right?"

"You're on, and already behind!" Collern said and disappeared into the jungle.

Rowan followed close behind, his feeling of camaraderie dissipating in the heavy odors that permeated the half-light of the jungle. Among the trees, he had to follow a different scent mingled with fire and smoke. The scent of new decay sank under the canopy, trapped and thickened by the moisture-heavy air. Those who perished had lain as they died for weeks. The scent overwhelmed the boys. They coughed and sputtered but continued forward.

Rowan faltered in his resolve, remembering the ghost ache of broken bones and the sharp pain of atrophied muscle. That's the worst he had to suffer. Even now, they drugged the pain out of him so he could be useful. However, the slaves aboard the QuellTruth had died horribly without ever knowing freedom. Rowan glimpsed the extent of his sin every day, as Scouts returned with news of no signs of life aboard the ship, until finally they stopped scouting that area. To keep his promise to his Queen and himself, he had to move forward, to face the QuellTruth one last time.

"I *thought* it was too early for us to smell the ship," Collern muttered. "Over here!"

When Rowan caught up to Collern, he found the older boy prodding a large mass of black fur with a branch he'd found. He grunted, lifting a massive front leg into the light. The long appendage ended in three long claws the full length of his hand. Rowan felt a prickling of fear and hung back while Collern inspected the carcass.

"Felzar cub," Collern said. He dropped the long front leg and pointed. Gashes on the creature's hindquarters and sides had resulted in its death. "Looks like the Chimeras got him, but he was running away. Silly thing." Collern tapped it with his branch. "You should have stayed out of the Lower Jungle!"

"There're more of those?" Rowan whispered. "And *that* one's just a cub?"

Collern grinned and threw down the branch. “Yep. And something *bigger* got it.”

“Can we go now?” Rowan asked, eyeing the dead animal.

“Sure,” Collern said. He adjusted his pack. “To the Lower Jungle.”

“You mean the place that thing should have avoided?”

“Yep.” His grin was full of mischief.

Rowan took a deep breath, then sighed. He gestured for Collern to lead the way, glad for his guidance. Rowan had a solitary mission that Collern refused to allow him to complete alone. Both boys carried shovels, kindling and flint rock. Collern also picked up a generous number of fire charges from Te-Dasuka.

It would be the planet’s largest funeral pyre, Maraba had said. Maraba offered to arrange a massive memorial service to the fallen slaves. Rowan insisted that celebration on such a large scale was for the living, and that, in his understanding, the dead needed rest. Traditionally, Unatans built funeral pyres and screamed the names of their comrades into the wind. He hadn’t witnessed the event, but it was sure to be loud. Rowan continued his heavy trudge along a narrow path through the undergrowth. He stared at the black soil and even stopped to run it through his fingers.

Collern stopped and turned to watch him. He looked puzzled. “What’s wrong?”

“My parents told me how their ancestors buried the dead in the dirt,” Rowan explained. He stared at his smudged hand, rubbing his fingers together, feeling the grit of the dirt. “Neither my parents nor I have ever felt real earth beneath our feet, let alone run it through our fingers.”

“Slavery,” Collern said, shaking his head.

"Hey, listen. I know it sounds kind of corny..."

"What? And what does 'corny' mean?" Rowan asked, wiping his hand on his dark pants.

"Well, it means kind of silly," Collern explained. "And since your family never got to do all those things, you can kind of... experience it for them, you know?"

Rowan looked at him, deep in thought. He nodded silently. "You're right. I can."

"And other than the 'Never die!' instructions you got from Queen Garyn, you should be able to do a lot of exploration," Collern said. "Maybe even off the planet one day, if the opportunity arises."

Rowan nodded. "But where would I go?"

Collern laughed and clapped him on the shoulder. "The good thing about freedom is that *where* you go is entirely up to you!"

The boys continued at a slower pace to the mesa edge and picked a slippery path down the cliff face toward the Lower Jungle. He showered Collern with rocks from above so many times that the more athletic boy laughed and found another route down. He left what he called the "Child's Path" free for Rowan to use.

As the Lower Jungle engulfed them, bright sunlight diffused into glowing green once more. Reaching the bottom, Rowan fought back the feeling of dread with a long look up at the top of the mesa. He hadn't realized he could climb that well. He stopped to adjust the odd leg brace, and then his arm brace.

The strain on his body started to show in his shaking, scratched up hands. He watched his fingers tremble and wondered if the shaking had anything to do with the task at hand. He clenched and unclenched his fist. The stinging of dirt in the cuts on his palms brought him around. Soon the wounds tingled and burned, and he didn't feel even that anymore. The drugs given him by the healer still worked, at least.

"We're almost there," Collern said with a solemn nod toward the northwest. "All the adrenaline from the last time... it seemed like a shorter trip. Half the day is gone already!"

Rowan nodded. A knot formed in the pit of his stomach. He remembered the day, weeks ago, when he felt ready to die. How could so much have changed in such a short time? At what point had he made friends and adopted a homeland? He frowned. *I don't deserve any of this*, he thought furiously. *Not after what I did!* When his heart returned to a regular rhythm, he opened his eyes on a concerned Collern.

The older boy turned and headed back through the undergrowth. Rowan followed with heavier footsteps. The fresh smell of decay choked him. This time, there was no denying its source. The weight of his sin sickened him. On the ground all around him, he saw shards of metal speared into the soft dirt, each ringed with charred vegetation.

A short distance away, the undergrowth gave way to ashes. Rowan stepped onto blackened earth wearing the first boots he'd ever owned. The trees and large leafed plants here lay broken and singed. Then, abruptly, all growth disappeared. The long scar that clipped off the top of the canopy for a mile ended in a great hulk of twisted metal and black ground. Black smoke rose to the heavens in several dwindling spires.

For a long time, he stared ahead blankly. Then Rowan's knees buckled. He fell forward onto his hands. The knot in his stomach turned to nausea. He vomited bile and then just heaved until he collapsed onto his side. Tears spilled from his raw eyes.

Collern stood silently, bearing the stench like a true warrior. Rowan rolled into a sitting position, drawing heavy, shaky breaths until he had calmed his stomach. His hands didn't stop shaking.

"Wow. This is... horrible," Collern said at last, offering a hand up to Rowan. "I'm glad we convinced Chard to stay and take care of Grandfather."

Rowan nodded and took the hand Collern offered. Collern dragged him to his feet. Then he stood still, waiting for some movement from Rowan to indicate where he wanted to start. Collern tensed abruptly, reaching for the battle-axe slung from his back.

Rowan reacted, too. He listened and looked around, but either couldn't hear as well as Collern or could not guess what he heard. He felt helpless again, with no more than a shovel to protect himself and no strength or skill to wield a weapon.

Collern lowered his stance, one hand on the battle-axe. "We're not alone," he whispered.

Rowan became more frantic. Had one of the Slavers survived? He wondered who would linger in such a disgusting pit of gore.

"You're remarkably slow, boys," rang a voice just outside the artificially created clearing. "I may show you a much shorter route if you plan on coming back here."

Collern relaxed, removing his hand from the weapon. Rowan felt confused. He recognized the voice, but why would Queen Garyn come to this place? From the edge of the clearing, she emerged, bearing an armful of bundled herbs. She was a short woman, much shorter than Maraba, Rowan noticed for the first time. That fiery personality made her seem so much larger!

She wore simple travel clothing and no armor save for the black and silver circlet across her forehead, which only partly tamed the wild hair spiking out around her head. She dusted her hands on the dark pants clinging to her slim thighs and stamped mud from her heavy pale-yellow notched boots. She adjusted the wide black belt that cinched her creamy yellow tunic. Her katana and war fans draped from her belt. She paused and leaned on a shovel.

Seeing his eyes on her weapons, she said, "My mother always said that living in peace is no excuse for living unprepared, Apprentice."

Rowan lowered his head in a short bow.

"Well, all I can say is thank goodness it was you!" Collern said. He whispered, "I know I'm pretty good, but we've been running all day. If we came across one of the big critters, we would've been in trouble!"

"I'm surprised you didn't," she answered. "It's their mating season around Festival time. And they use the blood of other big animals to attract a mate!"

Collern dutifully cringed. "They mate? I thought they had just the one mother. Aren't they all girls?"

Garyn laughed, but the sound echoed with mischief. "Yes, yes and no. It's a bit complicated, from what I understand."

Rowan looked from Garyn to Collern, then back to Garyn. Rowan noticed her bare, muscled arms for the first time. Rowan wondered about the deep red tattoo design on her right arm. Noticing his gaze, the Queen looked down at her right arm and twisted her wrist back and forth. The edges of the birthmark glimmered in the sunlight. She walked over to the two, seemingly unaffected by the surroundings.

"Aren't you supposed to keep the Royal Birthmark covered?" Collern asked, a look of concern on his face.

"The light won't harm it," Garyn said. "Would you have me wear that sweltering longcoat all the way out here, Collern?"

"Of course not!" Collern said, raising his hands innocently. "But folks talk like it's some sort of taboo."

"It's not, you silly lout." Then her severe smile cut into Rowan. She leaned against his shoulder. "This is not something a citizen of Unata should be allowed to do alone, Rowan Jun."

"You are very kind," Rowan responded. "However, I don't deserve..."

"That, Apprentice, is why this help is freely given," she said with her finger held in the air. "The worth of a person isn't in what they deserve, but what they do."

Rowan stared into her eyes. He felt her pleading with him to let go of his self-deprecating mentality. The Valkyrie called to him, saying he had a worth beyond price.

"You're not a slave anymore, Rowan," said Collern. He gave a genuine smile and shook him gently. "Now you get to learn what it's like being a Unatan."

Garyn gave him a challenging look and stepped away. She turned her back to him, facing the wreckage with her hands on her hips. "Now, command your Queen to help you in this small way."

"I... I want to find my family, if it's possible," Rowan said. He swallowed past the lump in his throat. Tears stung his eyes. "We can set pyres for the rest, but my family would have wanted a burial."

Collern, in a soft voice, said, "Do you know where to find them?"

"Yes," he replied, his voice breaking. In his mind's eye, he saw their desecrated bodies hanging against a glass partition. He closed his eyes.

"Lead the way," Garyn said.

Rowan nodded and forced his first steps toward the ship. He noticed the bodies of the Slavers, bloated from the heat and eaten upon by some small animals. Even so, someone had laid their bodies out head to foot in a triangle, with Dargin Imelda's body forming the third side. Sweet grasses had been piled all around in neat, tied bunches. Rowan glanced back at Garyn, who tore her eyes from the bodies to acknowledge his suspicions.

"I've been here for a while," she said.

The hatch door through which he had fallen still swayed in the breeze. He grabbed the control box for the zip line and showed the others how to operate it. Balancing his weight with one hand, he slipped his foot in the stirrup and pressed the Retract button. He gave a gasp of surprise that it still functioned. As the open door loomed before him, he drew a deep breath and plunged inside. *I fell so far!* he thought. *I can hardly believe I survived!* He looked down and sent the zip line back to the remaining two. Once they both joined him, he turned to them.

He looked down the dark hallways and accepted one of the battery-powered lamps Garyn offered. "There has been a great deal of damage to the part of the ship I need to get to. It'll be dangerous."

"You're not going anywhere alone," said Garyn Kei.

"Right," Collern agreed. "You're stuck with us."

Rowan sighed, but he conceded with a nod. His head cleared once the horrible smell of decay overpowered his olfactory sense and dulled the stench. Rowan faced down a hallway for a moment, trying to get his bearings. The upper decks held the Slavers and Slavemaster Quarters and storage. No slaves would have been held up there, except the few young boys Imelda held as personal servants. Rowan shivered. Those boys would have died quickly. And, from the rumors Rowan heard, they would have welcomed death.

"We're going to try and reach the ninth and tenth Lower Decks, where the breeding stock was kept," he said, pointing to lines on his hand-drawn map. "From what I can tell, the ship crumpled in the center and most of the lower decks will be toward the back now, well underground but mostly intact."

"Intact?" Collern asked, rubbing his chin thoughtfully. "Any chance there'd be survivors?"

"No," Rowan said quickly. "It's a sealed system. I think life support… terminated… there as soon as the directional controls locked up. Imelda activated a cargo preservation protocol. I doubt that means he tried to save them, but rather, preserved them in state for DNA retrieval."

"The system was designed to discard cargo to preserve the Slavemaster," Garyn said through gritted teeth. "Selfish bastard."

Rowan nodded grimly. "Most of the cargo…" and here Rowan choked on the word, "may have suffocated before and during the crash." He took a deep breath and closed his eyes. When he opened them, he adjusted his lamp and moved his finger to a new spot on the detailed map. "Most of the fires on the Middle Decks should be out by now. There are only two floors to this section—the navigation module and the life support control base. We want to make it here." His finger stabbed the life support control base.

"You think we can reactivate the life support for the lower levels," Collern concluded.

"If there's enough power left in the mainframe, probably," Rowan said. "Then we can head up to this section and boot up the door mechanisms while life support is regulating. The crash breached the Middle Levels, so there should be enough air to breathe in there."

"Rowan," Collern began. Rowan glanced up from his map. "Forgive me, friend. How does a slave know all this?"

Rowan stood silently for a long moment, controlling the surge of memories and emotions. Then, while staring at his map, he said, "Because I headed the Insurgency."

Collern clenched his jaw. "I guess I took you for a naïve kid."

"So did the Slavers," Rowan responded. "That worked for a long while."

"How did you survive this crash?" Collern pressed. He touched dried blood on the shredded metal.

Rowan raised his eyes to Garyn's, then stared at Collern with a sick expression. "I was on the Middle Levels, in the navigational control module, changing the ship's trajectory. The ship was supposed to do a standard emergency landing, but the gear didn't function properly."

Garyn spoke up. "You didn't know about Imelda's life support contingency." It was not a question.

"I told you," Rowan said, a tortured coldness gripping his heart. "I am a murderer."

Collern leaned in heatedly. "It's not murder

if you didn't know!"

Garyn gripped Collern's shoulder and shook her head. "Rowan has decided on this as part of his penance. You will allow him that. Know this, Collern. Cold logic will never convince a human heart."

"But, Garyn!" Collern whispered.

She tightened her grip on the boy's shoulder. He squirmed in pain. "Rowan is neither weak nor deaf, young man! Now, not another word!"

Rowan turned his back and took slow steps down the corridor. He had taken only a few steps amid several chunks of twisted metal when he heard a hushed whisper.

"You're dense! The whole world isn't black and white!" Garyn said. "It's bad enough you're going to have to eat your boot next summer!"

"You heard that, huh?" Collern responded sullenly. "Darn Royal birthmark!"

"I didn't need my hearing amplified to hear *that* cocky boast, kid!" Garyn said. "The whole forest cringed. Now come on!"

"Rowan," Collern said, approaching silently behind him. Rowan stopped. "Will you please consider forgiving me for prying, and for my cruel words?"

Rowan blinked several times, confused. He turned to Collern. Garyn hung back in the corridor, pretending to notice something on the smooth metal. "I've never been asked such a question before."

"Well, will you?" Collern asked. "I don't want to lose my new friend by my foolishness."

Rowan looked down, still feeling jostled about. "I... I wouldn't want to lose my first real friend, either."

Collern smiled and reached out his hand.

"Forgiven?"

Rowan took the hand Collern offered. "Forgiven."

"Is it okay if we move on now, Rowan?" Garyn asked from the shadows.

Rowan nodded. "This way."

The long, empty corridor didn't scare Rowan as much as he remembered. But anything would be less scary than the Slavers following him, ready to spill his blood again. He reached a corner and saw a dried blood splatter on the floor.

"This is where I collapsed before they found me. I came from this direction," he said, using his lamp light to gesture. "There shouldn't be that many dead where we're going right now."

Rowan arrived at a broken metal door. He traced his hands around the damaged edge. "I had to pry it open," he whispered. The fear he felt arose again in his heart. He brushed past the door. The hand that held the lantern began to shake.

Garyn watched the boy. She heard his insides churn and his heart pound. She couldn't protect him from reliving his last hours aboard the ship. To become a warrior, Rowan must overcome this obstacle. A Unatan life was a life of bearing hardship and learning to suffer. She watched his all-too-knowing steps as he made his way through the hallway and into a narrow, tall room labeled "Decontamination Chamber". Rowan moved in guilt, clearly ashamed that he knew exactly where his feet should carry him.

He angled them toward a narrow fissure in an automatic door. Rowan turned sideways and tried to slide through the crack. He set down his lantern and shoved at the door to no avail. He held such a comical look of confusion that Collern laughed.

"I can't believe I squirmed through here such a short time ago!" Rowan said with apologetic eyes. His hands paused on the door. "But Maraba's cooking tastes so good. I've been a glutton!"

Garyn and Collern shared a surprised glance. Rowan felt doubly confused.

Collern gasped as he suppressed his laughter. "My mother... a cook? She can't boil water!"

"Don't worry, Collern," Garyn said. Her eyes danced. "I'll have a word with her later."

"Oh, no..." Rowan began. "It's my fault. She never *said* it was her cooking!"

"Knowing my mother," Collern said, "she never admitted it *wasn't* her cooking!" He leaned against the stuck door with all his weight. Slowly, the metal creaked and began sliding back into the wall.

"I'll have Collern take you by the dining hall and kitchens starting tomorrow, so you'll be saved from Maraba's ego," Garyn said. "You can provide proper thanks to the *real* chefs there."

"Yeah. We barter skills and share artisans with other cities," Collern said. "Everyone trains for battle, plus another special apprenticeship of their choosing. So, our cooks *want* to be there! Makes the food better."

Garyn chuckled. "And his mother loves to eat more than she loves to plan. Maraba's the only one who would starve to death if all our cooks went on strike tomorrow!"

The boy looked up at her. "I'm sorry..."

"And stop," she said. "Stop apologizing for everything. You will eat until you're finished. You will train until you're finished." She paused thoughtfully. "Okay, that's wrong. You'll train until *Dresden* says you're finished. Apologize when it really matters. But never say you're sorry for who you are."

Rowan stared at her again, then down at her hands clamped on his bare shoulders. She felt his heart calm down again. Then he opened his mouth. He cast his eyes to the side and then closed his mouth.

Collern didn't miss the gesture. He grinned. "You were going to apologize for all the apologizing, weren't you?"

Rowan blushed. Garyn released him and threw her arms around both boys' necks. She sighed. She squeezed them both. Then she let them go. Rowan stooped to grab his lantern before leading the way once more. The room into which he led them had a steep floor, unleveled by metal buckling underneath. Rowan picked his way across the floor, avoiding tangled beams and dead wires. Garyn followed apprehensively. The room didn't feel right.

A low noise reached her ears before the others heard. She snapped her head up and screamed, "Boys! To the floor."

Rowan obeyed instantly, his lantern swinging light wildly across the metal walls. Collern crouched warily, watching his back.

Garyn snapped her katana toward the ceiling, flipped blood from it and replaced the weapon in its sheath in one fluid motion. A serpentine head the size of Rowan's foot flopped in front of his nose, its jaw working several times before the light left its eyes. Purple blood dripped from the ceiling, then a scaly body fell with a thud behind the head. Rowan froze in terror.

Garyn sighed. "They've been feeding."

The Queen stared overhead. When Rowan righted his lamp and turned it toward the ceiling, a hundred eyes flickered in the sudden brilliance.

She heard him gasp. “It’s my fault, Rowan. I should have left men in attendance while you healed.”

“Looks like they’re just juveniles. Their wings haven’t even started to develop,” Collern noticed. “I guess their mother couldn’t get in this far.”

“What are those?” Rowan stared wide-eyed at the green, black and orange mass of scales on the ceiling.

“We call them Chimeras,” Garyn said. “They’re one of the few predators left on this planet. Ah… They’ve live births, walk on four long legs, and later in life, they fly. And as you can see, they climb well and have armored scales. They get about this tall at the base of their neck before their wings sprout,” she said, holding her hand at shoulder level.

“They’re the monsters you were talking about? The one that got the big black cat?” he asked Collern. “I thought they’d be bigger.”

“Wait until you meet their mother!” said Garyn with a vicious grin.

Collern scoffed. “They’re voracious eaters and violent killers!” Collern said with some heat. “They almost died out until a few generations back. Now look at them!”

“Hmph.” Garyn cleared her throat. “Collern here has half a mind to make mounts out of them. Except they avoid his traps. I’m just content to have them scouting the Lower Jungle for me.”

“Why don’t they attack?” Rowan asked, still whispering, as he slowly drew himself to his feet. He stared at the glittering, moving mass on the ceiling.

Garyn smiled. “Because they smell my blood. They know better. Especially after my little talk with Primorda, their Sole-Mother. If she dies, they all die out to one again, and have to start all over with a new Sole-Mother. They *do* love their mother, so scouting isn't that big of an inconvenience."

"You mean you really have them *scouting* the Lower Jungles, don't you?" Rowan said, astonished. "And you can speak to them?"

"We have a mutually beneficial agreement," Garyn answered. "The Chimeras get the whole of the Lower Jungles for their hunting. They report any dangers from off-planet to me alone. They avoid any contact with Unatans, and I don't slaughter them all."

Collern groaned. "*You're* the reason the Chimeras stay away from my traps!"

"No, Collern." Garyn smiled. "They just inform me of how meager your attempts are. The Chimeras are offended."

"I'll show you offended!" Collern said, pulling his battle-axe from his back.

The creatures chattered and cringed in response, shrinking closer to the ceiling.

"Stand down, boy," Garyn said calmly. She looked above her head again. "Primorda will be terribly upset to hear that you have been scavenging. Especially if it's off-worlders you *knew* we had claimed." She felt Rowan's eyes on her exposed birthmark. It sparked and glimmered in the dim light as she spoke to the creatures and made them understand.

The ceiling rustled with worried movement. Garyn continued. "I count your trespass fulfilled in the death of your brother, and I entrust you with telling your sins to the Sole-Mother. Now, get down here and get out!"

Dark masses on the ceiling began to drop to the floor. Each Chimera landed lightly on four long, spindly legs striped in green and blackish purple scales. Their smooth, curved backs *did* look like they could take astride a Unatan. Their heads had a broad forehead and tapered to a spiny muzzle, with brow crests and sharp teeth. Scales and crests adorned their heads and tails, in vibrant orange and yellow. Rowan also noticed the purple, orange and yellow eyes that were dominant among the little guys. Their backs reached as tall as his hip now, but when they reached their full growth, he knew they could be perfect for riding! He could have sworn that two or three looked at him with the fondness of a pet, particularly one with imploring violet eyes. He watched them until all fifty had filed out, most with the drooping heads of scolded children.

He shared a knowing glance with Collern, and Garyn caught them. "Eyes forward, boys! These are not just beasts of burden to serve you."

She followed the young men to a sputtering control panel on the far wall of the room. As they walked across the crumpled floor, Rowan pressed a few buttons on the counter, then adjusted a keyboard and screen. After looking down at the buttons for some time, Rowan found the option he looked for and started typing rapidly. The board chirped with electronic tones. The sound fizzled out at the end in static. Collern stood behind the boy. Feeling stupid and unneeded, he craned his neck to see over Rowan's shoulder.

Garyn began scouting the rim of the room. Rowan had been right. She saw no evidence of bodies in this room. Other than the Chimeras leavings, Garyn only found one place that reeked of spilled human blood. She approached the metal wall, noticing broken glass on the ground and a dent in the surface at a point just over her head.

She reached for the burgundy stain that

streamed down the wall. Her birthmark sparked for an instant. The blood belonged to Rowan. He had been discovered in this room during the crash. Garyn guessed the Slavers had found him and merely flung him against the wall. Garyn saw blood prints made by bare human feet. Then he had run. A short while later, he had fallen to his safety among her men.

Using his new boot knife to strip wires, Rowan reconnected several to attach a console and keypad entry. The screen flickered to life.

"*Now* it works," Rowan said from across the room. An electronic hum vibrated in the air. He sounded disappointed. He looked up at her. "We can head over to the life-support module. It'll be easier on us now that at least some of the sliding doors function."

Garyn nodded and joined him. In contrast to the relatively pristine navigation module base, the life-support module housed a few corpses. The Chimeras had eaten their fill. Garyn noticed the haunted look that flooded Rowan's face when he saw the Slaver corpses picked clean of flesh and organs. He pressed his hand to his mouth and pushed a dead Slaver aside to type at the console. Nothing happened.

"They must have come here after the crash, after I ran away." Rowan ran his hand through his hair. "Pity that I ripped out all the input devices in the navigation module, and they couldn't stop the crash."

In a short time, the electronic hum that signaled a boot-up sounded overhead. Some of the lights flickered to life. Gushing air flowed through ductwork overhead.

Collern looked around and said, "Amazing that it still works."

"For now, it works. I don't know how long

the power will hold out," Rowan said. "Plus, it'll be much worse down there." He hung his head and walked past them.

In their descent to the Lower Levels, Rowan and his two companions found no other traces of the Chimeras. The scent of death welled around them as they trekked down crumpled hallways with sparking electrical work and flickering fluorescent lights. Garyn suspected that the human barely picked up the scent anymore. Unfortunately for the Unatans, their senses could not be so easily quelled. The Queen picked up all the nuances of death—the gender, age, and method of dying.

She shivered from the chill that carried them deeper underground. The metal she brushed with her fingers had heated and then cooled to near frost. She saw the white mist of her breath one moment and then her throat dried from heat the next. Collern plugged along, impervious and strong as always. Rowan trotted ahead and then skidded to a stop. Garyn and Collern peered around him.

Rowan swung his lantern forward. Before them, the floor took a sudden dive downward. The lantern light glared coldly across mangled gray steel, and then terminated in darkness. At the bottom of the pit, easily a hundred feet below, a red light blinked.

"What's that red light?" Collern asked.

"It's the decontamination chamber door," Rowan answered. "It leads to one of the Lower Levels."

"But which one?" Collern asked. "That drop isn't just a single hallway cave-in, from the looks of it."

Garyn stared over the ledge. Her Royal birthmark crackled in the silence. The darkness below illuminated in her eyes. She saw the broken metal walls in ivory-green contrast and two gaping holes between their ledge and the red light. And all around the red light, she could see the outline of an undamaged door. She blinked and refocused her eyes on Rowan. He stared at her intently.

"It looks like the higher two levels were crushed in the impact," she said. "Somehow, the very bottom level looks relatively undamaged."

"That's the one we need to get to," said Rowan. "It'll open on the mess hall, if memory serves."

His eyes remained guarded. He clenched his teeth on the wire that held his lantern. He turned his back on the blackness and grasped the edge of the floor. He groped blindly for his first foothold and began the slow descent to Level Nine. At the bottom of the shaft, the floor flattened out. Rowan turned from the unsettling red light to look above. Garyn and Collern descended nimbly behind him. Rowan turned again to stare at the door.

Rowan held up his lantern and pressed a series of buttons on a recessed computer station. He punched in the command for a full damage report. The computer hissed static, but the screen scrolled with dozens of pages of reports. Rowan read them all silently and then stopped the scroll when the lowest level appeared.

He pointed at the screen and read quietly, "Life support terminated, Sanction eight-six-seven." He stared at the time stamp, which was moments after he followed through with his plan. "Gravity engaged, livestock genetic sample control initiated, temperature regulation terminated." The timestamp for this activity ran from the life support termination time to just after the crash. "Complete system failure. Manual reboot required."

"What does all that mean?" Collern asked.

"It means that Sanction eight-six-seven both terminated life support and attempted to preserve the slaves by freezing them using the cold of space," Rowan answered in a clipped tone. "But not before they suffered."

"Rowan," Garyn redirected him by pointing at the last statement. "The system didn't fail until after the gravity part happened. You couldn't have done the manual reboot on your end because the second part was a function of this Sanction eight-six-seven command. It was still engaged until after the crash, wasn't it?"

Rowan agreed. "Seems so." Then he turned away from the blinking screen to the red light of the decontamination door. He set his jaw in a determined line and bit his lips together.

"That means Dargin Imelda killed them, not you." She stared at the back of Rowan's head for a long moment, willing him to understand. Then she sighed, resigned. "Are you ready?" Garyn asked.

"No," answered Rowan. Then he pressed a button sequence on the wall.

An electrical buzzing sounded. The door slid into the wall. Rowan entered and waited for Collern and Garyn before pressing another button sequence. He faced a new door with words that listed the room as a mess hall, leading to birthing chambers and sleep cells. Garyn pressed her lips together and stared ahead.

"It'll decontaminate us before we can move on," Rowan said. "It won't hurt."

Garyn watched the pale blue mist flood the room, shrouding them all with the smell of medicine and a light, powdery perfume. Then the vents pulled out the smoke. Garyn stood frowning. Collern worked his mouth open and closed and dug at his hair with open fingers. He hadn't kept his mouth shut. Into the flickering void beyond, Rowan sighed.

The door slid open. The stink of death immediately overtook the purified air of the decontamination chamber. Rowan didn't budge. Garyn knew that the blue mist had restored the boy's overpowered sense of smell. Garyn listened to the room beyond. The ineffectual ceiling air purifiers whirred non-stop. Though tainted with decay, Garyn found the air breathable. Otherwise, silence greeted them.

The harshness of artificial light streamed into the chamber from a round room. White walls reflected the brightness, blinding after so many dark passages. The nature of the air didn't settle well with Garyn. Because the room had been completely sealed and unventilated until that day, she expected the smell to be fresher. The freezing effect of space had long departed the sealed room, as she expected. However, mingled in the recent decay, she smelled much older death.

Past Collern and Rowan, both of whom stood a great deal taller than Garyn, she could see bodies of men and women, boys and girls, all piled around the door. They all lay prone as they had suffocated, pinned down by the command of increased gravity. Their hands had frozen into claws as they scratched at the door and floor. The only visible blood had dried around the victim's torn fingernails and had dripped from mouths and tear ducts of their tortured faces.

She stared at the horrific scene, realizing they had not stepped forward. She glanced up to Rowan. He had fixed his gaze on the far wall of the white room. Garyn pushed around Collern to follow Rowan's line of sight. There, suspended by winding ropes in front of thick, cracked glass partitions, hung three figures. A man and woman, rotting, defiled during and after life, and long dead. A smaller bundle, an infant, hung between them in the same state.

Rowan swallowed hard and took his first steps across the threshold. Garyn stared forward, frozen in shock. Collern followed Rowan, grasping the Queen's elbow and nudging her forward out of her trance. For once, the tall boy stayed wisely quiet. Rowan's eyes swept across the otherwise pristine room, pausing at each corpse. Garyn could tell that he had known each of them by name. His lips moved without sound every so often. Inevitably, his eyes returned to those bodies strung up against a glass wall.

Then the group stood before the cracked partition. Garyn heard Collern grinding his teeth. He shifted the pack from his shoulder to a clean spot on the white floor and rifled through the contents. He pulled out three compressed body bags. Deliberately, he cut the seal on each. Collern unfolded the white canvas material and opened the cinch closures, laying them side by side. The zip of the cinch closures drew Rowan's eyes to the floor, then to Garyn. She saw tears in the human's eyes. She understood his pain and guilt all at once. She trembled under his stare.

"Let's get them down from there," Collern rasped over the loud hum of the air purifiers. He caught Rowan's eyes. He pulled from his waistband a jagged knife. Rowan withdrew his boot knife. Both boys climbed up on the narrow ledge below Rowan's dead family.

They cut down the woman first. Postmortem, her frail bones had been broken several times, leaving dangling limbs. The bloat of death had left them all. However, Garyn saw through purple discoloration surgical gashes on the woman's lower abdomen, as well as a bullet hole in her chest, deep purple bruises, and a long gash on her throat to drain the blood. The scent of some preservative did little to mask the old death.

Rowan knelt on the floor and stared into her pocked face. He tucked her broken arms into the crisp white bag, leaving dark fingerprints as he pulled the cloth over her chest.

The man's body took the longest to retrieve, as he'd taken the most binding. A noose held his body upright. His arms hung from ropes where Slavers had no doubt severed them at the shoulder, well after death. Splashes of maroon all over the cracked glass ensured that little blood or fluid remained in any of the bodies. In fact, Garyn saw the paper-thin grayness of their blotchy skin as an unfortunate if successful preservation. The corpses were blissfully free from bugs in their sterile environment, ensuring slow decay. Her eyes snapped to Rowan. The Slavers had counted on that, she realized.

Garyn knelt and pulled the cinches closed on the bags that held Rowan's mother and father. She bound wide straps around the bodies to secure them for transport. She paused when a loud thud sounded in front of her. Rowan had collapsed on the floor. He clenched the knife in one hand and part of a severed rope in the other. The child's leg dangled free. And Rowan quivered in a pile, sobbing hysterically. Collern stared wide eyed at his Queen. For once, she saw the deep fury that had quieted him. His eyes asked her, "What creatures could have done this?" But she had no answer. She could only jerk her chin toward the child. Collern continued cutting at the ropes.

Queen Garyn knelt beside her new recruit as he cried, gasped, and shivered. She stared at him for a long while, unsure of how she could help and quite certain that nothing she could say or do would assuage him. *He won't just wake up and be okay, or put this behind him*, she thought. *Especially a human!* She rested her hand on his back and his crying reached a fever pitch. She heard him scream "Sorry!" between gasps, and "Sister!" Garyn cupped her hand behind the boy's head and tucked his face against her neck. She wrapped her arms around him, saying what she hoped to be comforting things. He put his arms around her and continued to sob inconsolably. He was just a boy again, no insurgent or warrior. Just a human boy who had seen tragedies rivaling her own.

"My Queen?" Collern said past the tightness in his throat.

She looked up as he knelt in front of Rowan. Collern's face held a horrible frown as he awkwardly cradled the dead child in his arms. With a stained finger, Collern stroked the infant's smooth cheek up to her forehead. There, his eyes darkened. In the side of her tiny head, a single hole bored through. He traced the edges of the wound.

Collern snarled. "Monsters." Garyn followed his eyes down the small form. "They shot an infant!"

"I couldn't get away!" Rowan gasped. He pushed away from Garyn, tears still streaming down his face. "I... couldn't... stop him! He shot our mother! Then Ayli screamed for my help. I ran with her. And still couldn't... p-protect her!"

"Rowan," Garyn said. "It's not your fault."

The boy nodded. Then he reached for the body in Collern's arms. His hands trembled. "Yes, it was." For a long moment, Rowan stared at the child. "The price for insurgency."

He held the dead baby, rocking gently like he had been taught. "I ran, holding her like this, when he killed her." His trembling lips stretched into a sneer. "And I see it all so clearly. Vividly, like it's happening right now. I held her. With these arms that protect *nothing.*"

The harsh lights flickered overhead. A red light flashed from the top of the wall. A speaker sounded a warning with a loud, monotonous tone, but crackled and sputtered. A piercing siren began in unison with the flashing lights.

"What's happening, Rowan?" Collern asked, working his jaw to release the tension.

Rowan answered with a distant voice as he stared at his kid sister. "Power's failing. I'm surprised it lasted this long." He closed his eyes and pressed the child against his chest. He drew a long, shaky breath. The siren wailed again. "Hear that, Ayli? We've gotta go, now."

He carefully tucked in her arms and legs, wrapped her in a cloth, and rolled the body bag around her. He secured her body with a wide strap. He rocked to his feet and looked uncertainly at the bundle. Garyn and Collern insisted on carrying his parents across their backs so that he could take his sister. Collern set the fire charges in the big round room. Rowan looked back once before they started a hasty ascent to the Middle Levels.

Rowan said, "There isn't much time left before the power's off completely." He ran to the life support room and pressed several buttons and turned a crank. "This should vent every room to the outside so the fire can breathe."

"What's *that* flashing red button?" Collern asked.

Rowan's eyes grew dark. "Not sure." He leaned over it, studying carefully, then gasped. "The bastards had a controlled fire-purge command, for," and he read, "*unsavory cargo.*"

"Well, that'll give us another reason to hate them," Garyn mumbled. "For now, can the command help with the pyre?"

"I think so," Rowan replied. "If the timer function still works."

"And if it doesn't?" Garyn arched an incredulous eyebrow.

"How fast can you run?" Rowan asked with complete seriousness.

Garyn's cynical laugh echoed in the metal room. "Quickly enough, I hope."

"Then I'll activate the command." He pressed a button. "Fire-purge, activated."

A ticking countdown was garbled overhead. Rowan froze. The sound came quickly, terminating to a long, piercing note. Garyn caught the panicked look in his eyes.

"Run?" she asked. Rowan nodded and led the way, with Collern having to slow his pace behind them.

7: PURGING FIRE

As they rounded the last of the Middle Level hallways, with the hatch open wide and sunlight beckoning, a loud explosion sounded behind them. Fire spilled around both corners, rolling toward its source of oxygen through the open door. Rowan slid to a stop in front of the hatch. He fumbled with the controls. The lift wouldn't work. He looked back toward the fire. Resignation crept into his bones. Suddenly, he felt very tired. Only his heart pounded furiously. He closed his eyes.

Garyn slipped past Rowan with her load and leapt from the height. Collern shoved Rowan out the door and jumped out behind him. As the top of his head cleared the bottom of the door, flames burst from the opening and climbed skyward. The ground rushed toward Rowan's head yet again. The taller boy wrapped his arm around Rowan's waist and threw him to a waiting Garyn, who caught the human and tumbled to break his fall. Rowan rolled several feet across the burnt clearing, then laid gasping for air.

Regaining his breath, Rowan rose to his feet and tested the metal brace. His legs shook from fear and strain. The strange tingling spread through his broken leg once more, telling him he'd injured something he couldn't quite feel. His heart still pounded, but the resignation and tiredness drained from his heart as he laid eyes on the smudged body bags lying in a row on the ground. Garyn and Collern started digging in the dense charred dirt. Rowan cast his eyes to the ship.

Smoke, fire and ash billowed from the open hatch and various vents along the sides of the crumpled ship. Silently, he joined his first real friends in digging a grave for his family. The sun set over the jungle. The intense light silvered the edges of glowing green foliage. Rowan laid his parents side by side in the hole and placed the bundled infant between them.

Rowan expected to break down again, to cry in front of the Queen and his friend. His eyes burned as he stared at the dead. However, his tears wouldn't fall this time. He felt as if they had dried forever. The fire overhead seared closed the wound in his chest. Still, his sin festered and ached, but he found it easier to breathe. He had done all he could at the end and didn't save anyone. But he slowly buried his past in some new future on Unata as he shoveled dirt over the soiled white body bags.

Wearily, they all raked the dirt back into the grave. Garyn made a quiet comment and laid down her shovel. She slipped off to the place where she had laid the Slavemaster and Slavers. The young men tamped the earth down and set aside their shovels. Collern remained silent the whole time. Rowan dragged three long, narrow rocks into place as headstones and packed dirt around them. Collern helped without speaking. At last the human looked up at the older boy.

Collern's face showed a mask of hurt and anger. His eyes flashed to Rowan.

"You weren't really considering staying back there, were you?" Collern asked, his voice full of venom.

Rowan remembered his crazy death wish and the way his heart had pounded. Collern had seen the look in his eyes. "It's what I deserve," Rowan said, staring at the fresh grave of his family as it was lit by the sky-high bonfire of the ship.

"I'm going to let you in on a little secret, *friend*," Collern said, grabbing Rowan's shirt. "You're my friend, and now a Unatan. You don't *deserve* the life Garyn's granted you. None of us do! But you damn well better *live* it! You better let go of what you think you deserve and start caring about what you *have*! Hear me?"

Rowan wiped his salt-tightened face with the back of his arm and cracked a tired smile. "I definitely have to live long enough to see you eat your boot!"

Some of the light returned to Collern's tired eyes. His face crinkled in a smile. He released Rowan's shirt and pounded him on the back.

They turned at the sound of flint cracking together. Garyn bent to nurse a small flame that licked at the sweet grasses piled around their dead enemies. Soon the bodies filled the air with light and white smoke. The aroma of burning incense flowers didn't mask the smell of burning flesh. The pyre burned savagely, easily reaching over halfway up the side of the ship.

As Rowan watched the last of his enslavement ascending into the evening air, Garyn beckoned him closer to the roaring fire. He stared at the crumbling ashes that were once his overseers. Garyn spoke up over the bellow of the flames.

"The pyres do more than dispose of the dead of Unata," she began. "In burning, we commit their bodies and spirits to the sky. We free them!"

Rowan looked back at the grave. "And their souls?"

"To their Maker's judgment, I suppose," Garyn said thoughtfully, looking back at Rowan. "To be honest, I just don't know. There are so many beliefs! But your family will know peace and rest in the soil of Unata. Of that I am certain."

"I would say," chimed in Collern, "that they are the only three to know peace on Unata."

Rowan sighed. "I think a kind of peace has found me at last."

"Then cherish it while it lasts, Rowan," Garyn said. Then she smiled. "At sunrise, you report to Dresden for training!"

"As weak as I am?" Rowan asked, suddenly perplexed. He backed away, returning to gaze at his family's grave. He placed a hand on the jagged stone and looked back at Garyn.

"If Collern is to eat his boot by next Proving, then you've no time to waste!"

"Hmph!" Collern swept by Rowan and gathered the shovels. He smiled at Rowan as he passed. "Lesson one, survival!"

Then he disappeared into the foliage. The moonless night suddenly loomed in the unfamiliar jungle. When he turned back to the flames, he saw Garyn back at the Slaver pyre. She danced and swayed near the flames. Then she threw her head back and screamed a name: *Dargin Imelda.* She committed the one name she had learned to the sky. Rowan stared, gaping, at the exotic woman. He felt ever the Unatan and a great swell of feeling for his Queen.

"Mother, Father, my precious Ayli, is it okay if I live a little longer as a Unatan?"

As if in answer, the breeze changed direction and swept warmly across his tearstained cheeks. *Live*, whispered the wind. And Rowan wanted to live, to truly understand living, for the first time in his life of slavery.

He pulled his eyes from the Queen and stared ahead into the forest. Collern unceremoniously left his Queen in a clearing in the middle of a jungle without worrying about her safety. Rowan felt determined to wait on the Queen, and to understand Unatan logic, at least! He crossed his arms and leaned his shoulder against a tree.

When he looked back to the pyre, the Queen had vanished into the night. *The nerve of these Unatans! Not doing what he expected of them!* He set his mouth in a determined line and trudged uncertainly into the forest.

The weak light of the electric lantern swinging from his hip did little to illuminate the utter darkness of the new moon. He'd only made it a few yards when the lantern light sputtered and died. He stared dumbly at the dead light for several long moments. Then the sounds of the jungle descended on him as heavily as the darkness.

During his ensuing panic, he felt his legs begin to give out from exhaustion. His arms quivered and his head throbbed. The tingling began in his belly, then subsided, taking with it the effect of Kadray's medicine. And the emptiness of his stomach protested loudly once he was fully away from the stench of death. The prickling crept slowly, advancing inch by inch through his midsection. He knew he had to return before that tingling reached his broken arm and leg.

He stomped ahead on the verge of an adrenaline crash. *Survival, Collern said!* He pushed aside a branch, then squinted at the blackness of a nonexistent path. The dark canopy loomed overhead. Claustrophobia, a fear he developed aboard the QuellTruth, made him panicky. Rowan knew the path, had counted his steps, if only he would pause to breathe and think. He pressed his hand to his chest, pushing away the sudden tightness there, forcing his brain to calm down. *Feeling sorry for myself isn't getting me home*, Rowan realized.

Twigs snapped behind him, and then again beside him. Afraid, feeling foolish and weak and cowardly, Rowan ran, counting his steps and accounting for his longer stride because he ran. He plunged down straights and barreled around turns until a stitch in his side doubled him over. He stumbled into a crevice between a large stone and a tree trunk. He groped for a sapling and sharpened it with his boot knife, all the while keeping his back crammed against the cold rock.

The image of a much larger Chimera drifted through his mind. Vicious, bloodthirsty, murderous. Unata's unwitting protectors. And Rowan knew he didn't have a drop of Unatan blood to dissuade the creatures from tearing him apart. How large could they get, really?

When he regained control of his breathing, all the normal buzzing of the forest had returned. He emerged from his hiding place with caution. The dim starlight above streamed through a gap in the canopy that terminated in a solid cliff face. Relieved to see the familiar stretch of cliff, Rowan had not only run in the right direction, but all the way to the cliff ascending out of the Lower Jungle. He backtracked many yards to find the climbing face they had used earlier. Rowan recognized the handholds and footholds of the Child's Path Collern had mocked.

Rowan tucked his makeshift spear into his belt. He began the slow ascent with quivering muscles and aching hands. Two-thirds of the way up, Rowan heard the bushes and limbs below him creaking under weight much larger than a bird. His heart pounded once more.

He scrambled over the ledge in record time and didn't stop to look down. He glanced around to get his bearings and recognized a small, twisted stump he had passed when he emerged from the Upper Jungle. He ran past the landmark and tried to bear north-east toward what he hoped to be Parisia, counting his steps.

The jungle twined across his path many times, but he managed to maintain his course. At least, he *thought* he maintained his course. He thought a small tree here and a rock there looked familiar and turned accordingly. Fear drove him onward with crunches and snaps of twigs. Whatever followed him, he could escape in Parisia!

The last of the old man's drug prickled down his arms and legs, past half-healed bones and deep bruises. Kadray had warned him to be in bed by that time, that the pain would catch up all at once, and that his body would shut down soon afterward.

Even as some horrendous creature hunted him, Rowan's fear gave way to the shock of a thousand dreadful aches, bones stressed to breaking over and over, and flesh torn by knives and glass and twisting metal—descending all at once in a wave of anguish. His legs would not move. He threw his weight forward and his legs crumpled beneath him. He landed on his belly on the moist earth, his hands clenched in claws of agony.

When finally he cried out, the sound came as little more than a whimper. He stared through bleary eyes at his drawn hands, and saw them as scarred, quivering ghosts in the darkness. Ayli's peaceful face filled his mind, followed by the memory of her wailing. And then the horrible silence of her death. *These arms that protect nothing.*

He cried out in frustration. Rowan forced his hands into fists and clenched his teeth against the pain. Dizziness swam at the back of his vision, darkening his eyes for a moment. *Not yet!* He squeezed his eyes shut, willing away unconsciousness. The roaring of a false ocean drowned his hearing, dragging him down toward darkness.

"No!" Rowan screamed in outrage. "I'm...I'm not finished yet!"

He dragged in his elbows, forced his knees beneath him and crawled to the nearest tree. Once there, he paused, heaving the cool night air into his lungs. Then he pulled his body to standing, balancing his weight against the makeshift spear. Anger filled him. He'd come so far and made so many promises!

"Come at me if you want!" Rowan hissed into the darkness. "I have work to do, and no stupid beast is going to stand in my way!"

He stood there for a long moment, the pain threatening to drag him down every second, and waited. He let his challenge hang on the cool breeze that drifted past his filthy body. When no creature answered it, he looked around and got his bearings once more.

His trailing hunter kept its distance after that. But Rowan wasn't foolish. *It's just waiting for the right chance!* He hobbled along proudly, ready to deal with that situation if it arose. He barreled ahead, letting his instincts guide him.

Parisia was close. He could feel it. The trees ahead parted onto a flat mesa, and the high wall of Unata's capitol city jutted from the sand. The real ocean crashed below the mesa. A flood of relief reduced him to jelly on the ground. Rustling in the brush behind him sent him to his feet again and into a dead run across the sandy clearing.

Rowan ran to the gate, but slowed to a walk when he didn't see the sentries at their posts. The metal gates swung freely, so he walked forward cautiously. *Something's not right.*

He pulled the spear from his belt, across his shoulder, and in both hands like a sword. He advanced slowly. No corner lights burned. No bunker lights shone out of narrow windows. The night mists crept through the streets as though the city had been abandoned. But even when the city slept, there were sentries and lights!

He walked through the central street, past the Throne Bunker, toward Queen Garyn's private residence. Light from a candle flickered in the window, but then snuffed out. Rowan's heart pounded even as his muscles trembled with exhaustion. Adrenaline flooded his body. With each tense step, he paused to listen. Hearing nothing, he advanced. He reached for the door lever with trembling fingers.

The next instant, the door burst open and electric lights gleamed brightly from within. A group of Unatans—led by the coordinator Maraba—spilled out of the Queen's home, cheering and chanting the warrior cry. All around, lights flared from all the other bunker homes.

Collern leaned on the door facing, shooting a cheesy grin his way. Rowan swayed on his feet from shock and nearly fainted with relief. The hand that gripped his spear quivered.

His broken ribs protested his stance. His leg and arm throbbed. His new bruises ached. His poor stomach growled above the cheers of his new comrades.

"What great timing!" Collern said, smiling fit to burst. "Congratulations! You're the quickest return we've had on Lesson One, probably ever."

"Ah! A spear! And pretty decent, too!" Garyn said with a laugh as she emerged from behind her home. She snatched it from Rowan's trembling hand. "Why is it that every time we abandon a trainee in the jungle, my future generations of trees suffer?"

Collern appeared at Rowan's side, more to support him than congratulate him. Rowan swayed against his friend, staring up at Garyn. "Looks like the meds wore off. Kadray said you'd shut down for sure. Pretty impressive, staying on your feet!" Collern chattered. "Sorry for running off on you. Dresden refuses to instruct anyone until they've gone through the survival training."

"What a welcome, huh?" sighed Rowan once he regained his ability to speak.

"A hurricane couldn't stop Mother when a party needs planning!" Then he lowered his voice. "Welcome home, Brother!"

Rowan muttered his thanks. The word *home* seemed such a foreign word to his lips that he whispered it. Home had always been a pristine white cell with glass along one wall and a fold down cot along the other. And no matter how he scrubbed, no matter how clean the room looked, he could never get rid of the toilet stench that permeated the whole ship.

But *home* meant something else on Unata. Rowan had inherited an entire society with this home. His heart thudded in his chest.

The feline-faced Chard appeared in front of Rowan. "Does this mean we'll be training together now?"

"I guess so," he answered with a woozy smile.

"Tomorrow will be fun!" And then Chard ran off to tell every awake Unatan about the new addition to the training roster.

Maraba walked over to Garyn, Rowan and Collern. "The look on your face says you finally understand! I hope you'll forgive me for torturing you so, especially tonight." She held his face in her hands. "But you'll also have to forgive our Queen for her horrible monster-in-the-woods performance." She called over her shoulder, "I'll pretend that you didn't just scare him in the right direction the whole way back!"

Rowan smiled at Maraba, then looked at Garyn. He felt deeply embarrassed.

"She knew the meds were wearing off. So, she followed you all the way home to, ah, 'ensure his fair survival'," Collern whispered. "And you came fast! I barely got here before you!"

Rowan felt quite the fool for being so scared. He also felt the guilt of being an inconvenience. But Garyn smiled, obviously unharmed by her efforts.

"Must be a real challenge to move *loudly* through the jungle, Garyn!" Maraba said with a jab of her elbow. "I know you were trained better than that!"

Garyn threw her head back and laughed, then brushed some leaves from her white hair. "I just pretended I was *you* trying to be quiet. It worked out wonderfully!"

"Son," Maraba nodded to Collern, "drag that boy in here to eat. He's going to bite a hunk outta you if we don't feed him soon!"

"Ha!" Collern whispered in Rowan's ear. "That's Mom's way of sayin' *she's* ready to eat!"

Rowan allowed Collern to help him into Garyn's chambers, which he'd never seen before. He didn't get to focus on the intricate weaponry on the walls for all the people in the place. They shoved exquisite food under his nose until he was quite near to bursting and content to do so.

"Let the boy rest," Garyn said to the assembly. "He's only got four hours until sunrise, and Dresden is expecting him! Collern, come fetch him first thing."

He felt his eyelids droop and struggled to stay awake. People started to obediently file out. He slumped to his side on the cushioned bench. Voices rose and fell in hushed whispers.

"I swear, Kadray!" Garyn whispered at one point. "He stayed conscious *and* got back up when those drugs wore off. In just minutes."

Rowan felt a presence over him. The old man harrumphed on occasion as he checked the boy over. He mumbled something about nothing being re-broken and swept out of the room.

The sounds of his surroundings faded to old dreams with faceless babies and indistinct white walls. The once vivid nightmares softened around the edges and he wasn't aware of what parts he found scary. The dreams faded for the night, and he slept in relaxing blackness.

Then all around him was silent and dark. He turned in his sleep and felt a warm blanket tucked under his chin. In that moment, he heard a low lullaby drifting through the room, in a woman's voice, soft and calming. Or did he imagine it?

8: DRESDEN

Rowan awoke to harsh shaking. He opened his eyes to bright, streaming sunlight and focused on the dark outline of Collern above him. Rowan mumbled that his head hurt and would Collern please stop knocking his head against the hard bench? Didn't Collern know how sore Rowan's muscles were? How much he ached?

"Rowan! We're late! *Late*... Dresden'll *kill* us!" Collern punctuated each word with a shake of Rowan's shoulders.

"Late?"

He saw a clean room around him and Collern's face near his. The Unatan held real worry in his eyes. Rowan jumped to his feet in that moment, looking down at his dirty clothes while groping for his boots. His hands tingled as did his muscles. In mere moments, his body stung all over with the excruciating pain of overworked and bruised muscle and barely mended bones. Four hours to sleep, Garyn had said.

"How late are we?" Rowan mumbled.

"When the night mists burn off, we're late!" Collern pointed to the window, to the last wisps of fog clinging to the thin foliage.

Rowan's heart pounded. He fumbled with the laces of his boots and darted for the open door. His fingers still felt numb, but he could see blisters forming under the dirt. Collern paused and shoved the sliding door back in place before he ran after Rowan, following on his heels.

"Rowan!" he panted. "You're going the wrong way!"

The human slowed only a little, which gave his sore body too much time to protest. He felt confused. Maraba had shown him a map indicating training fields outside the northern edge of the city.

"The Gauntlet trained there," Collern said with a nod in that direction. Rowan saw the Unatan cringe and decided to find out more about the Gauntlet later. "Way more advanced than recruits!"

"Dresden works this way!" Collern angled his run past Rowan and grabbed the boy's arm. He dragged the human west down a side path until he kept pace.

The boys crossed Parisia in record time. Rowan saw the intriguing buildings and fascinating citizens pass by in a blur. He felt the hot sun on his back and knew they couldn't be on time. Rowan stared at Collern's feet and matched his stride. He knew the older Unatan would have to shoulder the burden of Rowan's laziness.

He already failed his training order by the Queen. *Maybe she will change her mind.* Rowan's chest filled with dread. He ignored the pain of massive blisters on his newly shod feet. He squeezed his hands shut and ignored the stinging of blisters on his palms. The leg and arm brace still supported his bones, though he struggled to ignore their throbbing ache. He focused only on running behind Collern.

The boys mounted a low hill and saw the recruit barracks below on the left. On the right, Rowan saw a large, sandy field with wooden and metal devices along one side, under a shed. The devices looked like primitive versions of the exercise equipment aboard the QuellTruth. Older Unatans occupied the equipment now. The large, sandy field held two long rows of Unatans, one group at least half Rowan's age, and another group probably in their early teens.

"Whatever you do, don't apologize to Dresden," Collern said over his shoulder, barely above a whisper. "You think Garyn got mad when you did that! Whoo!"

Rowan nodded. He ran faster to catch up to Collern, keeping a wary eye on the assembly. He recognized Chard among the recruits.

"And don't say 'I can't.' He *hates* that!" Collern continued. "Answer loudly and honestly when spoken to, but look straight ahead. He'll ask questions, but not until I introduce you."

Rowan cringed with a stab of fear. A tall, athletic man stood with his hands on his hips, glaring at the assembled recruits and speaking in an animated way. Rowan couldn't yet hear him. The behemoth of a man, who Rowan could only assume to be Dresden, wore a close crop of white hair, heavy boots and dark pants. Old, thick scars streaked his face, neck and shoulders. He did look a trifle younger than Rowan expected, perhaps only around Maraba's age.

Then Rowan heard that clear, authoritative voice for the first time. Collern led Rowan through the gate and onto the field, never slowing a step. But the voice cut into Rowan, deeper than any knife.

Dresden's intense blue eyes snapped their way and followed them down to the lineup. He stopped speaking as they neared. Collern stopped and stood up straight, indicating that Rowan should do the same, a few feet from the group. Rowan tried to control his exerted breathing. But Dresden's eyes cut as deeply as his voice. Rowan stared straight ahead.

After a long moment of staring in silence, Dresden resumed speaking. His normal voice betrayed a smooth, calm, controlled tenor that belied his gruff appearance. "And the lesson can be easily remembered if you only recall our Queen's words: 'Logic is a foe of the learner, and a friend to the wise.' Tell me what it means, recruits!"

Dresden stared again at Rowan, who sweated and ached and tried not to waver on his feet. "Tell me the meaning, Chard!"

Rowan's ears perked at the young boy's loud, piercing reply. "As learners, we have to commit our action to muscle memory, to be automatic, because we don't have time in battle to think about basic things like our motion."

"And what of wisdom?" Dresden coaxed.

"And... once our bodies are wise enough, we'll be quick *and* be able to think at the same time!" Chard answered loudly enough for all Parisia to hear.

"Now, toward that goal, list for me the training order," Dresden said, allowing his strong voice to boom. Again, his eyes settled on Rowan. "Collern, let's see if you remember the basics!"

"Yes, Sir!" Collern answered. "First, we condition the body. Second, we train the mind. Third, we *discipline* the body and mind. Fourth, we extend our discipline with weapons."

"Fifth?" Dresden asked, striding over to Collern.

"Fifth," Collern faltered. "We... master the

body, mind, and weapons!"

"And the elusive sixth in order? Anyone?"

Rowan felt butterflies in his stomach. The silence nauseated him. He had a simple theory he would be rash enough to test. He shouted, before his head popped from the pressure. "Sir! Is it to ascend to the Gauntlet?"

Several young Unatans gasped. Dresden stood silently just two feet from him. Rowan felt the big man's eyes burning into his face. Collern groaned and mumbled something about Rowan keeping his mouth shut.

"Collern!" He still stared at Rowan.

"Sir!" Collern stood at attention.

Dresden looked at the older boy. "First, tell me why a new recruit born an alien shows a greater understanding of ascendancy than my own son!"

Collern faltered again, then spoke up. "Father, uh, Sir! I only spoke of the Gauntlet training grounds. Our Queen has informed me of the intellectual resourcefulness of humans in such matters."

"I see," said Dresden. His voice held some humor. "Garyn Kei has informed *me* that this young man will surpass his Unatan counterparts in time. Fastest back from survival, I hear?"

Rowan's throat tightened at his Queen's boast and at the realization that Dresden was Collern's father. He felt the heavy burden of living up to their expectations. His stomach turned. Dresden wouldn't accept any of his apologies and self-degrading comments. Collern had been specific on that front. Rowan bit his tongue to stop the torrent of habitual words from spilling out.

"Yes, Sir!" Collern was smiling. "He's our newest star!"

"What's this newest star's name, kid?" The tension in Dresden's voice released. Rowan could tell he was smiling, but he didn't dare look at the man.

Collern cleared his throat and announced, "Our new pledge, Rowan Jun, his Unatan status sanctioned by our Queen Garyn Kei, has been entrusted to you, Dresden Berzo, for immediate implementation of training in Order Basics until which time the Queen demands his presence for private training." Collern paused, sighing deeply.

"Private training, huh?" Dresden said for Rowan's ears only. His voice, despite the bite of surprise, sounded calm and kind. "I haven't heard that one before. It's time to earn that rank, huh, Rowan Jun?"

"Yes, Sir!" Rowan bellowed.

Dresden laughed at the abrupt voice from the new kid. "All right, eyes forward! Show's over. Rowan Jun is your brother now! Treat him as such! He'll be the one watching your back some day!"

Those assembled shouted in unison, "Yes, Sir!"

"Good. Now, on to our next activity! Run until you puke!" Dresden ordered. The group dispersed immediately, with Rowan close behind them. "Real puking! I'll break whatever finger you shove down your throat!"

Rowan believed he would do just that. He felt relieved to remove himself from Dresden's imposing presence, even if it meant pushing his already worn-down body. Rowan heard a final order before he rounded the bend in the huge field.

"Get goin', Collern!" Dresden yelled.

"But Father! It's mid-pledges!" Collern whined.

"Sounds like an excuse," Dresden's voice took on a warning tone. Then he smiled. "You only have to run until you remember all your Orders by rote. And after *that*, until you puke!"

Collern mumbled as he ran behind the group, but quickly his grumbling robbed him of breath. He caught up to Rowan halfway back around the field. He kept pace beside the human, who struggled to keep up with the slowest of the Unatans.

The recruits, many of whom were girls, jogged tirelessly. Through jarring of his voice as he ran, he commented on the female presence. Collern laughed, explaining that every Unatan trained, regardless of gender or social standing.

"Will one of them replace the Queen someday?" Rowan asked quietly. He shuddered to think of any one of them matching her on any level.

"Hmph. I'm afraid it doesn't work that way," Collern answered. "Unatan Royalty is a bloodline trait," he paused for a long breath as the group rounded a corner, "passed on from mother to daughter."

"But the Queen doesn't have a mate?" Rowan asked under his breath.

Collern laughed again. "Aiming for the Throne, too, huh?"

"No! Shhh!" Rowan replied. He felt the blood rise to his face, and Collern laughed again at Rowan's embarrassment. "Just trying to understand things that are common knowledge to you."

They ran in silence for several moments, passing several smaller boys bent over pools of their own vomit. Rowan hadn't realized how long they had run until that moment. By the next round, more boys faltered alongside the path with a few girls. They all wiped their mouths on their shirtsleeves or hands and rejoined the run when the group came around again. He wondered at the resilience of the planet's youth!

As the pledges passed Dresden, he yelled words of encouragement along the lines of "Did I see a finger down your throat, kid?" and "Keep it going! Run, run! Don't let the new guy beat you!" Collern kept pace with Rowan the entire time, though Rowan knew he could pass him. *Is it kindness or laziness keeping him with me?*

Rowan endured to be the last of the group to empty the contents of his stomach on the grass. The paltry bile and foam burned his throat, reminding him he missed breakfast that morning. He immediately jumped to his feet, ignoring pain and lack of food for the same goal they all sought. He doubled his speed, refusing to wait until the group made it back around to join. Collern maintained his lazy pace at the back of the group and grinned at Rowan.

"Well, new guy, now you're initiated!" he announced. "They all know that humans do, indeed, vomit!"

"Funny," Rowan said, his throat still burning from the bile. But he noticed that some of the pledges glanced back at him with friendly faces. His heart pounded from exertion and something more. He ducked his head timidly and turned his attention to the distance.

Another few laps passed in silence, with nothing but the pounding of feet on the earth and rhythmic breathing punctuating the air. Even Dresden had retired to the exercise machines that lined their path. Every lap, he would change machines. Finally, he resorted to pull-ups on a long metal bar. Rowan gulped past the dryness in his throat. What intimidating strength!

"Maraba teases her occasionally," Collern spoke suddenly. "I've heard them."

"Huh?" Rowan answered, confused. Then he realized the older boy took up their previous conversation about Garyn's sovereignty.

"Our Queen informed my mother that she'd mate if, and only if, a man *suited* her," Collern whispered.

"What does that mean?" Rowan asked, confused.

"I don't really know," Collern admitted with a smile. "But I'll be surprised if such a man exists!"

Rowan considered the immense power of his ruler. "Me, too!"

"And then," Collern continued, chuckling, "she *insisted* that Maraba shouldn't worry. That she refused to die until a proper heir was in place, so that Maraba would be able to plan the perfect coronation ceremony!"

Rowan nodded, admitting that it did sound just like Garyn Kei to make such a promise. Then he thought about Collern's other announcement. Did the Queen really plan on taking him as a personal trainee? Dresden's reaction made him realize what a rare opportunity she offered. He found it unsettling, even for a wonderful woman who had her whims. Then he shook his head. *This woman's whim saved my life!*

He hadn't looked up often enough to notice that only a few recruits still ran. Dresden had been dismissing them one by one as they reached his quota. The sun settled on the edge of the plateau, red and beautiful, before he even saw much of his surroundings again. He had been sick more than anyone by day's end, and glad of his already empty stomach that much more. He'd gotten his second, third and fourth winds, and struggled toward his fifth, when dizziness overcame him. He collapsed, quite unfortunately, at Dresden's feet.

He scrambled to his hands and knees quickly and retched repeatedly. Sweat dripped from his forehead to the ground. His wind-dried hair swayed stiffly around his face, the salt of his sweat forcing it into knots and spikes. And beyond his vision-obscuring hair, he saw Dresden's boots. Still his stomach heaved, but there was nothing to empty. He quivered and fell to his side. Again, he forced his body to his knees. His vision blurred.

"Don't worry, kid," Dresden said, but his voice held a little concern. "Puke's good for the greenery!"

"I'm sorr..." Rowan began, then cut off the words. He clenched his fists in the dirt and froze where he knelt. He cursed to himself over and over. Collern had warned him!

"Well, then," Dresden whispered. "We'll have to make sure you feel appropriately punished for your trespass. *And* for being late."

The coldness of Dresden's words pierced Rowan's heart. His breathing came in ragged gasps. He hauled his body to standing, ready to receive the appropriate punishment for his mistakes.

"All of you, except Collern and Rowan, dismissed!" Dresden bellowed.

The other boys and girls filtered from the yard, casting worried or haughty glances to the two who remained. Rowan saw anxiety etched on young Chard's face. The human forced his eyes forward and calmed his breathing. Collern glared daggers through him as he jogged over to join him. Rowan didn't budge.

Then Dresden stalked in front of him and

leaned toward his face. Rowan could feel the heat of Dresden's breath and smell his sweat. He also sensed the fury that radiated from the big man. Dresden cut an imposing figure. His proximity terrified Rowan. At the point right before Rowan needed to scream to release the tension, Dresden stepped back.

Dresden drew a deep breath and sighed. "I have a very specific reason for my actions," he began. "So should each and every Unatan. If your actions have reason and intent, and you protect Unata, you do *nothing* that requires apology."

Understanding dawned on Rowan. Dresden hated excuses and apologies with good reason. Rowan committed the statement to memory.

He turned to Rowan's mentor. "Collern!"

"Sir!" Collern said.

"There is no excuse for your lack of a thorough tutoring of Rowan Jun in procedures during his convalescence," the man informed his son. "Do you accept your duty, or no?"

"I do, Sir!" Collern said in a too-loud voice. By his tense tone, he hadn't realized his folly.

"We shall see," and Dresden shifted his gaze to Rowan. "And Rowan Jun."

"Yes, Sir!" Rowan straightened his shoulders.

"Your punishment is physical and mental conditioning," Dresden said. "You will run this track until you know everything about Unata, and I mean *everything.* Collern will teach you as you run. You seem perceptive, so let it serve you."

In Rowan's peripheral, Collern's shoulders slump a little.

"Yes, Sir!" Rowan answered.

"I'll quiz you at sunrise, or perhaps after training." The man picked up his coat from the raised-step benches and turned to leave. With a wave, he said, "Run until sunrise, or until you know Unata better than Collern. Whichever comes first!"

"Yes, Sir!" they answered in unison. Both boys, aching and exhausted and unfed, turned back to the long oval field and started a slow jog.

"Father's right," Collern said, his many aches and pains evident in his voice. "I failed you today. You had zero preparation, and it's my fault. Still friends?"

Rowan laughed as hard as the stitch in his side allowed. "Yeah. If we can make it through this day, and night, and morning," he took a couple deep breaths, "and tomorrow, without killing each other, then we're stuck with each other for good!"

"Good!" Collern replied. "I'd hate to lose my new rival first thing!"

"Then I'll forgive you if you get started on our assignment," Rowan said with a grin. "Learning the entire history and social structure of an entire world in one night isn't going to be easy!"

Collern laughed. "All right! One crash course in Unatan social studies coming up!"

Through the darkest part of the night, they paced their running to save breath for talking. Collern cited and repeated and tested Rowan. Then a loud, clear voice rang across the field to their tired ears. Rowan looked across to see a tall woman. Maraba had arrived carrying a large basket. She beckoned to them to come over.

When the boys looked around warily, Maraba kicked at the dust under the raised benches and called out to them. "Queen's orders that starving boys need to eat! Get over here!"

"Mother!" Collern simpered. "You brought food?"

"Oh, don't 'Mother' me, young man!" Maraba lashed out. "You're both in this situation because of your corner-cutting," she said, waggling a finger in his face.

Then she froze. Her eyes went wide. She abruptly burst out laughing. Tears rolled down her cheeks as she guffawed and pointed. When she could speak, she said, "You both look like you've rolled in the mud for a week instead of just a day." Then she laughed again. "Poor Rowan! Your hair!"

Though glad to hear some hearty laughter, he didn't understand. Then he lifted his hands to smooth back his hair. All his fingers met were a series of tangles, leaves, mud and untold nastiness matted in black hair that stood out at odd angles from his head. He patted experimentally at the mass and then dropped his arms, defeated. He shook his head. But he smiled a little at Maraba. He would have laughed if he didn't feel so exhausted.

"I see a long day of training has made even Rowan slap-happy!" Maraba cried. "Then you'll be even happier with tonight's dinner." She pulled a cloth cover from the basket top. The boys descended on her wares, wrenching the basket from her arm and tearing through its contents as she laughed at their antics.

They dug through bread, sliced meat and sweet cakes. Collern found two bottles of his favorite fruit juice blend and waved one glass bottle under Rowan's nose. Rowan turned to Maraba and mumbled a thank you around a mouthful of bread. Then Collern sprinted across the field to the eating tables with Rowan hot on his heels.

Maraba laughed heartily and called after them, "Back to your punishment as soon as you've eaten your fill!"

They waved at her in agreement, though reluctantly.

"And they were falling over dead just a few minutes ago," she said with a smile. "Collern's a lot like his father, all right. Is that why you're spying on them?"

Silence answered her, and then Dresden's whisper. He sighed and said, "You were always the only one who could find me. Well, you and Garyn."

"Oh, please! You breathe like a wounded redmeat!"

Dresden harrumphed. "I'm not spying, really."

She kept her voice low as she watched the boys. "Hiding and watching someone counts as spying, dear." She smiled. "Do you really expect them to disobey you?"

"No, I just want to make sure this one doesn't die before the Queen gives him *permission*!" In his excitement, Dresden couldn't keep his voice as quiet. "He outlasted most of the pledges who have been training for years! He's really got a future on Unata."

"I know," Maraba nodded, "and Garyn knows, too. She's got a feeling for this kid, and she's right!"

"She usually is," Dresden said with a chuckle.

Maraba snorted. "She said you'd be hiding behind the stands watching them."

"Then why didn't she send dinner to me?" Dresden whined like a child.

"Ahem... 'Children, we feed. Grown men know where to find the dinner table.' She also said that fasting with them out of guilt is something you've got to stop," Maraba grinned through the words.

"That's the only order I have trouble with," he sighed.

"As long as they don't know you're a cuddle-critter, your authority is absolute."

Across the field, the boys had thrown all their empty containers back into the basket. They looked up, realizing that Maraba was still there. Mistaking her continued presence, they headed back across the field with her basket.

She smiled at them and whispered to Dresden, "They've broken their fast. Now get outta here. They'll run until they pass out."

She graciously accepted her basket and waved to the boys as they immediately ran back toward the long oval track. When they rounded the far bend, she called to Dresden. Receiving no answer, she knew he had already left. Chuckling to herself, she turned and headed home as the night mist swirled around her ankles.

9: PARISIA'S FINEST

Dresden trudged over the slight rise that led to his training grounds. With sunrise still an hour away, the man begrudged himself a few hours of sleep and a hot meal before he hurried back under the pretense of ensuring that the boys followed his orders. The night mist draped like a silvered cotton blanket over the long field below.

He focused in the darkness to find either of the boys. Soon he saw a dark head bobbing above the mist, rounding the far bend and moving steadily toward him. *Rowan is still running?* Dresden thought. *I'd've expected him to be out by now!* The trainer allowed a smug, secret smile. Dresden felt strongly that Rowan's potential exceeded many of the stronger, sturdier Unatans. He saw a latent spark in the boy's aura like no other he had witnessed, brighter even than that of his own son. But when he looked for his lazy son Collern, he could not find him.

Dresden called Rowan to a halt. "Have you completed your assignment, Rowan Jun?"

The winded boy mustered the breath to answer. "Sir! I have to the best of my current ability!"

"Has Collern abandoned you?" Dresden let his disappointment show in his voice.

"No, Sir! Not really," Rowan began. His loud formal voice echoed in the pre-dawn quiet. "He collapsed some time ago. I paused in my assignment long enough to move him to the bench, so I didn't trample him."

Dresden nodded, since the boy couldn't see much below his waist in the fog. He still felt a little upset. His son hadn't handled a day and a half jog with a full meal as well as an off-worlder with a weaker constitution. And Dresden knew him to be one of the strongest pledges he had trained, meaning that the human ran on something that went beyond just conditioning and stamina.

Dresden stared at the boy, drenched with sweat and dew. He wavered only slightly, staying upright through a sheer force of will. But his eyes bored through the air before him, black and shining as coals. In only Dresden's eyes, Rowan's latent spark crackled all around him.

"I'll save your quiz for tonight, after your regular training day," Dresden said, impressed with the boy's resolve. "You have a little over a half hour before sunrise. I'm ordering you to the showers and to breakfast in the main hall. Do you think you can wake Collern, drag him with you, and make it back here before sunrise?"

"Yes, Sir!" Rowan exclaimed.

When Rowan swayed a little, Dresden gave him a shove toward the unconscious Collern. Rowan dragged the older boy to his feet and stumbled with him toward the showers in the barracks. When they disappeared into the gaping maw of the low building, Dresden heard recruits stirring within. He shook his head at the resilience of the little human. Then he went about preparations for his day's training.

* * *

Rowan dragged Collern back to the training grounds for another full day of hard work. Both boys survived the day, though Rowan looked a little gray around the eyes as he kept exhaustion at bay. Before dismissing the other pledges, Dresden, as promised, grilled Rowan about his knowledge. The questions came for an hour and, well-rehearsed, Rowan provided the answers without apprehension.

"And finally," Dresden began, "to whom do you owe allegiance, Rowan Jun?"

Rowan bellowed, "To Her Royal Majesty, Queen Garyn Kei, daughter of Kei Masali, daughter of Masali Rei. And to each and every Unatan in turn!"

A great cheer arose from the recruits. Several of the boys slapped Rowan on the back in camaraderie. Collern stood smiling with relief and friendly pride. But Rowan's face still showed all business. Dresden still leaned in with skepticism.

"That's a lot to take in for just one night of learning," Dresden replied, dismissing the knowledge with a wave of his hand. "Most of it could be available in a ship's manifest. Even that dirty trader knew about our Queen, after all."

Rowan flinched at the mention of Dargin Imelda.

"So," Dresden began casually, "tell me something that only a Unatan could know."

Rowan's brain ticked through everything he'd heard since he arrived on Unata. Then it all came spilling out. "Sir! Herder Jeshdin names his animals after past Royals, Fisher Kaleon says that he fathered two of his sons with a great fish so they'd be capable on the seas, and, Sir... Lady

Maraba cannot cook."

Rowan lowered his voice on that last bit but stood firm and straight shouldered. Several of the boys and girls gasped, but they all smiled at him. Rowan felt Dresden's eyes on him, but couldn't figure out the nature of the glare without looking at the man. Then from behind him, a woman snickered and laughed heartily. Rowan stiffened at the voice of his Queen.

"Well, Maraba," Garyn said, stifling her laughter, "looks like the boy's got you pegged right!"

Rowan didn't dare look their way. His face flushed, glowing in his embarrassment. Dresden looked away from Rowan to the new arrivals. He heard a shuffle of movement and everyone bowed to the queen. He followed suit, hoping his long hair hid his face from her scrutiny. He hoped he hadn't upset Maraba.

"We came, Dresden, because our Queen wondered if you were going to *starve* the pledges into submission tonight," Maraba said with an even voice. She sighed. "Rowan, I guess my secret's out. I beg your forgiveness if I misled you!"

Dresden harrumphed. But Rowan heard the smile in her voice. He straightened from his bow. She teased him! He filtered through what she said and how she said it. He still wasn't convinced he hadn't shared an inappropriate tidbit of information publicly. Then Garyn chuckled again.

"You've got him scared to even *accept* an apology, Dresden!" Garyn sighed. "Truth be told, dinner's been ready these past two hours. The cooks aren't happy to keep it hot for long."

"Just keeping my word to the boy, my Queen," Dresden said with a curt nod toward

Rowan.

"And I presume he passed your little test?" Garyn asked.

"This time, this time," Dresden replied.

Dresden gave the signal for dismissal to all the other recruits, requesting Rowan to stay. The others dipped forward in quick bows as they rushed past Garyn. Collern hung back with his mother.

"Then assign him a bunk and feed the boy," Garyn ordered. She fussed all around the two men, with Collern and Maraba talking quietly behind her. "I expect Rowan Jun in my quarters after dinner tonight to settle some unfinished business. Rowan, at *ease*! For crying out loud, dismissal of the others means at ease! And stop bellowing 'yes, my queen' all the time. You can just *say* it to me. It's Dresden with the pretend hearing impairment. Well, no use rambling. You have your orders!"

"Yes, my Queen!" yelled both Rowan and Dresden in unison.

She cringed, closing her pale eyes. With a heartfelt sigh, she turned and whirled past them, heading between the wooden posts and toward the dining hall. Maraba and Collern followed close behind. Dresden gave Rowan a bunk assignment number and dismissed him. The trainer rushed to catch up to his mate, leaving Rowan standing alone on the grounds. He stared after the odd group, feeling at once perplexed and content. He executed a deep bow to them, then hurried to catch up.

Rowan stuffed himself silly at dinner, once he realized that the other recruits did the same. He pushed embarrassment aside in the warm camaraderie of his peers around him. They didn't talk much to him directly but included him in jibes and waited for his reactions. Finally, a few of the girls beset him with a barrage of questions. Rowan's stilted, formal answers to the myriad questions they asked brought out the curiosity in the awkward few who hadn't yet talked to him. Collern and young Chard stepped in to shake Rowan of the formal stiffness and caution he had built up over years of slavery. By the end of dinner, Rowan felt very tired but felt the full embrace of being Unatan.

Maraba fetched Rowan as he finished his third helping of dessert. She led him out of the bright dining hall into the inky black of night. Only the creeping night mist and Maraba's silver hair caught the light cast by dim bulbs over doorways lining the street. He followed her in silence. At the end of the street, in the expanse between the main town and the Queen's dwelling, she paused and turned to the boy. Her face was masked by darkness, ringed by a silver halo.

"Rowan, may I ask you a personal question?" she said, her voice low and uncertain.

"Yes, Ma'am," Rowan whispered, warned by something uncharacteristic in Maraba's usually light voice.

She turned away and looked at the black sky—a new moon. "Do you like Unata?"

"Of course," Rowan said. "I've never had a *welcoming* home."

"Do you *love* Unata?" she asked. "Enough to release all others, even your own heart?"

Rowan stared at her back, trying desperately to give a true, honest answer. But he could not deny his humanity. "As much as this human heart can feel," and he brought his fist to his chest, "I am devoted to my Queen, and my Queen *is* Unata."

Maraba chuckled, but her tone was

somber. She turned and walked back to Rowan, looping her arm through his and leading him toward the Queen's quarters. "Garyn is worried about that heart, though she'd never tell you."

"Why?" Rowan asked, wondering what Garyn knew about his heart.

"Well, Unatans are more than just sturdy in body," Maraba began. "Our emotional capacity is singular, I guess. We have an experience, get our worst emotions out, and let go, usually."

Rowan nodded, aware that Maraba had slowed her steps. He waited for her to continue.

"Garyn says that humans don't deal with loss, sorrow, guilt, and the like—all the negative emotions—the same as Unatans." Maraba took a deep breath and sighed. "You know that you may have to *intentionally* kill someone to protect Unata?"

The emphasis on the word "intentionally" meant that Maraba knew about Rowan's actions aboard the ship. But her voice held no accusatory tone. She merely asked a logical question.

"I understand," Rowan said, his voice full of emotion. His shoulders tensed and he stopped walking. "I had to stand aside for so long, helpless, watching and waiting as people I cared for died—were murdered—for nothing. With Dresden's training, I have the chance to do more than just watch loved ones die. I maybe will save them, but at least I will be able to *try* to save them!"

"Oh, Rowan," Maraba said as sympathy welled in her voice.

"Then," Rowan continued, "I was ignorant. I caused so many deaths aboard that horrible slave ship and I can't fix that. I'll carry the pain of that guilt the rest of my life. I definitely can't, won't forget, because I'm the only one who *knew* them, who *cared* for them."

Maraba tightened her arm around his. "Then you know the Unatan path will be difficult."

"Isn't loss what makes humans stronger?" Rowan asked. "I can't change the way my brain works, the way I feel, anymore than you can." Rowan smiled up at her, his eyes gleaming. "But I'll surpass Collern, I'll do better than *everyone*, if it means that I get to protect just one person with this life!"

"Then I guess it's settled, huh, Garyn?" Maraba raised her voice, turning her head from the human boy.

Rowan heard a click. Light flooded the ground before them. Maraba and Rowan stood a mere ten feet from the open doorway of Garyn's house. The Queen propped her shoulder against the doorframe, obviously waiting for her company.

"I guess it *is* settled," she said with a longsuffering smile.

Rowan, feeling acutely embarrassed and cleverly trapped, glanced all around them to see who else had heard his ranting. Maraba chuckled at his reaction as Garyn strode over, hands outstretched to the boy.

"Don't worry, you weren't all *that* loud!" said the Queen. "Those in the city limits of Parisia who didn't listen intently to your speech were trying extremely hard *not* to eavesdrop. It's the Unatan ears." She indicated her own pointed ear with a flourish.

Garyn had to drag the boy into her house while Maraba cackled over his mortified expression. The Queen shushed the woman and shoved Rowan onto a bench in front of a wide table. She pulled up a stool for herself. Maraba fetched a long tray from Garyn's counter and set it before them.

Rowan gathered his composure long enough to stare at the items on the tray. He identified four small glasses and one large glass bottle. He thought the dark contents looked a lot like the superb fruit juice blend he and Collern had drunk last night. But the big bottle had sharp angles and intricate carving. A glass stopper plugged the opening, instead of the metal cap he remembered. He found himself salivating at the thought of more of the sweet drink when Maraba's sharp exclamation called him to attention.

"Ah! Te-Dasuka at last!"

"Lady Maraba," the regal old man inclined his chest to the Coordinator, "my Queen," he bowed to Garyn, "and Dresden's new pledge, Rowan Jun." Again, the man bowed.

Rowan snapped from his awe and stumbled to his feet. He knew about this man! And Dresden had told the man about him. He saluted Te-Dasuka as he had been taught, with such reverence that the old man blinked several times to get the moisture from his eyes. But he grinned.

"Rowan! I told you about the screaming! And at ease. At *ease*," Garyn bellowed, pounding her fist on the table. Rowan stiffened at her voice. He slowly forced his shoulders to relax. But Maraba and Te-Dasuka had already backed against the wall. Maraba recovered quickly and crumpled against the old man's shoulder, clearly wracked with laughter.

Te-Dasuka still offered a weathered grin. "Didn't work on him, Garyn. Did you notice it?"

Rowan looked up in confusion.

"You're just full of surprises, aren't you, Rowan?" Maraba slapped at Te-Dasuka's chest, leaking tears onto his shirt. Her laughter had gone delirious.

"It's just his blood," Garyn dismissed him with a wave of her hand. "I like it when I have one I can't bully around, anyway."

"You've used it on off-worlders before," Maraba said, sighing as she wiped her eyes.

"What are you talking about?" Rowan looked from one person to the other. He lost formality to curiosity.

"Garyn's voice has royal authority that manifests without very careful control," Te-Dasuka said. "She refuses to use it on her own people. It's more of a controlling weapon, when it works. It slipped out just then. She plastered us to the wall with it."

"And you just stood all calm and collected!" Maraba said with a cackle.

Rowan gazed back at his Queen. He saw the confirmation in her eyes. She didn't feel disappointed that she could not control him. But he saw no reason why such power wouldn't work on him. He puzzled over the ability for a long moment, until Garyn's voice brought him around.

"Now, to the point of our meeting," Garyn spoke evenly with an exasperated smile of apology to her charge and guests. "First item. Rowan."

"Y…yes, my Queen," Rowan forced his voice down from his salutatory yell.

She sat before him, gesturing the others to do the same. Te-Dasuka pulled the door closed and folded his big frame onto the short stool. Maraba propped her elbows on the table and her face on interlaced fingers. All eyes rested on Rowan.

"Did you mean what you said this evening, beyond the shadow of a doubt?" Garyn asked.

Without hesitation, Rowan answered, "Yes."

"I'm sure you've heard rumors about the

course of your training."

Rowan gulped and nodded.

"Dresden will take you as far as each day of basic skill training can go," Garyn said. "But I asked him for a formal evaluation of your potential for going *beyond* that training."

Rowan's heart pounded in his chest.

"You see," interrupted Maraba with a proud tone, "that's one of Dresden's special abilities. He isn't just sizing you up when he looks at you. He can evaluate your latent talent. It helps him to focus your training after basic."

"Point being," and the Queen stared at Maraba, "Dresden has confirmed my initial, ah, appraisal of your worth among our warriors. And I would like to test that appraisal."

Rowan formed the words carefully. "My Queen, I will excel in whatever task you ask of me."

Garyn Kei beamed at him. "I know. So here is my proposal to you." She lifted the decanter from the tray. As she filled each glass, she continued, "I offer you official training directly under the Queen of Unata, during hours above and beyond those spent with Dresden or on other official duties as they are assigned."

Rowan stared back at her, wide-eyed. "I-I accept, my Queen!" His fist on the table rattled the small glasses, the contents of which threatened to spill.

Garyn set down the decanter and replaced the glass stopper. She sighed, but her mouth stretched into a wide smile. "This is not an easy assignment, and it may well be lifelong. No one, in your Queen's opinion, ever completes training. You would start tomorrow, immediately following dinner."

"I accept your training, my Queen," Rowan

said with more vehemence. His heart lifted and his eyes filled with tears. He took the short glass Garyn Kei offered him. The others took up their glasses as well.

He looked at his glass. The odd, strong odor smelled distantly like the juice he drank, only soured. He cast his gaze up at his Queen and at those assembled.

"And, as a personal trainee of Her Majesty," began the stoic Te-Dasuka as he swirled the dark liquid in his glass, "protecting the Queen of Unata will be your primary task, to the detriment of all others."

Maraba laughed at Rowan, whose earnest nodding she found amusing.

"I accept, I accept!" Rowan cried.

"Then let us drink to a long, fruitful partnership!"

Garyn raised her glass, as did the others, and emptied her cup in one long draught. Maraba and Te-Dasuka did as well, without flinching. Rowan drained his glass. The drink burned like fire all the way down. He felt fumes akin to smoke flowing back up and out his nose. The heat settled like lead in his full stomach and spread quickly to his fingertips. His scalp tingled. He slipped to the floor from his low stool. Had they poisoned him?

With a hoarse voice, he asked, "What is that stuff?"

Maraba delighted in the young man's first drink of the sturdy Unatan brew, laughing heartily and smiling down at him. *So it can't be poison*, Rowan thought. *That's not the face of my killer.* Te-Dasuka offered him a hand up, which Rowan gratefully took. He felt a bit embarrassed.

"It's Parisia's finest, I'd wager," Te-Dasuka answered, with a spark of memory glinting in his eyes at his first drink. "With a long tradition of sealing words to action."

When Rowan stopped coughing, he indignantly said, "I don't think me and this 'Parisia's finest' are going to be good friends."

"Fair enough," said Garyn with a light laugh. "If the only problem you have with Unata is her alcohol, then I find no fault in you."

"Thank you, my Queen," Rowan managed to say. Then his stomach turned. He mustered every ounce of control not to vomit on his Sovereign's floor.

The Queen offered another round, which Rowan flatly refused. She continued around the table with her decanter, laughing and discussing a year-long timetable of Rowan's basic training. Rowan focused on the conversation, realizing that she aimed toward the next Festival of Proving as a demonstration of his skills. He couldn't focus much beyond that because his head grew fuzzy inside. Suddenly, he felt sleepy.

Garyn gently led him to the door, dismissing him so that he could rest for his training tomorrow. As she closed the door, she whispered to the shadows, "Come on out, Collern, and take the boy to his bunk."

"How is it that you always know where I am?" Collern whispered plaintively, emerging from behind a twisted tree and a building some distance away.

"You, my nosy little warrior, breathe almost as loudly as your father," she said with a smile. "Now off with you!"

Rowan did his best to answer Collern's specific questions. Quickly, the older Unatan realized that Rowan fell under the influence of Garyn's strongest toast drink. Collern chuckled, much like his mother, and saved the rest of his questions for tomorrow. Rowan seemed awake enough to slur a greeting to his bunk mates, one of which was Chard, before Collern left him. The warmth of Rowan's one drink of "Parisia's Finest" lulled him to sleep a moment later.

10: FEAR IS BLINDNESS

Rowan awoke to a ringing in his ears and throbbing behind his eyes, symptoms rooted in his first strong drink. He hurried from the bunks to breakfast, giving little consideration for his disheveled hair and sloppy clothes. Curious eyes followed him throughout the dining hall. The cooks gave him their same good-natured greetings, this time laced with some buried humor. The girls smiled and giggled as he passed. Some of the boys whispered but managed their usual hellos.

He wondered if everyone recognized the effects of his slight hangover. The last thing he wanted was to feel like even more of an outcast. *Or do they already know about the Queen's private training?* His heart sank. *What is she going to do to me?* Then Collern interrupted his thoughts with an elbow to the ribs. Rowan cried out in surprise, nearly dumping his tray of food all over his friend.

"Nervous yet?" Collern said, his silly grin splitting his face in two.

"Everyone's *staring* at me. I don't know what all they found out," Rowan whispered.

He glanced around the room. Many eyes snapped away, suddenly interested in their average-looking breakfast or an invisible spot on a clean tunic. A low murmur of conversation arose from the near silence in the huge room.

"You think they wouldn't know?" Collern waved to the assembled group—mostly pledges, trainers and other early risers—and threw his free arm around Rowan's neck.

Several grinning faces rose at Collern's loud question. Rowan felt he would drown in their intense scrutiny. But at least they smiled. Perhaps they expected him to fail. He was, after all, merely a human.

"Well?" Collern cried to the group. He gestured to Rowan, who remained ensnared in the crook of Collern's elbow. "What do you think about Rowan's new assignment, folks?"

The entire dining hall erupted with cheers, whistling and applause, and then the warrior yell of Unata. Rowan stood blinking. His jaw dropped. His ears rang. The nervousness welled in him, unbidden and nauseating. His fellow trainees looked upon him with layers of cheerful envy, worry and challenge. Among the group, Rowan spotted the familiar faces of Trayba, Chard, and even old Kadray. Rowan ducked his head in a brief, thankful bow and smiled at them all.

"And don't worry, friend," Collern said in a loud whisper, mischief in his eyes. "She won't have brought you this far just to carelessly kill you."

The room grew silent with a loud exclamation from outside. Garyn Kei heralded her arrival with the clanging of her katana against her war fans as she stormed into the dining hall. She trudged to the drink station and thrust a mug out to the smiling cook behind the counter, demanding the strong stuff. The cook filled her cup with sourroot tea. He crushed mint and ginger into a paste, stirred the paste into some plain whipped cream, and dumped a dollop into the thick tea. He shook his head as he returned her mug. She paused to stir the concoction, then sipped. Her comical grimace garnered a few hushed snickers before she turned on the assembly of diners.

"You all are *way* too excitable this early in the morning," Garyn griped as she stomped across the room to Kadray, brandishing her mug for emphasis. "Can't sleep through the noise, for crying out loud! Ugh! What a headache! Kadray, I need something for a headache!"

Kadray harrumphed. "Like I'd give medicine to a little brat with a hangover! Some of us have *responsibilities*," he wagged his finger at the queen, "that don't allow us to celebrate into the night whenever we please." Then he pointed at Rowan. "And don't go breaking that boy anymore with this *special training* of yours. His leg still hasn't healed completely, mind you."

She plopped down next to him, mumbling and stirring her tea sullenly. Maraba drifted in a moment later, leaning heavily on Dresden's shoulder. She pressed her free hand against her temple. Spotting Garyn across the room, she pointed and shouted, "This is your fault! Matching drinks with *Te-Dasuka*, of all people!"

Collern sighed and dragged Rowan to a seat. "This isn't going to be pretty."

"Maraba, stop," Garyn whispered, squinting across the room. "You're too loud. She needs one, too, Cook!" Garyn pointed to her mug. The cook nodded.

Collern whispered, "Only Kei Masali could out-drink Te-Dasuka."

"The Queen's *mother*?" Rowan pictured the burly Te-Dasuka collapsing, drink in hand, before a daintier version of Garyn Kei. In Rowan's mind, she cackled in triumph and planted her foot on his back. "Drinking *that* nasty stuff?" Rowan's headache had eased, but the memory of the taste made him cringe. He shook his head.

They bantered about imagined grievances until Te-Dasuka made it to breakfast, looking refreshed and bright-eyed. Then the women playfully turned on him to air their opinions about his tolerance for alcohol. The old man just grinned and shook his head, taking his meal and tolerating their jibing like he'd done a hundred times.

Rowan shook his head again, amazed by the bizarre behavior of the citizens of Unata, treating their royalty like misbehaving children and their war heroes like drunkards. Maybe he didn't know what to expect of such a culture, after all. He felt a twinge of comfort, though. The people—bizarre behavior or not—welcomed him as family.

Chard joined Rowan after breakfast. He attended to him constantly throughout the day's training and meals, excitedly asking questions to which Rowan couldn't fathom an answer. After dinner, he trailed behind a nervous Rowan on his way to Garyn's bunker for his first session.

"Wonder what she'll teach you this time?" Chard asked for the tenth time.

"I don't know," Rowan answered honestly. "Maybe it's just an initial meeting?"

"Maybe," Chard conceded. "But folks say she hasn't taken an apprentice because no one's come along who could survive her type of training."

Rowan winced. He halted and faced the

boy, distracted for a moment by how much taller Chard had grown since Rowan's arrival—at least a few inches. Then he scowled at the kid. *Unless my paranoia's making me imagine things.* Chard's cat-like face stared up at him, the picture of innocence and honesty. Then his mouth widened into a sly grin.

"But that's gotta just be gossip." Chard threw his hands up in defeat. "It can't be that bad, can it?"

Rowan blinked at the boy and then shrugged, working hard to imitate controlled indifference. Chard walked with him in silence after that. Rowan continued his slow pace to the edge of Parisia's main road. He saw the Queen's bunker and turned to say goodbye to Chard. The boy was long gone. Rowan scratched his head. With a sigh, he gathered his courage for a brisk jog across the flat expanse to Garyn's dwelling.

From a few feet out, he noticed that the sliding metal door had been left open a crack. He glanced around the space suspiciously, eyeing the door. Above, the low roof looked seamless, and the buried electrical conduit appeared undamaged. He stopped before the door and raised his hand to knock. A gentle breeze blew past his hand through the opening.

"My Queen?" Rowan pushed aside the sliding door and slipped through, into darkness. "I've come for training."

"Close the door," Garyn said from the far side of the room. "And we'll begin."

He complied with her order but felt uneasy as the darkness pressed all around him. He stood just inside the doorway, at attention as had become habit, and waited. He heard a light shuffling on one side of the room.

"As a human," Garyn said, "you arrive on

Unata at a severe disadvantage. Your hearing, your sense of smell and your sight are inferior. You agree?"

"Yes, my Queen," Rowan admitted. He swallowed hard.

"Your body is weak from disuse, even though you exercised, and even your structure is less dense than ours," she said.

"Yes, my Queen." The air seemed to drain from the room. Rowan felt beads of sweat trace paths down his face.

"On which of these senses do you rely the most?"

"S-sight, Majesty," Rowan stammered, realizing that she had deprived him of that sense.

"So to be blind is to be fearful?" Garyn said, immediately at Rowan's shoulder. He flinched.

He clenched his jaw in fear and tried to focus. "To be blind is to be helpless," Rowan answered finally. "And therefore afraid."

"To master your fear is to master your soul, and to master your soul is to conquer your enemy," Garyn chanted from across the room. "Repeat it."

Rowan repeated the statement.

"And who is your first enemy, Rowan?" Garyn asked.

"I don't know."

"You *do* know. Is it Imelda, the Slavemaster?" Garyn asked. "Is it the Slaver?"

"No," Rowan whispered. He bit his lips together at the flood of memories.

"Who did you curse first when your family died?" Garyn asked.

Rowan gasped, feeling the bite of pain before he could suppress it. "Myself." Rowan strained in the darkness but couldn't hear Garyn anymore. "My first enemy is myself."

"Now, what did you learn?" Garyn said.

"To master my *fear* is to master my soul, and to master my soul is to conquer my *enemy*," Rowan whispered. "But I *am* the enemy."

"The first rule of battle is to know your enemy," Garyn said. "What do you need to do now?"

"Take away my sight," Rowan answered, "so that I can conquer my fear."

Rowan closed his eyes then, though the darkness was absolute.

"Consider your sight taken, Rowan Jun." Garyn was beside him again and he hadn't heard even a rush of wind.

She instructed him to take the beginning position from his basic training, and then continue through each position in sequence, smoothly. He complied but tensed when he heard the distinct ring of metal in the air. Garyn had drawn her war fans against him. He froze in his movement. His heart rate doubled.

"M-my Queen?" Rowan's voice wavered.

"Fear considers consequences for each action, and the result is inaction," Garyn said. "Blades may cut you. You may or may not see or hear them. Fear is blindness."

He continued his movement, hearing the ring of steel through the air and feeling cold metal brush against his hair and face, down his back, across his arms and torso, and across his thighs. Garyn Kei always stopped a hair's width from cutting him in the middle of his action, but he didn't suffer a nick. His heart began to calm and his mind soon cleared. Even nearing exhaustion, he fought his invisible opponent—his own fear—diligently and smoothly, settling into the intoxicating rhythm of his Queen's war dance.

Then she dismissed him, late into the

night. Still in darkness, she tied a wide cloth across his eyes, instructing him to keep it in place always. She shoved him out into the night, completely blind, and told him to find his bunk and that she would expect him again tomorrow.

Rowan spent all day, every day for a month in the blindfold. He groped around for days to find his way, taking unexpected comfort in his slaveship habit of counting each step. He took his meals, completed his daily training, slept and showered—scrubbing his face beneath the fabric while keeping his eyes squeezed shut—in complete darkness. In the beginning, Collern made a big joke about Rowan's predicament. But he whistled in appreciation later when Rowan blindly dodged, blocked and rolled during his hand-to-hand combat training.

Other than the occasional good-natured taunting from Collern or the expressed worry of Chard, Rowan spoke to very few people during that month. At the outset, the Unatans would greet him kindly out of respect, but also to prevent him from running into them. However, by the end of the month, he could walk down the streets and navigate all the angles and back-paths with little effort. He used his ears, counting his steps, and the feel of the ground under his feet, as well as his knowledge of Parisia's layout. He knew the number of steps between landmarks and around the various running tracks used for training. By the month's end, the townspeople—especially the young girls—stood silently in his path to see if he could find his way around them.

During Rowan's trip to dinner on the last night of the month, Collern and Chard debated some point of training. As Collern had taken a higher training course, he insisted that the first order of Sovereignty was to produce an heir.

Chard argued that the first order was simply to survive. Rowan kept silent, though he felt sure of young Chard's answer. One could not do the former without surviving. As he mused this point, he paused in his measured stride.

The soft scent of warm beach lilies and clean leather flowed through his senses, mingled with the slightest scuffing of boots on pebbled pavement. The two boys argued on. Rowan dropped to his knees and inclined his head forward in a formal bow.

"My Queen, to what do we owe the honor of your presence?" Rowan asked quite properly amid the scraping of boots from Chard and Collern, who finally realized who they ignored and tried to bow before her.

Garyn Kei laughed aloud. Rowan sensed that she tossed her head back in the sort of wholehearted humor he had come to know so well. Then he felt a pang in his heart. He missed her face.

"Is it time to remove this mask, Rowan?" Garyn asked.

"My Lady?" Rowan began.

"Well, if you can hear *me* coming, then you've gone about as far as you can with this training in the city," she answered. "I've been busy lately, so I just came to see the spectacle of Rowan Jun walking through town and dodging people who stumble into his path. And appropriately greeting everyone he meets by the firmness of their handshake or the way they move and walk."

It is your scent, Rowan thought as he breathed deeply. He tried to hide his smile. Instead, he said, "I have learned much from this stage of your training, my Queen."

"Well, I've learned as well, Rowan," the

Queen answered. "And I believe I may have underestimated your ability."

"Is that why Maraba and Dresden have often followed me?" Rowan whispered, inclining his head to the shadows of a building where Dresden and Maraba hid at that very moment.

Again, she laughed. "So I'm found out, am I? Come on out, my spies! Your secret's out!"

"And how did you know?" Maraba demanded as she joined the group. "This one didn't tell you, did he?"

"Ow!" Collern yelled as his mother pinched his cheek hard. "I didn't tell him!"

"Actually," Rowan said, "Maraba always carries a small cake-roll in her hip belt, and..."

"You can smell that?" Maraba said with a grin. "It's emergency rations, I swear!"

"And?" Garyn urged him. Rowan thought he heard her cross her arms.

"And I can hear the rhythm of Dresden's breathing for quite a distance." His voice sounded sullen and apologetic.

The small gathering erupted in raucous laughter. Garyn and Maraba gasped for breath, caught in the humor of some private joke. Dresden grumbled in dismay.

"That," gasped Maraba. "That makes three of us." Then she laughed again with the others, nearly collapsing to the ground.

Rowan's face glowed with embarrassment, feeling sure he'd said the wrong thing again. Then a large hand clamped on his shoulder from behind him. He turned to the person, unsure of who the hand belonged to in such noise.

"Good job, kid," said Dresden without malice. "A very good job, indeed."

Rowan suppressed the apology he felt rising. He managed a bow to his trainer and thanked the big man. "Keep it up," Dresden said. "It only gets more difficult from here."

Garyn raised her hands to quiet the crowd. "Now, for your next task, Rowan."

Rowan turned back to the Queen and inclined his shoulders, then stood at attention.

"Most trainees spend a month of their basic survival training in the jungle with an assigned group of fellow trainees," Garyn said. Then she smiled, "But before I will permit *my* personal warrior-in-training to complete such a task, he must do this. I will escort Rowan Jun to an undisclosed location in the jungle. For the course of a month, he will survive on his own. He will hunt for food, find water and shelter, keep track of time, and maintain his physical conditioning. He will return after one month."

"Yes, my Queen!" Rowan answered.

"And oh, Rowan?" Rowan heard the smile in her voice. "I'll take your sight for the duration."

Though his heart leapt into his throat, he managed an affirmative cry. The gathered Unatans cheered along with his yell, drowning out the pounding of his heart. He wondered how she could have such faith in him, and wondered briefly if she kept him merely for her entertainment. Then he remembered her first order to him, to live, and pushed away his scrutiny of her motives. She willed him to learn and grow and survive.

From then on, Rowan's private training by Garyn Kei, Queen of Unata became a national point of public interest and a competition with himself that he had not been permitted to lose.

* * *

Garyn made a grand spectacle in the city of

having Rowan sit on a stool in the celebration circle. She pulled his blindfold up. "Stare straight upward. I said I would take your sight in the jungle, but not with this dirty cloth. It's quite gross. How in the world did you take my order so literally? But anyway... Kadray insisted that the blindfold would impede you there, so he offered something a little more practical."

The light of morning blinded Rowan for a moment. Still, Garyn hadn't given him permission to look upon her face, or any face for that matter. He took all orders literally, he realized. Her bare hand appeared in his vision, holding two small vials and a dropper. The crowd grew quiet.

"This will cleanse and prepare the eyes," she said, dripping a clear liquid into each eye. "And this one," she showed him the second vial of black liquid, "will create an air-permeable black lens that will take your sight. A liquid blindfold, if you will. Normally used by warriors to shield light from a damaged eye while it heals. Healthy for your cornea, but won't come off. I have the solution to dissolve it once you return to us."

The clear liquid felt cold and soothing in stinging eyes that hadn't seen daylight in a month. The black liquid felt slick and warm. Rowan felt mildly surprised that this medicine, like so many things Kadray provided, didn't hurt. He kept his own counsel on the matter, for he had grown to like the old man.

The inky liquid blotted out the morning sunlight one drop at a time, casting Rowan into a darkness that had become quite comfortable in recent weeks. He blinked as instructed, smoothing blackness evenly over his cornea, feeling the excess spill down his cheeks. Then the substance tightened for a moment as it bonded to his eye. Soon, he couldn't feel the membrane at all. He sat there, completely blind.

He choked down some rising panic. Before, he could have simply removed the blindfold. Now, blindness seemed absolute. He worked his jaw and focused on calming his breathing. Garyn bade him rise to his feet. The crowd cheered. Then she led him away, toward her next great challenge.

Rowan stood somewhere in the Upper Jungle with his small medpack, a boot knife, and two days' worth of traveltack rations. He'd counted steps to this point, knowing his path to be far removed from his route to the crash site. Garyn released his arm and walked away.

"My Queen?" Rowan said, his voice rising in panic.

"You know what, Rowan Jun?" Rowan felt the heat from her body as she peered up at his face. Her voice came out uncharacteristically soft. "I miss your dark eyes, my warrior-in-training. I want to be the first to see them when you return."

"Y-Yes, my Queen," he whispered.

Rowan's pounding heart drowned out the sound of Garyn's departure. The warmth of her closeness dissipated. Only the saturated heat of the jungle remained. *Why would she say something like that?* Rowan's face burned again at the thought of the Queen's words. He forced back the feelings that arose in him.

"*Everyone* loves the Queen," he whispered, remembering his conversation with Collern.

Rowan drew a deep breath, calming his heart. More pressing matters threatened him. *This is a different kind of blindness*, he thought. *No familiar roads except what I remember from maps. Maps aren't much good if you don't know where you are.* He groped for the nearest tree, aware that many predators of the Upper Jungle rivaled the Chimeras in size. In particular, he feared the Felzars. *No girls giggling and standing in my way. Only monsters.* He needed to sleep higher than they would bother climbing. Rowan leaned against a tree and reached for his rations-pack. He drew his knife and marked the tree. From there, he could make it back to Parisia without fail.

His pack contained no flint for fire and only enough rations for him to eat well for a couple days, or sparingly for up to a week. He also needed a source of fresh water, as he only owned one large bottle of water. Other than his boot knife, he felt defenseless.

Rowan wandered in a calculated pattern, counting his steps and creating a map in his mind. He listened for the telltale sign of running water, sure that several natural springs dotted the jungle. Eventually, as the warm sun dipped to the horizon and nocturnal animals replaced the daytime animals, he heard the rush of a stream. Following the sound, Rowan counted his steps and the trees, searching each trunk for an identifiable mark and struggling to forge a mental map of wherever the Queen had aban-doned him.

He became so absorbed in the sound of the water and mapping the trees that he dismissed the putrid stench that crept up around him. Some animal died here. He wondered what scavengers the Upper Jungle boasted. He imagined the rotting Felzar carcass Collern found. He saw the huge claws in his mind. Just a cub, he remembered. He heard the brush sway around him, just a slight noise in the breezeless air.

Five black-furred monsters slinked in the shadows, wondering that the strange smelling person didn't see or hear them, didn't turn to kill them. One of the predators made a snarling noise deep in her throat, much like a snort of laughter.

Rowan froze, the hairs rising on the back of his neck. Then he knew the smell of rot to be living Felzars, not just the dead. He heard their muted, calm breathing, felt their heat in the cooling jungle air. He sifted through what he had studied about the creatures. With just a knife, he could not be worse equipped to fight them. If he climbed, they would easily follow and devour him. He pictured the three huge claws on each huge paw. *But because of their peculiar shoulder and hip joints built for climbing, Felzars are slow to start running*, he remembered. *If I run, and could see where I'm going, I'd get a good head start. I'll stand a chance.* His trembling hand reached for his face. He touched skin, not blindfold. Realization dawned on him. His heart pounded in terror.

Fear considers consequences for each action, and the result is inaction.

Garyn's words cut into him. Rowan could not face the consequence of failure by removing this permanent blindfold, no matter how afraid. *This must be why Garyn blinded me with the liquid*, he thought. Clenching his fists and throwing his hands out before him, Rowan took off at a dead run through the vegetation. He vaulted forward off trees he ran into, stumbled across roots and low shrubbery, and barreled ahead with the recklessness born of desperation.

Before long, his pursuers began to catch up. Their slow, ambling gait hit three beats on the forest floor with each long stride. Rowan had a good lead on them. The sound of water became a roar that echoed too loudly in the night. Rowan tripped over a rock and flew headlong into a natural net of vines and young trees. He cried out in alarm. He kicked out with his feet, trying to find purchase in the dirt. His boots brushed off rocks that bounced down an almost vertical incline, a path also followed by a narrow waterfall. His bare arms stretched into nothingness. The vines held tight but swayed over a vast empty space.

Rowan's memory held one stark image of a natural tangle of vines between saplings. On their way to the QuellTruth, Collern pointed it out as a landmark of the Child's Path down into the Lower Jungle. The small relief he felt at knowing exactly where he landed soon paled as he heard the thudding of the Felzars' approach. Rowan heard their snarling and smelled their stinking breath. They paced at the cliff edge, waiting on him to climb down from the suspended vines, to come within reach.

Rowan gulped down his fear and reached for his boot knife. He couldn't go back to the Felzars, to his death. He couldn't climb down, either. *Fear considers consequences for each action, so I'll worry about how stupid this is later.* He grasped a thick vine overhead and began sawing at it with the sharp blade. His net shifted.

He hacked at the next vine and the next, until the whole structure gave way beneath him. He tugged the last vine loose, sheathing his knife at the same time. Then he fell, clinging to his lifeline. As the vines untangled above him, his fall slowed and stopped. He strained to reach the cliff. His vine vibrated as the snarling Felzars dug at the roots. He breathed heavily. He had no way of knowing how much farther he could fall. *Fear considers consequences. Crazy Unatans,* he thought. Then he released the vine, falling into familiar, more dangerous territory.

Rowan bounced off higher branches in the canopy of the Lower Jungle, glanced off small saplings in the understory and landed at last on the rotting vegetation on the jungle floor. The fall knocked the wind out of him. As soon as he could heave in air, Rowan took stock of his minor injuries. He'd only fallen halfway down the cliff. The trees and plants he grabbed had slowed his plummet. To his good fortune, he had only suffered scrapes and bruises.

He felt around for his knife and medpack. He still had his rations, as well. He opened that bag, pulled out a crumbling block of traveltack and crammed it in his cheek. Even the prickly expansion of traveltack in his empty stomach didn't comfort him. He reached for his water bottle. His heart skipped. The metal container—wrapped in thick leather—had been damaged in his fall. All his precious water leaked out onto the forest floor. He sighed heavily, then stood.

At the top of the cliff, the Felzars still snarled and simpered, having lost their quarry to the Chimera's territory. Collern had been right. Most Felzars were smart enough to stay out of the Lower Jungle. Rowan decided that they'd leave by sunrise, and perhaps he'd head up the cliff then. But the draw of familiarity—particularly the path to his family's grave—made him wish to expand the map in his head. He had a starting point, at least. Even the Chimeras didn't concern him much. He was, after all, Unatan—human blood or not. Maybe Garyn had extended her truce to include him.

The trees to his left shook and rattled. Branches creaked under some heavy weight. *Maybe she hasn't talked to them yet*, Rowan thought, the fear again raising the hair on his neck. But Rowan had a hunch they weren't just bloodthirsty and violent like the Felzars. Though he stood and waited—easy prey—the Chimeras never came closer. Counting his steps, Rowan made his way to a nearby spring and drank the cold water. He washed his shallow cuts and bandaged his arms and legs. The Chimeras, at least one larger Chimera, followed him. And soon, as the dark night dragged on, Rowan began to speak to his stalker.

"This would be a lot easier if you talked back," he said. "Unless you're my Queen again, scaring me in the right direction." Silence answered him. He chuckled, letting his fear drain from him.

"I think I'll stick around for a while in the Lower Jungle," Rowan whispered as he climbed a thick trunk in search of a sleeping branch. He carved in shallow depressions for hand and footholds as he went. "At least I feel like I can *reason* with you guys. Unlike those Felzars. Unless you get really hungry. But I must warn you. As much as I train, I'd probably be all stringy. Not tender at all."

Rowan yawned and settled into the crook of a high branch, firmly binding an ankle and a wrist to the branch with some twine he found in his pack. That way, at least he'd wake up before he fell completely. As he nodded off, visions of sapling spears bound to retrieval twine and clay bowls hardened in fire ran through his mind. *But how can I get fire without flint?* Then he'd have to figure out his extra training and mapping and even bathing. At the thought of bathing in cold water, he shivered, feeling the cold of the evening for the first time as he settled down. And some sort of sleeping blanket when he got around to it. He sighed, puzzling over his long to-do list until he finally drifted off to sleep.

Rowan managed a fire the next day by repeatedly and quickly twisting a stick into the cavity on a wider piece of wood. He nursed the fire with fallen wood and small tinder, keeping it going for days. The hunt for wood kept his mind and body busy, gave him purpose, and ensured that he could cook the small game he snared and speared. He had eaten a few reptiles and some small mammals, and an unfortunate bird-like creature that broke its wing in some accident.

At some point, near the freshwater spring, he came across some tall, fine grass that he wove into a rough sleep cover after much frustration and countless hours figuring out the weave pattern he'd seen in a diagram somewhere. Having no sight had advantages in his environment. Rowan had no need for daylight for any task. He could work during the cooler night to keep his body temperature up, and sleep during the heat of day. The nocturnal pattern seemed suited for his companion as well. The creature, whom he fancied a Chimera, came and went at will, making no sound save for that underfoot or in the branches of nearby trees. Sure that it wouldn't kill him, and sure after a while that the Queen had better things to do than attend him for a month, Rowan wiled away the hours chatting with the creature. Or rather, at it, since it never replied.

After a couple weeks wandering through the Lower Jungle, and returning each night to his sleeping tree, Rowan faced the cliff again. Across his back hung a thin spear bound with a piece of looped twine and a thicker sapling honed to a sharp point. He smiled, thinking that Garyn would complain about the loss of her future generations of trees again. He had packed an ugly homemade clay bowl full of the glowing embers from his campfire, then set that inside his modified leather bottle holster. The heat against his hip comforted him, and hopefully kept him from the grueling task of starting a new fire. He groped for the first handholds of the Child's Path and began his slow ascent back up into the Upper Jungle, bidding his constant Chimera attendant goodbye.

Two more weeks passed, each day bringing Rowan closer to some amazing revelation that always eluded him unless he found himself on the brink of great peril. But since he continued to survive, the promise of enlightenment slipped away. Ever since his fall to the Lower Jungle, he had the distinct impression that he had been followed. He also hadn't smelled the fetid stink of the Felzars' breath in days. A familiar musky scent lingered at a distance all around him. On occasion, he heard swift feet darting to and fro between the trees. He knew something hunted him—at least *watched* him. He considered it odd that the Chimera—for what other creature could it be—had ventured into the Upper Jungle at all. He picked up his conversation with the creature where he left off, though, since he talked to ease his loneliness.

Going in blind, Rowan estimated that he had researched and mentally mapped a third of the Lower Jungle and two-thirds of the entire Upper Jungle. He spent most of his time carefully memorizing each crag, cliff, tree arrangement, rock and cave so that he had generated a touch-sensitive map of the entire region of the jungle.

Unata's primary star, Paz, floated high in the sky on his last day in the wilderness. Rowan mournfully doused his campfire with the last water from his crude clay cup. *Today I return to Parisia, to my friends and to my Queen.* He turned the clay cup over and over in his hands, ready to pitch it into the ashes at his feet. He thought better of his work and tucked it into the leather holster at his side. He rolled his woven grass blanket and slung it from his bag. Then Rowan turned toward Parisia and started walking. His steps moved steady and sure. He didn't thrust his hands out before him or trip over rocks and roots. The path unfolded before him as the clearest beacon in his mental map—one that led him home at last.

Rowan paused outside the gate of Parisia, a strange and strong anxiety tugging him back toward the darkness of the jungle. He forced his feet forward and stepped through the gate, across to Parisia's main street where he heard many people milling about. When the scent of beach lilies and leather flowed before him in front of the Throne bunker, he knelt and bowed low to the earth.

"Welcome home, my warrior-in-training," Garyn whispered above him. "We've been waiting for you!"

The crowd erupted into the Unatan battle cry. Rowan lifted his head. Garyn placed her hands on his cheeks and slid her fingers up over his eyes. She steadied her hand over his face, and flushed his eyes with a smelly, thick liquid. As the Queen wiped his face with a soft cloth, the light overhead blinded him for a long moment. He squinted, then forced his eyes upward. Rowan laid eyes on Garyn Kei's smiling face first, after two months without his sight. All the anxiety drained out of him. All the relief of the world flooded into his body. The sky, the earth, and the beaming faces of the Unatans all looked beautiful to Rowan. And for the love of civilization and order, they fed him!

* * *

During his anti-climactic basic survival training with the other recruits in the jungle two months later, Rowan recounted many of the horrors he encountered on his own while he was blind in the forest. Chard and Collern listened intently, nodding on occasion and urging more from him as the boring nights wore on. He showed them how to make a string spear and hunt small game by sound alone. He didn't have the heart to tell them his blind adventure had been mostly luck and a great deal of deliberate, careful decisions.

Rowan turned the ugly clay cup over and over in his hands, watching the firelight dance across its uneven surface. The object had seemed beautiful to him when he needed it. But now it served a strong reminder about appearances. Rowan glanced at his new friends—most of them assigned as team members in his new break-group—and smiled.

Rowan's break-group—basically a support team for each battalion of soldiers—consisted of Chard, a rare set of twins by the names of Garlen and Deruk, and a tall, wiry girl called Beryl, who wielded a spear better than any boy in her age group. Collern volunteered as the ranked soldier in attendance, possibly as an excuse to get out of work.

"Dresden's got you on weapons and battle formation lately, I noticed. What's up with your special training?" Collern asked. "Haven't seen much of you lately."

Rowan shook his head. "This feels like a break, honestly." He smiled at his friend. "She's got me on internal cellular control. Was it painful for you guys?"

"Ugh. It hurts a little, but we all stop when we reach Dresden's individual potential limit." Collern wrinkled his nose. "All Dresden says is *you* haven't reached your limit yet. *That* can get messy, too. Mother says Garyn'll probably poison you and see if you can purge the poison before it kills you!"

Rowan blinked at Collern. His jaw dropped.

"Uh, of course that's just, ummm, hearsay." Collern feigned a cough to cover his laughter.

"Didn't you say she's doing paths of energy, too?" Chard asked, trying to save the light tone of their conversation.

Rowan winced. "I haven't wrapped my head around it, yet. Dresden says I have the same gateways Unatans have, but there are more keys for each gateway for me, whatever that means. So far, I've only electrocuted myself once or twice."

"Ouch!" Collern said. "But it's pretty advanced stuff. Makes me glad that it's optional training for the rest of us."

"Can you do it?" Rowan asked.

Collern laughed. "A little. No one but the Queen has mastered it. Something about the Royal blood. Te-Dasuka came close." He grinned. "But that's Gauntlet-level training. I'm jealous."

Garlen spoke up for the first time. "You told us he wasn't supposed to *know* that yet!"

Collern gave the boy a death glare. "Rowan isn't *supposed* to know that yet. But I doubt he's stupid."

"Oh, come on, Collern! If Dresden handles basic training, what *else* could Royal training mean?" Garlen said as apology. Then he smiled at Rowan. "How long have you known?"

Rowan stared at the fire, forcing down his excitement. "For about a month, when I started studying in the record vault. Dresden sent me there, saying I'd only have a couple months of history before the training got harder. I started with the oldest stuff and worked my way forward." He looked down at the clay cup. "Seems like she's going down a training list from her grandmother's time." He shrugged. "I just figured she's seeing how far I can go."

"Well, either she's *seeing* something, or she really is trying to kill you!" Collern harrumphed. "I'd be jealous if..."

"If you weren't so lazy, Caw-leen?" Chard asked.

Rowan smiled as Chard danced out of Collern's half-hearted grasp. The boy bounded out of Collern's reach, halfway up a tall tree. The others laughed as Chard taunted Collern. Rowan looked back at the flames, then at the cup in his hands.

"It's not like she's reinstating the Gauntlet anytime soon," Rowan whispered.

Rowan had rushed through the records, trying frantically to find out why the Gauntlet had only one remaining member. He knew the answer to his dream laid somewhere in those dusty records. The black-eyed human looked beyond future battle, into heroism and greatness far in the past within the warrior world he inhabited. He investigated toward his future, seeking reason and some final atonement for sins beyond his control. He sought to become one of the Gauntlet.

11: CORESTONE

Chard ran silently to the edge of the jungle, emerging onto the Parisian plateau with a triumphant yell. He waved a tangled mass of black fur overhead like a battle flag. Rowan walked behind him, shaking his head, followed by Garlen, Deruk and Beryl. All recruits were armed to kill and dressed in the tight black clothing assigned to stealth missions.

"Well," Garlen said, his pale eyes sparkling with mischief, "Dresden didn't specify how *large* the lock had to be." The twin raked his fingers through his long, sweaty white hair, grimacing at the feeling of grit.

"You all but shaved the poor thing," Rowan said with a sigh, his past fear of the creatures fading into pity.

Chard rejoiced, fur in both his hands and overflowing the wide leather pouch on his hip. The cat-boy smiled. He shrugged at Rowan and raced ahead to where the trainer awaited them. The tip of the boy's tail twitched back and forth in excitement.

Young Beryl yelled at Chard, "If it freezes to death, I won't forgive you!"

Chard turned to her and cried, "It's the

warm season! He'd probably thank me!"

"Felzar-stink sticks with you, too," Deruk said. He sniffed at his sweat-stained shirt and frowned.

Deruk stripped off the garment and threw it in Garlen's face. Garlen responded by tackling his brother to the ground and smearing his face in his armpit. They rolled in the grit and sand, plastering tan dust to their sweaty clothes and into their already dirty hair. Rowan stared silently until they regrouped, mumbled their apologies so that Dresden wouldn't hear, and joined Rowan at Dresden's side.

Dresden clicked the stopwatch. "And still ten minutes to spare. If you keep the wrestling at a minimum, you could shave time off that as well. Keep in mind this is a *team* exercise." He glared at the teenage twins. "But how did you do with the assignment?"

Chard set the fur on the ground for Dresden's inspection. The trainer cleared his throat, perhaps to keep from laughing at the absurd amount of fur. He nodded and sighed.

"Weapons?" Dresden asked. The team displayed their weapons—Rowan's sword, Beryl her spear, Garlen his bow and all his arrows, Chard his knife, and Deruk his daggers—and Dresden grunted. "Not a drop of blood spilled. And they didn't follow you?"

Rowan looked over at Chard. "They're all still sleeping like babies."

"Well, your break-group is doing well," Dresden said. "Garyn'll be glad you didn't have to kill any of her 'precious, stupid Felzars' today."

"We owe our progress to excellent training," Rowan answered, eyes forward, at attention. "And some natural talent at stealth." He nodded to Chard. "But we still need to fine-tune our group mindset." Garlen and Deruk dropped their heads.

Dresden gave a gruff laugh. "Still, it's hard to believe we grouped you just half a year ago. Pretty impressive teamwork in such a short time, especially in stealth."

Rowan agreed. Through months of practice, Rowan's group learned to use Unata's non-verbal communication system of hand signals. And with Chard's impressive skills, the Felzar wouldn't know it had been clipped until it caught a draft. Though playful, the twins proved loyal, serious when need be, and quite talented in their fields. Beryl had a wit as sharp and deadly as her spear. Rowan felt a swell of pride. He led a well-rounded break-group.

Dresden turned. "Let's get to the dining hall. The cooks kept our breakfast warm so far."

Chard gathered up his Felzar fur as the twins groaned. Beryl pinched her nose shut.

Deruk cried, "That's not going anywhere near my bunk, kitty!"

Chard made a face that bared his small fangs. Beryl sighed and swept past the three boys, catching up to Rowan. As Rowan followed Dresden toward the dining hall, he noticed an unusual amount of activity in the city. Armaments flowed through the streets, pulled by burly couriers and directed by Te-Dasuka's men. Forge attendants performed minor adjustments to armor outside. Maraba shouted orders all over the city center. The noise suggested a pending attack.

"What's going on?" Rowan asked, wide eyed at the frenetic pace of the laid-back Parisians.

"Just getting ready for a show," Dresden said. "The Communications Tower is tracking an unidentified spacecraft in our vicinity. They'll send out a notice when they get the ship's numbers. We're thinking it may just be our planned trade vessel making an early arrival. But you know our Queen."

Rowan gaped at the activity. "There's no excuse for living life unprepared."

"Exactly," Dresden said with a wink.

The vacant dining hall greeted the group. The on-duty cooks left a short note with their food on the warming trays, indicating the cooks had been called away for obvious reasons. Dresden and the break-group sat down with their meals, feeling the hollowness of the huge room. They stuffed their faces quickly, expecting to be called away at any moment.

Though Rowan's stomach fluttered in excitement, he felt a creeping nervousness. The Comm-Tower's alarm claxon sounded during the middle of breakfast. The pattern of sound reported an unsanctioned merchant ship outside its approved quadrant. Rowan jumped to his feet. Their trajectory indicated that the off-worlders would arrive in the atmosphere and head toward the main plateau.

"Stay calm, recruits," Dresden said in his quiet, measured voice. "That tick at the end of the alarm is a timer. We still have an hour and a half before they arrive. And you're not going to sneak up on *anyone* smelling like a Felzar."

Rowan looked down at his grimy skin and agreed. Dresden ordered them to the showers and to their break-group formations in front of the barracks in an hour. Rowan led his group to the empty barracks. Beryl broke off to the girl's dormitory and the boys headed right.

The boys stripped and stuffed their reeking clothes down the laundry shaft. They cranked on the hot water spigots and scrubbed away the filth of their morning assignment. Garlen and Deruk promptly started a soap fight and complained when the shampoo burned into their eyes, and when they slipped on the slick tile. Rowan wished he could be as carefree as the boys. They weren't more than a couple years younger than him, after all. Rowan breathed deeply beneath the rush of hot water, trying to calm his pounding heart.

"Don't worry," Chard said in his scratchy voice. "It's nothing we can't handle."

"How do you *do* that?" Rowan said, raking his fingers through his sopping hair.

"I could say it was my father's blood," Chard grinned, "but it doesn't take an Empath to figure out you're worried." He soaped up his long tail, digging his nails into the dense fur and frowning at the grit that foamed out.

"Hmph." Rowan resoaped his hair, noticing the stink of decay still lingered in his scalp. "Is that what your father's called? An Empath?"

Chard nodded, still focusing on cleaning his tail. "Garyn says the Empaths' planet was overtaken by some really nasty ruler. He killed most of the Empaths, and the survivors escaped into space. Some became psychic advisors. But *my* father was a pirate!"

He grinned, watching Rowan's confused expression. He finally rinsed his tail. "Anyway, he fell for my mother and here I am. His blood is why I've grown so fast. Empaths grow up fast and stabilize at maturity to keep up with the weird way our brains work. I have strong senses and balance like my father. And I'm sturdy like a Unatan. Garyn says I'm all Empath *and* all Unatan." He smiled.

A loud knocking jarred the shower room door. "Half hour mark, boys!" Beryl called in. "I can hear you chattering in there!"

Rowan stood under the spigot to rinse the

remaining soap from his hair. He turned off the knob and reached for a towel. Then he called out to Beryl that they were headed that way. Garlen and Deruk rushed past him waving their towels, bent on traumatizing the poor girl. Beryl was quicker, turning away and knocking their feet from beneath them with the end of her spear.

"Grow up, guys!" she said. "This is no way to get rid of your nervousness! Gosh! Why bother with towels if you don't use them?" Fully dressed for break-group duty, Beryl swept out of the room. "I'll be waiting out front for Dresden, *and* the rest of you."

Garlen and Deruk broke into fits of laughter. "I think we've found our wife," Garlen said, letting out a yell as Deruk jabbed him in the ribs.

"I don't think it works that way," Chard said with a frown. He scrubbed his wet hair with the towel and headed to his bunk.

"Move it, boys," Rowan said. "Fight later about who marries her. Get ready now!" He threw a discarded towel to Garlen. "You think *Dresden's* tough when we show up late. Remember the last time we made Beryl late for role call?"

The twins cringed. Chard shivered. Rowan clenched his jaw and toweled off. He reached for the thin-armored body suit hanging in his closet. He hadn't touched the undersuit in months, preferring to train without it. As he hauled up the skintight suit, Rowan realized his mistake.

Garlen and Deruk snickered, already fully dressed and buckling their belts. Chard pursed his lips in thought as he pulled on a boot. Try as he might, Rowan could not pull the zippered neck of the suit over his broad shoulders, let alone fit his arms in the narrow tubes that once hung loose on his wrists. The fine cloth just would not stretch far enough to accommodate his new muscles. Rowan peeled off the suit and kicked it to the side, feeling a stab of worry.

"Well, huh," he said. He threw on a fresh trainee tunic and pants over his underwear and put on his boots. "I guess I don't need armor, after all."

When the rest of Rowan's break-group finally scrambled out the door, arranging themselves around Beryl by rank, Dresden inspected Rowan. His sharp blue eyes flashed. When he met Rowan's eyes and asked about his undersuit, Rowan answered honestly that it didn't fit, and he didn't have time to find a replacement. Dresden furrowed his brow and turned away.

"Then I guess you'll just have to avoid getting hit," Dresden said, a shade of humor coloring his voice. "I guess you don't *need* armor."

Rowan took a quick look at Dresden's back. True to form, the trainer opted out of armor, even the sturdy undersuit Rowan had shirked. Since every fully-grown adult got measured for full armor, Rowan knew Dresden owned a set. He probably wanted to support his recruits, who didn't yet have full armor. *I guess I really don't need armor either.* Rowan stole a glance at his bare arms and belted dark pants. Adrenaline pumped through Rowan's body, amplifying every nerve's response. *I just have to get good enough to survive without it!*

Collern, in full armor, delivered an urgent message to Dresden from the Queen's scouts. With a stern, grave nod to Rowan, Collern headed off to the Throne Room. Rowan stood at attention, calmed by seeing his friend. Then he inspected his longsword, turning it again in the light, testing the sharp edge, before settling it in the sheath. He gave his heavy pack of support supplies a cursory inspection, and awaited Dresden's orders.

"You have learned that Unata's first greeting to an off-worlder is the presentation of steel," Dresden bellowed, eyeing each recruit in turn. "And the first order of a warrior pledge is to support the regular army with supplies, first aid, and the tactical spread of information. Under no circumstances are you to engage the enemy unless specifically provoked. Do you understand?"

"Yes, Sir!" shouted the group in unison.

"Any questions before you get underway in your groups?"

"Sir!" one young recruit spoke up. "Is it definite that the off-worlders are enemies?"

"I call upon Rowan to give you the textbook answer," Dresden replied.

Rowan's stomach fluttered. He said, "Sir! Unata treats each arrival with both courtesy and suspicion, because there is no excuse for living life unprepared!"

"And so, our Queen and her personal guard will meet them in full battle regalia," Dresden said with a fierce smile, "as will most of the city."

"Sir!" Chard peered across the city, focused on a scene only his sharp eyes could detect. "Soldiers form ranks around the off-worlders' vessel, and the Queen waits for their disembarking."

"All right, recruits!" Dresden bellowed. "Stay in your break-groups and flank your assigned divisions. Remember! You cannot do your job if you die out there! Now move out!"

The recruits split off in silent groups of four or five and headed to the perimeter of the city, gathering at the rear of each assigned division of soldiers. Rowan led his group toward division seventeen. He had learned that only ignorance or emergency led off-worlders to blindly land within the city walls. Unless, of course, they were enemies.

Rowan adjusted his pack, keeping a hand on the grip of his sword out of habit. Arriving at the rear of their assigned squadron, Rowan's break-group spread out in formation. Chard took a step up on a ledge to watch the events unfold before him. Apparently, the off-worlders had a navigation malfunction that took them off course. By the time they corrected the problem, they were within Unatan space and couldn't resist trading for some of the famous Unatan arms.

Rowan's gut filled with lead. Though his hearing could never be as strong as Chard's, Rowan heard most of the conversation. The strange words swirled in his mind. He didn't know the language, but he didn't like the tone of two or three of the traders. At least one of them sounded nervous. He gave his group the sign to stand ready, regardless.

Rowan caught Chard's eyes, giving the signal for enemy. Chard asked Rowan if the off-worlders weren't just nervous because of all the weapons trained on them. Rowan considered that. However, the overpowering sense of wrongness would not subside. If one trader sounded nervous, then their leader sounded full of false bravado. He listened again, keeping his focus on the pitch and timbre of the man's voice. *He's hiding something.*

All through the initial meeting, even as the full battalions followed the men and the Queen's Unit to the Throne bunker, Rowan's insides churned. He didn't like the feelings of suspicion and unrest triggered by the new arrivals. When the small group emerged from the Throne bunker sometime later, Rowan got his first unobstructed view of the man calling himself ship's captain.

Rowan couldn't tell if the man was Unatan or human, though he had the same basic shape. He called himself Nitch, according to fast-moving words from the front of the battalion. Nitch appeared to be sick, even to Rowan's weak human eyes and at a distance. His graying dark hair hung in greasy strings to his shoulders. The skin of his pale face sank into the bones beneath, shadowed further by gray and blue tones. He'd some scraggly facial hair that hung halfway to his chest and a gaudy assortment of flowing clothes that only accentuated the emaciated shape of his limbs and torso. Worse still was the cacophony of his too-loud voice. Rowan glared at the man, sure that his telling words fell on sharper ears than his.

At the thought of Garyn, Rowan sought her in the assembly and found her at the head of the group, a full line of warriors between her and the visitors. Rowan relaxed. *At least she is safe.* He gazed intently at her armored back and the distinctive outline of her Royal helmet. He spotted Collern as well, and worked his way to the edge of his contingent to get a closer look as the traders passed toward the dining hall. He heard Nitch chattering on in a broken version of the Unatan language, in that same nasal voice that grated on Rowan's nerves.

Break-groups ate in shifts, each one reporting the events at the head and guest tables as they rejoined their battalion. During Rowan's shift, he kept an eye on Garyn Kei. The Queen's voice seemed too light, almost playful. She laughed on occasion in a hearty way that knocked Rowan off guard. She laughed that way in private with other Unatans. He thought she would be more formal among strangers. She always had such a matter-of-fact manner that her behavior confused him. Dresden came to Rowan's table to check on his groups and chuckled at Rowan's obvious bewilderment.

"I forgot that you slept through our last trade ship. But staring at her won't make her act normal again, kid," Dresden said in a low whisper.

Rowan glanced at Dresden. "I didn't realize I was staring. Does she always act like this with visitors?"

"Only with the ones she doesn't trust," Dresden answered. "Throws them off guard."

"But I thought she doesn't trust *any* off-worlders," Rowan said.

"So far," and Dresden nudged Rowan in the back with his elbow, "just you."

Rowan mulled over that statement for the remainder of his meal, staring at the food in his plate. Word had it that the off-worlders planned to make an offer for Unatan close-combat weaponry—the best in rumor and in truth. The group would also depart after they completed the transaction. *Good*, thought Rowan. *The sooner they leave, the sooner I get back to training*. The sooner he could train, the faster everything and everyone would get back to normal. He had found a certain level of solace in his training routine. *Although this is why we train.*

Feeling the discomfort of being watched, he looked up, directly into the eyes of the Queen's dinner guest Nitch. He paused in his nasally dissonant voice long enough to affix his gaze on Rowan, who stared back, unblinking and unapologetic. Maybe he stared because Rowan appeared so obviously dissimilar to the Unatans.

Rowan felt a chill creeping up his spine. The young warrior sensed an air of challenge in the stare of Nitch. *What is that man thinking?* Rowan tilted his head slightly, curious that his feeling of unease increased. *He can't think I'm some kind of threat to his deal, can he?* Rowan shook his head imperceptibly, trying to figure out Nitch. *Then what else could he want?* Rowan narrowed his eyes at the man.

"Oh, Mister Nitch," Garyn interjected into the man's unexpected silence, "I see you've noticed our human citizen. It's amazing how these things happen. Shall I tell you?"

Nitch dragged his eyes from Rowan finally, forced by good manners to listen to a story that Rowan quickly recognized as a total fabrication. Garyn gave him a quick apologetic glance for the untruths and turned her full attention to her guest. Rowan tuned out that conversation, not much preferring the horrors of the true story either.

His group departed and Dresden ordered them to rest, that the off-worlders would depart within the hour and break-groups would be unnecessary. Try as he might, Rowan could not relax in the warmth of his cot. After an hour of tossing and turning, he heard a scuffling above him. Chard's head poked over the side of the mattress, backlit by the moonlight from outside the narrow windows.

"Can't sleep?" Chard asked. Without waiting for a reply, he said, "Me neither. Something's funny. They should be gone by now, but nothing!"

Just then, a group of returning trainees crept through the main hallway on their way to the bunks. Every trainee who had been ordered to rest skidded into the hallway at almost the same time for an update of the news.

"Well," Garo, a tall, heavily muscled young man with a soft voice, scratched his head, "when they tried to leave, their ship wouldn't work. Just stalled or something. Even though their team worked on it all day. Still needed repairs. Said if they worked on it through the night, they could leave by morning."

"Our Queen doesn't strike me as the type to welcome sleepovers," Rowan said.

"Is that ever an understatement!" another boy agreed.

"I don't really see a problem," Garo said. He ticked off the points on his fingers. "They're staying on the ship, not in Unatan buildings. They have the order they requested, and they've made good on their payment. New laser equipment for the anti-spacecraft devices!"

"Do you know Garyn at all, Garo?" Chard asked. "The problem is they've imposed themselves. Smells funny." He wrinkled his nose for emphasis. "I don't like it."

"We've been ordered to stand down and return to our quarters," Garo said with a shrug. "If they needed us to guard or fight, they'd've told us."

"Unless they're just protecting us," Rowan whispered. "Something's up, whether the Queen knows or not." Then he turned to the small group around him, his dark eyes flashing in the dim lighting. "Team?"

"Aye!" answered his break-group. "We're with you," added Chard.

"We're going to check it out," Rowan said, reaching for his equipment bag and grabbing the stealth darks from his clothing bin. His stomach fluttered and churned in mischievous excitement. "We'll report back before anyone sees us."

"Back from where?"

Dresden stood in the doorway, arms crossed with a harsh, strained scowl on his face. The large group of trainees shrank back as one, leaving Rowan's group standing alone. Rowan's heart leapt into his throat. The lanky girl Beryl stepped forward. She pushed her small chest out in pride.

"The off-worlders are planning something, and we're going to find out what it is!"

"Shouldn't you have some sort of strategy before you charge into battle, swords flashing?" Dresden asked in a tone of voice that was far too accommodating.

Caught off guard, Rowan rushed to speak. "I can't shake the gut feeling that something's wrong. That man Nitch is trouble!"

"And isn't it too convenient that their ship just happened to break down *here*, of all places!" Chard jumped in, struggling to justify action. The twins stood beside him, nodding vigorously.

Dresden held his hands out in a placatory gesture, an odd smile alighting on his lips. "Shhh! You'll raise the dead with all this wailing!" He shook his head. "She sent me to *you*, Rowan. But you've corrupted your whole team!"

"Sir?" Rowan, dumbfounded, blinked at the man.

"Garyn Kei," and he paused for reverence's sake, "has a special operation assignment for *you*, and it's a good thing I caught you when I did! Well, stop standing there half in and half out of your darks, boy!"

Rowan tugged on the black pants and pulled the long-sleeved shirt over his head. His mind reeled from Dresden's words. A special mission? What could Rowan do that the stronger, faster Unatans with better senses could not?

Dresden weighted the corners of a large map in the general use room of the dorm. Rowan's break-group gathered around. "Garyn has men posted all over Parisia, guarding various locations that house precious property."

"Didn't they already barter for weapons?" Chard asked.

"Unatans don't barter weapons of the highest quality," Dresden answered. "Word got out a few years back. Now every group that has ever traded with us thinks we slighted them."

"But even our bad stuff is better than their best!" Chard said, his eyes flashing to Rowan.

"I'd bet our best weapons would fetch a much higher price on the black market," Rowan said.

Dresden sneered in disgust. "Exactly." Dresden stabbed the map with his thick forefinger. "The men in this battalion reported stolen blades from old Kadray's private residence in their jurisdiction."

Deruk leaned over to Garlen and whispered so that Rowan could hear, "The old healer? Maraba's father, right?"

"Where's the hole in their defense?" Rowan asked, scanning the formation and seeing that it should have been effective.

"That's the problem," Dresden said. He leveled his concerned eyes on Rowan. "There *wasn't* one. The men apparently, ah, lost time somehow. All weapons here are locked away, as you all know. Old man Kadray doesn't take kindly to nosy people, intruders or otherwise."

"Is he okay?" Rowan asked. "I mean, I know he's skilled," Rowan stammered, realizing his implication of Kadray's age as weakness.

"He said he was sound asleep the whole time," Dresden said with a shrug. "Your instructions are to find out what happened and how, then report back. Undiscovered, if possible. Nitch had a keen interest in you for some reason, Rowan. Either he knows something we don't," Dresden said, grinning, "or he's just not a fan of humanity!"

"Likely both!" said Chard with a chuckle.

"You may need to use that to your advantage," Dresden replied. He held up a finger. "So gather information first." Then he held up a second finger. "Engage the enemy only as a last resort. Take your weapons, because..."

"There's no excuse for living unprepared?" Rowan finished his sentence and looked up solemnly at his trainer.

Dresden clapped him on the shoulder and gave the signal for dismissal.

The cold night air flowed into Rowan's lungs and across his forehead. He breathed deeply through the black cloth stretched over his mouth and nose. His loose hair flowed on the breeze as he moved through Parisia, the layout of the city keenly in his footsteps as habit after his blind training. He slipped silently with his group between buildings and through the mist. Black cowls covered the light hair of his teammates. Only an occasional sharp weapon's edge caught the moonlight. The rest of their stealth weapons had been blackened hilt to point.

Rowan's mind ticked through facts as he ran. How did the off-worlders infiltrate Kadray's home? There are few inept warriors on Unata. Rowan understood that those usually die quickly in battle or are repurposed in some career that is better suited to anonymity. The warriors' battle formations rely on perfect execution to preserve lives. And Maraba's father is known to be a light sleeper, with his noisy ring of keys securely around his neck. Had the lock mechanisms been damaged? He kicked himself for forgetting the important questions at a time like this. He couldn't figure out the missing factor.

He signaled his group to halt with a subtle gesture. On the outskirts of the city, unusual red lights swept steadily along an alleyway. Their path led back to the off-worlders' spaceship. To his amazement, Rowan spotted the gleaming blades of superior weapons carried in piles across the off-worlders' thin arms. They deposited their bounty inside the ship and exited again, their red lights leading the way down a more familiar path toward the Weaponmaster's forge.

Rowan's break-group followed silently as the thieves rounded a curve and headed into the gaping maw of the huge weapon facility. The doors stood unbarred and only mildly damaged. Unatan guards stood still, oblivious to the thievery. Rowan passed by, seeking another shadow in which to hide. Then he spotted Nitch, eyes closed, standing in the formation of Unatan soldiers. He held a bright stone to his forehead and spoke words under his breath.

Rowan gave the signal to Chard asking what the man said. Chard listened then squinted hard. He shrugged, telling Rowan it sounded like gibberish or that he didn't understand the language. Amidst the inattentive Unatan soldiers, another small group of off-worlders exited the building with many precious weapons in tow. Rowan recognized the silhouette of an exceedingly long, wide sword he favored from the Weaponmaster's forge. One of the smaller aliens pulled on the heavy sword's handle, barely scraping it along the ground.

Rowan heard Deruk's foot slip behind him, and a few pebbles tumbled down the low incline.

Deruk cursed under his breath, for the damage had already been done. The off-worlders paused in their exertions and peered into the shadows, trying to pinpoint the sound. An older thief appealed to Nitch, whose final words resounded as he redirected his concentration. Nitch lowered the glowing stone and gestured to one of the Unatan soldiers, a man named Dron. The group's comrade-in-arms stalked toward the shadows as he drew the short swords at his sides.

His heart pounding, Rowan signaled the others to stay still and silent. He stood and emerged from the shadows. He sidestepped the large soldier from Dresden's most recent contingent. Formidable in sparring when he controlled his own body, Dron's arms and legs moved stiffly, unsurely. Nitch merely used him as a puppet, Rowan noticed. Nitch either lacked control or knew nothing of war. Rowan moved behind Dron, encircling his neck with skilled arms. He applied pressure to his arteries and airway. In seconds, Dron crumpled to the ground, unconscious but otherwise unharmed. He didn't get up again, but his chest rose and fell in rhythm.

Never slowing a step or speaking a word, his heartbeat doubling in controlled anger, Rowan continued toward the man who stole from his new home. In the dim moonlight reflected off the night mist, Rowan clearly saw the thin man's drawn face. He clutched the glowing stone with trembling fingers. *Of all the warriors on the planet, why is he afraid of me?*

Rowan grasped the sword grip over his shoulder and drew his weapon. *Dresden said not to engage the enemy.* The sharpened edges of his black long-sword reflected the odd light of Nitch's glowing stone. Rowan settled into an easy battle stance, each muscle remembering its place, just as he'd been told. His stomach fluttered. This wasn't another exercise or sparring match. His opponent stood before him. Nitch looked physically weak. Yet somehow, he had frozen all the Unatans. Rowan focused on the glowing rock. *That rock must be the key to Nitch's control.* Rowan set his jaw. *All I may need to do is destroy that stone!*

The thin man held out the stone like a shield. He glared at Rowan, keeping his mouth pressed tightly in concentration. Rowan glanced all around him, looking for more Unatan attackers.

"I can't get *through*," Nitch yelled to his fellow thieves. He gave a low growl of frustration. "Stupid human brain won't accept it!"

So that's it. During Nitch's outburst, Rowan tried for a non-lethal attack, knowing that Garyn's summary trial and execution of the man would be in high demand. He almost knocked the glowing object out of the man's hands. However, Nitch moved shockingly fast for such a sickly man.

As the other man dodged, he pulled more Unatans between Rowan and himself. If Nitch couldn't fight with them, he would at least use them as shields. Rowan leapt over his comrades and slipped past others that lurched toward him, unaware of their actions. Rowan finally got close enough to strike out at the stone again. He pulled his sword down with all his strength. At the point of contact, the stone's light doubled and coursed up Rowan's blade. Then the sword shattered. Rowan threw his arms to shield his eyes, feeling the hot metal tear through his skin.

Rowan cursed when he opened his eyes. Nitch fled. His men followed close behind. All but one off-worlder seemed to disappear into the shadows. The smaller trader still tried to drag the great-sword behind him. Seeing Rowan bear down on him with his blood dripping all over the sandy ground, the trader dropped the blade and ran for his life toward his ship. Rowan stared at the ruined sword hilt in his hand. Frowning, he set it on the ground. Then he eyed the larger great-sword through the swirling mist. Rowan picked up the weapon, testing its immense weight against his strength. He decided that he could wield it, at least in a short battle. He liked the more substantial feel of the great-sword.

"I've got their scent," Chard whispered as he crossed the ground toward Rowan. "They're going all over to throw us off. But the only place they have to go is back to their ship. And it's my job to *remind* you that our orders are to report back with intel. Not engage the enemy." He grinned at his leader.

Rowan deftly adjusted his shoulder strap for the sword, hanging it slowly against his back. When he felt sure the strap would hold, he signaled to the others. Turning to Chard, he nodded in the direction of the foreign ship.

"You heard the man." Rowan sneered. "That thing won't work on me."

"Yep," Chard answered. He pretended a heavy sigh. "Thought you'd say that."

"Lead the way," Rowan said. "Keep your ears sharp for an ambush."

Chard shook his head at the mischievous glint in Rowan's eyes. Then he took off running, casting a broad grin over his shoulder. "Te-Dasuka would find it *very* interesting that you'd pick that sword of all swords."

"It's his?" Rowan asked, following on Chard's heels. The rest of the team silently appeared behind them.

"More than that. It's *hers,*" Chard answered. "The former queen's. He couldn't bear to use it after her death. So it's hung as a constant reminder of her ever since. That's the story, anyway."

"What a waste," Rowan mumbled.

Condemning a weapon to disuse didn't sound like Te-Dasuka. Other than a loyal servant, who was Te-Dasuka to the former queen? More questions than answers flooded his mind. Then Chard gave the signal for silence. He signed "enemy" and their direction. They had arrived near Queen Garyn's home, thinking they'd lost their pursuers.

Nitch stood at the edge of the building row, just inches from at-attention warriors. *They must see him,* Rowan thought. But they didn't. Already, the armored warriors stood too still, their mannerisms frozen by the power of the off-worlder's glowing stone. Even Te-Dasuka the Weaponmaster stood stock still, with Collern close by his side. Te-Dasuka's strained face showed that he somehow fought against the power that held him. Collern didn't have the blank eyes of the other soldiers, but he could only struggle unsuccessfully against the power.

Nitch's thieves worked swiftly to breach the metal doors of Queen Garyn's private bunker. Rowan held back the urge to yell at the man or the warriors, preserving his advantage over the thieves. He turned to direct his team in a flank maneuver around the man.

The twins and Beryl had disappeared. He found them a second later. Rowan stared in horror as they walked stiffly from their hiding places to where Nitch leered back at the shadows. *He can't see me.* Rowan gritted his teeth. *But I can't hide here while he takes my team!* Rowan felt the anger rise from deep within as he stepped boldly from the shadows into moonlight, into the direct gaze of the off-worlder Nitch.

Rowan gripped the handle of the large sword and took several half-running steps toward Nitch. Rowan swung the sword from his shoulder and toward the off-worlder with surprising speed.

"Foolish human!" Nitch said with a smirk.

Responding to Nitch's quick gesture, the twins moved to restrain Beryl. She didn't resist. Garlen drew his dagger and pressed it to Beryl's throat. Rowan, with a mighty effort, checked the sword and diverted it to the ground. He glared at Nitch, then cast his eyes toward Beryl. A thin trickle of blood followed the tip of Garlen's blade and dripped down her chest. Rowan raged internally, fighting hard to keep his emotions in check.

"They may not fight *you* for me, my friend," Nitch spat out the last word, drawing Rowan's glare once more. "But against a *willing* victim. You know the outcome. Step closer and they die one by one. And let go of the oversized meat cleaver."

Rowan stared at the sword, dropping the weight of it to the ground with an impotent thud. Then he straightened his shoulders again and waited. He used the moment to breathe deeply and calm his anger. He decided that he wouldn't hesitate to kill the man when the opportunity came again. He forced down the stab of worry for his controlled teammates. But he glared at Nitch, waiting for him to falter, to show his weakness.

The groaning metal of the Queen's door as it slid open diverted Nitch's attention for a moment. Rowan had a hand on the sword and lurched forward under its weight. Nitch noticed

Rowan's stumble and lifted his hand toward Rowan's break-team. Rowan's stomach flipped in fear. In those few seconds, Rowan felt dazed. He saw the feet of a shadow descend to Nitch's shoulders and saw a gloved hand rip the glowing stone from the man's bony fingers. In the next instant, the shadow zipped around the twins and Beryl, flinging all three to the ground, safely away from each other.

Rowan's focus sharpened when Nitch wailed and drew some type of projectile weapon from his robe. He leveled the small device at the human's chest. Rowan regained his balance and swung the sword before him in a long arc, splitting the off-worlder a long diagonal through his chest. Though heavy, the sword cut through flesh like a thin razor. The hollow cry that tore from Nitch's throat hung on the night air for a long moment. He clawed at the wound and fell to his knees, dying with his face turned to the heavens. Rowan stared into the dead man's open eyes, torn by a dozen feelings he struggled to suppress.

Then his attention snapped to the shadowy figure that saved the lives of his break-team. Rowan grinned in gratitude at the cat-boy Chard, who pulled the dark hood from his head. The young one smiled back, full of the child-like enthusiasm of accomplishment. Rowan hadn't heard a whisper of Chard's movement. He shook his head. Then he nodded to the Queen's bunker.

"We're not done yet," Rowan whispered. "The other off-worlders got into Garyn's. She's in danger."

"Not anymore," echoed the Queen's familiar voice.

Rowan looked beyond the warriors to Garyn Kei's doorway. She stood in her thin metal under suit, wiping off-worlder blood from a long katana.

"I could hear that blasted stone trying to shut me down," she said. "But it didn't work. On just us three."

"Is it our half-blood?" Chard wondered. "And Rowan's human blood?"

"It would have to be, I suppose," Garyn conceded. "We're lucky after all!"

"But you don't believe in luck, Queen!" Chard said breathlessly.

"Would you have me call it something else?" Garyn said as she resheathed her sword. "Blind, dumb luck determined our genetic makeup."

"What about the ones who ran away?" Chard cried. He looked toward the Parisian plateau.

"I had a stealth division confiscate our stolen goods." Garyn joined the two boys. She studied the odd glow of the stone over Chard's shoulder. "We'll detain the off-worlders and send them in stasis aboard our *official* trader guests' ship to the High Courts. We'll prepare a full report on the ship's contents, and send that as evidence. I'd wager ours wasn't the only planet looted by Nitch and his men."

"The warriors are still affected," Rowan said, standing before Collern. He saw emotion in his friend's eyes, but Collern could not move. "Collern and Te-Dasuka less than the others."

Garyn looked into Te-Dasuka's eyes. She strode over, taking the pulsing stone from Chard's hands. "This looks like an Azelan corestone. It's something only Azelan royalty can possess and use without side effects."

Chard dropped his head, staring at the dead Nitch. "Is that why they looked so thin and sick?"

Garyn nodded. “These guys really were being sucked dry by the power of this thing.” She gritted her teeth. “Ugh. It’s reacting with my birthmark. Burns a bit.”

“So they’re Azelans, at least?” Rowan asked.

“Hardly,” she chuckled. “You’ll know an Azelan when you see one.”

“Do we have to destroy it, then?” Rowan asked. He rested the huge sword on his shoulder.

Garyn stared at the corestone. “If we can.” She glanced at Rowan, then noticed the big sword. Her eyes glistened. Then she said in a low voice, “If any weapon can crack this thing, that sword can.”

The Queen laid the glowing object on the ground, on a wide rock. She gestured, indicating that Rowan aim at the stone. Rowan swung the sword forward from his shoulder, in a wide arc, and brought the edge down full force on the corestone. The impact jarred his body. Lightning leapt up the blade and fizzled before it reached the sword hilt. Rowan swung again with all his might. This time the corestone split neatly down the middle, protesting with a loud crack of thunder and blinding light. Rowan dropped the sword and threw his arms in front of his face.

When the glare and lightning subsided, Rowan opened his eyes. The small stone lay in two pieces, one on either side of the wide blade. The fierce, pulsing glow of the halves ebbed and finally ceased completely. As the last glow died, warriors regained their consciousness all around the three. Te-Dasuka rushed over first, followed closely by Collern.

“Majesty, I couldn’t make it to you!” Te-Dasuka said, his voice shaking with emotion. “I couldn’t protect you. Forgive me!” He prostrated himself before her.

"Silly man, get up!" Garyn answered, tugging at his shoulder. But her voice cracked. "There's nothing you could have done to prepare for this! And obviously, I'm fine."

Collern came to Rowan's side. He threw an arm around Chard, then gripped Rowan's shoulder firmly. His voice was full of relief and gratitude. "Good job, my friend. Good job."

Rowan nodded to his first friend. A swell of emotion rose in his throat, flooding behind his eyes. But he suppressed it. "I am glad to protect my new home."

The other man smiled and moved aside when Te-Dasuka approached Rowan. He made a great show of formally sizing up Rowan. "We shall have to make another sword for you, it seems."

"My other sword broke, Weaponmaster," Rowan answered as he straightened his shoulders. "I retrieved the most effective-looking weapon from those the thieves dropped."

"Effective?" Te-Dasuka laughed. "Aye, it is that, if nothing else."

"Sir?" Te-Dasuka regarded Rowan, awaiting his question. Rowan cleared his throat. "Sir, may I have permission to use this sword until the Weaponmaster provides a new weapon?"

Te-Dasuka stared at Rowan for a long while. Rowan nearly retracted his request when the old man finally spoke. "Fine Unatan weapons should not be displayed to collect dust, but used. I have neglected the weapon in resigning it to disservice. Until which time the Queen orders your new weapon, you may wield my Cainslayer."

Rowan retrieved the weapon from the dirt and bowed before Te-Dasuka. As he stood, cheers erupted from the assembled warriors—exclamations of relief and gratitude. Garyn debriefed and sent runners all over the city with their reports. She set workers to fixing the various buildings' minimal damage. Someone carefully piloted the old ship to the scrapyard, with instructions to inventory the contents for transport. The hull would be disassembled later for use throughout the city.

"I'd send the whole ship, but in that shape, it's a liability. A miracle they made it this far," Garyn smiled at Chard and Rowan. "We survived today because of you, my precious recruits."

Chard beamed at her, his tail twitching in pleasure. Rowan fell thoughtfully silent. He felt the sticky blood coagulating on his arms, listened to the productive industry around him, and drifted in his mind for some time.

Then Maraba whisked the Queen away to attend to funeral rites. Unatans reverently built funeral pyres for their enemies in plain sight of the prisoners. Rowan rushed to help. Rowan folded Nitch's arms across his ruined chest and, with help, laid his body across the others. Garyn handed him the flaming torch. Rowan lowered the torch to tinder and stood back to watch the fire reach toward heaven. He joined Garyn and called Nitch's name into the roaring flames to be carried to the sky.

Afterward, he felt sick with melancholy. A man died because of him, by his hand, that day. He stood leaning against a corner, staring once at his hands, then at the pyres. He ignored the well-wishers so often that they finally gave him leave to mourn. As the evening commenced with an impromptu celebration, Beryl, Garlen and Deruk scrambled to find Rowan. When they saw him leaning against the building, Garlen called out. Rowan didn't respond. They moved to rush forward when an arm barred their passage.

Collern looked down at the twins, and at Beryl. When Deruk protested, Collern shook his head. “Chard’s with him. Give him a few minutes.”

On the roof above Rowan’s head, Chard paced back and forth, tail atwitch. Then the boy knelt and bounded to the ground, landing lightly on his feet by Rowan. He glanced at the human from the corner of his eye and leaned back against the building next to him. Rowan stood staring into the flames, arms crossed, sullied with ashes, and face streaked with dirt and possibly tears.

Chard sighed mightily. “The first kill is hardest, and it doesn’t get easier. That’s what Dresden told us from Day One.” He gauged Rowan’s reaction before continuing. Seeing the forced blankness in the human’s eyes, he continued, “As a half-breed, I learned something you need to know. You can still be Unatan *and* who you are, Rowan.”

“I’m a murderer,” Rowan mumbled. “The slaves and now this man.” He nodded toward the fire.

“If you protect something you hold dear, and your heart is pure, you will never murder,” Chard said. “Queen Garyn told me that a long time ago.”

At the mention of Garyn, Rowan’s eyes focused again. “She may be right. But why does that knowledge still allow me to hurt inside?” He rubbed his hands across his midriff as if to massage away the hurt there.

Chard kicked at a pebble on the ground, then watched it skip across to the fire. “Full Unatans feel sorrow, regret and pain, but these are fleeting. Even half-Unatans like me. Our hearts just aren’t as big.” Chard leaned forward, staring into Rowan's face. "Since I'm half Empath, too, I can *hear* that agony clanging around inside you." Chard frowned, clenching at his chest. "Garyn said that humans sometimes carry heart-wounds all their lives because their hearts have more room inside."

Rowan smiled despite his sorrow. "That sounds about right. I guess I'll be a Unatan *and* a human. All I have to do is bear it all!" He turned to Chard, letting the mask of indifference fall. "I'm sorry I worried you."

Chard whispered, "Apology accepted."

Feeling less nauseous and more determined than ever, Rowan pulled himself from the side of the building. He stood quietly for one more moment, staring at the flames and then skyward. "Do me a favor, Chard."

"Yeah?"

"When I die, don't burn me. Bury me. I get to stay with you guys, then, right?"

Chard swallowed past the lump in his throat and whispered, "Right."

Rowan clapped his hand on Chard's shoulder and looked in his eyes. The sadness sank deeper in Rowan's black eyes, along with the resolve. Chard sighed and beamed up at the man. With that look in Rowan's eyes, Chard knew he wouldn't have to fulfill his promise for a long time.

Rowan threw his arm around Chard's shoulders and turned to his waiting group of friends. "Let's get a bite to eat." Then he called out to Collern. "Tell your father he can stop spying on me now. I'll be okay!"

The whole group caught the quiet confidence of Rowan. They laughed infectiously as Dresden straightened up from the shadows just inside the city gate, cursing his loud breathing and Rowan's too-good training.

Dresden continued in the same friendly and scolding banter as he dragged Collern and Rowan toward dinner, with the rest of Rowan's break-group rushing to catch up.

Rowan laughed and danced more than he had in his entire life. Those he had ignored earlier took heart from his display and came to speak to him again. The Queen and Maraba raised their glasses to Rowan, their hero. He pushed his pain deep into his stomach where it could only rumble on occasion. He felt emotions akin to joy, belonging, and purpose. Always waiting in the wings were the guilt and sadness. But the festivities celebrated survival and honor. He would show them his appreciation and happiness at being one with the Unatan people.

Garyn Kei caught Rowan's gaze. She watched as he buried his human soul in the heart of a warrior. Rowan never doubted she could see the pain in his eyes, in fact experienced similar pain. But he smiled. He determined to live up to her expectations at whatever cost.

The Queen understood, and rewarded Rowan with a mysterious, mischievous smile, just for him. Rowan read her lips as she mouthed a word, "Live!" Then he knew there could be more to her order than mere survival. He, for once in his life, really protected something. Rowan Jun lived.

12: ORICHALCUM

Garyn felt disoriented, standing before warriors from the past. They loomed over her, as if she had become very small. She watched them draw weapons against her. Garyn's hands tightened convulsively. She realized that she, too, held weapons in both hands. Then the group descended, bent on killing her. Her birthmark sparked and glowed. Her blood burned in her veins. Fear left her shivering, even as she whirled in the war dance ingrained in her muscle memory. Man after man fell at her feet—strong men the likes of which Unata would mourn. Yet they kept coming.

Once her fear subsided into dizzy familiarity, Garyn knew she relived events of her past. The powerful men who bore down with ill intent were members of the Gauntlet, the best protectors on Unata. Only eleven at the time, she fought with the power and precision necessary to bring down Unata's most powerful fighters. Masterwork weapons broke in her hands. She retrieved more. Blood splattered at her feet, but she managed to keep her footing. Even in her dream, she could feel the gore seeping up through gashes in the thick soles of her boots.

When only one man remained, she flicked the blood from her katana and sheathed the sword. The last of the Gauntlet—a tall, strong and proud man. He knelt before her, proclaiming her Queen before the Gauntlet and all Unata. Te-Dasuka served as her mentor ever since. But in Garyn's dream, this time, Te-Dasuka walked away, into the shadows, and left her standing in the blood and bodies of his comrades.

The electric lights flickered, and the floor tilted beneath her feet. She finally slipped and fell into a wide puddle of blood that splattered all around her. The blood began to trickle between the shifting floor stones. Then she cried, the sorrow welling beyond her capacity to control with her Unatan side. She pressed her bloody hands to her tear-streaked face and sobbed uncontrollably. *This isn't how it happened,* Garyn interjected in her own dream. *Unatans can't be seen to cry like this!* But the little girl still cowered and wailed in her pain. No one would see, anyway, for the child stood alone in the blackness.

"I'm nothing more than a killer," little Garyn said between wracking sobs.

"No, you did what you had to survive," rang a quiet baritone voice over her shoulder.

Garyn jumped up and turned in the direction of his voice, expecting Te-Dasuka. She scrubbed at her eyes so she could look at her unexpected company. The man lounged on one of the benches placed around the room, his feet propped on the back of a straight-backed chair. He sat up and leaned forward into the flickering light.

Young Garyn looked at the strange man with intense curiosity and confusion because she didn't recognize him. He wore a black tank shirt, dark blue pants and black boots. He had paler skin than hers, long black hair, and black eyes. The depth of those eyes entranced the child. She stepped toward him to get a better look. Adult Garyn, buried somewhere in the girl's subconscious, gasped. Rowan Jun, perhaps ten or fifteen years older than his current age, leaned into the garish brightness with a battered smile that barely reached his troubled eyes.

"You're wise," the girl said.

"I had a good teacher," the man said, with a mysterious smile. His eyes sparkled.

"What did your teacher say about murderers?" little Garyn asked, staring down at her blood-drenched hands, flexing her fingers as the stuff dried to a sticky burgundy.

He looked up at the lights then. "She said that if you protect something you hold dear, and your heart is pure, you will never murder."

The girl furrowed her brow, nodding vigorously. "Then why does it still hurt here?" she asked. Garyn pressed her hand over her chest.

"Maybe your heart has more room in it than other hearts," he answered with a fond resonance.

"But how do I forget the pain?" little Garyn asked, a clearly disturbed expression on her face.

"Mnemosyne sings an abrupt song, and often/ When the Furies alight, and Aries descends/ When the Firebird flies, and the Unicorn dies/ When Valkyries ride at sunrise, yet we live on 'til Dark/ Mnemosyne sings high above all," Rowan recited softly in answer.

Garyn looked about her, and when she turned back to Rowan to ask him to explain, he had vanished. But the darkness lightened. Her floor no longer shook. The deep dream-breath she took didn't roil in her lungs and threaten to rip out. And with the long exhale, she relaxed into abrupt wakefulness.

Garyn Kei opened her eyes, alert in the darkness. The ache from her past welled again. Something in her gut made her wary. Her ears twitched, seeking evidence of an enemy's footfall. Only the salty smell of her sweat and the ocean below filled her nose. She sensed nothing amiss in the room or the building.

She reached farther, feeling the twist in her stomach. Faint light traced a glowing pattern around the intricate curves of her royal birthmark as she focused on the source of her uncharacteristic anxiety. She could hear no more than a few particles of sand drifting over the mesa on the faint breeze. The sleeping bunker city lay silent in the heavy mist. At the edge of the great city, the sentries stood vigilant. Their light breathing and murmured conversation floated through her heightened consciousness. All that lay beyond the city's walls—the dense jungles, the rushing, formidable rivers, and the sheer cliffs around Parisia—rested in rare stillness.

Satisfied for the moment, Garyn took a deep cleansing breath. She relaxed her grip on the katana. Dreams always came, dark and crimson with the blood of others. This lucid vision felt different. It lingered in her consciousness. Why had Te-Dasuka left her? Why had Rowan shown up? The Rowan Jun in her dream had looked so confident and powerful, so comfortable in his skin—a far cry from the burgeoning youth in her employ. Garyn smiled at the thought of him. *If only he had a few more summers on him*, Garyn thought with a chuckle.

Paired with her mother's warnings about lucid dreams among those of the Royal bloodline, Garyn's gut told her something big headed their way. But Unata felt safe for now. Garyn closed her eyes, listening to a redmeat's soft breathing in a holding pen across the city. She smiled and relaxed, allowing her Royal hearing to dissipate. With a busy day ahead of them, the Unatans slept soundly. No need to disturb their rare peaceful rest.

Dawn arrived, reaching the Parisian mesa an hour after Garyn's strange dream ended. The unforgiving mists hung over bunker houses and other fortified structures of the hauntingly beautiful landscape of Parisia. Garyn strolled to the east wall of her bedroom.

"Morning, Parisia," she whispered. She leaned into the narrow window. Her favorite natural sight—the mist glowing in the early brightness—often proved a moment so brief she dared not look away. Her mood lifted as the haze swirled and shifted, glittered like diamonds and then sank back to silver shadows. All at once, the mist blazed with the full refraction of the dawn.

Rays of yellow sun cut through the heavy mist. The vapor then drifted upward to reveal the violet shadows of her kingdom. Garyn admitted that her great-grandmother had built a glorious capital city, and no doubt laughed as she bestowed the delicate name. Morning formed a yellow outline around the low military-style buildings made of heavy stone slabs, cement and metal. Threads of fog clung to the base of each archery tower and sentinel nest.

Garyn Kei tore her eyes from the eastern window and crossed to her restroom. She dipped her calloused hands into the shallow water basin in the corner and scrubbed at her eyes. By habit, she traced a path across the slim, horizontal notch above each eye that marked her racially as Unatan.

"Obviously their kind. And yet they tried to deny me," she told her memories. "To keep me from the Throne."

She raked her long wet fingers through the thick, wild white crop of hair, remembering the day she cut it short in mourning her mother's death. The incoherent warning from her dream ebbed as memories of her mother rose to the surface.

"It's a day full of the past, Mother," she whispered. "Bloody memories."

The gray stone walls echoed the padding of Garyn's feet as she walked to her armoire in the opposite corner. She pulled her black undersuit from the wall and slipped into the sheath of fitted thin metals. She drew on her high-collared longcoat—a ceremonial affair in Royal yellow. The edges, trimmed with stylized black notches—the Royal three notch and cabochon emblem—indicated her lineage and rank.

Garyn cinched and buckled the wide weapon belt and crammed her feet into cuffed high boots. As an afterthought, she grabbed the ornate forehead band—a metal protective circlet enameled in black and silver-gray—worn by Unatan monarchs in times of fleeting peace. Shoving the band over wild cream-white locks, she faced the huge, polished metal shield that served as her mirror. For a moment, she saw her mother's stern expression staring back. Then she smiled at her own reflection.

She gripped the right edge of the shield and pushed it aside. The mirror swung on a hinged peg and opened into a narrow corridor of rough-cut stone. Garyn strode through the entrance and descended a steep flight of narrow stairs. Pulling back a heavy curtain, she entered a room carved into the stone. Weak electrical lights glowed above her, revealing a shocking array of masterful weapons. On the far wall, she placed her war fans and sword on pegs and stand. She made her way to the back of the room, finding a special carved alcove. Black and silver weapons hung in this space. Her hands traced the sleek edges of weapon after weapon.

"In my hands, which among you will spill the blood of my enemy?" she whispered.

She gripped the sheath of an exquisite long katana. "My thanks, Masoliethiel." She pulled two war fans from their pegs. "And also, thanks to Bastielkir and Montrab. Be swift in my hands today."

Then she smiled, full of mischief, and turned back to the stairs. Garyn Kei burst into her ready-room, startling several of the guards who waited for her. The tension in the room brimmed with lighthearted excitement.

"So, Collern, have you seen your mother today?" Garyn sighed with derision.

Collern scoffed. "On the Festival of Proving? You must be kidding! Her Majesty *may* qualify to seek audience on her Coordinator's biggest day of the year."

Garyn smiled. "And what of our warrior pledges?"

"Ready and nervous," Collern answered. "Father has drilled them in custom."

"Have you washed your boots today, my young warrior?" Garyn asked, her tone full of innocence.

Collern's sigh rattled past his teeth. "No need, my Queen. At least, not on last year's bet. Rowan's gone as far as he can go, I'd say. And I still beat him regularly in sparring."

"Hmph! With the right motivation, Rowan could be quite a challenge," Garyn said, "but I can tell by that heartbeat that you're excited. So what do you know that I don't?"

Collern met Garyn's eyes with a winning smile. "Today will be the best Festival you've ever had, Majesty!" He crammed his helmet over his white hair and called the guards to order.

Garyn brushed past the men and through her door into vibrant sunlight. She hurried across the grounds to the Throne bunker, breathing the enticing aromas from her feast kitchens. She turned in a circle at the door, taking in all the excited Unatans as they hurried about their Festival tasks. Collern shook his head a little and smiled, wondering if Garyn's reversion to childlike excitement helped her overcome the real past that created the day.

Two warriors pulled the heavy metal doors along their oiled track. Garyn swept into the room with such a commanding presence that the attendants and festival planners startled from their posts to bow to their queen. Garyn Kei mounted the wide stone steps to her black marble throne. She sighed and plopped down with such comic excitement that the others wore huge smiles.

Into the ensuing silence, she rang out, "Well? Let's get this thing underway!"

The planners lined up, displaying goods, entertainment and food for her approval. She rushed them away with enthusiasm, attacking each item of business with a glint of mischief in her eyes. When the last business had concluded before the noonday meal, her stomach growled audibly in the emptying hall.

"Queen Garyn Kei!" a scolding voice split the fresh silence.

"Maraba! You've made your way here!" Garyn said with an impish whimper.

"Don't you 'Maraba' me, Your Majesty!" Maraba seethed with a frenetic energy. "Here!"

Maraba shoved a basket under her nose. "Eat! When the breakfast cooks hadn't seen you, I *knew* you would be so foolish as to hear business before you ate! They don't make lunch on Festival Day!"

"I was fasting for dinner!" Garyn said mockingly. She had become famous for her festival appetite. But she obediently laid out bread, juice, cheese and fish patties on her top step. She pursed her lips at her least favorite breakfast item. "Bet you haven't eaten yet, either," she mumbled like a scolded child.

"It's different if *I* don't," Maraba answered, her voice rising. She brandished her writing plates like a weapon. "You're the Queen! I have to make sure you're okay first. Then I've got a lot to do before this evening!" She tapped the stylus on her writing plate. "We're nowhere near finished with the sparring platform, and Collern tells me we have to outfit the thing with special seating for his 'main event' with Rowan. There's no way we'll finish in time!"

"So *that's* what Collern was so excited about!" Garyn laughed. "So that old dust bowl is an arena now! Haha!"

Maraba's jaw dropped. "Oh! I forgot his surprise!" Then she growled her next words. "You *better* act surprised and pleased and thrilled!"

Garyn waved her hands in innocence. "What top-secret sparring platform?" She smiled up at Maraba. "You get all worked up every year, and you pull off this festival without a hitch every year, and neither of us ever eats early on Festival day until we're forced. So stop worrying, and sit!" She gestured to the wide step beside her. "Eat!"

When Maraba started to protest, Garyn

pointed to the place beside her. "If I have to eat these nasty fish patty things, you do too!"

"Oh? You don't like them?" This time Maraba adopted the innocent voice, pretending she didn't know. But she sat next to Garyn. She smiled after her first big bite of fish patty. "You remember? You're the one who ordered a simple fast before the festival, and this is what your cooks came up with."

Garyn's eyes glazed over as she chewed. When she swallowed, she said, "Mother loved these things, gross as they are. She said they were good for reminding folks about humble beginnings."

"She was a wise woman," Maraba said, her voice sober for the first time. "It's a good thing she passed it on to you."

Garyn shook her head. Her feelings from the dream rose to overtake her. "Passing things on is what we're good at. Drowning the past with industry. Thank you, Maraba, my friend."

Maraba cleared her throat. "Well, I'll get on with it if you don't mind, my dear friend," Maraba said past the tightness in her voice. She stood abruptly. "It'll be perfect. If we can just find and prep Rowan for the rites."

"He's missing? Well, given the day, I can guess where he is."

Maraba smiled wistfully. "Collern said the same. He spoke with Te-Dasuka earlier, but he was busy. So Collern and Chard are, um, taking a bit of a walk."

"It's a good thing Te-Dasuka was busy. He doesn't go for walks," Garyn reminded her. She grinned. "He overdoes things. He goes on epic quests of reverence or salvation or what-have-you! And the speeches! I think I know every one of them!"

“All I can say is that they all three better be back by sundown!” Maraba said as the Coordinator’s fire returned to her eyes. “And *you* gave the poor old man a commission at the last minute, I hear.”

Garyn shrugged. “Queen’s prerogative!”

Maraba tapped a scratch-pen on the thin metal plates and rushed toward the door. “Now you’ve got activity progress checks with me until well past noon, so don’t go wandering off!”

Garyn sighed. She stood, placed her makeshift tablecloth and glass drink bottles in the basket and joined Maraba. She playfully scuffed her boots all the way to the door.

Maraba continued talking between each stop along their route, and sometimes the subjects caught Garyn’s interest: “From here to the Weaponmaster’s. He said he has a special gift for you that he didn’t have finished in time for today’s *very early* business call.” Then she said other things, Garyn thought, but in the mid-morning heat and grit, the last one caught her interest most of all: “And then you’ll have your ceremonial bath. The attendants are making preparations already, and you are to relax until,” Maraba looked over her itinerary, “an hour before sundown, when we’ll practice your speech and rites.”

“And then we can eat?” Garyn asked, her voice a plaintive whimper.

Maraba eyed her for a long moment. Then she broke from her serious banter. “And then we can eat ourselves sick! I’m so excited! Did you see those desserts?”

With that, Maraba’s hardest work ended. She needed only check on progress and usher the Queen about with her. Garyn wondered how her establishment of the holiday had become such a complicated event. She wanted only to remember her past. When she saw how fired up Maraba became, how much the organization of the day proved her passion, then Garyn relaxed and let the Coordinator's excitement run its course. Every event had a purpose, and every rite had a reason. Maraba had created a stunning festival full of duty and memory. So Garyn turned her concern to reciting and practicing the newer ceremonial words and actions she needed to remember.

And occasionally, her mind returned to the attractive man from her dream. Her heart fluttered. She thought about her too-young, favorite recruit. Then Garyn felt guilty wondering how young Rowan Jun fared at his family gravesite.

"I know it must be important," Maraba whispered. "But we're here."

Garyn blinked at Maraba, jumping at the Coordinator's elbow in her ribs. "Hmm?" She looked around, seeing Te-Dasuka and his many assistants crowded around them and a table in the Weaponmaster's work bunker. Then she felt keenly embarrassed and selfish.

"Weaponmaster Monarch!" Te-Dasuka saluted. "Your commission is finished, but first, your gift." The burly man bowed, his outstretched hands bearing a long, cloth-covered object.

"I know the commission was last minute! How in the world?" Garyn asked. "I was fickle and should have let you know ages sooner!"

"It is our duty to be at the Queen's whim. Besides, it was the best all-nighter we've pulled all year!" Te-Dasuka smiled up at her, his pale eyes crinkling.

His face looked drawn and red from wear and heat at the forge. She chided herself for working the man so hard at his age. Then she clipped that line of thought. *Te-Dasuka is the last member of the true Gauntlet!* she thought. *He'll live on for spite!*

Another jab in her ribs refocused her. "Get on with it," Maraba urged. "I'm sure they'd like to get a bath, too!"

Te-Dasuka chuckled, indulging his Queen. "Eventually, perhaps. But my Queen is..."

"Nonsense, Te-Dasuka!" Garyn quipped. "I'm being extraordinarily rude today, Queen or not." She laughed and reached for the covered weapon he bore. "Now, gimme!"

With a sigh and shake of his head, the old man removed the shroud from his newest weapon. He placed the battle axe in Garyn's hands. Garyn tested the weight and gave an appreciative whistle at its lightness. The grip fit her hand perfectly, and the broad axe head was thin as a razor. She dutifully inspected the fine carvings along the blade.

"Ikaria's work?" Garyn asked.

Te-Dasuka beamed, his leathern face brightening at the mention of his daughter's name.

"We came across the metal formula when a foreign trace element made its way into our melting tanks," Te-Dasuka began. "We noticed that the metal appeared polished before we touched it. The first blade held a perfect edge and could only be sharpened by the mineral additive that created it."

"Perfect edge?" Garyn glanced up, interest piqued.

"Once sharpened, that first blade never became dull." Te-Dasuka's eyes twinkled. "And believe me, we tried."

"So, naturally, you identified the

'accidental' compound and reproduced it," Garyn said while turning the weapon over and over in her hands.

"Naturally," he chuckled. "But it's a complicated alloy to reproduce en masse. We were able to improve the formula and make that axe, which finally broke the first one."

"What're you calling this stuff?" Garyn said with a challenging grin.

"We think we've rediscovered orichalcum," Te-Dasuka said in all seriousness.

Garyn blinked at him. "As in *Atlantean* orichalcum?"

Te-Dasuka grinned back and shrugged. "Perfect edge, no polishing, nigh unbreakable. What would you have us call it? That's Stage Two orichalcum."

Garyn flipped the large weapon on edge and flung it past Te-Dasuka's ear. To her pleasure, he didn't flinch. When one of his assistants gasped, he sighed and grinned. She cuffed him on the shoulder as she walked past. "Throws pretty well for a battle-axe. If you don't mind, Collern'll love it!"

The blade had sunk up to the handle in the thick stone pillar that supported the room, straight through an assistant's shirt with a hairsbreadth between the metal and him. With much effort, Garyn unpinned the boy and ruffled his hair. He blushed and bowed clumsily, embarrassed by his fear. Garyn couldn't find a scratch or smudge on the curved blade. Seeing the potential—and proof—of Te-Dasuka's genius, she threw an arm across the much larger man's broad shoulders.

He laughed heartily. "I thought you may like it. We've got a new katana and a couple war fans in the works for you, but given the nature of your commission, we ran low on our existing alloy. Wait until you see what we did with the Stage Three orichalcum!"

Te-Dasuka took heart in Garyn's excitement. They followed him to the back wall and a huge table he used for assembly. A heavy side of leather covered the surface of a large weapon. When the Weaponmaster removed the cover, Garyn gasped.

Maraba whistled. "Wow! Are you sure anyone can even *carry* that thing?"

Garyn laughed. "I'm sure he'll manage!" She clutched the long handle. With a grunt, she hefted the metal slab from the table. "I thought you said this stuff was light!"

"You wanted your commission to be solid, if I recall correctly," Te-Dasuka said, his eyes glistening in pride. "Steel would have been unbearable, even for him. But he should get a few good years out of this one!"

Garyn judged that the weapon was as wide as her shoulders at the hilt and taller than Te-Dasuka. The black and silver blade caught the red light from the forge fires. The queen's notch emblem had been carved along the guard to indicate her special training.

"Hmph! This one outsizes old Cainslayer twice over!" Garyn said, turning a sympathetic eye to Te-Dasuka. She saw the flicker of emotion at mention of her mother's sword. Wistfully, she said, "That old thing will be returned to you at long last. I expect it to be of use?"

"As you wish, Majesty," Te-Dasuka said with a tired smile.

"So, what name do you give this sword, Weaponmaster?" Garyn regained her authoritative bearing.

"With your permission, Weaponmaster

Monarch, I bequeath the name Godslayer, a translation of Masalikir, in honor of your mother."

"Godslayer, it is, Te-Dasuka." Garyn set the sword down, her eyes glistening. Masali, a name shared by her mother and grandmother, was a word meaning 'divine', and 'kir' was from 'kirna', the Ancient Text form of 'killer'. "If you'll be so kind as to help with the honors tonight?"

"Collern will be so jealous," Maraba said dotingly.

"He has every right to!" Garyn laughed. "Now, is it time to bathe yet? This place is sweltering! Wonderful jobs, everyone! I thank you. Now go! All of you!"

She ushered everyone out and pulled together the double doors against prying eyes. Garyn insisted that Maraba join her for the so-called ceremonial bath. Against her micro-managing will, Maraba consented. Soon, they were soaking off the dusty grit of a long day in the luxury of a mountain of soapy foam. Their attendants spoke in excitement about the evening's events, who was the most attractive new recruit, who was the most powerful, how wonderful the food smelled. Rowan's name came up often in their discreet whispers.

Garyn smiled again at the memory of her dream. Rowan's dark eyes peered out at her, older, stronger, smoldering. She giggled in her childish giddiness, enamored of a man who didn't yet exist. When Maraba stared and demanded to know the joke, all Garyn could do was blame the heat for her red face and the evenings' fun for her good mood.

13: AT MEMORIAL

"Right where we expected to find you," Collern said. He pushed aside vines and peered into the clearing at Rowan, who knelt on the ground before three headstones.

"I intended to return in time," Rowan answered, casting Collern a tired smile.

Chard joined Collern, standing over a foot taller and ages wiser than when Rowan first met him. Chard had said his father was an Empath, giving him his catlike grace and appearance as well as his accelerated growth. Rowan watched him, finding it hard to believe the young man looked barely older than a toddler a year ago. Chard stared somberly all around the clearing.

"You promised to show me where you came from," Chard said as an apology.

"I did promise," Rowan said. He gestured expansively. "And this is all that's left of it."

All around them, the jungle reclaimed the burnt scar left by Rowan's fiery entrance into Unata's society. Vines climbed over the charred, crumpled metal of the Slaveship QuellTruth. Rust gnawed at the raw edges of the ship thanks to the high moisture under the canopy. Rowan cleared the last of the greenery from around his family gravesite and placed a tied bunch of beach lilies before each stone. Then he poured water from a glass vial over the graves.

He smiled down at the stones. "You never got to see the ocean, so I brought it to you."

Collern knelt beside Rowan and produced a flask from his kit. He poured the strong liquor over each stone as tribute, took a swig and handed it to Rowan. The human accepted and drank to his memories, raising the flask as he stared at the stones.

Coughing, he handed back Collern's container. Then he laughed, shaking his head.

"Not used to Unatan spirits yet?" Collern whispered.

"Never will be, I think," Rowan answered. "Chard?"

The young man appeared silently through the vines, carrying several round objects. He stopped before the kneeling men and set his armload on the ground. The large fruit, native to the Lower Jungle, had a smooth rind and sweet liquid core. Chard took out his boot knife and cut a hole in the top.

"I wanted to pay tribute as well," he said with a genuine smile. He poured the green sweet juice over each stone and topped three others for the men to drink.

After a long draught to rinse away Collern's liquor, Rowan thanked Chard.

"The nearest stand of greendrop is easily a mile away," Collern said thoughtfully, eyeing the sphere in his hands.

Chard's eyes danced with mischief. "I'm fast!" He winked at Rowan.

They lounged in silence for a long time, listening to the daytime buzz of the jungle and sipping their greendrop juice. An occasional rustling at the edge of the clearing roused them. The thick air and heat sapped the energy from them in a pleasant way. Rowan drew deep breaths, unable to pick up the slightest smell of human death or pain. He felt the sweltering heat trapped under the shading canopy, a far cry from the raging fires that burnt away the flesh of the dead. He found it remarkably peaceful in the place of so much suffering. Soon, all that would be left of his past would be memories.

Chard sniffed. "There was a pyre over there?" He gestured to the far left of the clearing, where the telltale signs of body-burning remained.

"Queen Garyn built a pyre for the fallen Slavers and the Slavemaster once they were defeated," Rowan answered, mildly surprised that he noticed it under the new growth. "They were the ones who kept us, who bred us for selling."

Chard's face grew distant for an instant, then he asked, "Were they going to sell you, too?"

"Not immediately. I was to be breeding stock, to make more like me," Rowan answered, letting the lazy heat quell the old contempt that rose in him. "But I didn't like the idea of being a slave. Especially if that meant making more like me, to be subjected to the same or worse fate."

"No one would, I imagine," Chard answered heatedly. "Breeding stock or not."

"I guess not," Rowan replied. "But an unpopular mentality among slaves."

"What did you do?" Chard asked.

"I started and led the Insurgency," Rowan said with a glance toward the ship. "We lived under lock and key, and we were all very young. But we got a hold of information the others couldn't."

"Didn't they suspect you?" Chard asked.

"Like I said, we were young and they mistook youth for stupidity," Rowan said with a crooked smile. "We did little things, like snatching extra rations for the weaker ones so they wouldn't be killed off at the next appraisal. Then we got more ambitious and slowly created logs of ship knowledge from snippets of things we heard."

"How did you avoid getting caught, if you kept things like that? Wait, I'm sorry! This is bringing up bad memories," Chard said, responding to feelings that Rowan had not voiced, waving his hands in worry.

"No, I promised!" Rowan stared at the boy, willing him to understand. Then he turned back to his memories. "We didn't have paper or tablets or anything. Everything was stored up here," Rowan said, tapping his temple with a finger. "They told me everything and I remembered. We would stand on the appraisal blocks with the Slavemaster and he would talk candidly with the Slavers. That's how I knew their language. I learned it slowly. All while they poked my face, checked my teeth and squeezed my limbs regularly, looking for any imperfection that would render me worthless."

"By the time they suspected me, a kid, I already had all the information I needed. And when little Ayli was born, I ramped up the plan so that she could grow up free," Rowan said. He dug his fingers into the dirt before him. "They got to one of my followers first. They beat him until he talked, and they killed him afterward. But not before he suffered."

"They took me away the next day." Rowan rested his face in his hands. "To prove their point, they killed my parents and then my baby sister as I held her."

Rowan rocked back and forth over the

grave, quaking, but he couldn't cry. Collern wrapped his arms awkwardly around his friend while Chard wept openly into the dirt before Rowan.

"That's why you still cry out in your sleep," Chard sniffed, scrubbing at the tears flowing down his face.

"The same nightmare every time I close my eyes!" Rowan straightened his shoulders. "I was so hysterical; they were sure they'd broken me. I had to look at the desecrated bodies of my family for so long, the way they strung them up as reminders."

Chard gasped. Collern touched the boy's shoulder with a sympathetic shake of his head. He shuddered despite the heat, feeling the fury afresh at the memory of those pathetic bodies tied to the glass wall. He gritted his teeth again as he pictured the infant girl as he had found her.

Rowan sighed. "They were right. But when the announcement came about a rendezvous with the SlaveBlock after passing Unata, I saw my opportunity. I'd hoped to just delay the meeting and escape on Unata, but that went horribly wrong."

Chard sniffled. "And they all died," he whispered. "I understand more now," he said, "why Garyn wanted to take you in."

When Rowan looked up, Collern nodded. "You have more in common with our queen than you realize."

Rowan inclined his head, waiting for Collern to continue.

"Do you know why the Gauntlet training grounds are empty?"

Rowan's eyes grew wide. He shook his head. "I found it curious that I had only met one great warrior from the Gauntlet."

Chard piped up, nodding vigorously. "Te-Dasuka's the only one left!"

"Some history, then?" Collern asked. "The kind I wasn't allowed to tell you about when you had your first big lesson?"

"Definitely!" Rowan answered, with a vibrant gleam returning to his eyes.

Collern drank the last of his greendrop and cast the hull into the forest. Then he leaned back against the tree again. "Mother told me a story from when she was very little. The Gauntlet were warrior assassins of advanced skill, beyond even the Weaponmasters. And they were traditionally trained by the Queen and the Head of the Gauntlet. That's why people acted a little weird when Garyn chose to train *you*."

Rowan nodded, suppressing the flush in his cheeks. She had chosen him above all.

"Well, when Garyn Kei was small, her mother the queen died in battle," Collern began. "That left the Throne open for Garyn. But because she was a half-breed, the older Unatans denied her claim. Even after the Royal birthmark—her bloodright—manifested, most of the older warrior men, filed an official challenge against her sovereign right to the Throne."

"But the birthmark is proof she could rule!" Rowan's impression of Unata remained one of a no-nonsense, incorruptible, and unified kingdom. The black-and-white dealings proved a comfort to him. He never thought Unata could be any other way.

Collern smiled and said, "It's not all that simple. The traditional prize for winning the challenge was the Throne. And permission to father Garyn's first-born, to finalize the blood claim through a child as soon as Garyn was physically capable of conceiving."

Chard coughed, a little embarrassed and just as appalled as Rowan with the process.

Seeing their shocked expressions, Collern shook his head. "Hey, listen! It may not be pretty, but it serves a purpose. This kept the powerful Royal Blood alive and prevented any of the warrior women from issuing a challenge. Since characteristics of the dominant Royal Blood guaranteed a daughter from that first union, the cycle continued. It's just genetics, I guess." Collern shrugged and threw his hands in the air.

"How did she handle it, then?" Rowan asked. "She has not birthed an heir yet!"

Collern smiled, "Well, she accepted their challenge."

Chard spoke up, "She told me that none of the old warriors chose to challenge her personally. Their plan was obvious—tradition forced her to select her suitors, requiring the approval of the original old guys." Chard smirked, an odd expression for such a kind boy. "They assumed she'd pick inferior warriors."

Collern ruffled the young man's hair. "Knowing they would reject any challengers they felt she could destroy, she assembled the Gauntlet as her suitors. Of course, the geezers were, ah, surprised at her decision, but they couldn't reject it."

"Mom was there, just a little girl herself," Collern said, his voice lowered by the serious turn the conversation took. "She said Garyn Kei was shivering in the Throne Room that day and just stared at that stone seat. When the fight began, she moved like a war goddess. At just eleven years old, she killed them all. Except for the one Gauntlet who bowed at her feet."

"Te-Dasuka," Rowan whispered.

"I think her half-blood lets her still feel

guilty," Chard said. He cast his eyes to the graves before them. "Te-Dasuka lives only because he refused to go along with the challengers' plan."

"Does that mean he's her suitor?" Rowan asked.

"No," Collern said. "Mom told me the challengers would have chosen a suitor from among themselves, not whichever Gauntlet member defeated her."

"But why did she deliberately kill them all?" Rowan asked, his heart in turmoil.

Collern smiled with real sympathy. "They were in on some deal with the geezers, except for Te-Dasuka. Proving is supposed to be an exhibition series that ends in first blood. But they all turned on her, aiming to win without honor. And because, like you, Garyn wanted to control her own destiny for once in her life."

Rowan slumped as if he had been kicked. The whole thing made a sick sort of sense to him. It really had been Garyn's only choice and she had to act. If she had chosen an inferior opponent, even at her age, she would have undermined the power of her sovereignty. *We truly are alike in that we had to act and risked everything.*

"She really is the most powerful, amazing woman I'll ever know, isn't she?" Rowan said to his friends.

Collern laughed. "Most likely."

Chard beamed at Rowan. The cat-boy leapt to his feet, his tail swinging out to support him. He reached down to give both Rowan and Collern a hand up. "We'd better head back, before that most powerful, amazing woman kills us all for being late!"

"The smartest thing you've said, kitty-cat!" Collern said. He threw an arm around Chard.

"Don't call me that!" Chard said, pulling away in defiance.

"You'll always be a kitty-cat to me, kid!" Collern laughed and headed after the boy.

"See if you can catch up, Cawl-een!" Chard disappeared into the forest then.

Rowan spared one more look back at his family grave-plot and smiled toward his new friends. They would be really surprised when he beat them back to Parisia this time. He chuckled in anticipation, and then headed off at a jog in the near-opposite direction.

14: WHITE NOISE

Maraba excused herself from the Queen after Garyn had forced her absence from important Festival of Proving duties. She insisted that Garyn relax until the Coordinator sent for her, much later in the evening. The Queen smiled and closed her eyes obediently, waving a sudsy hand at the woman to dismiss her. Garyn drifted in the foaming bath, lulled by the heat and soft scents of bath oils. At long last, she fell asleep.

She slipped into a familiar nightmare. Rain poured in a sudden torrent on Parisia. Young Garyn Kei rushed onto the battlefield, screaming, sword in hand as her mother fell at the hands of her powerful adversary. Te-Dasuka's scream reverberated in Garyn's memory, a touching melody of anguish and rage. The enemy who killed the Queen fled from Te-Dasuka, but Garyn moved faster. Garyn slashed at the pirate's heels, severing the tendons just below his calves. He cried out in fear and pain. Crippled, he sprawled on his belly. He turned to her and raised a gloved hand in front of his catlike face. *He's an Empath!* Garyn saw the terror rise in his dark eyes.

"Tell me your name before I kill you," the girl ordered.

"No, please!" he sobbed. His voice grew shrill. "I had no choice. They have my family. They'll kill them!"

"There is always another choice! Because of *your* choice, my mother is dead," Garyn screamed.

She kicked him to his back in the mud. Then she gasped. Garyn's mother had already dealt a severe injury across his stomach. He tried to scramble backward. His heart faltered. The sorrow on his face gave way to defeat. Blood dripped from his mouth and washed away in the swift rain.

"I can't reverse what I did," the man cried over the roar of the rain. "Kill me! I deserve death. I don't have long anyway. But please save my family! I'm all they have. Tell them Chard loves them very much!"

"You're in no position to make requests, *Chard*," young Garyn said, leveling her sword at him.

His last, long look into her eyes pleaded for her help, though she was only a child. *What can I do?* When she brought down the weight of her sword, he closed his eyes, never making a sound as he died. *He killed her, and I can't forgive him.* Garyn avenged her mother with the malice of sorrow, staring into the dead man's face long after his heart stopped. The rain stopped. Everything stopped. *And now I'm all alone.* She couldn't tell if rain or tears dripped off her chin. Then Te-Dasuka knelt before her and wiped the blood from her face. The look in his eyes haunted her.

"Weaponmaster!" yelled a scout. "You're not going to believe what we found."

He turned from Garyn's grief-stricken face to his scout. "Report."

"We found two children, one is a boy

thirteen years old. The girl is around eight."

Garyn roused from her numbness to look at the scout.

"Well?" Te-Dasuka's voice dragged with sorrow.

"Sir, they're *Unatan*!" whispered the scout. "The two children who were kidnapped when those raiders tried to snatch Garyn years ago. They know our language. One's named Dresden."

"Berzo's boy?"

"Has to be," the scout said with a nod. "The girl won't speak to us, but we know she's Gonder's. Dresden says the girl just wants her Chard."

Te-Dasuka's eyes snapped to Garyn. Her jaw dropped. The pirate Chard was a protector and father to lost Unatans. He claimed them as family. Killed to free them. And he killed *her. And I killed him.* Garyn stared in horror at the first man she ever killed. Then she gazed numbly as Te-Dasuka's concerned face blurred. Tears coursed down her cheeks into the mud and gore. Garyn shuddered and fell uncon-scious.

The memory shifted, swirling into the stark walls of the Throne room. Blood surrounded her again and all the members of her mother's Gauntlet lay dead at her feet. The onlookers were gone, and she bawled. Her dream was muddled with indistinct impressions and echoing voices. One voice rose clearly above them all.

"What troubles my Queen?" Rowan—the *older* Rowan—asked.

Garyn scrubbed at her eyes, but her hands came back covered in blood. Sniffling, she turned to look at him. He stood before her, scarred, muscular and calm. Then he knelt before her, took a cloth from his bag and wiped the blood and tears from her face. Adult Garyn's heart raced as she looked through a child's eyes at this man.

"There, now," Rowan said, casting a winning smile her way. "Do you feel better?"

Garyn ducked her head. She couldn't nod. "Rowan?" She searched his face for recognition.

His eyes danced at the mention of his name. His smile faded a bit. Silence.

"I should commemorate this day, right?" Garyn's child voice asked the question.

"If my Queen so wishes," he answered, the softness in his voice full of understanding.

"But, I killed so many!" she cried. Garyn threw her thin arms around the man's neck. He held her tight, whispering comforting words.

"We all have killed," he said, pulling away to look at her. "To protect who we love."

"Ha!" Garyn cried, wrenching away from him. "I protected no one but myself!"

"Darkness hides in us all, Garyn Kei," Rowan said. "And so does greatness."

My words, Garyn thought.

"But there is danger now," he said. "Time for the Valkyrie to fly."

Then he was gone, and bright lights replaced the red of blood. Someone shook Garyn and yelled her name. Her eyes opened on the genuinely concerned face of Maraba.

"I hate it when you sleep like that!" Maraba yelled. "Stupid birthmark sparking, keeping you under for who-knows what reason!"

"Actually," Garyn said with a groan, running a hand through her wet hair. Thankfully, the shaking stopped. But the bath water had cooled significantly. "I think I was in the process of being told to wake up before your arrival."

Maraba's look of worry had nothing to do with her fussiness over the festival. With no apologies, Maraba thrust a thin robe at the queen. As Garyn climbed out of the bath, Maraba paced before her.

"Our sentinels intercepted a garbled transmission," Maraba stated. "Our translator could only make out a bit of the message."

"What bit did they get?" Garyn asked.

She gestured to Maraba to follow her into her ready room. The woman took a deep breath. Garyn stopped toweling off and looked at her Coordinator.

Maraba met her eyes with concern. "Arrival on Unata," she said, "and another word... *slaves*!"

Garyn narrowed her eyes. "Humans, then? Or Gangre-tan? When?"

"The words were corrupted, or the language was unfamiliar," Maraba said. "Plus, our regular analyst is out on Kadray's orders. Some type of sickness in her bones."

"I'll have a listen," Garyn said. She crammed her soak-wrinkled feet into her boots and threw on her royal longcoat. Lastly, she grabbed the ceremonial sword and war fans. "Let's go."

"Slaves!" she said in a harsh whisper. "There's one they won't have, I guarantee it!"

Maraba nodded and handed her the circlet. Garyn crammed it over her damp hair. "Garo's on duty in the transmission tower? The recruit?" She took longer strides to match the taller Maraba's hurried pace.

Maraba smiled pleasantly. "Yes. Dresden says he 'lacks the fighting spirit of a warrior'. He realized it after Garo refused to fight in the Nitch battle."

"He *refused*, huh? It's a shame, though," Garyn snorted. "He's a big boy."

Maraba laughed, releasing some of her worry. "I think he is one of the vomiting-in-fear types. And 'big' doesn't win battles. You know that better than anyone!"

"Short jokes can wait until I've eaten this festival dinner," Garyn said with a sigh. "Up we go!"

She bounded up the circular steps of the communication tower. The two sentinels on duty scrambled to bow as she crashed through the door and demanded to know all they could tell her. Garo, a large young man with a heavy jaw, called her over to the playback equipment. He pointed to the voice spike pattern on the small screen.

"Took me all morning to decode it just so we could get some decent playback," Garo said in a soft voice mismatched to his looks. He jabbed a smaller section of the pattern. "These spikes are overlapping and dropping where other spikes bottom out. Shows that it's damaged. Not live, but a recording, probably from a beacon with a timed playback."

"You can already tell that much just from looking at the visuals?" Maraba said with an appreciative wink. "Not bad for such a short training period."

Garo smiled at her. "Before my reassignment, my specialty was laser engineering and operation. So, the technical side, I understand. The languages, I don't."

With a sigh, Garyn said, "Let's hear the playback. All silent!"

Garo flipped a switch and adjusted the tuning knob. The recording was indeed heavily damaged. The white noise filters could only do so much. Garyn translated most of the message.

"Gangre-tan, with the same high-echelon inflection spoken by Imelda. 'The slaveship signal is gone,'" she said, pausing the playback after each statement. "'No evidence available. Avoid all contact with Unata. Rendezvous with SlaveBlock in seven days.'"

"My Queen, this code took all day to crack, and my trainer says I'm a natural at codes." Garo chewed on a fingernail, staring at the screen. "So if it's just a recorded *retreat* notice, why would they encode it under a class nine encryption?" Garo said, sinking into another desk chair.

"Why, indeed?" Garyn Kei grinned viciously. "Sounds to me like we're expecting company soon."

Garo nodded. His voice trembled. "I-I analyzed the digital components of the message, but none of the new records tell me how to find the timestamp," Garo began. "Since they composed it on an outdated device, I haven't had time to search *older* records, yet."

"Then I'll consult the walking storehouse of records, here." Garyn nodded to Maraba. "She was quite the Comm Tower brat as a child. Garo, I want you to go," she said. "Bring Te-Dasuka here. He needs to hear this. Say nothing to the others!"

Garo leapt to his feet, executed a sharp bow, and turned on his heels. Garyn heard the steel door slip back together in mere seconds. *The boy's fast, at least.* The other recruit stared openmouthed after Garo. Garyn gestured to him.

"Bring me your noteplate and stylus," Garyn ordered. The boy complied. Garyn scribbled briefly on the surface and signed the note. "Take this note to Rowan Jun. Don't stop, and don't speak to anyone."

"Does Milady have a suggestion where to look?"

"He had *better* be back at the recruit barracks by now." She cast him a warning glance meant for Rowan. The boy bowed and ran off with his secret letter.

Garyn stared out the high window of the tower toward the barracks. She focused her strong eyes on the side of the building, where a thin, dark figure leaned against the wall with his arms crossed. *He beat them back*, Garyn thought with a smile. Two winded figures ran through the gates of the training ground, making wide gestures of shock and what appeared to be laughter. When the bobbing figure of the tower boy appeared before Rowan, she turned away.

Maraba set her jaw and stared at the voice patterns. "They didn't expect us to break the encryption, did they? Otherwise, they would have used something better than reverse psychology wording."

Garyn smiled. "Or they may think there's a slim chance that we're smart enough to break the code and even less of a chance that we're stupid enough to dismiss it as a retreat message. They planned on arriving on and leaving Unata before it ever started broadcasting! It's a timed playback to notify their boss of a successful mission."

"If that's right, we either have lots of time or no time. So, we need to focus on the number seven. Seven days?" Maraba frowned.

"A Gangre-tan day is about the same as a Unatan day," Garyn said.

Maraba snorted. She turned the dial back and listened to the beginning of the message again. "Something keeps drawing me back here."

She repeated the first few seconds, cranking the volume to maximum. "Hear that?"

Garyn gasped. "It's the timer blip! These things beep once for every unit of time they are to wait before transmitting. A term transition has no leading timer blips. This *is* old technology! No wonder the kid had trouble."

Maraba dialed up a harsher filter and counted six beeps. "This thing was damaged with six days left. According to Garo's notes, the buoy's location is just inside our farthest sensor range, and *that* is about five days out. So, they've only really been traveling from the beacon for at least one day. Now who's your favorite Coordinator?"

"My Maraba, of course," Garyn smiled, grabbing her shoulder and shaking her.

"And now my head hurts," Maraba said as she plopped into the cushioned office chair. She rested her face in her hands.

Garyn leaned over the small screen again, her eyes narrowed in her calculations. Her fingers drummed on the table. "So we've got some time. Given the signal's point of origin and the timestamp, we know how long it'll take them to get here. We'll assume that they're hostile and prepare, starting tomorrow. Full scans starting in three days, in case their full week was a bluff."

"Not tonight?" Maraba's face was the picture of innocence. Maraba had relaxed with the Queen's decision. But she still held the hint of worry about her preparations.

"And waste all your planning and the good food? Not a chance!" Garyn said with a wink. "I'll let them know after the ceremonies, though."

"Let them know what?" Te-Dasuka boomed from the open door. His short hair stuck out at wet, tangled angles.

Maraba instantly cackled at the old man. She pointed at him. "Looks like you're not the only one who got dragged out of the bath, Garyn!"

"To hear this Garo kid talk, it's war and battle and the end of times!" Te-Dasuka adjusted his belt and tugged his shirt into place. "Doesn't even act like a true Unatan! Doesn't he know that he lives on Fear Planet, the originator of war-terror!"

"I'm sure, my dear Te-Dasuka, that he has been well reminded of terror if he's seen you angry just now!" Garyn said with a winning smile. She walked over and hugged the old man. "I'll not expect him back at post until you've gone, don't worry!"

"If you weren't horribly overworked and under-rested," Maraba began with a smirk, indicating Garyn's fault in his foul mood, "then I'm sure our news would be of greater interest to you."

Te-Dasuka took a few cleansing breaths and relaxed into his controlled demeanor once more. Then they let him hear the transmission and told him their conclusion, with which he agreed. Garyn solidified their plans and dismissed them both for the festivities. Then she headed down to the fairgrounds to take up her traditional post. She was all smiles again, even in the face of the coming battle. She chuckled when she remembered the note she sent to Rowan, sure that it would perplex him more than most things she'd said to him.

15: WARRIOR IN TITLE

Rowan frowned at the thin metal plate the kid put in his hands. The boy bowed politely and scurried off in the direction he came. Folding out the thin plate, he read silently.

Darkness hides in us all, Rowan Jun. But so does greatness! I expect Collern to dine on leather and rubber tonight!

—Garyn

"Whadusitsay?" Chard bounced around like he hadn't just run through half the jungle.

"I don't think I'm supposed to tell you," Rowan answered, clearly confused. He refolded the plate and slipped it into his back pocket.

"Getting love letters on Festival day, huh Rowan?" Collern elbowed his friend in the ribs.

"No," Rowan said. He absently rubbed his sore ribs.

Those types of letters had been coming at inopportune times in the last year, just as Maraba had predicted. Rowan couldn't hide his embarrassment and awkwardness around the Unatan girls. But perhaps he felt so connected to just one woman, he couldn't wrap his head around the others' advances.

"If you keep acting so focused, distant and

mysterious," Collern said with another jab to Rowan's ribs, "they'll *never* leave you alone!" Collern laughed heartily and threw his arm around Rowan's neck. "Ready for tonight's battle?"

"Not yet," Rowan answered. He coughed and struggled in Collern's headlock.

"Getting nervous?" Collern jibed. He poked his face with his forefinger.

"No," Rowan wrinkled his nose, "but you stink like a wet Felzar in summer."

"Hey, now!" Collern said with a laugh, releasing Rowan. "You don't smell like flowers, you know! Maybe it's that manly jungle sweat the girls love so much!" He stalked into the barracks toward the showers, followed by Rowan and Chard.

"I don't think it works that way," Rowan called out to Collern.

Chard asked plaintively for the tenth time, "So are you going to tell us how you got back so quickly?"

Rowan chuckled. "Nope!"

"Rowan!" Chard whined before the door swung shut.

Later, Rowan followed Collern and Chard out to the fairgrounds. He had to adjust the chest strap of his sword holster yet again to accommodate his muscle growth. Then he settled Cainslayer through the wide strap on his back. The great weight proved a comfort to Rowan, who felt naked without the weapon. Against the chill of the evening, he wore a black tunic open to the waist, dark blue pants and black boots. Collern wore his white officer's longcoat with the stiff collar, sleeves removed, and the single notch of Warrior cut into the corners. Chard bounced around them excitedly in his tan trainee uniform.

Rowan understood that many of his fellow pledges would be vouched as warriors tonight, which included a crossing-swords initiation with Queen Garyn. He coveted the symbolic notches on Collern's coat more than he admitted, but since he'd only been training for a year, he knew the goal should be far off.

As the sun sank on the horizon, the sandy mesa housing Parisia cooled noticeably. An alarm claxon sounded the call to order for the festivities, and with the sound, every Unatan rang out in their battle cry. The simultaneous roar vibrated through Rowan's chest. He took up the cry with his brethren. When the noise died down, Collern elbowed him in the ribs.

"Dresden'll vouch for warrior pledges first, then we eat, then the weddings." He had a twinkle in his eyes. "Then current business and special announcements. And then blood matches!"

"Blood matches?" Rowan asked.

"Warriors don't kill each other, and they don't fight during the year," Collern explained. His voice trembled with excitement. "They settle scores honorably through first blood matches on festival day."

"So that's what we're doing?" Rowan asked, a pang of nervousness rising in his gut.

"Yep," Collern said, digging Rowan's ribs with his elbow again. "Mother's got us listed as the last fight." Collern laughed heartily. "The main event, your first time out. Let me show you the platform I designed. Hurry, before Garyn does her kick-off speech!"

Rushing like kids, they wove through the throngs of Unatans who had gathered in the great court. Rowan gaped at the enormous feast tables erected in the huge cobblestone circle. Unata's black and silver banners—streaked in red, the color of Proving—floated on the evening breeze. Torches mingled with twinkling electric lights, casting flickering shadows that lapped at the edges of darkness.

Folks from all over Unata braved the long trip to Parisia—the Herders from the east, Fishers and artisans from the northern islands and western shore, and Farmers from the south. Sporadic dancing, singing and cheering reverberated through the crowd. Even the frail, esteemed elderly and smallest children danced bravely on the border between light's safety and uncertain gloom. Faltering, Rowan felt a firm hand on his arm, dragging him away from the mesmerizing chatter and down a path lit by torches on poles.

He followed Collern to a wide concavity—a small meteor pit—that sank not fifty feet from the border of the old Gauntlet training grounds. The torches around the pit had been placed but remained unlit. He scrambled down the smooth slope to the bottom of the bowl.

Rowan paid no attention as the murmur of the huge crowd slipped away behind them. The platform before him rose ten feet from the ground and curved in a huge circle that covered most of the depression. The sides had been built like a stone wall held with cement. Rowan saw an arched doorway leading under the raised area, and the dim outlines of beams and floor supports. Narrow slabs of stone jutted from the cement, rising along the curve of the platform and forming the lifts of a suspended staircase.

Into the rock all around, the workers had carved bench ledges for spectators, drainage ditches, and two or three alcoves for supplies. Rowan saw a more ornate seat carved on the opposite side, and he knew it must be for the

Queen. As he stood gaping, Collern laughed again.

"I'll take that to mean you like it," Collern said. "Mother told me, 'I'm tired of having them set up a platform every year just to have them take it down a couple days later.' A few years back, Garyn told her to make use of that 'ugly bowl down the hill'. So Mother remembered this crater. And, well, I had a say in the design, at least. And this is what we get. Quaint, huh?"

Rowan shook his head. "Your design is amazing! Maraba doesn't do anything halfway, does she?"

"My mother? Never!" Collern snickered. Then he listened hard. "Crap! She's started, and of course we're late!"

Rowan hadn't noticed how silent the faraway crowd had become until that instant. He turned away from the construction before him and sprinted up the sloping path behind Collern. They both skidded to a stop on the outskirts of the gathering in the middle of Garyn's last sentence.

"...and with each shed life, another is made new!"

Rowan's heart pounded. He stared at his Queen. Garyn wore her full longcoat and metal undersuit, with some impressive ceremonial weapons at her side. Taking an easy stance atop the stone wall surrounding the cobblestone court, she appeared a vision of power and beauty. As the crowd erupted in a cheerful ululation, Garyn's eyes snapped to Rowan. Still holding his eyes, she raised her hands to call for silence.

"Just one early announcement: our *late* arrivals," she gestured to Rowan and Collern, who groaned, "are going to entertain us tonight with my special protégé's first official duel! Good

Festival!"

The warrior chant soon rose above the initial cheering. Men clapped Rowan on the back with good-natured jibes and words of wisdom and wishes of good luck. Rowan felt awkward and gangly, now realizing that every eye followed him to that spectacular platform at night's end. He swallowed hard and managed appropriate responses to the well-wishers.

Still, he felt the prickling embarrassment that reddened his face. Collern basked in the attention. Rowan shrank from it. As the young ladies pushed their ways through the crowd to find him, Rowan pulled Collern in their paths and ducked between the tight press of bodies and back out to the shadows.

He ran through Parisia's streets, having no need of light. When he reached the main wall of the city, he leaned against the cool stones, heaving in the cooler night air. After a low chuckle, he whispered, "I got away."

"From who?" whispered a scratchy voice overhead.

"I should have figured *you* would find me, Chard," Rowan gasped.

"Not that hard," Chard replied. "Now, you sound as loud as Dresden!"

The cat-boy leapt from the roof, landing silently in a smooth motion two feet from Rowan.

"I'm relieved you're on our side, you know? Your stealth is beyond most Unatans." Rowan chuckled a bit and relaxed his breathing. "Thought you were getting ready for vouching tonight."

"That's still a *long* time away. And I'd already seen the platform, so I got bored," Chard explained. "Why do you run away from them? The girls?"

Rowan ducked his head, knowing that Chard could probably sense his embarrassment. Now halfway through his eighteenth year, Rowan still felt awkward around the young ladies of Unata. Most proved strong. Many appeared quite beautiful to Rowan. He didn't understand his feelings.

"They won't bite," Chard said, baring his own mini fangs with his smile. "At least, they *really* like you. Both Collern *and* you are marrying age, you know!"

"But," Rowan said, "they're not..."

Chard giggled. "Not Garyn Kei?"

Rowan blushed and rubbed his hand across his face, mumbling a failed rebuttal.

"Heh!" Chard said, jabbing a finger into Rowan's shoulder. "We *all* love the Queen," Chard thrust out his narrow chest, "and she loves us, too. But if anyone's gonna marry her, it'll be me!"

"Like hell!" Rowan said, playfully shoving the boy. "She doesn't want a pet!"

"What? You think she wants a puny human?" Chard drawled. Then he threw his head back and laughed. He scrambled behind Rowan and shoved him toward the street. "Challenging the natives, tsk tsk. First to be the best warrior, then for the hand of the Queen. That's some ambition you've got!"

"Eh? I just want to save everyone! Is that too much to ask?" Rowan dug his heels in and insisted on walking under his own power.

"Hmph. If anyone can do it, someone with your luck can!"

They jogged back to the court and found the space empty.

"Oops!" Chard said. "I'm going to be late for my own pledging! Dresden will kill me. Let's go!"

The whole of Unata squeezed onto the stone

benches or stood on the bowl floor around the new platform and up the slope leading to the grounds. The torches now blazed merrily on innumerable faces. Rowan politely pushed his way down the slope to get a closer view. When he had resigned to stand, someone called his name over the chatter. Collern and Maraba gestured frantically to him, indicating an ideal seat on the bench halfway up the stands.

Squeezing through the press of bodies, Rowan's saving grace seemed to be the width of his sword and the good festival nature of the Unatans. He felt rather winded when he finally plopped next to Maraba and her son. Maraba had relaxed considerably now that the festival moved smoothly on schedule.

When he couldn't hear their excited words over the sudden warrior cry, he turned to the platform. Garyn stood in the center of the circle, her hands spread in welcome. Dresden and Te-Dasuka stood at attention behind her. Garyn called for silence, and then began to speak.

"Dresden Berzo, Master of Warriors, step forward," she ordered.

Dresden stepped forward, his piercing blue eyes boring holes into the space before him.

"How many pledges do you offer for the rank of warrior this festival?" Garyn asked.

"Fifteen are fit warriors, Your Majesty," Dresden bellowed.

"Call them forward to pledge!" Garyn cried.

A knot of excitement fluttered in Rowan's stomach. He knew he wasn't among the fifteen pledges eligible for warrior status. He just hadn't trained long enough. But he didn't stop hoping that they'd make an exception, just this one time.

"Deruk Sin, come forward!"

Rowan's heart leapt with joy for Deruk. He

cheered loudly, immediately on his feet for his break-group grappler, who'd been training for the better part of ten years with his brother. When Garyn drew her katana and leveled it at the young man, he didn't crumple, but drew his daggers and took a battle stance. Rowan felt such pride at his friend's courage.

When their weapons clashed, Rowan's heart raced. Deruk held his own, and the Queen held back but a little. And after a few tense moments in mock battle, the Queen flicked her wrist and disarmed the boy. An old warrior in the crowd caught one of the daggers as it came flying. Another section dodged the second dagger with shrieking laughter. Garyn sheathed her sword and extended her hand in congrat-ulations. Deruk, as custom dictated, kissed his Queen's hand and knelt before her.

"To pledge Deruk Sin, I hereby grant the title of Warrior!" Garyn announced.

The crowd erupted enthusiastically, and welcomed each of the fifteen warriors in kind. The other three members of Rowan's break-group made their ways across the stage to face the Queen. Rowan made little effort disguising his good-natured jealousy. Collern and Maraba both encouraged him that his status would come in time, with patience and training. But Maraba's eyes glinted mischievously. Or had Rowan imagined that?

Finally, Chard stood before the Queen. A broad grin spread across his face, the joy evident in his sparkling amber eyes. He faced her barehanded. Garyn laughed and tossed her weapons to Te-Dasuka. Both took relaxed beginning stances. From the first strike, Rowan had trouble following their movements. Chard vaulted over Garyn, landing behind her only to duck her swift elbow. He kicked her feet from beneath her, but she flipped away from the strike of his fist. Then something changed about Garyn's movement. Suddenly, she *knew* where Chard would move, and caught him. Garyn pinned him finally, drawing back her fist for a finishing blow. She tweaked his flat nose instead. Standing, she offered Chard a hand up.

"Ha! Made you use your birthmark!" Chard cried as he took her offered hand.

"That you did, my little brat!" Garyn answered. Then she looked down at their still-linked hands. Garyn smiled.

"The day you were born," Garyn said, her voice barely audible, "I swore on the blood of your mother to protect you with my life. And now, you stand here, nearly a man, looking more like your handsome father every day, with as much spirit and heart as the other man whose name you bear."

Dresden cleared his throat quietly and looked away from young Chard toward the sky. Maraba leaned on Collern's shoulder, seeming melancholic for some reason. Rowan caught Collern's stern expression. He gave the signal for 'later.'

Chard knelt before Garyn, still holding her hand. He received full warrior status with her wholehearted approval of his skills. She placed her hand on her fosterling cat-boy's shoulder and dragged him in for a long hug. The crowd applauded for the duration.

As genuinely happy as he felt for his break-group, especially Chard, Rowan's stomach still bottomed out in disappointment. The warmth of the moment cemented Rowan's resolve to reach that platform and bow before his Queen. His heartbeat drowned in the volume of the next announcement.

"And now," Garyn yelled, "we eat!"

The crowd erupted in cheers and started to vacate the bowl. Rowan hung back, staring at the platform. Garyn left quickly, but Te-Dasuka looked intently at Rowan. The stately old man saluted Rowan, who returned the gesture. Then the Unatan took the winding steps two at a time and disappeared into the crowd. The warmth of such a respectful gesture from a man so deserving of his rank comforted Rowan. He knew what he wanted to achieve, and nothing would get in his way!

In the great festival court, the feast cooks piled the huge tables high with redmeat, fowl, fish, vegetables and breads prepared in ways Rowan had never experienced. He suddenly realized the roaring in his belly, since he had left before the cooks prepared their meager morning meal. As he stared stupidly, Collern dragged him to the table occupied by Maraba and Dresden.

The beautiful woman with silver eyes and hair ate with none of the delicacy implied by her looks. Rowan watched her tear through a whole redmeat flank without apology, then she reached for more. Then Collern punched him on the shoulder, shoving a full plate under his nose. The older boy laughed at Maraba's wanton gluttony.

"Garyn told her that she only goes through all this for the food!" Dresden excused Maraba with a smile and a shake of his head.

Dresden alternated looking around expansively with taking small bites. After a few minutes of trying not to notice, Rowan looked down at his plate. His overwhelmed feeling kept him from eating. He sat with the knife in one hand and a fork in the other, wrestling with some unfamiliar emotion that fought to choke him up. He thought it must be happiness, or something like it, but couldn't be sure.

Collern gave him a sharp jab in the ribs and leaned in for a loud whisper, trying to be heard over the roar of people all around them. "Old man won't eat until his recruits eat."

Rowan's eyes snapped to his trainer. He had barely touched his food, either. *Not quite sure why Dresden would wait on me!* Feeling clumsy and insensitive, Rowan tore into the cooling meat on his plate with the same enthusiasm Maraba showed.

After the fire of his guilt ebbed, he tasted the most delicious food he had ever eaten. A relieved Dresden piled on Rowan's second and third helpings. Dresden alone took to eating with gusto surpassed only by Maraba. Maraba paused only for a moment here and there to shove something new in front of Rowan that he "absolutely *must* try." Rowan felt bloated and stuffed when he finally turned away from his fifth helping of meat.

Above the jovial roar of conversation and merrymaking, Rowan heard Garyn Kei's lilting laughter. She had apparently eaten her fill, because she circulated in the role of gracious hostess, waving a half-eaten poultry leg to punctuate her words. In the large group, Rowan eventually lost sight of her. Surprisingly, most of the people fit at the huge tables or were accommodated around the court. He faced forward again, enjoying the laughter and conversation of Collern and Dresden, occasionally joined by Maraba, who had slowed down her eating.

Collern tried to explain to him over the noise that Chard's Empath namesake died twenty years ago and had been Dresden's rescuer and foster parent after off-worlders kidnapped him years before that. Rowan wouldn't have imagined that Dresden lived a life so like slavery. The other Chard must have been an amazing man to leave such an impression on the trainer. There was something else, something important that Rowan still couldn't make out in the conversation. Collern wouldn't speak up on that point. Something about how it was related to the death of Garyn's mother. He'd have to remember to ask again later.

Then the scent of beach lilies and leather flowed around him. Rowan breathed deeply. He turned to see Garyn standing behind their table.

"You're getting good at that, aren't you?" she asked with a smile.

"I am well-trained," Rowan replied with a short bow to his queen.

"You're getting there, I will admit. Quicker than some. Are you ready for your bout tonight?" she asked.

"Perhaps," Rowan patted his belly, "If I have some time to digest first."

"That is a problem," she said, laughing lightly. "Collern, did you intentionally stuff your opponent to gain an advantage in your fight?"

"The thought *did* cross my mind," Collern drawled casually, taking a long draught from his cup. "But after he tasted the stuff, we couldn't have stopped him if we wanted!"

"Surely you saved room for dessert?" Garyn asked.

"Well, no," Rowan answered, feeling particularly inept.

Collern's cackle caught them all off-guard. When Rowan looked around to see what amused Collern, Maraba stared at him, the last bite of a roll halfway to her mouth. Her eyes were round with sorrow and tragedy.

"Really?" Maraba asked in such a piteous tone that even Dresden chuckled. "But it's the best part!"

Though Rowan felt fit to burst, he gave in to Maraba's insistent plea when the cooks brought around dessert. *Just one bite*, Rowan thought as he struggled to take a deep breath. The dessert looked simple enough, even kind of unappetizing—a thick, smooth yellow paste over brown cookies and white fruit. But his "one bite" turned into many. He managed to finish the whole thing. And when he pushed away the plate, Maraba beamed at him.

"Told you," she said.

"I never should have doubted you regarding food, Lady Maraba," Rowan replied earnestly.

Garyn laughed first, then Collern and Dresden, and finally Maraba laughed along. Rowan shook his head but allowed a smile to creep onto his lips. Then the heaviness of his huge meal weighed on his stomach. With the food came an unyielding sleepiness, to which he succumbed, even in such good company. He laid his head on the table. He curled his arm around his head and drifted until darkness replaced the festivities, and silence reigned.

Nitch, the emaciated off-worlder who counted as his first intentional kill, plagued his shadowy dream. The drained look in Nitch's eyes had never been far from Rowan's thoughts. Swinging the sword had been effortless, taking the man's life had been easy. *Of course*, his guilt whispered, *you had already killed before*. The face of his sister filled his vision, her pink, vibrant, healthy cheeks and peaceful, sleeping eyes. Then her eyes opened, and they were black, empty, and haunted. They were the eyes of Nitch. And then little Ayli started wailing. Rowan reached for the glowing Azelan corestone in Ayli's hands, and soon, its light was all he could see. But Ayli still screamed.

16: BLOOD MATCH

Collern's hand on his shoulder awakened him. Rowan jerked upright with a groan. Rowan shook his head and blinked hard.

"Another one?" Collern asked with real sympathy.

Rowan nodded, rubbing at his eyes. "How long have I been asleep?"

"You missed the weddings—there were a lot of them this year—and the current business," Collern said. "Chard looked everywhere for you, but I told him to let you sleep. There's been a transmission that we intercepted."

"What's the message?" Rowan felt the stab of worry. "Another attack?"

"Yes," Collern answered. "But we have a few days to prepare before the ships arrive. We'll be ready. And Rowan?"

Rowan stared at Collern, waiting. Collern's tone went uncharacteristically worried.

"They're high-ranking Gangre-tans," he said softly.

Unbidden, the fury rose in Rowan. The Slavers—the Gangre-tan—made their way to Unata. All the possibilities ran through his mind.

Did they want to search out the lost QuellTruth? Did they know about the lone surviving human? What would they do to his comrades-in-arms? The thought of even one Unatan dying rankled in him.

Collern tapped him on the head with a finger, bringing him around. “Hello?”

“I…I just don’t want anyone else to die,” Rowan growled. “What if they know about the crash? What if they found out about me?”

Collern gave a knowing smile. “I wouldn’t worry about that. So what if they lead the Slavers? You’re a Unatan now. And Garyn’s already decided that you’re more important than a thousand people like the Slavers. We protect our own.”

“But people will die. I don’t want people to die protecting me!” Rowan’s voice shook with rage and worry.

“Yet you’re willing to die protecting us?” He smiled at the paradoxical Rowan. “Listen. They’re bringing the fight to us. They want money, or goods or maybe even Unatan slaves.” He laughed at that prospect. Collern plopped down on the bench beside Rowan. “And we’ll fight to protect our homeland. *We* can’t just avoid fighting because there will be casualties. You know that much.”

Rowan nodded.

“And listen around you,” Collern ordered. “Do *they* sound worried to you?”

Rowan listened. The crowd had taken on an even livelier tone than before. News of impending battle had bolstered morale instead of set them to worrying. *So this is their strength*, Rowan thought, looking around in amazement. *To face the uncertain future without fear.* Rowan smiled, again glad to be grafted into such an enthusiastic race.

"Point taken," Rowan said with a tired smile.

"So, are you fit to fight?" Collern asked.

Rowan sighed, rubbing his stomach. "Ready as I'll ever be," he said.

He stood with a grunt and walked with Collern to the new tournament arena. Maraba had just finished the special announcements and announced the first set of blood match participants.

"Trayba Heronia, Warrior Scout, eldest son of Kaleon the Fisher and Lady Heronia Destine of the traveling Healer tribe against Dron Deresti, only son of Jeshdin the Herder and Deresti Sana, assistant to Te-Dasuka," Maraba said. "First blood wins the hand of Te-Dasuka's youngest daughter, Ikaria, to be consummated in marriage at next year's festival."

Rowan looked to the front of the group. On the sidelines below the platform stood a tiny, frail-looking young woman with shoulder length wavy white hair. She stood dwarfed by the huge man at her side—Te-Dasuka—who stood solemnly. Both men on the platform looked intently her way occasionally. She showed little interest in either of them.

"I remember her from that day at the forge. Is this normal?" Rowan asked. "To raffle off a daughter in the result of a duel?"

"With Te-Dasuka's girls?" Collern chuckled. "It's not so much a raffle. Word has it she told the silly boys to stop competing for her attention and prove themselves worthy of her. She may not look like much, but that Ikaria girl carries the full weight of her father's talent in her blood. If she were stronger, Te-Dasuka would appoint *her* as his replacement."

"As Weaponmaster?"

"Yep. She's not much for fighting, though," Collern said. "But you should see some of her weapon designs!"

A huge uproar signaled the start of the fight. Dron outsized Trayba in height and bulk. He moved quickly enough to keep the other man on his toes. He swung his short swords at the other man's belly. The crowd hissed their displeasure. Going for a kill must be distasteful in the blood matches. The other man stood tall, too, but looked thin and more athletic. Rowan saw the grim set of his square jaw from far up in the stands.

"I met Trayba that day, too. And Dron just graduated Basic. I knocked him out when Nitch controlled him." Rowan cringed. He took a deep breath. "So these guys are going for status?" Rowan asked. That didn't sound right.

"Dron is. Other than fighting, there isn't a talented bone in his body," Collern said with a chuckle. "But Trayba, he's been a scout for Queen Garyn for a few years, personally selected by the Queen to oppose Dron."

Rowan gave him a confused look. Then the crowd roared again. He kept his eyes on the platform while listening to Collern.

"He's liked the girl forever, too," Collern whispered. "And Te-Dasuka doesn't want to 'thin my blood with an uncreative dullard.'" He laughed outright. "No word if Ikaria has a preference. However, if there's no one to oppose a union, then the rule is that it is permitted. She can certainly decline if she has no interest, but if she's indifferent..." Collern shrugged. "Looks like Garyn's throwing in her lot with this one, though, with Trayba."

Trayba dodged another death blow as the

crowd hissed again. Then he rolled upright and sprang to Dron's back, tipping the larger man forward onto his face. With a knee between Dron's shoulders, Trayba deliberately drew his boot knife and cut a shallow wound across the back of Dron's neck. The man grunted. Trayba stood and backed away from his enemy. He wiped the blood from his knife and sheathed it. The applause deafened Rowan.

Dron bellowed his defeat, pounding on the wooden floor. Then with a roar, he retrieved his short sword and lunged at Trayba. Rowan's heart leapt to his throat. Unatans didn't behave like this! Rowan gaped as the floor beneath Dron's feet trembled and quaked. The man lost his footing and went flailing again. Rowan felt a tremor in the stone seat beneath him. *That was odd.*

As soon as the quaking stopped, Dron reached for his weapon again. This time, the floor shook with such force that even Trayba fought to keep upright. From the left side of the stage, Maraba appeared. She stalked across the stage to where Dron tossed and rolled. The movement ceased. She grabbed him by the front of his longcoat and drew his face close to hers with surprising strength. Rowan could clearly see the fury blazing in her silver eyes, even at a distance. He shivered.

"Unatans do *not* kill other Unatans," she screamed into his face.

"He's not been acting right since the corestone controlled him." Garyn leapt to the stage, then approached cautiously. "I'll have Kadray look into it."

At the mention of her father, Maraba's temper cooled. "You've lost your match. Get outta my sight." She flung him down. He scurried across the wooden surface and hit the ground running.

"Haha! Mother hates an unfair fight more than anything," Collern said, unmoved. "That, and wasting food. Scary, huh?"

Rowan nodded. "Did *she* do the thing with the floor?"

"You felt it through the rock, didn't you?" Collern asked. "It's worse when you're standing near her on solid ground. That, and her speed." He shivered. "Has to control that temper at all times."

"Even Garyn was careful with her," Rowan noticed, amazed.

"Garyn's not a fan of earthquakes." Collern scratched his chin. "But mostly, she just trusts Mom not to go too far. Chances are *she'd* have done worse to Dron for breaking the rules!"

Amazed, Rowan stared at the stage again, at the tall man named Trayba. He remembered his first outing, when he ran into Trayba outside the Weaponmaster's building. Young Ikaria had come out and scolded him severely. Rowan shook his head at his memory of her shrieking voice and wondered why Te-Dasuka would approve of such an ill-suited couple.

On stage, Maraba had fully regained her cheerful composure and lifted Trayba's hand in victory. The crowd screamed and whistled. Trayba descended from the stage and walked to where Te-Dasuka stood. He bowed before the old man and his daughter. Te-Dasuka took Ikaria's hand and placed it firmly in Trayba's hand. Te-Dasuka visibly sighed in relief and even smiled at the couple. Ikaria leapt into Trayba's arms, kissing his face.

"She seems to have a preference, after all," Rowan mused.

"Hmph!" Collern shifted on the bench,

clearly irritated. "That's a surprise. She didn't seem all that interested a minute ago!"

Rowan gaped at Collern. "Are you jealous?"

He smiled unapologetically. "You'll have to get to know her. She's really something!"

"You're unbelievable!" Rowan sighed. "Why didn't *you*...?"

"For reasons. Ah, she is a little *too* perfect for me, I guess," he answered, spreading his hands in a placatory way. "I got scared. I screwed up. Besides, it doesn't matter anymore."

Collern inclined his head to where the two young betrothed stood. Rowan heard the tinge of sadness in his voice. Trayba held Ikaria tightly. She wrapped her thin arms around his neck, burying her face against his throat. Collern wiped the hurt from his face and stared at the platform again. Maraba announced the next match and it soon started, taking their thoughts away from sad things. The time flew by with the excitement and drama of fights that resolved year-long quarrels.

Somewhere deep in his heart, Rowan had a nagging feeling. Did anyone else have abilities like Maraba? How did they get them? Also, Unatans released negative emotions quickly. What part of Collern allowed him to hold on to his suffering over Ikaria? Rowan looked from Collern to Dresden. Did Collern inherit his father's traits after all? What a mysterious family!

17: THE GAUNTLET

Then Maraba stood in the center of the platform again. “Okay,” she said with a clap of her hands. “Now we have just a couple more announcements before our final blood match.”

“That’s odd,” Collern said. “Mother never forgets an announcement. Unless...” Then he stifled a chuckle. “I thought something was wrong when you didn’t even get first level warrior after your performance with the off-worlders.”

“What do you mean? I’d only trained for less than a year. *You* admitted that much.” Rowan felt nervous enough over the brief delay in his fight with Collern, without his know-it-all attitude.

Collern sighed. “Just wait.”

“Will the final combatants please come forward?” Maraba sang across the crowd.

Rowan and Collern stood and made their ways toward the platform, amid wishes for good luck. Racing up the suspended steps, they stopped side by side on the platform, facing Maraba. Rowan’s heart pounded. He knew every Unatan must hear it. But he stood at attention, willing his breathing to slow down.

“Tonight, an announcement that is a long

time coming for many," Maraba began. "These powerful young men have a duel for succession. Our underdog newcomer, Rowan Jun, the special trainee of our Queen Garyn Kei, holds my Collern to avowal that Collern must *eat his boot* if Rowan bests him in this friendly fight." Scattered cheers and laughter filled the air.

Maraba let the noise die down. "As you all know, Rowan just arrived this time last Festival, and has made great progress in his training since. But Collern is powerful as well," she said with the doting voice of a mother, "and *he* is eligible next Festival for the esteemed three-notch title of Queen's Guard."

Again, the crowd cheered. Rowan had no idea how far along Collern had come. His nervousness redoubled.

Garyn ascended the narrow staircase, carrying a hide-covered package. Te-Dasuka arrived behind her with a leather-bound, much larger object. Ikaria followed her father.

"First, the Queen's gift for each warrior," Maraba said, "in honor and appreciation for your past service, Collern, and your expert defense against the corestone off-worlders, Rowan."

"Te-Dasuka? Ikaria?" Garyn handed her package to Ikaria as she walked past.

Rowan greeted the two with a bow. He stared at the cross-notch on the hem of his longcoat that marked Te-Dasuka as the Weaponmaster. The Ikaria girl wore a similar longcoat with apprentice notching.

"My Ikaria carved the designs herself," Te-Dasuka said, beaming a loving smile at the frail girl. "Made this gift from smelt to finish. It is only fitting that she presents it to you, Collern."

Rowan stole a glance to his left. Collern awkwardly lifted the package from Ikaria's hands, muttering sweet words that made the girl blush. *And she is cute*, Rowan admitted. Beneath the delicate scars striping her cheek and forehead, Rowan saw a determined, pretty face. Then she shoved Collern and stomped off angrily. *Frail but fiery.* Rowan wondered what Collern had meant about being stupid. She really seemed to hate him.

Te-Dasuka rasped a short laugh. He gave a harsh whisper. “Raise up, boy, and receive your gift. You can ogle her later!”

Rowan felt blood boil into his face. He raised his eyes to Te-Dasuka and clamped his mouth shut. The old man just smiled down at him. Ikaria gazed around her father’s shoulder to look at Rowan. Her indignant face softened when she caught his eyes. He smiled at her long enough to get an elbow to the ribs from the enamored Collern.

Te-Dasuka smiled, shook his head, and laid the long, wide package in Rowan’s hands. Rowan braced against the weight of the object. But his heart beat faster when he realized it was a sword. He stood patiently until the old man laughingly gave him the signal to open it. He untied the leather straps and folded back the leather. Collern whistled his appreciation somewhere to his left. But Rowan only heard something about an axe. He stared in awe at the huge blade he held.

The slab of metal held a silver double-edge, black sides, silver guard and intricate carving down the blade and across the hilt. The carving had been inlaid with red enamel. He heard nothing of the world around him as he recognized the three notch and cabochon design representing the Queen. He traced his fingers along the other, somehow familiar markings. He wrapped his fingers around the solid grip. Of course, it fit brilliantly. And, in testing the weight, Rowan could tell the sword felt superbly balanced, despite its bulk and weight.

"It's Garyn's Royal Birthmark design," whispered a soft voice to his right. He glanced that way. Ikaria smiled up at him.

"You did this?" Rowan asked. She nodded. "Amazing!"

She ducked her head. Then she puffed out her small chest proudly. "Of course I did! If I'm going to take over the shop someday, I *have* to do the best job."

"I can't imagine a better job, Ikaria," Rowan answered, giving Ikaria his full attention for the first time since he saw his sword. His heart pounded. Ikaria's face brightened and her jaw went slack in surprise at the simple acknowledgment. "I'll be honored to wield it!" he announced to Te-Dasuka and Garyn Kei with a bow.

Rowan reverently laid his new sword down before him and pulled Cainslayer from his back. Kneeling before Te-Dasuka, he placed the big old sword in the last remaining Gauntlet member's hands. "Thank you for letting me use her weapon for so long," Rowan said. "She served me well."

"Indeed she did, son," Te-Dasuka said. He indicated the new weapon, which was twice the weight, width and height of Cainslayer. "Her name is Masalikir, the Godslayer," Te-Dasuka whispered.

Rowan beamed at Te-Dasuka. "After Garyn Kei's mother? She meant a lot to you."

"That she did," Te-Dasuka said with a kind smile. "Now do her name justice. I doubt you'll be able to break *this* one."

Rowan bowed before the man and stood. "I

will accept both of those challenges, Weapon-master!" he cried.

The crowd whistled and clapped. Maraba and Garyn both waved their hands erratically to quiet them. When the noise lowered to a rumble, Garyn spoke.

"I provide an additional stipulation," said the Queen. She paused for silence. "The winner of this bout will receive all privileges, honors, and responsibilities as the first member of *my* new Gauntlet."

The crowd paused for a collective intake of breath, letting the news sink in. Rowan gaped at Garyn Kei. He pretended not to notice the moisture in Te-Dasuka's eyes, but the proud smile on his face appeared unmistakable—he supported the Queen fully, as always. Cheers came tentatively at first, and then others took heart. Soon the stadium roared with anticipation. Everyone leapt to their feet, jumping and embracing one another. Rowan felt as if the Queen's announcement had begun a healing ripple in her people. She brought the taboo to light in reestablishing the Gauntlet.

And then Rowan felt stupid. He blinked again and again. Rowan fully realized the offer she extended. To be a part of the legendary Gauntlet, he only had to defeat his best friend, who had trained his entire life. Without killing him. With a weapon he'd never used. Suddenly, all the nervousness and worry, all his awkwardness, even the weight of extra food in his belly faded. His heart returned to a strong, steady beat.

Collern picked up on the change in his opponent. The broad smile faded from Collern's lips into an intensely focused glare. Rowan hadn't seen his friend in such a state before. But he still wasn't afraid. The Gauntlet lay before him. He didn't want it for status, honor or privilege. He would ascend to the Gauntlet for the power to protect his Queen and his fellow Unatans. Even Collern could not stand in the way.

Rowan lifted Godslayer high overhead, his arms straining against the weight. The crowd cried out in the Unatan war chant. The platform shook with the cry's reverberation. Across the platform, Collern dipped into a battle stance, with his old battle axe in his right hand and a thin, light axe in his off hand. When the platform cleared and Maraba signaled the beginning of the fight, the arena vibrated beneath his feet.

Collern flanked him in the next second. Rowan hefted the sword to the side, knocking away the old battle axe with the flat of his blade. With each deft movement of the extensively-trained Collern, Rowan managed to block him. Collern fought expertly while duel-wielding the axes, catching Rowan off-guard. They fought and clashed, neither one gaining ground for the better part of an hour.

Attack as he may, Collern never received a return blow. Yet Collern never backed off in arrogance. He knew his opponent too well. Rowan just waited for an opening.

Rowan felt inefficient swinging a sword much heavier than Cainslayer. Soon he ached all over just trying to fend off Collern. But he soon had a feel for the sword, struggling though he did against the constant weight. He wanted to be quicker. Otherwise, sheer will would have to win the fight. By the time Collern realized that Rowan used his attacks to acclimate to his new sword, Rowan went on the offensive. Then the real battle began.

Another hour later, Rowan twisted his

sword and cut clean through the inferior metal of Collern's favorite battle axe. Collern was quick to change weapon hands and avoid the huge blade that could have cost him first blood. On a fluke, Collern lost his footing and slipped to the ground in the path of the Godslayer's downward swing. He flung the new axe on a long, spinning arc toward Rowan. As Rowan's sword sliced into Collern's exposed shoulder, the thin axe made a razor cut across Rowan's chest.

The crowd sank into stunned silence, waiting for the official ruling. Meanwhile, Rowan dropped his sword and ran across to check on Collern's wound. Blood flowed, but Collern began to laugh.

"Stop! You're hurt, too!" Collern shoved him away. "Damn, you cut me deep!"

Rowan noticed the burning in his chest. Collern's new axe held such an amazing thin edge, he hadn't even felt the wound until then. And for such a thin cut, it bled profusely.

Maraba cackled from across the platform. "*That* was fun. Whaddaya say, Garyn?"

"*Definitely* a draw, I'd say." Her eyes held the mischievous twinkle of a woman with a plan.

"Second a draw!" said Te-Dasuka, having snatched the spinning axe from the air.

"A draw it is!" Maraba announced. Then she whispered to Garyn, "I guess we're starting out with two new Gauntlet members, huh?"

Garyn smiled. "I guess. It'll give the old man something to worry about, other than his eventual Weaponmaster replacement."

Basking in the announcement, Collern pulled the medpack from his hip. Rowan wouldn't stop apologizing, though he cringed with each apology. Though Rowan expected him, Dresden didn't descend to punish him for these apologies.

Rowan saw nothing of Collern's prior intensity in his friend's smiling face. Collern grinned up at him and flung his searingsalve at Rowan's head. Rowan caught the tube. Collern gestured emphatically at the blood dripping all over 'his' new platform until Rowan took the hint and began to close his wound.

"Stop being so modest," Collern gasped for air. He tried to chuckle, but coughed violently instead. "Never saw you that focused. If you were using Cainslayer, I'd've been down ages ago."

Te-Dasuka offered Rowan and Collern up as Gauntlet trainees later that night, grumbling that Collern may finally do something more suitable with his life than lazing about in the lower ranks. Especially since he would have Rowan to teach him about real dedication. Collern laughed off Te-Dasuka's teasing.

Garyn officially bestowed crossing-swords honors with a delighted Rowan. He even delighted in her complete and utter victory over him. He delighted in bowing before her and receiving her blessing to train in *her* Gauntlet.

Then the music and laughter rang through the night, into the uneasy hours of the morning. They all slept soundly. Upon waking, they would prepare for the next battle for Unatan peace. As the Queen says, there is no excuse for living life unprepared.

18: PRIMORDA

Thirty enemy ships burned into the atmosphere at sunset and glittered on the horizon, heading straight toward the Parisian mesa. Hordes of festival attendees delayed their return home to join the regular Parisian forces, all still gathered in the great city. All Unata's finest warriors stood armored and assembled, awaiting orders and battle. Maraba issued some instructions to a battalion leader, stabbing a finger in several places on her chart. Then she arrived at Garyn's side.

"That's a lot of ships for a mere inquiry, no?" Maraba said to Garyn.

"Mmhmmm," Garyn responded. The queen stared westward at the advancing ships, swinging her war fan to and fro from her finger. She tucked her helmet under her arm and turned finally to Maraba.

"Your scouts should be in place any moment," Maraba said. "The break-groups are in order as well. I have it on good authority," Maraba paused, and Garyn knew she spoke of Dresden's bragging, "that Chard is handling leadership of

Rowan's group admirably. Or so I'm told."

Garyn smiled, though her eyes drifted back to the horizon. "In just two days. Of course. That boy oozes tenacity. He wouldn't dare fall any farther behind Rowan."

Maraba laughed. "Speaking of which, where *is* the Gauntlet?"

"Each is delivering a very important message for me," Garyn said.

Her cryptic grin sent Maraba into giggles. "All three of them? Errand boys?"

Garyn shrugged, already settling into the quiet calm before pending war. She closed her eyes. The ships would arrive in moments. Te-Dasuka and Collern would return in time, but Garyn doubted that Rowan could make it so quickly. She had sent him much farther than the other two. Her heart fluttered in the odd worry she stifled with resolve. He knew the jungle better than any of the others. She had no reason or room for silly emotions involving Rowan. He remained strong and battle-proven, and well-trained. A fine Unatan.

Te-Dasuka and Collern arrived in unison, announcing their successful missions. The older man looked winded but managed a clear report that the Queen's Guard would serve as decoys for the stealth team. Garyn appreciated the composed stature of Collern. He hadn't even broken a sweat after all the running. His Gauntlet training would do wonders for him now that he had proper motivation.

Collern smiled. "Team Leader Chard gladly accepts your challenge for enemy scout interception and execution. He is suited in stealth blacks as we speak, and his team members will provide support. He is posted at the southern city wall."

"Good," Garyn said. "We know what the enemy will *say* they want. Now we'll figure out what they *really* want. What reports do we have from the Comm Tower?"

"Majesty!" gasped Garo as he arrived before her. The big boy wrung his hands. "Interceptions indicate that their fleet numbers thirty-*two* ships. Thirty are those non-civilian warships. The remaining two," Garo glanced away and bit his lips together.

"Get on with it, kid! Time is running out," Garyn ordered.

He buckled under her glare, then looked into her eyes. "The remaining two are their mothership, SlaveBlock, and a civilian support vessel. They brought their actual *slaves*!"

"Will they land?" Maraba asked.

"No, Ma'am," Garo answered. "They've been ordered to orbit and not an inch closer. They don't want to lose any more *precious cargo*."

Garyn saw the stirrings of real anger in the meek boy. She nodded her acknowledgment. "You've done a good job, Garo. The slaveship and civilians are out of our reach to help, then. Transmit the location of SlaveBlock to our friends in the Alliance, so they can catch them at their illegal trade and arraign them. But, now, we'll make sure our opinion is clear on their *business*. Dismissed!"

She flicked her fingers toward the communications tower. Garo executed a brief bow, then fled back toward the security of his post.

"It's about time," Maraba said with a sigh. "You sure you don't want to talk to them first?"

Garyn gave it the briefest consideration. Garo reported no attempts to contact Unata for peaceful negotiations. The Slavers even ordered their cargo ships to the safety of orbit, knowing there would be conflict. And they brought a *fleet* of Gangre-tan warships. The sparkling dots on the horizon took on large angular shapes flying in a tight formation that threatened to blot out the sky.

Garyn shrugged and pointed. "*We* know those are warships. *They* thought we'd be defenseless. Shall I offer to let them surrender now?" Garyn gave Maraba a challenging smile.

Maraba arched a pale eyebrow at her Queen and best friend. Then she shook her head. "Oh, well. I should have known better."

"Ready the anti-spacecraft lasers," Garyn called out to her gunmen. "When they're calibrated, we'll fire a warning shot. And by 'warning shot,' I mean shoot down the first wave of ten ships before even one of those green-skinned bastards can set foot on my dirt!"

The Unatan battle chant vibrated the ground beneath Garyn's feet. "When those ships are down, the first battalion will descend on any survivors from the wreckage." The loud affirmative from that battalion sounded. "That'll cut our enemy by a third. The second barrage of lasers should get the second third of enemy ships. Destroy, decimate and demoralize them! If we have any luck, their leaders will be foolish enough to be among the casualties."

"Garyn, we've only got two rounds of laser to shoot before the weapons have to recalibrate," Maraba said.

"I know," Garyn said with a grin. "I'm counting on our unwelcome company to start their ruse at that point. They don't know we can't fire a third time, so it'll get them shaking. Don't worry. I have a hunch."

Garyn winked at Maraba, who threw her

hands up and stalked off, yelling for a percent-charge on the lasers. Receiving her requested report from the head-gunner, Maraba went about her feigned angry spell until she felt assured that all preparations were in place. She returned to Garyn's side as the gunmen prepared their first assault on the incoming enemy forces.

"Fire!" cried Garyn Kei.

* * *

Rowan ran beneath the canopy and soon descended into the Lower Jungle along an oft-traveled path. Garyn had told him that the recipient would find him, as long as he held the scratch plate tucked into his belt. But even with an imminent war on his mind, he couldn't imagine how that would work. Nor did he realize that any Unatan lived in that part of the Lower Jungle. Rowan hated doubting the Queen, so he dove through the undergrowth obediently, merely concerned with meeting the one in question as soon as he could.

A rustling up ahead stalled his movement. The footsteps sounded nothing like any animal on Unata. He had been careless, with his loud running along a direct course. But Garyn had not ordered a stealth mission, so he had figured that silence didn't matter. He skipped aside and leapt to the low branches of a great tree, glad for once that he at least wore dark clothing in the canopy-shaded twilight. He crouched on the branch and gripped the handle of Masalikir. Rowan waited to attack.

A loud, demanding voice rang out through the trees. Rowan's heart skipped and he felt faint. The Slavers—no, these *Gangre-tan*, Rowan corrected himself—had arrived separately of their main convoy. Perhaps the QuellTruth had a homing beacon, to bring them to the Lower Jungle? They'd wandered far off course. Also, they would have no need to take such a long route to Parisia. But then again, Rowan already knew their radio transmission had been coded, meaning they were planning something from the beginning.

Rowan patted the message plate in his belt, feeling the first pangs of worry. What if they already found the person to whom Garyn's message was addressed? Rowan clenched his jaw as the first of the Gangre-tan scouts broke through the undergrowth onto the path. They yelled again, and Rowan knew they had heard him. He recognized the dialect. He didn't answer.

The large green creature walked erect and proud, clothed in an odd assortment of bright fabrics. His long braids swept forward as he breathed deeply of the thick jungle air. Rowan ducked silently out of sight. Sure they hadn't seen him, Rowan looked for a silent path down the back of the tree so he could gather as much information about them as possible. He briefly contemplated an attack since he held the element of surprise. More and more Gangre-tan scouts poured onto the path behind him. With such a large group, and with the enemy carrying projectile weapons, Rowan wouldn't be at an advantage for more than two kills.

A muffled shot rang through the air and splintered the wood two inches from his nose. Rowan tensed in surprise. Was that just a lucky guess?

"Come out, spy!" said the nameless scout leader. "We'll not have you hindering our mission."

"What mission?" Rowan snarled in their

tongue, moving quickly and silently from his current position.

"Well, your anger is justified," the Gangre-tan said. "We did fire on you without provocation. And I suppose we *are* trespassing."

The other scouts grumbled, and one leaned in to whisper to the leader. "My colleague is curious about your knowledge of our language. Also, we're looking for a ship that we lost in this area. Perhaps you can assist us?"

"Perhaps," Rowan answered. He couldn't run away now. He stepped around the base of the tree and settled Masalikir on his back again. Matching the Gangre-tan's dialect, Rowan said, "If you can provide an acceptable answer as to why you came uninvited and unannounced to this place."

"You're—not Unatan! And you're barely a boy!" the leader said with a sigh.

"You shouldn't judge me so easily, off-worlder!" Rowan growled. "Since I'm the future champion of Unata."

The man laughed. "One your age should give up childish dreams! A weakling, a *human* by the looks of you, making such bold claims in *this* world!" Then he glared at Rowan. "You entertain me. It's a shame you'll never leave this place to accomplish that dream!"

He made a ready gesture to the men behind him and then signaled them to fire. Rowan ducked and rolled to the leader, sidestepped his long dagger, and drew Masalikir across the Gangre-tan's throat. He held the man up as a shield against the raining bullets. The larger, dumb underlings shot their own leader. Rowan backed against the trunk of a huge tree, tying their hands against a counterattack.

The Gangre-tan leader coughed up dark

blood and cursed the shortcomings of his group. He struggled in Rowan's viselike grip but grew weaker. Rowan stared at the dumbfounded Gangre-tan scouts. He could smell their fear.

"Now tell me what you *really* want from Unata," Rowan demanded. "Before you die, give me your name and your mission!"

"Bastard! Human bastard!" the man cried and broke down in a fit of coughing. "The ship..."

Rowan clamped his teeth shut. Then he leaned in close to the dying Gangre-tan. "The Slaveship QuellTruth crashed here. I am the only survivor. I killed *every* living slave."

The Gangre-tan twisted his face around to Rowan's. The look of shock on the scout leader's face settled into wary belief as he considered the telling expression on the young human's face.

"I...I see." The man gave a grim chuckle that turned into a wet cough. "We didn't have a chance from the beginning if *you're* one of the weak ones! Then it can't be helped. I'm Lieutenant Deker in the Gangre-tan scout division two. We're after the orichalcum."

"The new metal?" Rowan asked, glancing at the length of Masalikir. "How did you find out about it? What do you need it for?"

A solid impact rammed into Deker's body, knocking Rowan solidly against the tree. Deker's chest splattered all around Rowan. The Lieutenant slumped to the ground. Rowan scrambled to his feet and swung his sword all around him, slicing through each of the gun nozzles aimed at him. The disarmed Gangre-tan scouts trembled and scattered. Then he sought the source of the heavy shell weapon that killed Deker.

A large man stood under the weight of a large weapon. He wore muted colors and his steel-gray braids tied behind his back. Rowan saw the dark green organic plate armor through the open front of the flowing robe. "I am Captain Berisson. And we *need* the orichalcum to wage a grand war, little human. The QuellTruth was a minor financial loss, in comparison." Berisson chuckled. "Is that true about the slaveship? Well, Imelda was a sentimental fool, after all! Figures he'd let something like this happen."

Rowan fought the perverse desire to defend the Slavemaster. To have his ordeal dismissed as a mistake of sentimentality infuriated Rowan. But he forced himself to stay silent and focused. More Gangre-tans poured out of the forest—larger, stronger men. Among them, only the Captain had the refined features of an Elite. Still, Rowan stood steadfast.

"All that loss of cargo caused by a silly, weak human!" Berisson said. "It's a good thing that the manufacture of orichalcum will make this side excursion more lucrative than the slave trade ever did!"

"How did you find out about it?" Rowan demanded. "Tell me!"

"So impatient to die, little human?" Berisson asked. His yellow eyes crinkled in amusement. His crooked smile wavered at the look in Rowan's eyes.

"If you want orichalcum that badly, I'll give you a taste now!" Rowan settled the Godslayer before him and strode toward the larger man.

"Haha. So, the rodent turns on the cat," Captain Berisson said. "Men, don't interfere!"

Rowan's first strike left a long nick in the huge gun Captain Berisson wielded. *If only I were stronger, I could have cut through it!* Rowan dodged a heavy kick from the Gangre-tan warrior and swung Godslayer at his ankles.

Even in his battle-focus, Rowan heard the Gangre-tan scout to his right cry out in terror. He stole a peripheral glance. The man was gone. Forcing himself back to his fight with Berisson, he ignored the sounds of scouts disappearing right and left. Something zipped them away into the forest and silenced them in seconds, until the shrieks sounded monotonous.

"What the hell is going on in this jungle?" the Captain bellowed, finally pinning Rowan to the ground in his distraction. "Tell me now, human, or die!"

The unarmed seven that Rowan first attacked were all that remained of the original group, and barely ten of Berisson's men. They huddled in terror. Rowan had no answer for the off-worlder. Was Chard out there in his stealth blacks? Had Collern followed him? No, they were given specific missions that directly protected the Queen. Rowan still sought an answer for the man and himself when he heard deep, soft breathing from the forest ahead. The breathing rolled into a snarl that increased in pitch to an unnerving hum. Rowan gathered his senses enough to roll out of Berisson's grasp. But he pulled Masalikir in front of him and stared beyond the Gangre-tan man to the suddenly still forest. Only the rolling hum remained.

"Tell me, now!" Berisson demanded. "Where are my men?"

Raspy chittering surrounded them and blended with the humming. Rowan heard small things moving in the branches. Then a bloody pile of bones and flesh splattered on the ground between them. Rowan bit his lips together. *Well, that answered the Captain's question.* His pulse quickened with fear. Sure that some creature would claim him next, he kept his eyes on the forest behind Berisson.

Then a shadow loomed behind Berisson and blocked the fading sunlight. The creature's head reached nearly to the canopy. Its arched neck and wide body pushed aside large trees, snapping some like they were mere twigs. Rowan trembled on his feet.

Captain Berisson turned from his human enemy to face the new arrival. On impulse, he fired the huge weapon over and over at the huge creature. The creature squealed in pain. When his weapon only clicked, he threw it down and took up a smaller weapon. His remaining ten men took heart in their leader's actions and fired on the creature as well. The smaller ammunition proved ineffective against the creature's thick hide. It swiped the ground with a huge forepaw armed with talons as long as Rowan's leg. Another two swipes and most of Deker's men and all of Berisson's men fell, either maimed or dead. Two of Deker's men screamed into a handheld communication device about monsters and killings before two smooth green heads snapped out of the undergrowth and ended their cries.

Berisson managed a final reload of the big gun during the loss of his final men. He emptied it once more on the creature just as Rowan got a handle on his terror and recognized her by description. Rowan lunged at the man, knocking him headlong toward the creature. She promptly sank her talons into his back and smashed him into the forest floor.

She took two graceful steps forward and lowered her great head before Rowan. He trembled before her, struggling to keep his footing. Her eyes sparkled with cool violet. Rowan dropped his sword and stared in awe of the creature he had never seen before that day.

"P-Primorda!" Rowan managed. He bowed before the mother of all Chimeras.

Primorda snorted and her hum reverberated in a questioning tone. Rowan raised his eyes to hers again. Her head easily the length of Rowan's whole body, she sniffed and exhaled, keeping an intelligent eye trained on the human. Primorda snaked her head around behind Rowan and gently nudged where Rowan had stored the scratch plate.

"*You're* the one who would find me," Rowan said, gulping in fear. "I wish Garyn Kei had been a bit more specific."

He retrieved the plate and held it out for Primorda to inspect. She sniffed the plate and looked at Rowan expectantly. Rowan got the feeling she needed him to open it, so he did. He stared at the plate with wide eyes. There were no words on it. The surface had been smeared in blood. If he guessed right, the blood belonged to Garyn Kei. But why?

Primorda flicked out her pink tongue and tasted the substance. Her hum rumbled in her throat. All around the path, the undergrowth came to life with movement. Juvenile and older Chimeras spilled out onto the pathway, ranging from four feet to eight feet tall at the shoulder. Many of the larger ones had the beginnings of wings developing at their shoulders. Traces of dead Gangre-tan scouts dripped from their muzzles and claws. Two Chimeras that rivaled the size of their Sole-Mother arrived at each side of Primorda. Rowan noticed something catching in her breath. His eyes followed the spiny curve of her neck. The dim light finally revealed Primorda's full extent of injury. Dark blood gushed out of her chest, sides and neck. The Gangre-tan special weapon had punctured her lungs as well.

"Oh, no! You're hurt!" Rowan cried. He rushed toward her side. "We have to stop the bleeding or you... you'll die!"

If the great Sole-Mother of the Chimeras didn't speak directly to Rowan, she at least hummed a sorrowful tune for him. Rowan laid his hands on her sides and fumbled for his medpack. The blood came out in such volume that his small medpack couldn't even stem the flow of one shell wound. Rowan fell to his knees before her, daring to lean against her neck. He cried hot tears of frustration.

"But you did *this* saving me!" Rowan cried. "I don't want you to go! Not like this!"

Primorda drew her form up and leaned back, trying to get a better view of the little human. She breathed deeply at his face and finally lapped at his tears. Her hot breath and warm saliva smelled like the forest after a long rain. Then she nuzzled him with her spiny muzzle. He draped his thin arms across her broad nose and tried to control his pounding heart. Rowan felt the ache in his chest, and something else, a billowing swell of peace. *I knew I would die someday, silly.* He looked up into her glowing eyes, having felt the words from her rather than heard them. *Better doing this than nothing at all!*

One of the juveniles dragged Rowan's sword to him with great effort. Pushing away from the wounded Primorda proved difficult, but he managed. Rowan finally reholstered the weapon and thanked the little creature. A much larger Chimera trotted up beside him. Smaller than the two with Primorda, this one had familiar glowing violet eyes that matched her mother's and broad wings tucked by her ribs.

"You're from the QuellTruth, aren't you?

You've grown!" Rowan's realization startled him. He inhaled deeply. Rising above the scent of blood and the other Chimeras flowed a familiar musky scent, unique to this Chimera. "And *you* followed me when I was blind in the forest, didn't you?"

She paced near him. She nudged his hand and released it on her shoulder, moving her body toward him. Her spirited insistence encouraged Rowan to climb to her back. He rubbed his eyes with the back of his arm, then turned to Primorda for permission. She snarled an encouragement. He pressed his lips together and nodded to Primorda, his heart rent by her sacrifice and great honor.

Rowan mounted and flipped his sword sideways. He had barely grabbed onto the Chimera's neck crest before she flitted into the jungle, back toward Parisia. The trees blurred; twigs snapped over Rowan's face. Though determined to maintain his somber battle-readiness, his heart rose at the thrill of the ride. Somewhere in the distant back of his mind, he remembered Collern's dream of capturing and riding a Chimera. Rowan sighed, sure that he'd have to contend with Collern's envy.

Soon, Rowan settled into the swift rhythm of the Chimera. He had nearly adjusted to the speed as well, until they neared the cliff base that led to the Upper Jungle and Parisia. When the Chimera gave no indication of slowing down, Rowan's heart leapt into his throat. Rowan heard the creature's insistent croon. His hands convulsively tightened on the mount's neck ridge.

Fifty feet from the base of the plateau, the Chimera leapt straight at the rock face. She landed on a foot-wide ledge nearly a hundred feet in the air and continued hopping from ledge to ledge until she ran out of footholds. Then, with

Rowan clinging to her neck and screaming every breath, she leapt straight up and cleared the final hundred feet with the mighty pumping of her undeveloped wings. As soon as her feet hit solid ground again, she barreled ahead along the narrow path toward the city.

She nickered again at Rowan. His heart pounded almost too loudly to hear her. He managed to loosen his death grip on her neck and settle onto her bare back again. But as the many gorges, ravines, precipices and high rocks presented themselves in their path, his stomach flopped. She bounded over the wide cracks in the plateau and used tree trunks and branches as bridges and springboards. She glided with her wings over one ravine. Rowan held on through it all, deciding that maybe he would rejoice in battle for once, just so he could get his feet on solid, unmoving ground once more.

Finally, the great perimeter wall of Parisia loomed in the last rays of sunlight. Smoke and fire rose from the grounds in unsettling quantities. Rowan gritted his teeth and, for the first time, urged the Chimera forward even faster. She hummed in pleasure, leapt over the wall with ease, and set out by scent to find Rowan's goal: Queen Garyn.

* * *

"Ah, I see he's made it back in record time," Garyn said with a cackle. She beheaded one Gangre-tan and slit the belly of another. "Making an entrance is starting to become a habit of his, I fear. But he's only a few minutes later than our 'breakdown of negotiations'."

"What 'negotiations', Garyn?" Maraba asked. The ground beneath several enemies rumbled and quaked. She stabbed her rapier into the midst of the Gangre-tans. "You just told them that you hoped they didn't think you were 'stupid enough to believe their petty lies' and signaled the attack."

"Mmhmm. Negotiations," Garyn said, punctuating with a swipe of her war fan.

Rowan's Chimera dove into the midst of seventeen low-level Gangre-tan warriors and scattered them. She reared up, pawing in front of her, talons flying, then turned to kick two warriors with her back feet. Rowan sat upon her back, swinging the Godslayer to and fro, slicing through enemies with reckless abandon.

"He's back already?" Collern asked, wheeling about, looking for Rowan. "That *bastard!*" Collern cried, gaping and instantly overtaken with the worst kind of jealousy. He swiped with his new axe. A Gangre-tan fell with a thud. "On a frickin' *Chimera*? That's it! He'll answer for *that* after this war!"

Rowan dismounted and stalked past the defeated enemies to where the Queen fought. The Chimera followed close behind him, turning her violet eyes on the enemies. Some of them cowered and hung back, too injured to move. The battle lulled for a moment as the enemy attempted to regroup for a counter offensive.

"Your message has been delivered, my Queen," Rowan reported at attention. "And all the enemy scouts who searched for the QuellTruth have been defeated."

"I guessed as much," Garyn said. "Where is the recipient of my message?"

Rowan lowered his head, intensely regretful. "She took heavy fire. She may dead by now, severely injured while protecting me."

"Are you sure about that?" Garyn asked as

three gliding shadows blocked out the last rays of sunlight.

"Primorda!" Rowan screamed. Rowan's Chimera trilled a greeting, torn between staying by Rowan's side and running to her mother and sisters.

"No, little one," Garyn said to the creature. "She wants you to stay here, with him, where it's safest."

Garyn Kei heard the shrieking of the enemy before she saw the reason. Primorda and her daughters returned many of the dead Gangre-tan scouts to their brethren, in pieces, one bloody regurgitation after another. Even Garyn had a rough time watching them. She turned to Maraba, who stared, mouth agape.

Their diversion effectively muted the enemy's morale. After knocking aside enemies, the three Chimeras descended on the enemy ships and large guns, tearing the metal apart and gashing through spaceship hulls with their talons. The Gangre-tans cowered and fled in terror.

Rowan reflexively placed his hand on the Chimera's shoulder to comfort her, even though his stomach turned. Primorda trembled, in horrible shape. He could see her weakening with each rake of her claws. The Gangre-tans fired on her and her two large daughters, switching to the larger guns when the smaller ones proved ineffective.

Primorda gave the Unatans time to recover and move their incapacitated injured to safety. She gave Garyn and Maraba enough time to plan the final phase of the battle. She died slowly and in agony. Rowan wanted to run to her.

"She chose this path long ago, Rowan," Garyn said. She hoisted a heavy pole bearing the red, black and silver flag of Parisia. “Primorda doesn’t really fight for me out of fear. She made her pact with my Grandmother, to protect Parisia and the Queen of Unata whenever she spills her blood.” Garyn showed him a white bandage on her palm. “This war is beyond us, alone, even after destroying two thirds of our enemy before we ever met them.”

“So she chooses to fight to her death?” Rowan fought back those hot tears again. “I don’t want her to feel like she’s fighting alone, then.”

Rowan drew his sword and headed toward the largest fray of enemies.

“She won’t!” Garyn called out. A messenger interrupted Garyn and delivered a hasty message. Garyn furrowed her brow and sneered. “Bastards!”

“Another scout team?” Maraba asked. Garyn nodded.

“Rowan, let Maraba handle it!” Garyn said. Maraba turned to follow the Queen’s orders. “I have an assignment that requires speed. Chard needs you!”

Rowan set his jaw and frowned. Rowan stared at the painful scene of destruction and the snuffing out of a powerful life. Then he turned away from Primorda. Chard lived for now and needed him.

“Maraba,” Rowan said, touching the woman’s arm, a horribly pained expression on his face. “Tell her thank you for me. I didn’t thank her!”

Maraba nodded and jogged across the field toward the majestic creature.

“We’re okay here, for now. The enemy is trying to escape,” Garyn said. “Take Collern and go.”

Rowan received Garyn’s instructions and

turned to Collern. He stared up, all sparkly eyed, at the Chimera that followed Rowan. She ducked her head, indicating they should ride. Rowan thanked her and climbed to her back. He gave Collern a hand up behind him.

"I'd talk about how awkward or cool this is," Collern said, looking for something to hold on to, "if I didn't want to kick your ass because of it. You don't think I'd forgive you, just like that, do you?!"

Rowan shook his head. "I wouldn't imagine it." He spoke to the Chimera, giving her directions to the Weaponmaster's private home, where Chard had encountered enemies.

Then the Chimera raced onward through the city at twilight, easily skirting the wreckage and outdistancing any enemies, until they arrived at the darkened dwelling of Te-Dasuka and Ikaria.

19: BEROKON

"You expect me to believe that you, the Weaponmaster, have no knowledge of it?" bellowed the larger man.

"I didn't say *that*," replied Te-Dasuka in an even tone. "I simply said that you'll hear nothing about it from me."

"Do you know what it means to be an Admiral among the Gangre-tan Elite?" the man asked, punctuating his question with a firm backhand across Te-Dasuka's cheek. "I'm Fleet Admiral Berokon du Loche, and I will get what I came for!" With each word, he struck Te-Dasuka a solid blow to his unprotected face.

"I don't care if you're God Himself." Te-Dasuka spat blood in the man's face. "I'll pass that secret on to one man before I die, and it sure as *hell* won't be you!"

"Have it your way, pathetic old fool," Berokon seethed, his low voice full of warning. He pulled a metal object from his belt pack and drew it onto his right hand. Blunt spikes lined the knuckles of the heavy glove. "I'll beat the truth out of you!"

"Heh. Heheh." Te-Dasuka coughed once. His

eyes twinkled when he set them on Berokon. "Only one person could ever do that, and all *she* had to do was ask, Gangre-tan bastard!"

The blunt spikes crashed into the side of Te-Dasuka's head. He grunted in pain, reeling in the chair to which they tied him. Again and again, the spiked fist railed against his head and chest, until the old man felt he would finally lose consciousness. When Berokon drew back his fist one last time, the force from the blow sent Te-Dasuka toppling over, chair and all. His sudden impact with the stone floor jostled his brain.

"Do you have anything you'd like to tell me, Weaponmaster?" Berokon loomed over him, tugging on the wristband of the spiked glove. He dripped Te-Dasuka's blood across the floor, where the drops joined with wide pools that sank into the smooth stone and between the cracks.

Te-Dasuka slurred, "Not a word. Looks like you're going to have to kill me, after all!"

"Gladly," Berokon answered. He drew a black weapon with a long nozzle and shoved it against Te-Dasuka's scalp. He pulled back the hammer and settled his finger over the trigger.

"No!" cried Ikaria from the low rafters. "Don't kill him! Don't kill my daddy!" She leapt down and shoved aside the gun barrel, guarding her father with her small body. She trembled all over in fear but held her eyes steady with the Admiral's.

"What do we have here?" Berokon asked in a falsely kind voice. "A little girl? Is this the one you've told your secrets, old man?" Berokon stared at the girl.

She openly scoffed at such a suggestion. She drew her thin body up to her full height and glared up at the Gangre-tan man. "Will you spare his life if I tell you?"

"No, Ikaria!" Te-Dasuka cried.

"It'll be okay, Daddy," Ikaria said with a brave smile. "All this man wants is the secret to orichalcum, right? They'll leave us *all* safely alone if we do what they say, right?"

"I'm sure we can reach a mutual arrangement, girl, if you'll be so kind..." Berokon lowered his weapon to show his sincerity.

"Very well, then," she said, meeting the man's eyes. She extended her hand, which he accepted. "I'll hold you to it, too, Admiral Berokon du Loche."

"Of course," he responded, squeezing her tiny hand with the slightest pressure.

"You!" Ikaria pointed at the two attendants with the Admiral. "I have your leader's word that my father will be unharmed. I'll take you to the secret now!"

Berokon signaled for them to follow.

"Don't!" Te-Dasuka bellowed after her.

Berokon laughed. "She's as weak in the mind as she looks!"

He heard her saying as they left, "It's really simple, actually, I guess. But we have to go to the forge to get the formula plate. Gosh! You guys sure are strong, making my daddy bleed that much!"

When they were far away from the door, Te-Dasuka chuckled. He spat out the blood that oozed into his mouth. "She's weak, all right, in some ways."

"Hmph! Then why do you laugh?" the Admiral asked.

Then Te-Dasuka laughed again, tears overflowing at some private joke. Berokon, feeling bewildered at his behavior, stemmed the laughter with his fists, until the man lay on the ground, still chuckling occasionally.

A flash of black in the darkness outside drew Berokon's attention. He rose from his crouch over

Te-Dasuka and walked to the door, gun in hand. He scanned the wide flat field before the house, satisfied that he had seen no threat. When he turned his back on the open doorway, a shadow descended behind him. From within his stealth darks, the cat-boy Chard withdrew two daggers and jammed one blade into each side of Berokon's weak throat.

The Admiral roared in pain and fury, turning to glare at his attacker. Chard slipped past him into the house, skipped outside the angle of the Gangretan's gun, and began picking at the locks binding chains to the Weaponmaster. When suddenly the Admiral was quiet, Chard looked up, expecting to see the man dead on the floor.

Instead, Berokon was standing with both bloody daggers in his hand. He dropped the blades with a rattling on the stone floor. His other hand pressed a steaming cloth against one of his open wounds. The cloth stemmed the flow of blood and seared the edges together, just like Unatan searingsalve. The fine hairs rose on the back of Chard's neck. He had underestimated the Gangretan Elite.

"Now, runt, you know what it's like to feel helpless," rasped the Admiral. He leveled the gun at Chard. "Move away from my ticket to fame. I wouldn't want him to get shot before he tells me all his secrets."

Chard froze. His heart pounded. He didn't have time or room to draw his sword without hurting Te-Dasuka. If he moved, the other man would mow him down with the gun. If he didn't move, he endangered Te-Dasuka. He blinked hard, trying to focus on the best choice. What would Rowan do right now? He couldn't think. Rowan would do something reckless. Chard wasn't good at reckless.

Then he realized that the man didn't plan on killing Te-Dasuka yet. He saw an opening into the dark night to the Gangre-tan's right. He may be able to slip out before getting shot and get word to the Queen. He kicked off the ground with frightening speed and leapt through the narrow passage.

The Gangre-tan Elite was quicker. He snatched Chard out of the air like a falling leaf and pinned him to the door facing. The man holstered his gun and drew a curved dagger. He carved a long cut across Chard's face, from his right cheek across his nose to his left cheek. Chard clenched his teeth and did not scream. Blood poured from the deep cut, across Chard's lips and down his chest. The man gave a self-satisfied laugh.

"Now I *could* stab you." He threw down the blade. "Or shoot you," he pulled the gun and jammed it into Chard's ribs, "but there are worse, more *painful* ways to die. You're lucky, you know." He forced Chard's face to stare out onto the flat field. "You missed them all."

Missed them all? Fear gripped Chard. At first, his sharp eyes couldn't pick out anything in the field. Then he noticed regularly spaced, flattened mounds of upturned dirt. Something had been buried all over.

"But I'll bet you won't miss them if I aim *just right*," the man snarled into his ear.

Chard shivered. Adrenaline flooded his body again when the man pulled him away from the doorway and prepared to fling him. Instead, the Gangre-tan smashed the gun aside Chard's head, completely disorienting him. Then he threw him into the midst of the little mounds of dirt.

Chard hit hard and rolled across the ground, unable to stop his fall. A loud pop and an explosion of dirt came behind him. Chard felt searing pain as something tore through his flesh, all over his back and hips. Another explosion tore through his gut. The smoke choked him, and the pain threatened to draw him into unconsc-iousness. He pulled out the comm device on his belt and, thankfully, it crackled to life.

Before he lost consciousness, he relayed his position and situation to the communications tower for the Queen, hoping the device delivered a clear message just this once. Then he slumped to the ground, feeling his strength drain out with his monumental effort. He held his eyes open as long as he could. But the darkness soon rose to take him. He couldn't fight it anymore.

* * *

Ikaria led the Gangre-tan grunts down the road through the double doors of the forge and weapons hall, chattering nervously all the while. When they had cleared the doorway, she jammed her hand against a lever set into the wall. The doors slammed together. In their confusion, the two Gangre-tans threw their bodies against the door. It wouldn't budge.

"Silly men," Ikaria said. "Underestimating your enemy. I am just a young, frail woman, you know." Her voice had leveled, losing its nervousness. She pressed a series of buttons alongside the lever. "And you won't see the light of another day!"

"What the hell are you playing at, girl?" screamed one of the enemies.

The other enemy lunged toward her. She ducked under the wide table after she flipped a final switch. Electricity shot along a conduit and directly into the fine metal net in which the man became entangled. The lights dimmed and flickered. The man screamed and writhed and jerked, and finally became still, hanging from the net that electrocuted him.

The overhead lights buzzed and went dark, leaving only forge fire flickering through the iron grates. The other Gangre-tan bellowed in anger and dove under the tables after her, skirting equipment and the body of his dead kinsman. Ikaria climbed to the rafters and retrieved her wide leather strap studded with throwing daggers. She took aim and lodged a dagger to the hilt above his collarbone. He bled out from his main artery, cursing her with every weak breath he drew until at last he slumped to the ground.

Ikaria realized she trembled all over in fear and with the shock of adrenaline. She picked a careful path down to the floor and looked about, plotting her next step to save her father. With the electricity down, she would need to manually latch the door so she could make her way to the underground labyrinth.

She had her hand on the door latch when a shadow blocked the moonlight on the other side. Then the door slid open and three Gangre-tan scouts filed in silently. She stood with her mouth hanging open in fear, knowing that no one would hear her screams.

* * *

Collern saw the slumped body lying in the sandy field first. He signaled to Rowan that he thought it was Chard. *Are we too late?* Rowan thought. Smoke drifted across the field toward the Upper Jungle. The smell of an explosion or gunfire lingered in the air, explaining the bang they'd heard on the way. So much of the war in Parisia drowned out other noises! *It's a wonder we heard anything*. The Chimera slowed to a silent walk. She, too, was wary of the utter silence all around Te-Dasuka's home.

The rattling of metal in the forge building drew their attention. Collern drew his battle-axe and slid from the Chimera's back. He crept around the building to the front as Rowan circled from the back. The door slid open and two Gangre-tan soldiers filed out, carrying a sheaf of metal plates bearing Te-Dasuka's mark. They said something in Gangre-tan to one another and made for the Upper Jungle with surprising speed.

A third soldier dragged a limp body behind him through the doors. His fingers were entangled in wavy white hair above the bruised and cut face of Ikaria. Collern managed to control his fury until the other scouts disappeared out of sight. Then he swung the orichalcum axe with full force at the junction of the man's neck and shoulder, burying the blade up to the handle. The man died without a sound, never seeing his assailant. As he slumped, Collern stooped to catch the uncon-scious Ikaria, quickly checking her for vitals, reassured that she lived.

Rowan rounded the building with a quick signal to Collern that he headed toward the other scouts. Collern signaled that he would take care of Ikaria and Chard and wait for him. The Chimera bounded toward the Upper Jungle silently with Rowan astride. Collern took only a moment to treat Ikaria, as her injuries were mostly deep bruises. Nothing life-threatening, he realized with some measure of relief. He traced the edges of the small, odd cuts above and below her left eye. Then he ran a finger down her cheek to her chin. He smiled in a longsuffering way, then laid her safely out of the way.

Collern crept across the field toward Chard's

prone body, using the cover of small buildings until only the expanse of night mist and sandy dirt lay between him and his objective. Then he cautiously walked into the open, his weapon drawn and at the ready. Something smelled wrong. Perhaps they thought a dead Unatan served no purpose.

Halfway across the misty field, with his next step, Collern realized his mistake. Chard's body was a trap. His boot settled on something that gave off a light hiss of air. He froze, but his foot trembled slightly. His trembling set off the trigger, sending a loud pop of an explosion—with untold amounts of burning shrapnel—up through his foot and into his body. His last thoughts centered on warning Rowan about the danger of the field of bombs. But he found it hard to focus and harder to stay awake. He collapsed on the ground, a hand outstretched to the cat-boy Chard, clinging to the last moments of his consciousness as darkness threatened to overtake him.

* * *

Rowan and the Chimera slipped quietly between the stalks and trunks of the Upper Jungle's understory along a path of their own making. The dense rotting matter absorbed the sound of the Chimera's claws. The fleeing Gangretan warriors moved less gracefully, crashing through greenery and flailing recklessly. Their swinging handlights punctuated the thick, moist blackness in an easily followed pattern toward the Lower Jungle.

"Oh, no," Rowan whispered. The Chimera stopped short, looking from the ground to the handlights disappearing through the forest.

Rowan dismounted in front of a bloody Unatan. He found a strong pulse and unlabored breathing. Recognizing him as Garlen, his break-group's sniper, Rowan scoured the area for the remaining members of his team. Beryl groaned nearby. Rowan dragged her from beneath a splintered tree trunk.

"Garlen! Wake up!" Rowan hissed. "Beryl needs you!"

The sniper rolled to his knees, clenching his ribs. "They did a number on us, huh?" He drew back in fear at the Chimera, but she purred at him in encouragement. With his eyes on her, he crawled to where Beryl lay and pulled out his medpack.

"Making friends again, Rowan?" he asked. Then he whispered, "How did they get past us so quickly? How is Chard?"

"I don't know," Rowan answered to all questions, remembering Chard as he lay on the ground, unmoving.

The Chimera danced over an indentation in the crushed greenery. Deruk lay still, a crumpled mass of cuts and blood. His stealth darks had been shredded earlier by the very scouts who ran away now. His breath came in a gurgling hiss. Rowan knew he would die if he couldn't end the fight with the fleeing Gangre-tans and get him to Kadray soon.

Rowan ripped the boy's shirt from him and pulled medicine from his healing kit. He wiped at the blood with the tattered shirt. Grabbing two fists full of sealing powder, he set to work closing the largest wounds. Then he filled his palms with searingsalve and smeared it over Deruk's chest. Smoke billowed from his chest, but he still didn't move.

"Stop staring!" Garlen cried, wiping the caustic salve from his hands. "Here!" He handed Rowan the cleaning cloth. "You've done what you can! I'll handle them from now on. We'll wait here on you." Garlen stared down at his brother, expecting Rowan to obey him, and got to work.

Rowan turned to the Chimera. He mounted in a fluid motion and leaned to whisper to her. The lights had been swallowed by the jungle. Could she still find them before they escaped? She nickered and took off with the frightening speed that left Rowan clinging to her in terror. But soon the lights came into view again, shining up from the base of the cliff leading into the Lower Jungle. The Chimera didn't bother slowing. Instead, she leapt from the cliff edge into the twilight, spreading her small wings to glide in overhead of the oblivious creatures.

When Rowan saw the Gangre-tans pause and hold their lights over a crude map, he leapt from the Chimera's back, swinging his sword with the full force of his fall. The first creature died immediately, split down the center in a spray of dark gore. The second stood in such shock that Rowan made short work of him as well. By the time their bodies lay cooling, he had retrieved the sheaf of metal plates—now drenched in blood—and headed back up the sheer cliff astride the Chimera. Below him, the juveniles swarmed over the Gangre-tan corpses. Rowan swallowed hard, too occupied with clinging to his mount to worry about anything else. He stopped only briefly to load up Garlen and the others before barreling toward the old man's house.

The Chimera, bearing the load of Rowan and his wounded break group, slipped between the trees silently and was within seconds of emerging onto the field in front of Te-Dasuka's home. Rowan told the Chimera to stop and he dismounted, asking her to stay behind with the others. Rowan heard heavy feet trampling the ground. Collern's distinctive voice rang through the air as Rowan caught sight of the field through the last stand of vegetation.

"You'll not hurt our future Weaponmaster, off-worlder scum!"

Collern stood before the prone body of Chard. He had draped Ikaria's limp body across his left shoulder and wielded the orichalcum axe with his free hand. He bled profusely from dozens of puncture wounds. Gravely injured, he wavered on his feet. The man he faced had the size, features and bearing of a Gangre-tan Elite.

They both turned at once to where Rowan emerged. The Gangre-tan spun with his weapon ready to fire. Rowan had already drawn Masalikir and poised to charge the field.

Collern stepped forward and screamed, "Rowan! Land mines! Be careful!"

Rowan froze, glaring at the enemy. He swung his sword in a slow arc along the ground, swirling through the night mist and catching the exposed triggers. He hefted them up from the loose dirt and set them aside, making a broad path for himself.

"Stop showing off," Collern said with a cough.

Rowan cast a worried look at Collern. Then he addressed the enemy.

"Cowards fight with hidden weapons, Gangre-tan!"

"A human with a sense of honor? Ha! Shouldn't you be a little more subservient? More like a *slave*!" Berokon bellowed.

He leveled the big gun on Rowan and fired. Rowan stabbed Masalikir into the ground and crouched, shielding his body from the barrage. Each projectile rocked the sword but didn't damage the metal. When the big gun clicked and clicked, Rowan stood and pulled his sword from the ground. Berokon threw his weapon aside and drew two long, curved daggers from his belt. Rowan circled in slowly, keeping his eyes on every movement the big man made.

"Collern! You're hurt!" Rowan said without taking his eyes off his enemy.

"This?" Collern answered. "It's just a few scratches. Nothing!" He spat out blood and straightened his shoulders.

"Get them ready for transport, then," Rowan called out. "Chimera!"

The creature trotted out of the forest, stepping lightly around the remaining land mines hidden under the thin mist, and stopped before Collern. Garlen climbed down and helped Collern heft Chard and Ikaria onto the Chimera's wide back. Then Collern collapsed. With the Chimera's help, Garlen managed to drag the unconscious man across the Chimera's shoulders, and then climbed up behind her. Rowan stole a glance at the Chimera and nodded. She was to go to Kadray's camp. She sped off through the darkness with the night mists flowing around her ankles.

His enemy stood stunned as well, gaping at the huge creature as it left. Rowan used his distraction to close the distance between the Gangre-tan and himself. He swung his sword at the man's face, but the enemy danced out of the way at the last second. Te-Dasuka lay unconscious in the doorway, bound in thick chains and strapped upright in a chair.

"You'll get nothing if you kill that man," Rowan said. "Especially since you're just stalling now, *brave* Gangre-tan leader!"

"Stalling? Whatever for?"

Rowan held out the metal plates with Te-Dasuka's mark he had retrieved from the runners. "Looks like you'll have to get these from me if you want them," he said. "Since your thieves are

Chimera food."

The Gangre-tan's look of innocence turned to a snarl of anger. "Then I'll take them!"

"You should tell me your name, off-worlder!" Rowan shoved the plates into his belt and dove at the Elite's chest.

Berokon knocked the heavy sword aside with both daggers. "Admiral Berokon du Loche, at your service, kid. Though what use will it be to know my name when you're dead?" He hurled a small sphere at Rowan's feet, which erupted into billowing white smoke.

"I want to commit the name of my fallen enemy to the sky," Rowan answered calmly.

"Bah!" Berokon scoffed. "Let's see how well you fight without your eyes!"

Rowan eased the tension in his shoulders and closed his eyes. He heard the man dashing at him from his left. He heard the ringing of metal through the air and brought up Masalikir to solidly block Berokon's every attack.

"I don't need to see to defeat you, *great* warrior!" Rowan whispered.

"You insolent brat!" Berokon bellowed.

Rowan turned to the sound and stood ready to attack. The smoke began to clear. Then he felt a spherical object bounce off his thigh. He scrambled to kick it away. As the sphere flew back through the air toward its source, it exploded, sending fiery shrapnel flying in all directions. Rowan guarded his eyes and gritted his teeth, glad that he suffered only shallow wounds. *Had it been any closer,* he thought, *I would have been hurt like Collern.*

But Berokon wailed. He'd taken the brunt of the attack. He bled through jagged cracks in his organic armor. Rowan took the opportunity to rush in, cutting a long diagonal across his chest. The organic armor—and his midsection—split open in a spray of blood.

"You can't fight anymore," Rowan said. "Leave this place with your life."

Berokon clutched at the wound, forcing it closed with trembling fingers as the daggers clanged to the ground. His yellow eyes grew red rimmed in pain as he stared at Rowan. He dumped a fine black powder into the fissure and struck the flint on his gun. Fire shot down the wound, searing it closed as Berokon wailed in pain. Rowan lowered his chin in determination, gripping Masalikir with renewed vigor, willing the blood from his wounds to stop flowing.

"No, human," Berokon gasped. "I won't leave without what I came for. My life is forfeit if I fail, after all. And your life is forfeit if I succeed!"

Berokon went on the offensive, driving Rowan back toward the edge of the clearing. Rowan lost his footing and barely rolled away to avoid Berokon's daggers. The jungle loomed behind him. He heard crashing through the understory. He hazarded a glance, hoping the Chimeras came to help. But the Gangre-tan relief troops had arrived. Rowan saw five of them in the odd glow of fire, war and twilight.

Berokon stared up in abject relief. That's when Rowan cut him across the belly. The man dropped to his knees and clutched his waist, struggling to shove his intestines back inside. He stared outward, not at Rowan but at his sword, with an expression meaning he had finally realized its worth.

"The sword!" he cried to the new arrivals. "Bring me his sword!"

"You'll not have her," Rowan answered. He settled into his battle stance.

Four of the biggest men Rowan had ever seen came forward, drawing their guns, as the fifth smaller Gangre-tan knelt at Berokon's side. Rowan tried to keep an eye on them all. He kept Te-Dasuka at his back.

"You won't survive long at this rate!" said the short Gangre-tan who looked too young to be in battle. "Uncle, did you have to be so careless?"

"Shut up! We need to get to the ship's medic now! Get me out of here!"

"Hey Boss?" said the biggest man. "This little human did that to you?"

"Shut up, shut up!" Berokon screamed. "It's his sword! Trust me, it's what we came after! Bring it to me, and I'll see to your reward!"

The largest Gangre-tan dug at his ear with his finger. Then he scratched his head. "If you say so." Then he ambled with his group toward Rowan, unconcerned, while Berokon roared something about not underestimating him.

The young soldier dragged Berokon to his feet, casting a wary glance over his shoulder at Rowan. In the young Gangre-tan's eyes, Rowan saw fear and awe. As they reached the edge of the clearing, the boy tore his eyes away from Rowan and leaned into supporting Berokon's weight. A thin streak of silver zipped through the air past the boy's neck. He faltered one step then fell to the ground, sending Berokon tumbling again. Blood spurted from the young one's throat. A thick black arrow lodged a foot deep in a tree on the right. The poor boy grabbed his neck and sputtered as he bled out. Rowan's heart went out to him.

Rowan relaxed, took a signaling stance and nodded imperceptibly toward two warriors. Two more arrows hit vital marks in the necks of half the remaining Gangre-tan warriors. In the confusion that followed, Rowan hacked apart the guns of all four Gangre-tans. Those who were mortally wounded cursed him as they died. A rolling hiss rumbled across the open field.

Berokon stared in horror, looking all about for the assailant. Finding no one, he scrambled to his feet, still clutching his stomach. He wavered and stumbled toward the forest and under the shielding cover of the trees. He ran for his life, in an erratic course through the jungle.

The Chimera arrived then, hissing her indignation at being absent from the fight. She turned and kicked one of the remaining creatures and slashed at the other with her front talons. He jumped back out of her reach. Then she turned in the direction of the fleeing man.

"Let him go," Rowan said. "He shouldn't get far with those wounds, and the other Chimeras will clean up the rest, won't they?"

The Chimera gave an encouraging croon.

"What the hell is that thing?" the big man said, holding his daggers out like a shield. "It's bigger than the others!"

The others, thought Rowan. *Had the juveniles delayed the big men?*

She stared at the big man. Her croon deepened into a rumbling hiss, answering Rowan's question. He guessed that the Gangre-tans had killed many of them. The Chimera turned to the man at her feet. She sank her talons into his back. He screamed, then whimpered, and then screamed again when she flexed her talons. Her violet eyes bored into the larger man's face, a clear challenge to retribution. She crushed her prey's throat with a swift bite. His screaming stopped. The Chimera began devouring him in sight of the other warrior, who quaked violently in fear.

"Name yourself, warrior," Rowan said, pulling Masalikir up in front of him. "If you don't die by my hand, *she'll* leave nothing for the pyre."

"N-Name?" the man shrieked. "Don't pretend

you care about such a stupid thing as my name!" The remaining Gangre-tan slipped by Rowan's sword and toward the old man slumped in the doorway.

Another arrow zipped through the air and pinned the Gangre-tan's foot to the ground. He wailed, clutching at his foot. Rowan stalked around in front of him. From behind him came the grinding of bones and sloppy tearing of flesh as the Chimera feasted.

"Attacking an unconscious man is a foolish decision," Rowan said. "If you don't run, the only thing that awaits you is death. And you've made enemies in the forest. If you run, they'll show you real suffering. Your only choice is an honorable death in battle."

Rowan waited while the Gangre-tan thought that over. The human gave him time to consider and a chance to redeem his honor. Finally, the Gangre-tan sighed hugely. He grabbed the arrow and slowly pulled it up from the ground and out of his foot, gritting his teeth and then sighing as it came loose. He stared at the fine black arrowhead dredged in grit and his blood. His green face was a mask of concentration. The man looked all around him. He cringed at the Chimera's feast. He dropped the arrow and his daggers, and stood with his head bowed. His long black braids swung in the breeze.

"My superiors said not to expect mercy, but here I stand before a weaker human who offers it. I have my orders in case of failure... He said, 'I won't tolerate your presence'." The Gangre-tan looked up at the sky as dawn peeked over the horizon. "Nothing you can do to me would be as bad as my father's disapproval, you see," the Gangre-tan man whispered. Suddenly his face livened with a deep sorrow. "Even Berokon forgot my father's orders. I pity him, if he makes it back home."

"Your father?" Rowan whispered. "Who is he?"

The man shook his head with a smile. "I'll take that secret to my death. Honor doesn't matter much to me, just his approval. So I'm afraid I can't let a wild animal or even a strong human take my life today. I'll go by myself. That way I can face him on the other side."

"Wait!" Rowan said. His grip on Masalikir loosened and the sword clanged to the ground.

The Gangre-tan's smile finally reached his yellow eyes. "You know, human, you're really something. And my name? It's Gilder," he said with a rush of breath.

Then he dove head-first on the nearest landmine. As the smoke cleared, Rowan still stood helpless, one hand outstretched and trembling. His eyes burned and itched. Then he dropped his arms. His face fell forward. He couldn't cry. The ache welled up and he couldn't shed a tear for Gilder. The Chimera walked over to where Gilder lay, still and shredded. She bent her head to him.

"Don't," Rowan murmured. "Please let me burn him."

The Chimera crooned and joined Rowan. She shook the blood from her tapered muzzle and pressed her cheek against his. He patted her face, ignoring the stench of fresh blood from her meal. She crooned again. Rowan shook the fog from his head and turned to Te-Dasuka. The old man had roused enough to complain about his restraints, so Rowan set to work on the chains.

In the next second, Rowan froze. A dozen metal spheres had been tied all around Te-Dasuka with their pin triggers set to pull if he moved.

"Weaponmaster, you've got bombs on you," Rowan said, hands frozen in place.

Te-Dasuka harrumphed. "Then get 'em off, *Gauntlet* recruit! I have to see Ikaria!"

As Te-Dasuka cursed the name of Berokon du Loche to all eternity and wondered at his stupidity in returning to his house unarmed for just a moment, Rowan focused on disarming and removing the grenades one by one. When finally they set in a neat pile with the Weaponmaster freed, he helped the man to the waiting Chimera. Te-Dasuka stood blinking at the creature, his battered face a mass of purple and red. The old man chuckled again, and that turned into a cough. Then he laughed again. Rowan couldn't be sure why he laughed. Perhaps the old man was more injured than he realized. Rowan gathered a few items into Collern's discarded satchel and climbed up behind the old man.

"We have one more stop to make on our way to the city, Weaponmaster," Rowan said.

Then he nudged the Chimera to where his sniper awaited transport.

20: VALKYRIES AT SUNRISE...

"If Garlen hadn't shown up when he did, I would have been in trouble," Rowan said with real gratitude. He nudged the boy with his elbow.

"The idiot insisted on going, even with his injuries!" old Kadray called out from inside the tent. "I told him not to crawl back to me, bleeding, if he went off to act the fool!"

"He still saved the biggest, meanest one for himself," Garlen answered.

Rowan shivered in remembrance of Gilder's death. "Not as big and mean as I thought."

"Wow, Te-Dasuka!" Garyn said, rushing from eastern Parisia. "You really are a mess, huh?" She gingerly touched his face, draped as he was across the back of Rowan's Chimera. He swatted her hand away.

Kadray came out of his tent, wiping his bloody hands on a rag and shooing them all away from Te-Dasuka. The old healer didn't bat an eye at his mount, but had his assistants drag the old man off the Chimera and onto a stretcher. He cursed when Te-Dasuka complained about the rough treatment.

Kadray ranted on and on. "Hmph! You'll be one big bloody scab, you old fool! My guess is your blood pressure's up again, too! And running off, just because you forgot that fool's charm, while there's a war going on!"

"You knew those plates were fake, right?" Te-Dasuka said to Rowan, ignoring both Kadray and the Queen.

"Not for sure. I assumed you wouldn't just leave them out, Sir," Rowan answered. "But if they found that out, they'd never..."

"Did you read them?" he interrupted with a cough. When Rowan shook his head, Te-Dasuka replied, "You should."

Rowan pulled the plates from his pocket and stared dumbly at them for some time. He couldn't read the language, but made out an ingredients list and instructions. Garyn snatched it from him and laughed as she crumpled in a heap on the ground, her armor clanking.

"They wouldn't have made orichalcum," she said, "but they would've made the best banana pudding this side of the universe! Though why you'd write it in Earth's Latin, I have no idea!"

"My grandmother's favorite!" the old man answered with a laugh.

"And mine, too!" Maraba chimed in. "We've got 'em on the run, by the way. But we can't figure out how to damage their shipside weaponry. You said leave them with only life support and directional controls, right? Well, the lasers would just kill them outright." A loud explosion sounded from the battlefield. Maraba cringed. "Correction. The lasers *did* just destroy a couple more ships. Hope their occupants had sense enough to run away."

"Let me help with that," Rowan said. He produced a sturdy case from the wide bag across the Chimera's hips. He opened the case and pulled out a grenade and a disarmed landmine. "There's more inside. Use their own medicine against them?"

"You *kept* those things?" Garlen cringed and shied away from them. "What the hell for? You were carrying those the whole time?"

"Get to it, Rowan," Garyn ordered. Rowan saluted her, then looked past her to Garlen.

"Just in case, friend," Rowan said with a mischievous smile. He slung the case by a strap across his left shoulder and headed out across the battlefield of Parisia.

Distant explosions sounded from the Lower Jungle. The Chimera screamed and reared, pawing at the air. Her scream turned into a pitiful whimper. She paced back and forth.

"Some of her family just died down there," Garyn said.

"That bastard made it to the river, to their damaged boat!" Rowan cried. "Berokon! Let's go, Chimera!"

He grasped her neck frill and threw his leg up when Maraba caught his arm. "No Rowan! Don't go! He's just one enemy. We need you here! Even Primorda waited for you."

"She's right, Rowan," Garyn said, looking toward the smoke on the horizon as it filtered the morning light. "There are still Unatans to be saved."

Rowan bit his lips together. He stroked the Chimera's smooth neck. Then he turned, bowed to the Queen and hurried back toward the battlefield. Most Gangre-tans fell back to protecting their ships, gathered in desperate throngs around the remaining functional vessels. Unatan forces still fought the enemy all through the city, protecting the storehouses, private armories and hidden passages to the underground labyrinth where noncombatants—the elderly and smallest children—waited for the end of the battle. Break-groups scurried around, acting as couriers and informants. He nodded to those he saw, but felt despair creeping up on him. He had yet to see a single uninjured Unatan.

He sobered with the sight of so many corpses, enemy and Unatan alike. Many Unatan scouts took on misery duty, killing off wounded enemies who couldn't flee. Others built pyres, even before the battle had been declared a victory. From Parisia's town center, a large black mound blocked his view of the enemy ships and cast a long dark shadow across the celebration circle.

He entered the darkness of the shadow and recognized the horribly mutilated body of Primorda. She lay dying and still, her two largest daughters dead by her side. The enemies left her alone when she couldn't move anymore. He saw their broken daggers and spent ammunition cartridges littered across the ground. Primorda purred a greeting to Rowan as he approached.

"My new friend," Rowan said, a mournful tone filling his voice. He laid a hand on her tapered muzzle and stared into her violet eyes. "I'm sorr… I know you must go, though I'll miss you. You know, your daughter's eyes are just like yours. She's strong and beautiful."

Rowan's eyes filled with tears he refused to let fall. Primorda purred again, but the sound gurgled as her lungs filled with blood. She nuzzled his hand.

"Don't worry. I'll take care of her, of all of them," Rowan said.

The dying Sole-Mother blinked at him. Her breath sounded like a chuckle of irony. Primorda, in that instant, chose her successor. *All my children will grow weaker and die off even if you protect them, little human. But for your offer, I thank you. You care!* Then she settled down to her rest. The great eyes closed with a contented sigh. And just like that, the mother of all Chimeras died.

Rowan forced down the surge of emotion he felt. He simply rested his hand on her face a moment longer. He turned back once and saw the speck of Garyn staring back at him. Then he plodded on ahead, across upturned paving stones and toppled pillars and over bodies and blood to the few remaining enemies. The death piled higher for both sides as he approached the spaceship. He thought he wanted revenge, but mostly he wanted them to leave, to disappear from his new life. The Gangre-tans enslaved many of his race. Then they killed many of his new brethren. They deserved death. *But I've killed enough for today*, he thought.

As that thought occurred to him, he heard a gun click on his right. His hand gripped Masalikir to fight. The wounded Gangre-tan grabbed at his throat before Rowan could budge. He turned to see Garlen waving at him from the communications tower roof two hundred yards away. He nocked another arrow, drew back the huge longbow and waited for his next target. Rowan sighed in relief.

Rowan stared at the closest hulking ship, looking for all the places he could plant the bombs. He skirted the wreckage of another ship that had been shredded by Primorda and her younger daughters. Still three hundred yards away from his first objective, he searched for a path he could follow that would allow him a measure of stealth.

Rowan advanced to the other side of the wreckage. Two of the remaining ships still billowed smoke, destroyed as they were just moments before as Maraba had mentioned. The edges of the melted metal still glowed orange from the lasers.

The three functioning ships—all that remained intact of the thirty-strong fleet—had landed five hundred yards apart in a long row on the sandy field at the edge of town. Gangre-tans swarmed all around, some screaming and running, others shouting orders, still others struggling not to break formation. The scene stank of a retreat. But their leaders looked alert. He could not sneak up on them.

Nine shadows appeared from behind the ship to greet him. They carried daggers and guns and blunt-spiked clubs. Again, his hand settled on Masalikir's grip. Under his boots, he felt tremors as the ground shook. Ahead of him, the earth bucked and roiled beneath the Gangre-tans feet. They could not take aim. Soon they toppled over. Seven streaks in rapid succession rained down on them from his left.

"Your aim's getting better, Ikaria!" Maraba cried. Rowan stared into her silver eyes. She smiled brilliantly. Quietly, she said, "I knew you had this one, Rowan. I just got... bored!"

The warrior Trayba loped over. Ikaria perched on his shoulder, her head and ankle heavily bandaged. Above and below her left eye, the Gangre-tans had gouged deep grooves. Trayba set down Ikaria gently and clamped his hands on his knees. He heaved in air. "God, you're fast, Maraba!"

"You all came here?" Rowan asked. "To help?"

"Of course!" bellowed Dresden from up ahead. He swung an oversized warhammer at the heads of the remaining Gangre-tans with a resounding crunch. "You missed two, kid! Taught you better'n that!"

"I was making an entrance!" cried Ikaria as Trayba laughed. "Just ruin it!"

The soft scent of beach lilies and leather filled his nose. He closed his eyes and inhaled deeply. Rowan turned to Garyn, who appeared silently at his right.

"You didn't really think I'd send you out here all alone, did you?" Garyn asked.

"I didn't think," Rowan said. His throat tightened. A feeling gripped him, swelling to drown out the sorrow.

"Now you're starting to sound like Collern," Maraba said on his left.

Ikaria hobbled over on a splinted left leg. She smiled up at Rowan. Cuts above and below her left eye had been cleaned but left without bandages. Her scalp looked like mostly gauze and tape, yet she was still quite pretty. Rowan thanked her for her help.

Garyn glanced up at some movement beyond Rowan's shoulder. An arrow whizzed past Garyn's ear, through Rowan's hair and through the eye of the Gangre-tan who crept up beside them, pinning his body to the stone rubble behind them.

Maraba laughed, her voice echoing above the murky dawn. "Betcha Garlen was sweating *that* shot! The Comm Tower's almost a mile away by now! Lucky boy."

Rowan stared at her in shock, feeling his short life of freedom flash before his eyes.

Garyn tugged on his hair. "Not luck, just good training and the best weaponry. Right, Rowan?"

Maraba leaned in to whisper. "You could fall over like you've been hit!"

"Too late, now," Garyn pouted. "He'll know!"

"Ummm, ladies?" Dresden said. He gestured to Rowan and then to the big ship, whose doors all opened at once. "Company's coming back out!"

Rowan shook himself loose of shock and returned to his task. The surviving Gangre-tans weren't following a retreat order. Most of them just fell back to their supply ship! Many Gangre-tans who fled into the ship seemed to emerge with fresh weapons.

Maraba and Dresden ran point, leveling the battlefield with rippling quakes and that huge warhammer. Garlen handled the stragglers. Ikaria and Trayba guarded the rear. And Garyn personally dispatched enemies that got past the others.

Rowan's heart pounded. Arrows flew past him with lightning accuracy as he walked. The ground trembled under his feet with Maraba's power. He turned away from the brutality of Dresden's swinging warhammer. A few feet from the closest ship, he jumped onto a small ledge. He grabbed at bars and ridges along the side and scrambled on top. The Gangre-tans who followed him up fell just as quickly to Garlen's arrows or Garyn's quick assassinations.

He searched for the battle system nodule that even the merchant-class ship QuellTruth had. Rowan found the tell-tale depressions in the ship's surface that housed air-to-ground weaponry. He drew Masalikir and threw his back into slicing through the re-entry armor that sealed the weapons' function. The armor was thicker than any other he had seen. Rowan guessed that thicker armor protected their ammunition.

Once Rowan had breached the hull, he set down and carefully opened the case of landmines. He rigged three to explode when weapons were activated again, to tear through the wiring and computer controls. He planted another four behind the huge environmental controls panel. They'd lose gravity, temperature and atmospheric controls when the ship shifted to travel mode.

"All clear!" Rowan called to Garyn as he closed his pack and slid down the other side of the ship.

She signaled the others and resumed their formation on toward the next ship. The Gangre-tan split in unorganized groups. Ranks had disintegrated. Half the enemy ran away, piling into the ships, fearing the onslaught by just a few elite Unatans. The other Gangre-tans rushed foolishly to their deaths. So many of the remaining Gangre-tans looked young, barely warriors and hardly on the level of the Elites.

Rowan planted the bombs in both weapon bays and environmental controls. For good measure, he dislodged several panels of the thinner re-entry armor on the second, larger ship, ensuring it would have more trouble than the smaller weapons ship. Then their group headed toward the third ship.

Maraba sidestepped Garlen's incoming arrow. She drew her rapier for the first time, slitting the Gangre-tan's throat. She sighed. "He's just now out of range. Seeing that, we won't have any more help from him."

"*Whining* because you had to bloody your sword again?" Garyn scolded. She smiled viciously. "That's what they're for, you know!"

"But my little Finistir is such a frail baby!" Maraba said, hugging the ornate guard to her face. "And Garlen's *daddy* could pick off a gnat at just over a mile!"

Rowan marveled about that, secure in his tight group of protectors, as they approached the final ship. He scouted the points of attack and got ready to climb up. *Just over a mile?*

Dresden piped up at that mention. "Garlen's father is dead, Maraba! Don't think the boy doesn't know he has a long way to go." The stocky man swung the warhammer at another enemy. "Besides, almost fifteen hundred yards is pretty good with a bow!"

Maraba sobered, ashamed of her selfishness. "I'm sorry."

Rowan cringed at the word, even as another wave of Gangre-tans bore down on them. Collern's words rang in his head, *No matter what you do, don't apologize. He hates that!* But when he hazarded a glance at Dresden, the man worked his jaw and kept his mouth shut, bending to his work with renewed energy. Maraba sent out a shockwave of earth that broke over the group of enemies, pinning them to the ground. Then she drew Finistir again and began slaying with as much grace and skill as Garyn.

Garyn, sensing Rowan's distress, whispered beside him, "Don't worry, Rowan. It's the only apology he will accept. Especially from her."

He nodded as they trotted across the field. "She's an amazing fighter."

Garyn laughed. "She should be! She trained with me. You think *my* training is rough, wait 'til Te-Dasuka really gets on track with you and Collern!"

Rowan liked the perverse way his heart thudded in his chest. His heart anticipated the challenge even as his mind dreaded it. When he lived through this battle, he had a much tougher one to overcome!

The oversized bays on the side of the last ship grinded open as they approached. A horde of Gangre-tan soldiers spilled out. They held their guns steady, holding their fire. Rowan and his group stopped short a few yards before them.

"If you can kill them, kill them," a familiar voice rang out. "All I want is that big sword!"

The large Gangre-tan, mostly bandages and wide metal staples, leered around the shoulder of a soldier. He survived the Chimeras and the trip back. An impressive accomplishment. But Rowan seethed at the man.

"Berokon du Loche!" Rowan growled. He gripped Masalikir. "If you want her, get her yourself, coward!"

Berokon shrank back from Rowan. He cast his yellow eyes on frail Ikaria with her Trayba, on Maraba and Dresden, then finally on the Queen. After a moment, he realized her rank and trembled.

"Hurry!" Berokon cried to his assembled men. "What are you waiting for? Fire! Kill them!"

"Ah," Garyn sighed. "The only one who got away. Let's remedy that, Maraba?"

Maraba tucked her chin down in concentration. The ground before them rumbled and quaked, knocking armed Gangre-tans off-balance right and left. The fifteen enemies who recovered and charged ahead met Dresden's hammer and the Queen's katana. The ten who flanked them died by Ikaria's hand.

"I'm out!" she called back to Garyn.

Trayba laughed. "Sorry, I can only carry so much!"

"Then fall back to the Comm Tower!" Garyn grunted as she hefted a Gangre-tan's body off her sword. "Trayba! Take the jungle path. Get word to Te-Dasuka to assemble fifty scouts to scour the jungle for stragglers. Pattern three. Let 'em know we're almost finished here. Go!"

Trayba bowed. He grabbed Ikaria and sprinted into the jungle. Garyn covered them.

Rowan still glared at Berokon tumbling across the ground, crying out and scrambling for purchase underfoot. The Berokon said he was an Admiral. He alone admitted his responsibility for injuring his closest friends and helping bring war to Unata. He knew the man should die a slow death for his sins. Then Rowan remembered the QuellTruth and his murder of ten thousand innocents. He remembered Nitch and all the others who died by his intent. His hand fell from Masalikir's grip.

His head fell back. He wanted to give in to the sorrow. Too late, Rowan saw movement on top of the ship, where only tremors reached. The dozen Gangre-tans fired on his group before he could alert the others. A gray and silver blur appeared from Rowan's right. Metal flashed in the yellow morning sun. The monotony of gunfire droned on and on. Sparks flew all around Rowan and Maraba. But Garyn deflected every bullet.

When the weapons clicked, empty, the Gangre-tans attempted to reload. Rowan looked around him, checking on his fellow Unatans. Garyn glanced back, her wide eyes on Maraba.

"It's okay, Maraba," Dresden said, holding his hands out to placate her. "It's just a nick. Kadray'll fix you right up."

Maraba clutched her arm. Blood spurted from a bullet wound in her shoulder. Rowan mistook her gritted teeth for pain. But her silver eyes flashed, livid, never leaving the enemy. Then her eyes blanked and her mouth went slack. Rowan shook in his boots. Collern's words echoed back to him—*she has to control that temper at all times!* She slowly raised her arms from her sides. The ground trembled as before, but the sound of a guttural roar rolled up from deep underground.

"Maraba, calm down!" Dresden cried, torn between fighting the enemy and facing his wife.

Garyn faced Maraba, then threw up her hands in resignation. "Ah, hell, Dresden!" Garyn said. "Let her go!" Then to her chief Coordinator, Garyn said, "Maraba, let's end this!"

Dresden fell back to Rowan's left, guarding the rear. Garyn guarded in front of them. They stood behind Maraba. The woman threw her arms wide. The ground rippled at her feet and spread in a shockwave that sent every Gangre-tan to their backs. Maraba swept her arms left and right. The huge ship rocked as if on the ocean, flinging the armed Gangre-tans from the top. Re-entry armor clanged to the ground, crushing some unlucky Gangre-tans. The whole shape of the ship twisted to and fro, ripping fissures in the smooth metal. Slowly, the ground ceased heaving. Maraba dropped her arms and sank to her knees, drawing deep, ragged breaths. Dresden dropped beside her and took her into his arms.

"Well, you won't have to plant bombs on *that* one," Garyn said to Rowan. She absently patted her friend's head and sighed.

Rowan stared in terror at the upturned soil and destruction. A siren wailed from behind the cargo doors. The few Gangre-tans still alive after the quake scrambled toward the safety of their ship. The doors closed against the injured and dead. With a groan, the ship heaved and rattled into the air, spraying the Unatans with dirt and rocks.

Explosions sounded behind them. The first two ships rose into the air, bucking against Unata's gravity and billowing smoke from their damaged environmental nodules. The Gangre-tans signaled a retreat at last. The airborne ships tried to fire on the Unatans. Loud explosions signaled more damage, this time to their weapon systems. Helpless and hopeless, they angled for the glowing star on the horizon that was their mothership.

Dresden pulled Maraba to her feet. She cast an apologetic smile at Rowan, looking exhausted and shaken. Rowan stared at her with unveiled worry.

"I'll be fine," she said. She ruffled his dirty hair with a weak chuckle. "Seems I've scared you a bit."

Rowan shut his gaping mouth.

"Hmph!" Garyn said. "*My* Rowan's not so easily shaken by a mere temper tantrum, is he?" She leaned on his shoulder. Then she laughed, feeling him tremble under her hands. "That's a good first reaction to seeing her mad. You didn't pass out or run away. Looks like you're a keeper!"

Rowan shook his head in dismay. Maraba laughed then, sounding more like herself. He relaxed, watching the sky light up with the fire of the remaining ship's exit toward freedom.

Garyn stared back toward the thin Comm Tower. "Company's coming!"

A message flag hung from the window of the communications tower. Garo hit the ground running to the battlefield. He skidded to a stop before them several minutes later. He held up his hand, begging them to give him a moment. "I think," he gasped. "I think I'll work on," Garo paused for a deep breath, "our two-way radios so they'll work better with this planet's crazy magnetic field. *If* my Queen would like more efficiency in her message delivery." Garo stared up at her with an exasperated sigh.

"Not a bad idea," Garyn admitted. "Report?"

"The damaged ships have survived leaving the atmosphere and have picked up a bearing. Toward the Gangre-tan home world," Garo reported.

"We're letting them go," Garyn said with a shrug. "They missed their objective by a long way. The Gangre-tan are a proud race. Let them return home in shame, in defeat, to warn the others. Let them remind the world why Unata is called Fear Planet."

The sunrise cut a glowing outline around Garyn's backlit figure, glinting off her black and silver armor. She sheathed her katana in a fluid motion, clapping the hilt to scabbard with a note of finality. Unata had won this battle. The Valkyrie stood straight and proud, watching her enemy flee to the stars.

21: ...YET WE LIVE ON TIL DARK

"Every last able-bodied Unatan—get these wounded to Kadray's unit!" Garyn called out. "Healers, report to the old man immediately! If you have a drop of medic blood in you, and you're not a patient, he'll need your help!"

Rowan dove into getting patients and materials to the old man, for once glad that his injuries were just cuts, scrapes and bruises. He hardly noticed the hours slipping away. Kadray grunted orders and received supplies without an upward glance at any of those working under him. He muttered constantly when he wasn't shouting, his sharp gray eyes and deft fingers flying masterfully through the work of healing. Rowan stared at the old man's hands for a moment too long, feeling suddenly drained. Kadray looked up finally, when the tray of supplies did not arrive quickly enough to suit his speed. He paused long enough to appraise the boy, his gray eyes seeing every injury old and new.

"Rest," he said with a nod and a jerk of his head toward a cot in the corner of the tent. "Don't move an inch until you've eaten," Kadray muttered as Rowan staggered off.

Rowan slumped down on a cot beside Collern. His friend had awakened to the worried face of Ikaria, and couldn't have been happier. The pungent aroma of medicine hanging over Collern's bed spoke volumes of his condition. Rowan glanced over his friend's extensive bandages, some of which had seeped, despite heavy use of sealing powder and the smelly searingsalve. Collern put on a brave face for Ikaria, but he looked all but dead from blood loss. She fussed over his silliness at getting injured in a way Collern was too injured to fully enjoy.

Rowan wondered at the absence of Ikaria's betrothed. He glanced around to find Trayba balancing stacks of materials for Kadray, looking energetic and strong. Rowan marveled at that Unatan stamina. Collern managed a half-hearted salute to Rowan and an exhausted smile.

"Gramps finally retired you for the night, huh?" Collern said with a pained sigh.

Rowan nodded. "How do you feel?"

"Like I stepped on a land mine," Collern answered, wincing. The smile he gave Rowan hid little of the pain he felt. "The old man threatened dosing me up if I can't sleep through the night."

"On Unata's finest?" Rowan said, wrinkling his nose and sticking out his tongue in disgust.

Collern glanced at the old man. "Or worse! Chard hasn't woken up yet." Collern nodded to the bed where the kid slept. "Gramps said it was best he slept through the stitching. He caught two mines. He landed stomach-first on one with only his undersuit as armor. The metal tore through some important internal stuff. He took the longest in surgery. He took a few transfusions too, so he's got more Unatan blood than half-blood for once!" His short laugh turned into a cough. "We almost lost him a few times."

"Collern, look what you did! Think before you speak!" Ikaria said, seeing the grief in Rowan's eyes. She punched Collern in the shoulder, sending him into a coughing and laughing fit, crying about how she was supposed to be taking care of him. "Doc said he'd be back to normal in no time thanks to his other blood. Because he grows fast, he *heals* fast, too."

Rowan sighed in relief.

"Oh, by the way. We felt the aftershocks," Collern said. Mischief glinted in his eyes. "Mom musta been mad."

Rowan shrank back, remembering his fear. Collern laughed at Rowan's reaction, groaned in pain from laughing, and then laughed about that. Finally, Collern wiped at his eyes. Then, in an abrupt mood swing, he shook his fist in anger, yelling across the tent at Kadray.

"Hey! What did you slip me, old man?" he cried. "I'm slap-happy over here!"

"Not enough of it, since you're supposed to be sound asleep!" Kadray yelled back. Then he muttered something about Collern's resistance being as annoying as his mother's.

"I'm just trying to follow sleep-orders over here," said a drowsy Garlen. He sat up, rubbing his eyes with his knuckles, and yawned. "Kinda hard to do with all the yelling!" He cast a mock warning glance at Collern, who clamped his hand over his mouth in a teasing apology.

Rowan perked up. "Wow, Garlen! You're amazing. I had no idea about that range!"

Garlen ducked his head, rubbing his pale hair in embarrassment.

"He's right. You've really improved, Garlen," Maraba chimed in. She appeared silently and sat on the edge of Garlen's bed. "Good genetics breed that kind of talent."

Garlen's grin dropped and he scrambled to bow from his bed. "Please forgive me, Lady Maraba! I could have injured you badly!"

She sighed. "You didn't. Let's just leave it at that. Besides, I know you'll be as good as *him* one day soon!" She ruffled his hair and threw an arm around him.

"You really think so?" Garlen's eyes lit up.

Maraba leveled her eyes in rare seriousness. "You're close now. And your father was the best sniper I've ever seen, and Dresden's best friend. Those two, along with Garyn and myself, were unstoppable as a break-group. These guys should count themselves lucky to have you, Garlen," she said.

The tears in Garlen's eyes spilled over. He hid his face behind Maraba's shoulder. Then Rowan smiled and lay back on his cot again. He stared at the rippling tent fabric and then around at the surrounding cots. The rest of the break-group were blissfully unconscious.

"We *are* lucky to have each other, Garlen," Rowan said.

Collern said, "From what I've heard, I'd have any of you watch my back anytime!"

"Oh, and speaking of watching your back," Maraba said to Collern, excusing herself from Garlen so he could pull himself together. "Father sent this to you." She held out a small paper pouch. "This is to go into the next thing you drink, and you are to finish that drink even if it kills you. Then you are to settle down and stop fighting sleep. And if you do *not* follow the doctor's orders, he has my permission to have Trayba render you unconscious by *any* means necessary." She leaned in to whisper harshly. "*After* he assigns you a different nursemaid."

Collern took the envelope, staring piteously at the blackish-green contents, like a man condemned. Then he folded the flap back down, heaving a sigh of malcontent. Collern, already medicated to the point of erratic emotions, settled in for a long pout. Maraba chuckled and continued her rounds.

Ikaria hobbled around on her injured foot, tugging at her charges' bandages, blotting at faces with cold cloths, and checking temperatures with her wrist. When she made it back around to Rowan, Ikaria stared down at him for a long moment. He had fallen asleep with his arm draped over his eyes to block the light, his breathing low and rhythmic. She pulled the blanket over his lean chest. Then she sat back down on Collern's bed, ready to keep him company until she forced that medicine down his throat.

Rowan smelled the evening meal before it ever arrived. The loud protest from his empty stomach woke him up. The kitchens delivered carts full of hearty soups loaded with meat and spices, and fortified with pureed vegetables and seasoned broth to the wounded. They brewed the native tea strong for its healing properties and mixed in heaping spoons full of additives according to each patients' needs. Kadray directed them just as shamelessly as he ordered his assistants, with hardly an upward glance.

Rowan tore voraciously into his dinner. Even the bitterness of the strong sourroot tea felt welcome in his starving body. Garyn Kei watched him from across the tent.

"I think I did well in saving him, huh, Te-Dasuka?" Garyn said to the old bandaged-up man. She shoved him back down on the bed.

"Ouch! That you did," he replied. "That's twice he's changed the course of a battle with blind luck and will alone. Three times if you count his arrival."

She chuckled. She pushed him down again. "Stop trying to get up. You're ordered to *heal*, Weaponmaster. No dying until we've an appropriate replacement, remember?" She paused, deep in thought. "He won't think of it that way, will he?"

"I doubt it," Te-Dasuka said. "That's why he's got potential, I'd wager."

"Wager, huh?" Garyn's eyes sparkled. She looked across the huge tented arena Kadray's men had set up.

"He'll do it again, I bet." His laugh turned to a cough. "He'll go beyond what even you dreamed up for him!"

"It's funny that you should mention dreams," she said with a girly giggle and a duck of her head.

"You've seen him?" Te-Dasuka turned serious. "Was it a vision?"

Garyn smiled at his turn of personality. "He was doing quite, ah, well. Very strong. But that sadness was still deep inside. I could see it in his eyes." She sighed.

Maraba appeared behind them. She leaned in and whispered, "Well, if Kei's daughter is *that* smitten with a man who doesn't exist yet, then there's really no hope for her, huh?"

"Shhh! He'll hear!" Garyn whispered. She waved her hands for silence.

Maraba threw her head back and cackled outright, drawing eyes from many in the medical tent. She leaned down again and whispered into Garyn's ear. "It took me a few days, but I *knew* I'd find out. Just be careful with that transparent fool's grin. Don't worry. Your secret's safe with me!"

"Fiend!" Garyn hissed.

Maraba simply laughed again. "What's the

report from the Chimeras?"

Garyn sighed. Her eyes unfocused for a second. Her birthmark sparked. "There are no more enemies in the jungle, and there's nothing to put to pyre." She furrowed her brow. "'Except *his,*' and Rowan's face. I guess Rowan claimed a few enemies for the pyre."

"We were lucky today," Maraba said. "If not for the Chimeras, Rowan and our festival guests," Maraba shrugged, "things could've gone badly."

"Luck again, huh?" Garyn grinned. "My guess is they just didn't expect the entire populace of Unata to be gathered in Parisia! Let alone the monsters in the jungle and a single human that would take them all on."

Maraba saw the glint in Garyn's eyes. Mischief danced in the look she gave her Queen. She laughed again, and then wandered directly to where Rowan sat with her son and husband.

Te-Dasuka cough-chuckled again. "Things will be interesting from now on."

"She won't say anything," Garyn said, her tone tinged with doubt. "Hopefully."

"Definitely not," Te-Dasuka said with a wide smile. "But she'll have fun tormenting you. You know it's the prerogative of a best friend!"

"Let her! I'm not afraid!" Garyn stuck her chest out proudly and squared her jaw.

"Oh, Rowan, dear," Garyn heard Maraba's singsong voice and she froze, "Garyn Kei would like to speak with you."

"I'll kill 'er!" Garyn hissed as Te-Dasuka laughed. Maraba caught Garyn's eyes and blinked innocently.

"My Queen?" Rowan stopped before her and gave a brief bow.

Garyn gave her best smile to the boy, and gave in to the whim to brag on him. "You really were amazing today. I'm incredibly lucky to have such a warrior, you know."

Rowan blushed, making Garyn's smile wider. He bowed again. "I am nothing without the support of my fellow warriors and my Queen."

"I can't wait to see what your future holds, Rowan Jun," Garyn said in all seriousness. Then she fought the blood that rose to her cheeks. "And I'll hang your worth on that future."

"Yes, my Queen!" he said with a salute.

She sighed again. "You're not going to stop the yelling and saluting, are you?" Her voice was soft, teasing.

"I'm sor—no, my Queen!" Rowan bellowed.

"Someday, you will," she said cryptically.

"If so," Rowan answered in a low voice, "that doesn't change anything."

In his earnest expression, in his black eyes that met hers, she saw the glimmer of the man from her dreams. Her heart pounded, and she knew every Unatan in the room heard it. She heard his heart pounding, too.

"No," she managed, "it doesn't!"

He took her hand and brushed her knuckles with his lips, feeling the blood rise to his cheeks. Then Rowan bowed and excused himself outside the tent. The Chimera, too tall for the entrance, waited for him. She offered her knee as a leg up, and he climbed to her back, brushed aside the flowing neck frills and leaned against her smooth neck. He smiled, willing his heart to slow down. *So, this is devotion?*

To the Chimera, he said, "You didn't have to wait."

She nodded. Rowan noticed the blood on her muzzle. She jerked her head to the corpses of her family. The sun had circled back toward the horizon, and the corpses swarmed with the living bodies of juvenile Chimeras. Rowan turned away from the voracity of the feast.

"You eat them?" The Chimera purred in response. Then Rowan remembered something Garyn had mentioned, about the Chimeras all dying off to one so that a new Sole-Mother could emerge. He realized what Primorda meant in her cryptic thoughts to him.

"No!" he said. His soaring heart plummeted. "I promised her I'd protect you all!"

The Chimera turned to him and nickered. "She knew, didn't she?" Rowan asked. "Try not to leave, will you?" The Chimera smugly tilted her head and settled down to stare at the feeding frenzy again.

"Don't worry, Rowan, not yet," Chard said from the door to the massive medical tent. "Garyn said it may take a couple years for them to die off, but that the strongest one will remain, and retain all their memories. It'll be like before, almost. It's only happened once before, that we know of."

He turned in surprise toward Chard's voice. "I thought you were bleeding internally and ordered to sleep," he said softly. Even so, seeing Chard awake filled Rowan with a flood of relief.

"I was and I did," he answered. "Collern's meds just made him louder, so only the dead could sleep in there. Maybe not them, either," he said with a smile. "But I heal fast."

With the boy's face scrubbed of blood, Rowan noticed the long cut that grooved the top of his nose and notched a horizontal line across his left cheek. He'd left it unbandaged, unlike the rest of his tattered body. Even his tail had been wrapped in places.

He noticed Rowan's scrutiny and pointed to his face. "First official battle as a full warrior. We usually let these kinds of wounds heal on their own. Don't you think it'll be a cool scar?"

Rowan smiled down on him. "Probably." He looked down at his own chest and arms, already striped with scars from his arrival, and various fresh cuts. "Scars, huh? I think I'll wear them all as reminders."

Chard gazed up at him, nodding wisely. "You're more of a Unatan than you know."

Rowan stared back at Chard, contemplating his words that sent his heart soaring again, then out at the frenzied eating. "Have you eaten your fill, Chimera friend?" She nodded and pranced around.

Rowan gave Chard a hard look. "How're your wounds, according to Kadray?"

"They hurt less before he got a hold of me," Chard winced. "But I 'won't die as long as you don't do something stupid'!" He smiled.

Rowan laughed, knowing full well what he meant. "I think we should do some scouting, y'know, just to make sure everything's okay out there." Rowan grinned. Noticing Chard's quick pouting, he laughed again. "I need some help setting up a pyre!"

Chard's face lit up and he laughed. "Pyres, I understand." Fires already burned all around Parisia, piled high with nameless enemies and beloved Unatans. Smoke and ash drifted in the evening breeze. "But scouting? In addition to the fifty men Te-Dasuka already sent out?"

"Two, ah, three more couldn't hurt, right?" He patted the Chimera's neck.

"Riding when it's *not* an emergency? I would not pass up the chance to get one over on Collern, any day!" Chard cried, grabbing his weapon belt from the long wall of weapons relinquished by the injured.

Rowan gave the cat-boy a hand up behind him and off they rode, toward Te-Dasuka's place again. He gently dug up the remaining land mines, disarmed them and set them aside.

Chard stared at the huge burgundy stain that soaked into the earth. “That’s mine, isn’t it? And that’s Collern’s. He came for me?”

“Of course he did. We both came for *you* as much as Te-Dasuka and Ikaria,” Rowan said with a smile. “You think we don’t love our favorite kitty?”

Chard crossed his arms and pretended to be upset. Rowan knelt over Gilder’s body. He pulled on the big man’s shoulder until he lay on his back. Gilder’s tattered face appeared peaceful. He died by his own will, saving him from his father’s disapproval. Rowan folded the Gangre-tan’s arms across his chest and stared around the field.

“Hey, Chard? Are you up to taking him somewhere else?” Rowan asked.

Chard looked down at the body. “Your memorial?”

Rowan nodded, surprised that Chard understood him so well.

“Sure,” Chard said. “Let me help with him.”

He climbed down gingerly from the Chimera’s back. With some effort, and with the Chimera’s help, they draped Gilder’s body across her back. Then Rowan directed her toward the Lower Jungle, toward his private memorial and the fading scar in the jungle that heralded his arrival on Unata.

22: MERCURY RISING

Sometime later, Chard pointed out that even the jungle had quieted in mourning. Rowan offered that it just breathed a sigh of relief after the threat had passed. The Chimera and her smaller sisters grouped around the edge of the clearing to watch them pile sweet grasses and fallen wood around Gilder's body. Their curious chirping blended with the larger Chimera's piteous purring. She seemed to understand the somber tone of each task, and bade her sisters gather and bring more grasses and fallen wood to the pyre. After Rowan reassured her that he would be okay, she settled at the edge of the clearing with the others, examining his every move. Having her eyes on him and scent around him, a familiar feeling from his blind days in the jungle, gave him great comfort.

Rowan knelt and sparked his flint on the tinder. He nursed the small flame until it caught the sweet grasses and wafted an intoxicating smoky aroma across the clearing. Chard joined him in the ritual, joined him in screaming Gilder's name into the wind around his enemy's pyre.

Rowan, face sullied with the Gangre-tan's ashes, turned away from the heat toward the graves of his family. Firelight glinted off something metal draped across his mother's stone. He leaned in closer and recognized the crushed golden locket, the only remaining tether to his past. The golden chain sparkled while the locket reflected a more somber glow. Rowan had been sure he lost the locket upon his abrupt arrival on Unata. He stared at the flickering flame as it danced across the crushed oval. *Who could have found this, and who would have brought it here?*

"Garyn," he whispered. *When did the Queen have time to visit the grave?*

Rowan felt compelled to touch the locket once more, to be sure it felt real in his hands. Then he saw a new symbol carved into its surface. He leaned closer. In his mother's native language, the word etched thereon appeared pure and simple. And meant just for him.

Live, he read. He drew a deep breath and glanced skyward, toward Parisia. But the scent of beach lilies and leather already drifted away on the evening breeze.

* * *

The rattling of the damaged ship almost drowned out Berokon's shaking voice. He spoke through the secure line when well out of range of Unata's scanners.

"I'm sure the QuellTruth crashed there, but we didn't have time to do a full scan of the area. Some unexpected enemies stalled our progress," Berokon reported. He released the button on the handheld device.

Static crackled on the communications line. Then a silken voice drifted from the speaker. "What unexpected enemies?"

"They have monsters guarding the jungles!" Berokon cried. "We killed the biggest of them that came at us, but the rest just kept coming! *He* called our men 'Chimera food'!"

"Monsters? And Chimeras, huh?" the voice crackled. "Were they serpentine and shaped like Old Earth's equines?"

"Yes! Mean, those!" Berokon said. "Vicious, too! They have sharp teeth and—"

"You said you killed the biggest? Did it have wings?"

"Ah, uh," Berokon looked to the men who had shot it down. They nodded. "Yes."

Laughter sounded on the line. "Good, very good. I've heard of those creatures. You've killed their mother," he said. "You've set us up for a perfect counterattack, if what I've heard about those creatures is true!"

"But Admiral Visett—what does it matter? There're thousands of them!"

"Just trust me," he said with a laugh.

"Aye, Admiral."

"What of Gilder?" Visett asked. The speaker crackled in silence for some time.

Berokon gulped. "D-dead by now, sir. Likely killed by that vile human. You see, he arrived, allowing me to escape."

"So, escape you did, without my son," Visett said, a note of warning in his smooth voice.

"W-What about that damn human kid with his sword?" Berokon asked, his voice trembling in fear.

"Human?"

"Yes, just one, though," Berokon sighed, glad for the subject change. "He may be the only survivor of the QuellTruth, but I doubt it. No one could go from weak slave to that strong in just a year!"

"Perhaps," Visett answered. "But he's just one human. What damage could he really do to the true Elites we will send?"

"R-Right, sir!" Berokon answered. "Against the real deal, he'll fall easily."

"So how many of your men did this one human kill?"

"S-Several, at least. It was that sword! It *had* to be made from the alloy!" Berokon rubbed a hand across his stapled stomach armor. "Cut through our armor like it was regular flesh! And our guns like they were paper!"

"What of the *formula* for the new alloy?" Visett asked. "The second purpose of your mission? Your *orders*, Captain?"

"Yes, they have the secret, but we... we lost it!"

"That's unfortunate. Very disappointing," Visett answered. "But we'll have the upper hand next time. They'll never know what hit them, I guarantee!"

"Y-Yes sir!" Berokon saluted. He was replacing the receiver on its hook when Visett spoke again.

"Oh, and Berokon?"

"Yes, sir?"

"Take care not to throw around the title of Admiral lightly," Visett warned, poison dripping from his voice. "Even to our enemies. For one who hasn't made it to that rank, you can only make us look bad."

"Y-Yes, Admiral! Forgive me, b-but this can work to our advantage!" Berokon stammered through his apology. "Won't they underestimate us now?"

Visett sighed audibly. "Perhaps, but you miss the point. Failing to meet your objectives is bad enough, but impersonating an Elite officer is a major offense. *Perhaps* you didn't think I would find out. I expect your full report *in person* on your arrival planetside."

"S-Sir!" Then he replaced the receiver on its hook, contemplating suicide over facing his superior with a failed mission, lost supplies and men and other charges, on top of the preventable death of Visett's son due to his cowardice.

"Captain! We've arrived at SlaveBlock!"

Berokon slumped into his seat at the helm. "Then take us in. Prepare for docking." He sighed. "And have SlaveBlock set a course for home."

Visett's disappointment reached out across the expanse of space, strangling Berokon with dread. The Captain shivered and quaked, even as the comforting bulk of SlaveBlock loomed on the viewscreen. The deaths of his men and destr-uction of ships meant nothing to Berokon in the end, in the face of failure. If only one had survived and returned victorious, the Gangre-tans would have rejoiced. But lacking success, only his immense terror remained.

We return in shame, he thought. *But absolute victory awaits us in the future!*

Berokon clung to that hope as fervently as he clung to what could be the remaining days of his life. His dreams of victory had to wait. Visett awaited his report. And Visett made it clear that he would be *extremely disappointed.*

###

Ready for more? The story continues in
Silver Empress, Book 2 of the Pathos Series,
Available in Kindle Unlimited, Audible, and
Paperback!

ABOUT THE AUTHOR

Tamara Henson lives in Kentucky with her precious little family, and all the people in her head. She's devoted to her son Elric and her man Will, and her kitty-brat Twitter-pater. She's a Sci-fi/Fantasy Author and Artist, Anime/Manga Fan, Legal Stabber of Tattoo and Piercing Clients, a Directionally-Challenged and Incompetent Gamer Gal, and a Workaholic Entrepreneur. Always improving, except in gaming, probably.

She is likely working on something creative, when she should be sleeping.

To access exclusive info and offers related to Tamara's PATHOS universe, go to her website:

www.tamarahenson.com

Discover other Pathos Series titles by Tamara Henson:

- Silver Empress (Book 2)
- Solana (Pathos, Book 3, A Novella)
- Ariana (Pathos, Book 4, A Novella)
- Primorda (Book 5) *Fall, 2026*
- Incarnata (Book 6) *Spring, 2027*

Discover 3 NEW Romance Series by Tamara Henson (Series Titles TBA):

Cryptid (w/ a JACKALOPE SHIFTER!!), *Fall, 2026*
Dystopian and Dark Fae Romance Series
TITLES TO BE ANNOUNCED, COMING SOON!

ABOUT THE PATHOS SERIES:

Tamara Henson's ever-expanding Pathos universe spans space and dimensions beyond the waking world to bring fresh life to mythologies, folklore, and legends, spinning epic original locations and memorable, multi-dimensional characters in rich detail with her playful dialogue and direct writing style.

Join Rowan Jun in his path toward redemption from slave to warrior.

Walk the path of Briescha, a born diplomat so dedicated to her sister that she would shatter the cosmos to keep her safe.

Follow Solana into the wilderness as she escapes those who seek to harm her, and follows the voice of the mysterious Taiyo of the Flames.

Let Ariana guide you through her new life in the Mansion in the Mountain, where the mystery of her family is finally revealed, and her true trial begins.

Tread the path toward life and redemption, where suffering and pain hold the promise of a brighter, more joyful future. The Pathos Series!

Join the tamarahenson.com newsletter for updates on all Tamara's Upcoming Projects!

www.ingramcontent.com/pod-product-compliance
Lightning Source LLC
Chambersburg PA
CBHW030019060826
49398CB00031B/148

9781968677022